C000057694

THE LONDON SPYMAKER

BOOK 7

THE RESISTANCE GIRL SERIES

HANNAH BYRON

Copyright © 2024 by Hannah Byron

All rights reserved.

No part of this book may be reproduced in any form or by any electronic or mechanical means, including information storage and retrieval systems, without written permission from the author, except for the use of brief quotations in a book review.

This is a work of fiction and not a history book. Names, characters, businesses, places, events, and incidents are either the products of the author's imagination or used fictitiously. Even though actual facts and names have been used to serve as a backdrop to World War 2, any resemblance to actual persons, living or dead, or actual events is purely coincidental and should be read in the context of a fictional story. For more info, see Author's Note.

ISBN eBook: 978-90-833027-1-3
ISBN Paperback: 978-90-830892-5-6
Book Cover Design by Ebooklaunch
Editor: Amber Fritz-Hewer
Website: Hannah Byron

I am not this hair, I am not this skin, I am the soul that lives within.
  RUMI

PREFACE

Dear Reader,

Welcome to Book 7 in *The Resistance Girl* series: "*The London Spymaker*", the last real 'resistance girl book', which is packed with intrigue and courage. If you've been following the series from the beginning, you'll remember our journey started in 1918 during World War I with "*In Picardy's Fields*", setting the stage for a tale of resilience and bravery featuring Agnès, Alan, Madeleine and Gerald.

From the ashes of the Great War emerged two remarkable couples, whose daughters, Lili Hamilton and Océane Bell, stood up as young resistance fighters during World War II in "*The Diamond Courier*" and "*The Parisian Spy*". Their stories intertwined with those of other brave souls like Austrian Esther, Scottish Sable, Dutch Edda, and German/English Anna, all alumnae of the prestigious Swiss finishing school Le Manoir, over the course of Books 3-6.

In "*The London Spymaker*," we delve deeper into the shadows of wartime Europe, drawing inspiration from the real-life exploits of Flight Officer Vera Adkins CBE . Through the lens of our fictional heroine, Anna Adams, we embark on a riveting adventure, navigating the treacherous landscape of espionage and sacrifice.

Vera Atkins, WAAF squadron officer, 1946

While rooted in historical events, this story, like the others, weaves fiction with fact, allowing me to explore the untold stories of female courage and cunning which shaped the course of WW2 history. As our characters grapple with the weight of their choices, we're reminded of the indomitable spirit of those who fought against tyranny.

In the interest of storytelling, certain liberties have been taken with historical facts, though my commitment to historical accuracy remains paramount. The Nazis mentioned in this book are listed with their real names, but the resistance fighters' names have been slightly changed due to the fictional nature of the story. Allied politicians, such as Winston Churchill and General de Gaulle, also appear with their real names.

As we bid farewell to *The Resistance Girl* series, there's a promise of closure and continuation. Book 8, "*The Resistance Girls Revisited*", will unveil answers to lingering questions, including the mystery of

Madame Paul's behavior and the post-war reunions of our beloved characters. *The Resistance Girls Revisited* will mark the 40th anniversary of Madame Paul's tenure at Le Manoir, promising a reunion of all our girls.

But my passion to write about female resistance fighters doesn't end with the conclusion of *The Resistance Girls*. In my upcoming *Timeless Spies* series, I will explore the real lives and missions of the 40 female SOE agents in France during WW2. Through the eyes of interesting contemporary women, we'll uncover the untold stories of these courageous agents, shining a light on their active contributions to liberate Europe from German occupation. Stay tuned for a riveting new dual-timeline series.

Please join me once more as we embark on this final *Resistance Girls* book, where heroes are forged, and legends are born, amidst the chaos of war. And remember, behind every act of bravery lies a story waiting to be told.

I hope you'll find as much joy in immersing yourself in Anna's journey as I did in lovingly crafting it.

Hannah Byron

PROLOGUE

Hanover, October 1937

A bluish-pink halo of a rainbow settled over the *Neues Rathaus* on Trammplatz in Hanover, lighting up the green-copper dome like a large colorful hat. All day, it had rained long and hard and the cobblestone square shone with a treacherous, wet gleam.

The sun, sparse since the beginning of fall in Lower Saxony, came out, first tentatively, then stronger, as the late afternoon pushed towards evening. The dancing sea of umbrellas, dripping black circles moving unevenly across the square, came down and people, mostly men in suits, appeared from underneath them, rushing hither and thither to home and hearth.

A small boy, no more than ten, pulling a cart, with one wheel on the brink of coming off and a dirty cloth over it, was begging along one side of the square.

"Some bread to spare? A *pfennig*, please?" His voice was small and shrill and persistent. The shop door of *Der Brotmeister* opened, followed by a waft of freshly baked pastries and the stout, blonde baker's wife appeared. Sturdy and broad-faced, with sleeves rolled up above her elbows showing fleshy arms, she stood squarely in the door opening, looking displeased.

"*Juden Raus! Auf Nach Palästina!*" She shouted, shooing the boy off with dismissive, flabby hands. Away with the Jews. Go to Palestine. The dark-haired boy jumped, then scurried away, pulling his squeaking cart behind him. A little farther down the square, he started calling out again, "Some bread to spare? A *pfennig*, please?" seemingly unperturbed.

Quite perturbed was Ansel Grynszpan, passing by *Der Brotmeister*, the cotton satchel with her schoolbooks pressed against her chest. Half hidden under her waterproof coat, still dripping with rain, she walked with steps as swift as if the German baker's wife had scolded her. Ansel sensed the hostile atmosphere more than she saw it, keeping her eyes fixed on her shoes, good black leather shoes and white socks that were clean and not yet needing mending.

She wasn't a beggar. She was Yehuda Grynszpan's daughter. Her family had money and repute. There was nothing to fear. None-theless, safely hidden under the hood of her raincoat, fearful eyes watching from behind her dark-framed glasses, with shoulders hunched, Ansel slipped off the square and into the warmth of *Bücher-laden im Herzen*. Her father's main bookshop, on the corner of Trammplatz and Friedrichswall, he'd aptly called 'Book Haven in the Heart'. The familiar clacking sound of the mechanical types being hammered against the carriage told her her father was working on his other job, being a journalist.

The typing stopped the minute the shopkeeper's bell rang with her entrance. Shuffling feet and her father appeared from his office at the back of the shop.

"Ansel? You're early?" Slim and wiry like his daughter and sporting dark-framed glasses of his own, clad in a black suit of good quality gabardine, Yeduha Grynszpan smoothed the worries from his forehead as he caught sight of his drenched eldest daughter. While he rubbed his ink-stained hands and smiled, Ansel didn't miss the worry in her father's eyes. The shop was quiet as dreaming trees. Customers were few and far between these days.

"Take off that wet coat and let me make you a cup of tea."

"I *am* early, Father," Ansel replied with quiet stubbornness, still standing with her satchel clamped against her, dripping onto the doormat. "I wasn't allowed to take part in the gymnastics hour."

Again, that worry in her father's eyes, which he quickly camouflaged with another smile.

"What are you telling me, Ansel? I pay for your tuition at the Friedrich Schiller Gymnasium, just like all the other parents. That includes your physical wellbeing."

Ansel shrugged, took off her coat and hung it on the coat rack. "Never mind, Vati. I'll have that tea with extra sugar. I got caught in the rain."

She followed her father to his office, that also held a small cooker. Yehuda was already busying himself with kettle and teapot, every movement economical, as if he measured the space he had to move in. Ansel sat down at the table that also functioned as her father's desk, finally letting go of her satchel, watching him. Even in motion they were similar. Not theatrical or grandiose like her mother, but reserved, regulated, almost reclusive.

Father and daughter didn't talk until the tea was ready. Ansel thought of all the times she'd come in here after school. First when she was at primary school, *Die Sonnenschein-Grundschule*, and then at age twelve when she'd transitioned to the Friedrich Schiller Gymnasium for secondary school.

It had always been her father with whom she'd shared her friendship perils and her academic questions. She'd often stayed with him in the bookshop until closing time, six o'clock sharp. Reading books or doing her homework, while her father wrote his articles or talked with customers.

Vati seemed to always have the proper answers for Ansel's inquiring mind, whereas Mutti was often preoccupied, certainly after the birth of the twins, Sarah and Eva, two years earlier.

"Mutti's sweet and loving but her nerves sometimes get in the way," her father had explained to Ansel when she'd fallen off her bike and, instead of comforting her daughter, her mother had started screaming at the top of her lungs at seeing the blood oozing from Ansel's knees. To the seven-year-old, this had been a lesson in caution and many more had followed where she'd been more concerned about her mother than seeking her help. Of course, Ansel loved her mother as dearly as her father. The relationship was just different.

"What's happening to us, Vati? There seems to be one decree after another against Jews. We have to do something!" Ansel looked up from blowing on her hot tea. The question was frank and open, as the discussion between them always was.

"I know, Ansel. Hitler's dedication to corner the Jewish population keeps me awake at night. But for now, I have no solution. I have been here since 1911 and built up a good life for us. Once upon a time, being the chief editor of the 'Judische Rundschau' was an esteemed position. The whole Jewish community in Germany depended on our newspaper. And I own two bookshops. That's a lot more than my father had in Warsaw."

"So, you don't think we should go back to Poland?" Ansel took a tentative sip of her tea. It was very sweet and very good. It warmed the coldness in her chest.

"I have nothing left in Warsaw, dear, after Oma and Opa Grynszpan died, and I brought your mother here in 1919. She was quite on her own already. And after my only sister, your Tante Riva, followed us in 1922, and settled here with Onkel Sendel, I considered our life was here for good. We belong in Hanover. For Heaven's sake, we are Hanoverians."

"I think we're still considered Polish Jews, Vati, and it doesn't help us." Frank, amber eyes behind spectacles, scanned equally brown eyes. Yehuda couldn't bear her inquiring glance and cast his eyes down. He heaved a deep breath.

"What would I do without you, Ansel?" he mumbled. "I feel so bad for not having the answer."

"Doesn't Mother have a brother in London? An Onkel Benjamin?"

"Benjamin Bittermann?" Her father looked up again, a vague

smile around his lips, "I'm afraid he's a league above us, my girl. And he's your mother's half-brother, anyway."

"What do you mean? A league above us? Is he in Parliament?"

"Heavens no, child. He's a merchant. Diamonds I believe. Hasn't stayed in touch with your mother since our marriage. Maybe he thinks Judith's married a 'typesetter', a boring intellectual. Who knows?"

"You're not a typesetter, Father. You're a business owner yourself. And an editor-in-chief. Why do you think Onkel Benjamin looks down at us? Did he say so much?" Ansel insisted.

"No, he didn't, but as far as I know, Benjamin Bittermann severed all ties with Poland and Germany. If you want to know the truth, you'll have to ask your mother."

"I'd still love to see London," Ansel mused, "I have a feeling Jews don't have to watch their every step there."

"I wouldn't be too sure about that, child. Jew-hate is widespread in all of Europe if I believe the newspapers from my colleagues in other European countries."

"So, there's no way out for us, Vati? We just have to bear the brunt of the German defeat in 1918 forever and ever?"

"We'll find an answer, Ansel. And it's not as bad as that yet."

"Oh, Father, don't play the fool. It's bad! Very bad. I hate being a Jew, not inwardly but outwardly." Ansel didn't raise her voice, but she spoke her words with conviction. If she could have un-Jewed herself in some way or other, she would have chosen that route.

"I promise you, I'll come up with a solution." The conviction in Yehuda's voice was less, though.

Ansel finished her tea. It was getting dark outside. No customer had come in. She got up from her seat to close the shutters in front of the windows, a routine she loved to do when she was in one of her father's shops. It meant they would soon go home, where their house-keeper, Greta Schmidt, would have prepared the potatoes with thick gravy and lamb chops and green beans. After dinner, Ansel would play with Sarah and Eva before they went to their little cribs for the night.

Simple moments of family bliss. Maybe her father was right. He'd always come up with a solution.

Side by side, father and daughter Grynszpan walked amicably to the large family residence on Leibnizstrasse. A house with a view of the river Leine, a house filled with books and good quality furniture and food on the table. The house where Ansel was born in 1920.

PART I

POST-WAR GERMANY

NOVEMBER 1945

1

THE WOMAN IN BLUE

Nuremberg, Germany, 21 November 1945

The November wind howled around the majestic Nuremberg Palace of Justice, tearing off the last yellow-brown leaves from the trees along Fürther Strasse. The sprawling limestone walls and red-topped roofs looked as grim and resolute as the skies above. Demanding answers, not accepting guesses. The steady rain that belted the cobblestone Strasse made the droplets splash back up in the air, producing swashes of tears. As if the whole world would weep. For a very long time.

The Palace of Justice, or *Justizpalast* as the Germans called it, stood in Nuremberg's city center. Since its completion in 1916 - in the middle of that other big German war - the palace had sought to be a symbol of justice, playing a central role in administering the rule of law in Germany.

Understanding its symbolic importance, the Allied conquerors had chosen this city and this building on purpose to hold the first International Military Tribunal in human history. The Justizpalast was in the middle of Hitler's beloved Bavaria, the birthplace of his National Socialist Party, only a two-hour drive from Munich.

Here, the Nazi monsters he'd created over the past twenty-five years would be put to trial. Inside these walls, prominent leaders of Nazi Germany would be persecuted for war crimes, crimes against humanity, and other heinous acts committed during the six long years of World War II.

The chief criminal himself would escape an irrefutable death sentence in these chambers, having committed suicide in his bunker in Berlin in April 1945, only days before the final German capitulation.

From under a black umbrella, a frail, dark-haired woman with an oversized leather coat over her navy-blue WAAF uniform stood looking up at the bulky building as if assessing its strength against hers. Though the amber eyes betrayed no emotion, the slight lifting of her chin made clear she considered this her 20th-century version of David against Goliath. Behind dark-rimmed glasses the glance was vigilant and steely. Nothing was missed, not a word would slip by unnoticed, while her smooth, young face remained as stony as the walls she was about to invade.

Closing the umbrella with the routine movement of an English-woman, she shook the water off it and stepped quickly under the parapet. There she stood for a moment, glancing in the direction from whence she'd come. With the same cloak-and-dagger expression that had made her look ahead, at the Justizpalast, her gaze now fixed itself on the sheets of rain pelting Fürther Strasse. She stood in absolute stillness, lost in thought, lost in the rain.

I am Anna Adams.

And the rain whispered 'yes'.

Then she shook herself as she had done her umbrella, with fierce, determined jolts. Drawing the strap of her red military bag closer to her, the umbrella over her forearm as a gun pointing downwards, Anna directed her feet with measured steps towards the building's entrance. The cadence of her high heels on the marble archway created a staccato clicking that echoed against the opposite wall.

A drenched flock of men, some in civilian clothes, most in their respective Allied uniforms, which Anna could identify, rank and all, pressed forward to gain access through the narrow entrance. For some reason only one of the double-doors was open, leading to a tussle of bodies among the wet and waiting victors, struggling to be the first to get entrance. Rank didn't seem to play its international role here, though Anna knew the high-level officials had their own receiving area.

As she took up her position at the tail end of the crowd, Anna's sensitive nose picked up a mixture of wet wool, cigar smoke and excess Eau de Cologne. The scent disagreed with her stomach, and she regretted having breakfasted on just two cups of black coffee. But the Bratwurst and black bread had not seemed like an appetising option.

Scanning the participants, a routine habit when surrounded by people, Anna was pleased to spot one female amid the sea of men. The blonde woman with fierce blue eyes and a scar down her right cheek, dressed in overalls, was working her khaki elbows to get ahead of the crowd.

Her clothes and hair were wet, indicating an umbrella was not part of her outfit. A satchel as khaki as the rest was slung over her shoulder. Army boots on her feet. A pencil stuck between healthy, white teeth and a notebook in her hands. Clearly one of these battle-hardened, war correspondents.

"Good for her," Anna mumbled under her breath as she waited her turn to show her entrance pass to the weary British porter who blocked the other half of the open door. She thought the man looked as if he was personally carrying the entire burden of the Nazi trials on his frail old shoulders. But he greeted her with a chirpy, "Morning, Miss Adams."

"Morning, Mr Clarke. Beastly weather." And she squeezed herself past him into the corridor.

"Beastly country," Mr Clarke observed, looking as sour as an unripe grape. Anna shrugged but smiled. What else could one do? This country had brought the wrath of the world upon it. Once inside the entrance hall, she took off the heavy overcoat. It was hot, with too many damp bodies and overanxious overheating. She felt faint but steeled herself.

"Anna, over here!" The familiar voice of Sir Reginald rang out behind her. Anna sighed. Her London boss was also staying at *Das Bayerischer Gasthaus*, in fact next door to her room, but Anna had managed to escape his presence at breakfast by having her coffee upstairs in her room.

Major Reginald Owens, whom everyone at SOE called Sir Reginald, was loud and pompous. Generally, SOE staff were expected to keep a low profile at these trials, but the man had no switch to turn off his loudness, nor his sense of misplaced superiority. Both had been ingrained in him since he took his first aristocratic breath in his parents' Belgravia, London residence at the turn of the century. He was the only one in SOE who could get away with anything but a low profile.

"Of course, you're the first to spot me, when I'd much rather slip in unnoticed, and take a back seat," Anna muttered, as she turned to face her superior with an impeccable smile on her rosy lips.

Tall but hunched in the shoulders, which made his neck disappear in the back of his head, the former Navy-officer-turned-bureaucrat was – for reasons Anna didn't know - clad in civilian clothes, a tailored three-piece navy suit with a pompous, pink tie.

The Major's blue eyes, slightly bulging and red-veined due to his penchant for copious amounts of late-night liquor, observed his right-hand staffer from Section F from under bushy gray eyebrows. But the gaze in his black pupils was steady and straight. That was the problem with Sir Reginald. He liked to come across as dumber than a pillar-post, but not one of his five senses missed anything. Ever.

Anna was just not in the mood for the constant bombardment of her boss's clever repartees in which he liked to involve her at all hours. She was tired. She was here for the answers. The war may be won, but it was far from over. And maybe, just maybe, she was tired of the cigar-smoking, old boys' network, whether in uniform or in suit, proclaiming they were now the new masters of Germany.

Germany. Anna swallowed.

Sir Reginald had already grabbed her by the elbow, firm and possessive.

"And here I was thinking you were still in Berlin, Miss Adams. Did you shorten your tour?" He was meanwhile directing her towards the courtroom as if she was the one standing trial. Anna shook his hand off.

"Yes. It was cut short on my request. Major Jaffe drove me down yesterday. Berlin can wait. I need to be here." Her voice was clipped, and her eyes were on the crowds around them. People were pushing and shoving as if on their way to the circus, eager to secure a front-row seat.

"Aha, I see. Not much left of Hitler's Reich, huh? Just cratered streets and Nazis in cuffs. Our RAF bombs and boys taught them the proper lesson before our armies scootered in." Sir Reginald paused a moment before adding, "you got the permit to go to Recklinghausen and Paderborn, I presume? To interrogate the scoundrels?"

"Who told you?" The amber eyes shot fire, but then she shrugged. Sir Reginald was a highly trained security officer, just like she was. It was his job to know what his subordinates were up to.

"Your driver." He played his innocent card as usual.

"Jaffe?"

"Do you have more than one driver?" One bushy eyebrow went up and Anna shrugged again. The man was hopeless.

She lingered before confirming what he likely already knew.

"Major Jaffe drove me straight from Berlin to Bad Oeynhausen. I told him I wanted to see the head of the war crimes unit. He told me not to expect anything, grumbled his dissatisfaction most of the way." A thin smile appeared on Anna's face. "However, Group Captain Summers was very forthcoming and gave me permission to interrogate Fritz Suhren about Pearl, Maureen, and Madeleine. And perhaps get the story about Yvonne from Suhren's own mouth. As long as I took one of his war crimes investigators with me."

"You went to Bad Oeynhausen, huh? Quite a trek on these bloody roads. That's North-Rhine Westphalia, right? Close to Han..."

Anna interrupted her boss sharply, feeling her cheeks redden. No going there! To divert his attention, she added, "I might apply for a job with the war crimes unit in Bad Oeynhausen when SOE dismantles. It may take years before we trace all our missing agents. Being on the ground here might help."

The bulging blue eyes were rather penetrating now.

"I see. You're dead-set on this, aren't you, FA? Finding them all?"

Sir Reginald hardly ever said or did anything without purpose. Using her country abbreviation was one of them. The first letter stood for their country section within SOE, France, followed by the first letter of the desk officer's first name. So, Anna was FA. Sir Reginald, as the head of the country section, was the only exception to this rule. He was simply F.

"You know I'll never do anything to harm SOE and will always protect its secrets, F."

He nodded.

"So, your first target is the Ravensbrück's camp commander, huh? Good work, Squadron Leader. No looking for Major Pilecki then?" The red-veined eyes bored into hers. Anna stiffened. The name hurt but it was not the time to be hurt.

Rather primly she quipped, "strictly speaking, Major Pilecki is the Polish Section of SOE. However, Summers has also given me permission to interrogate Anton Kaindl, the commander of Sachsenhausen about Peter Suttill. And of course, about Francis Churchill."

Anna took a deep breath before continuing in as neutral a voice as she could muster, "...as Maurice told us he last saw Major Pilecki in concentration camp Sachsenhausen in January 1944 and he *is* ... was an SOE agent, I don't see why I couldn't mention him to Kaindl as well if I am already there. The visit to Paderborn, where Kaindl is now interned in a British jail, will be sometime next week. The war crimes unit is rather busy as you can imagine, and Summers couldn't spare another man to accompany me sooner."

Anna hoped Sir Reginald would leave it at that. She'd given him the information he requested, now it was just hoping he wouldn't decide to accompany her on her trips. Her boss was the last person she wanted trailing along, looking over her shoulder.

"Good for you, old girl! Let's just hope for Jaffe's and your sake that bloody rain stops falling. The roads are atrocious and you'll be trekking through the Huns' country for quite a bit."

For once Anna agreed with her boss. The incessant rain made this search for her missing agents even more dreary and depressing, while the road conditions meant she and Jaffe would be travelling all Friday to get to the internment camp in Recklinghausen.

They'd finally come to the front of the crowd to be allowed inside the corridor that led to the courtroom after showing their passes to an exhausted looking British official.

"Well, let's get at it!" Sir Reginald boomed merrily, "you sit with me so you can have a clear view of the crooks. I'll tell Maurice to shuffle down a seat." Though she'd rather have preferred a seat in the back obscured from view, Anna could think of no excuse to turn down his offer.

"Thank you." It was the least she could say. Maurice Stonehouse, one of the few agents from the French Section of Churchill's Special Operations Executive who'd survived three concentration camps and managed to return to England in the early days of May, stood waiting for them inside the door.

Maurice, whose code name had been Shadow, had been a successful barrister before the war, a friend from Sir Reginald's vast network. He'd been the organiser of the Papillion Network in Lyon until his arrest by the Gestapo in August 1943.

Still pale and nervously smoking but at least with filled-out, freckled cheeks and a firm crop of red hair topping his head, rather than shaved to nothing, which is how he'd arrived at Tangmere Airport in Chichester six months earlier. Clad in borrowed American clothes, he'd stood on solid British soil, forlorn, too exhausted to even understand he'd survived. Then falling to the tarmac and kissing it, crying out, "Liberté!"

The flash of remembrance was as bright before Anna's eyes as the sun on that May morning. She'd been that close to tears, that close. But no. No tears for Anna.

Maurice smiled as he saw Anna approaching with his friend. Anna smiled back, inwardly suppressing the gnawing feeling of guilt every time she encountered him, or any other surviving secret agent. "Miss Adams!" Maurice shook her hand with gusto, "you should've told me our London spymaker was coming too, Reggie."

"I didn't know myself, Maurice," Sir Reginald lied. "Well, let the show begin. We've been waiting for it for too long."

Anna knew that Maurice was one of the witnesses during the tribunal but apparently not yet today.

The men let her pass down the corridor first. Taking a deep breath Anna stepped into Courtroom 600, which was about to write history. Or rather rewrite it.

2

THE NUREMBERG TRIAL

The first thing Anna observed as she entered the crowded courtroom with Sir Reginald and Maurice Stonehouse on her heels was the charged atmosphere in the large rectangular room. The space was not just filled to the brim with officials from the four conquering countries and large groups of journalists, it also oozed a poignant sense of historical significance, the gravity of the situation written over everyone's face.

"Third row. British section," Sir Reginald boomed and squeezing past Anna took the lead. The air in the room made her positively sick as she slowly zigzagged through the crowds trying to follow the Major's tweed jacket. Her stomach shot angry cramps through her entire belly and the leather coat weighed her arm down as if filled with lead. She also struggled to keep the dripping umbrella and her evidence-laden bag by her side.

"You're okay, Miss Adams?" Maurice's polite English voice with that lovely French lilt asked behind her. "Let me take that coat for you. It's like a hothouse in here."

"Thank you, Mr. Stonehouse."

Somehow, they'd never reached first-name basis and it wasn't likely they ever would. Anna was glad to slip into her seat and took a deep breath, steadying herself as Pearl had proudly taught her after her Gestapo interrogation training at Beaulieu. *Oh Pearl, where are you now?*

Using her lace handkerchief to fan herself, Anna pressed her lips together in dogged determination, all the while pushing the dark-rimmed glasses up the bridge of her nose as they kept sliding down from perspiration.

Squashed in between Sir Reginald and Maurice, she scanned the room for familiar faces, but she knew none of the men, nor the secretaries. Directly around them everybody spoke British English but, in the distance, she picked up French, Russian and American English. All the non-English attendees wore headphones through which, no doubt, interpreters would translate everything in their respective languages.

She spotted the blonde reporter in her overalls, also with headphones, which hung over one ear and half entangled in the blonde curls, sitting on the overcrowded journalists' bench. Anna wondered which nationality the blonde was.

In a flash, Esther Weiss's sweet face loomed before her. Somehow this reporter triggered the image of her roommate from the Swiss finishing school. The stylish Jewish girl from Vienna, on her way to Norway, hoping to marry her Carl. Anna had given her a copy of Daphne du Maurier's *Rebecca* in the train to Paris as they'd both travelled north.

What had the war done to resistance fighter Esther? A Jewess. A shiver went through Anna's slender frame. The last she'd heard about Esther was from Sable Montgomery, who'd met her when she was training for the Norwegian Resistance in Shetland. Raven-black Sable. Another brave agent. One of her Section F 'girls.'

Both former finishing-school girls had been so much more courageous than London-based Anna, who'd only had to make sure not to be hit by one of Hitler's bombs during the Blitz. But at least the Highland Raven had returned to her base and was now happily married to her Scotsman. And Sable had found her missing daughter.

Oh, the war! The wretched, wretched war!

Stop the past, Anna! It is no more.

Maurice handed her a peppermint, which Anna accepted gracefully. The minty sharpness in her throat pepped her up. Even her stomach seemed to agree. Suddenly the courtroom hushed as the defendants were brought in one after the other, handcuffed, marching in between two solemn guards in identical white helmets.

Anna counted twenty Nazis - the civilians dressed in crumpled suits that had seen better days and the military men still in their hate-triggering uniforms. Some, like Hermann Göring and Karl Dönitz, wore sunglasses to protect people from trying to read their souls through their eyes.

Anna's gaze, like everyone else's, was fixed on these middle-aged and elderly men taking their seats in two rows in a box opposite the judges' bench. The air in the courtroom was stifling, as if the audience's collective breath was taken from them. The awareness of being in the same room with them made it impossible to breathe.

These men, now looking bored and tired, had sent millions of innocent people to their premature death. The regime they'd embraced had brought the whole world teetering on the edge of extinction, freedom and safety no more than vague concepts from life before the war.

How the crowd had hoped to see the real architects on trial - Adolf Hitler, Heinrich Himmler, and Joseph Goebbels - but the cowards had taken their own lives and let their henchmen wear the post-war responsibility.

Most eyes were on the biggest defendant of them all, both literally and in Nazi rank, Hermann Göring, puffed-up and haughty in his gray battledress, sitting in the corner as if he still reckoned on a free ticket out.

Anna peered at the high-ranking Nazis through her glasses, taking in every detail, storing and filing as her mind was programmed to do. Nothing escaped her attention, and nothing would be forgotten. Not the keenness with which Alfred Rosenberg, the NSDAP's racial theory ideologist, scanned the public in his turn; nor the fidgeting of the restless Rudolf Hess, Hitler's Deputy Führer who'd made a mad dash for the United Kingdom to reach a peace agreement at the last minute. Early signs of mental illness were written all over him.

The one man she couldn't read as easily was sitting in the back row, behind Joachim von Ribbentrop. Also behind sunglasses, his slick, black hair carefully combed backwards and using headphones, the tall uniformed man was unknown to Anna. She shuffled through her papers to find he was Baldur von Schirach, Hitler's Youth Leader.

Before she had time to take more notes on where or how these Nazis were connected to the camp commanders she intended to interrogate, the door opened.

"All rise, the Court of the International Military Tribunal is now in session. The Honorable Justice Lord Geoffrey Lawrence of Great Britain is presiding."

The courtroom rose as one and in strode the American, British, Russian, and French judges in their formal attire, followed by the chief prosecutors of the respective countries. Each country sat in front of their own flag.

A bespectacled man with receding black hair, wearing a black suit and tie and looking as if he was carrying the weight of this tribunal on his slender shoulders took to the stand. He briefly looked at the defendants and let his eyes glide over the packed room. He nodded, checked the microphone, then lowered his eyes to his written speech. The whole room went silent as a tomb.

Justice Robert H. Jackson, the American prosecutor addressed them with his opening statement. Anna knew immediately that this speech would make it into the history books. She was glued to every word.

"May it please Your Honors.

The privilege of opening the first trial in history for crimes against the peace of the world imposes a grave responsibility. The wrongs which we seek to condemn and punish have been so calculated, so malignant, and so devastating, that civilization cannot tolerate their being ignored, because it cannot survive their being repeated. That four great nations, flushed with victory and stung with injury stay the hand of vengeance and voluntarily submit their captive enemies to the judgment of the law is one of the most significant tributes that Power has ever paid to Reason." [1]

It took the great orator, Justice Jackson, three hours to recite the entire speech, but everyone continued to listen with full attention in whatever language befitted them. The atmosphere inside the courtroom remained somber and tense as the words of horror rippled over the attendees. No one had yet really comprehended the extent of the evil they'd lived through. It was too colossal and staggering to understand.

The defendants, brought before the tribunal to face charges of war crimes, crimes against humanity, and crimes against peace, seemed deaf and mute, though Anna saw Walther Funck, the Nazi Minister of Economics, regularly mop his eyes with his handkerchief. Repentance? Or a show?

She couldn't feel sorry for him. These individuals were responsible for orchestrating and implementing the Nazi regime's policies that had led to the suffering and death of her agents.

She vaguely heard Lord Geoffrey say, "the Tribunal will now adjourn until 10 o'clock tomorrow morning," before she fainted.

"Anna?" It was Sir Reginald. "Have you eaten?" He was shaking her arm vigorously.

She looked around her, bewildered. Thank God, she was still sitting up straight, next to Maurice. She hadn't slipped to the floor.

"I'll never go without breakfast for the rest of my life," she promised, as Sir Reginald fed her a piece of chocolate.

"You silly goose," he said in a rather paternal voice. "Well out with you. Fresh air and some bread and bratwurst. No excuses."

She smiled at him, a genuine smile. For once Anna was thankful for her boss's bossiness. Maybe Sir Reginald's bark was worse than his bite. But she would never forget the investigation he'd ordered into her background in 1942.

---

1. *Justice Robert H. Jackson's famous 25,000-word Opening Statement can be found here

3

THE FIRST MISSION

Two days later - 23 November 1945

Aweak sun rose in the chilly, November morning, casting rayless light over Germany's war-torn landscape. At least it was dry after the heavy rains earlier in the week and the traffic was light. Anna counted her blessings after another sleepless night, tossing and turning in her bed at *Das Bayerischer Gasthaus*.

She was glad to leave the gloom and doom of Nuremberg behind her, though she didn't exactly expect her visit to Fritz Suhren to resemble a party. Two more stops and back to Britain. At least for the time being. Gosh, she was so tired of all these criminals.

Major Angus Jaffe, a seasoned British officer with a stern demeanor, who – in early 1945 - had fought the Germans tooth and nail at the Siegfried Line with the British Second Army, gripped the large steering wheel of the Humber Heavy Utility "Box" as he maneuvered the khaki-colored, armoured vehicle through the narrow streets of Nuremberg.

The engine rumbled with a sense of purpose, its tires crunching over rubble and debris left in the wake of conflict. Anna sat beside him, her blue WAAF uniform pristine against the muted backdrop, her gaze behind her glasses focused on the road ahead with a mix of determination and unease. An unfolded map of Germany, marked and torn at the edges, rested in her lap. Her red bag sat securely between her silk-stockinged ankles.

In the back seat, Major John Stewart, the war crimes specialist that Group Captain Summers had assigned to her from the headquarters in Bad Oeynhausen, was sifting through a stack of documents, his elongated face with narrow nose and hawkish eyes illuminated by the pale light filtering through the windows. At times he would curse under his breath when the Box hit a pothole sending his papers flying from his briefcase.

Every bump in the road was inevitably followed by a "so sorry, Sir!" uttered by Jaffe. Anna clenched her teeth and forcibly calmed her stomach. At least she'd eaten this morning, which oddly enough had turned out to be a full English breakfast.

Bayern certainly wasn't the flourishing Bayern from the before the war, but the Germans were as good as always to spot an opportunity for commerce when they saw it. With the influx of British army personnel, they'd simply crossed out the words Bratwurst and Schinken from the menu and replaced it with sausages and ham.

The hum of the engine provided a steady rhythm for the journey, punctuated by the occasional distant rumble of demolitions. For the rest the city was eerily quiet on this dreary, November morning.

The journey was also marked by the silence inside the car. The lack of conversation seemed to carry the weight of Anna's mission - to uncover the truth behind her missing agents. The dozens who hadn't returned to Britain at the war's end and whose fates hung in the balance.

As the Box rolled on, the landscape shifted from the ruins of Nuremberg to desolate countryside, where skeletal trees and abandoned farmhouses told tales of displacement and loss. The road stretched without end, mirroring the uncertainty and emptiness that filled Anna's heart.

At a fork in the road, she offered directions while following the journey with a finger on the map, but Jaffe appeared to know the way by heart, having been stationed in the British part of Germany since its surrender. Major Stewart in the back had closed his suitcase and his eyes. He snored lightly.

For Anna the uncomfortable expedition in the Box went on forever. They'd made just one pitstop near Frankfurt for lunch and bathroom break. It was only towards the end of the afternoon when the outskirts of Recklinghausen finally came into view. A watery sun was setting in the west.

"What's the name of the hotel again?" Jaffe asked. Stewart opened his eyes and yawned.

"Engelsburg," Anna replied, suppressing a yawn herself.

"Nice name," Jaffe chuckled. "I suppose the Germans will want to change it, now we govern this part and they hardly see us as angels."

"Probably," Anna agreed, gazing up at the old castle coming into sight. It had that unmistakable robust, and yet refined, sense of Germanic architecture. Seeing the proud, centuries-old building stand undamaged in the fading daylight somehow brought the essence of this war to Anna. And it hurt. The way this once great nation had come to its deserved ruin.

Despite all the horrors that had passed in this country, the Germans generally weren't better or worse than other people. They, too, created beauty and style. And just wanted to live their lives.

How had they been led astray by the wrong people, the ones she'd encountered in the dock at the Nuremberg Trials? But this was not a thought she could share with her companions. The pain between the nations was too big, the rift too deep. She opened the door of the Box to stretch her very stiff legs and take a breath of cold winter air.

"Dinner in an hour?" It was one of the first things Major Stewart had contributed to the conversation. The middle-aged military man was exceedingly tall, with sparse sandy hair and a limp, most likely from a war wound.

The war investigator, Major Summers, had assured Anna that the man he'd sent with her wouldn't be in her way but could be helpful, as Major Stewart already had an extensive file on Nazi Commander

Fritz Suhren. Anna had nothing against taciturn men, on the contrary, she appreciated the quiet as she preferred to spill as few words as possible herself.

"Sure," Jaffe and she agreed. Major Stewart pushed one of his files into her hand.

"You might want to look through this before you go in tomorrow morning, but I warn you it's gruesome." It was a simple gray folder with Fritz Suhren typed in bold letters on the cover.

"Thank you, Major. I'm grateful for your help." She wondered how much there was in that dismal-looking folder that she didn't already know. Probably a lot. Her London research into the Ravensbrück commander, albeit thorough, had lacked the on-the-ground research the war crimes investigators were able to assemble. Now she could act with even more forethought, which was the way Anna liked to do things.

4

THE RAVENSBRÜCK
INTERROGATIONS

The Humber Heavy Utility Box passed under the iron framework of what had been a small *Konzentratsionlager,* the former concentration camp was now a detention center, *Internierungslager Recklinghausen.* The first thing Anna noticed was that there were all sorts of German prisoners here. Nicely dressed ones, who'd obviously had enough time to pack a decent suitcase, while others were haphazardly dressed, being no doubt caught whilst on the run, or arrested by surprise.

The next thing that made her swallow was the humility in their eyes. If they wore any kind of headgear, they took it off as the British car passed them and stared at their shoes. Were these the proud Nazis that had caused so much suffering, or the smaller fish that had just followed orders? They seemed as lost as the last autumnal leaves that whirled around them.

"Straight ahead, and park close to the main entrance," Major Stewart instructed from the back seat. Only then, Anna realized, the investigator had been here before. Jaffe brought the heavy vehicle to a stop and immediately two British soldiers posted themselves on each side, as if they feared the prisoners would peel off with the Box if they got a chance.

The trio emerged from the vehicle, their breath visible in the cold air, and exchanged brief nods with the guards before entering the low, sprawling building with its many offshoots of barracks. The sun was still fighting the angry fall clouds and had won so far, but the wind was sharp with the acrid scent of pines in the air.

Anna hesitated a moment before crossing the threshold. A concentration camp. She had narrowly escaped being sent to one. So many, so, so many hadn't. She was one of the lucky ones and needed to remember it.

Stop such senseless thoughts! I wouldn't be here, doing what I'm doing if I had. The agents' families deserve answers. And I will provide them.

Anna shivered for the second time that morning. Most of the families she was reporting back to hadn't even known their loved one was sent into France and had been caught.

It was only at the war's end – and an agent was reported missing – that Anna confessed to their families that postcards she'd sent on behalf of the agent hadn't been real but written in stacks before departure. That was the first painful hurdle. Then admitting to these same misled families that only a handful had managed to avoid or escape the Gestapo and make it back to Britain alive. Of all those who hadn't returned, she now had to extract their fate from no doubt unwilling torturers.

"You're okay?" Major Stewart must have seen the struggle on her face. "My first time inside these hellholes wasn't smooth sailing either. I even vomited."

With surprise, Anna looked up into the elongated face with the narrow, hazel eyes and saw only friendliness. And understanding. The Major shrugged.

"I know. It's sheer cowardice and that from a military man but..." His voice dropped, "it was Ravensbrück, Miss Adams, the rustic dwelling of this chappie we're about to see. The first thing we encountered as our battalion went into the camp were heaps of dead women's bodies. Everywhere, and a burning crematorium. The stench, and the flies. I'll never be able to get rid of that encounter as long as I live. By God, what has humanity come to?"

"Sunk to its knees," Jaffe grumbled angrily, as he showed their passes to a sentry waiting for them in a secured corridor. He led them to a cellblock with small, barred windows.

"Don't expect much from Suhren." Major Stewart had found his professional voice again. "Hard as nails. No conscience. Denies everything. Hopes to get out with just a prison sentence."

Anna nodded. She'd read his statement word for word.

The interrogation room they were led to was dimly lit, casting long shadows across the grimy white walls. A wooden table stood in the center of the small space, flanked by three chairs. On the table stood a clean ashtray, a bottle of water and three glasses.

"Should I go?" Jaffe asked, looking around him.

"Would you, Major Jaffe?" Anna was relieved. She felt that two British military men present might be too intimidating to the German camp bully. Bullies were generally sensitive to being outnumbered.

"No problem. I'll wait in the Box and take a much-needed nap." Jaffe was already out of the door and Anna sensed the Brit was relieved to avoid the orbit of the nasty individual that Fritz Suhren no doubt was.

Major Stewart pulled out a chair for Anna and, after taking off her leather coat and straightening her tie and jacket, she sat down, crossing her feet at the ankles. A notepad and pen ready with a list of names and pictures of mostly her female agents, as she had been responsible for them. Major Stewart glanced over her shoulder as he sat down next to her.

"What a list," he sighed. "And that's just the women."

"The ones we assume were in Ravensbrück. Then we have Mauthausen, Sachsenhausen, Dachau, and Auschwitz."

"Don't forget Natzweiler in France," Stewart added.

"They're all engrained in my brain, and I intend to visit them all." Anna's mouth pressed so thin her lips were white. She pushed her glasses up, a habit that always helped to steady her.

"What's taking him so long?" She was tapping with the backend of her Parker pen on her notebook.

"Security measures," her companion explained. "Don't forget he already escaped once and was brought back by the Americans. They're dead set on keeping him locked up now."

Suddenly the door swung open. Two guards jogged in who posted themselves on each side of the opened door. They were heavily armed.

A third guard brought in Fritz Suhren. Anna studied him intently. He looked younger than the early forties she knew he was. Pale-skinned, with reddish hair that was well-kept. Of medium height. A peculiar, round face. Eyes far from dumb.

What struck Anna was that he only wore socks, trousers, and a shirt. Were they that afraid he'd take a runner again? The next surprise was that he stood to attention for them, acknowledging his war was lost.

"Sit!" the guard that patrolled him most closely ordered in English. Suhren took the seat opposite the two Brits. He didn't look at Anna, but his eyes darted towards the photographs she'd deliberately spread out on the table for him. His glance betrayed nothing. It was just that. A glance.

Suhren's face remained a mask of emotionless stoicism, but he clearly jumped when Anna, instead of the war investigator who'd questioned him before, addressed him.

"Any familiar faces, Herr Suhren?"

"No. I don't know who they are, Ma'am." His voice was tentative but even. English with a heavy German accent.

"Do you remember any English women in Ravensbrück?"

"No, I don't. Dutch, German, French, Polish. But not English, Ma'am."

"Denise Damerment was French." Anna dropped her finger on the photograph of a young woman with an open, friendly face and mid-length, wavy, dark hair.

Suhren shook his head again. "Sorry, Ma'am."

Anna wished the Nazi would stop "ma'am-ing" her in that emotionless voice, but felt it was not her place to tell him so. The Nazi's eyes went from the photograph to Major Stewart, perhaps hoping he'd shut the English woman up and give him a less arduous time. But Stewart's face was as closed as a locked safe. He scribbled away in the gray Fritz Suhren file, pretending not to see the prisoner's silent plea.

Anna was surer than ever the camp commander was lying but interrogation was a technique she'd not yet mastered.

"Do the names Maureen Knight, Pearl Baseden, Madeleine Bloch, or Yvonne Churchill ring a bell?"

"Churchill? Yvonne Churchill, yes." Suhren sat up straighter, even allowed himself a slight smile.

Of course, you despicable man, Anna thought bitterly, *you'll trumpet your one so-called good deed, which was only to save your own skin.* She'd already read Suhren's account of his "helping the Englishwoman." Though she'd not been able to speak with Yvonne, who was still convalescing in a Manchester hospital, Sir Reginald had confirmed Yvonne's miraculous escape from Ravensbrück.

Wearily Anna remarked, "so first you tell me you don't remember any English women, Herr Suhren, and now you admit to knowing Yvonne Churchill? Well, tell me your version, and let's have it over with."

"I thought you only wanted information on .... uh...prisoners who passed, Ma'am?" Again, that tentative, even voice. It made her blood boil.

"Just tell me." Anna fought to control her anger. A new emotion to her, who prided herself on her own evenness of mood.

"Yvonne Churchill was a special prisoner. HQ in Berlin made me especially responsible for her, as it was rumored she was Winston Churchill's niece."

"She wisely created that rumor herself, but she wasn't related," Anna snapped, but silently grateful that the Churchill name saved at least one of her agents in the most unlikely manner.

"I learned that later, Ma'am. When it was clear that the Allies were coming and the war was lost, I personally drove Miss Churchill to the American lines..."

"... where you used her as a hostage to negotiate for your own life, telling the Americans not to forget your good deed."

"Officer Adams!"

It was Major Stewart looking at Anna with a steely expression.

"Sorry!" she bowed her head. *Be more impartial.*

"That's right, Ma'am," Suhren said unperturbed. "That's exactly what I told them, but it didn't do me much good, did it?"

It was the first time Suhren's façade showed a small sign of a crack. Anna saw beads of sweat forming on his forehead, and his hands trembled slightly. But he quickly regained that infuriating detachment.

The room seemed to grow colder as the interrogation unfolded, leading her nowhere. Even Major Stewart's helpful prodding only made Suhren more defensive.

"Please bring in the two female guards I've requested to interview as well. See if they can help refresh Herr Suhren's mind," Anna said with as little exasperation as she could muster. Another crack appeared in the camp commander's façade, but he gave nothing away yet. He'd clearly not anticipated that the Englishwoman had another card up her sleeve.

The room became very crowded when the two German "Erstaufseherinnen", chief wardresses, were brought in, and two more chairs wedged into the tiny interrogation room. The first one was a young, fair-haired woman with an impressive bosom and a defiant look in her light blue eyes. She tried to tone her fierceness down, but captivity had only made her more angry. Anna recognized her as Dorothea Guhl, who was "known to look for the weakest or the most fearful prisoners, whom she then showered with lashes or blows, along with a leashed German Shepherd," as the investigation report had read.

A face from hell indeed.

The other woman was Dorothea's boss, Luise Brunner, a dark-haired woman with a softer, round face, pronounced eyebrows and dark eyes. She seemed to want to disappear in the shadows.

Don't be fooled by looks, Anna, she reminded herself. This creature had been trained in Auschwitz II and was chief Oberaufseherin of Ravensbrück in the last months of the war when the death toll rose and rose. "If they noticed a shawl, a pullover, or stocking with which the women prisoners tried to cover themselves, she would beat them half-dead," from the report on Luise.

Anna groaned softly. Surely, not all Germans had shown themselves to be sadists, but these creatures seemed the lowest of the lowest.

"*Gab es englische Mädchen und Frauen in Ravensbrück?* Anna asked Luise in flawless German if there had been English girls and women in the camp. It was the first time she addressed them in their native language. Everyone in the room, including Major Stewart, seemed utterly surprised that that thoroughbred Englishwoman happened to speak German slick as a whistle.

Anna pretended not to notice. Her quest was more important than the fact people found out she knew German. The woman would hardly speak English and she wanted to get down to business.

"Yes," the older woman affirmed., "There were several English women in the camp. They wore red triangles on their shoulders with the letter "E."

"What happened to them?" Anna asked the woman, all the while with her eyes on Suhren sitting across from her. He squinted but shook his head. She continued the entire conversation in German, knowing Major Stewart had had a language course prior to becoming a war investigator and would be able to follow the conversation.

"They were killed."

Anna shoved the photographs of her agents towards the woman. The light was getting dimmer, the cell was only lit by a fluorescent strip. It made Suhren look even sicklier than he already did. The woman was clearly short-sighted. She peered at the photographs for a long time. Then a fat finger landed on Maureen's face. "Shot." Then on Madeleine, "shot." Then on Denise. "Shot".

Anna held her breath as the finger went to her friend Pearl. "No, dear God," she prayed, though she knew there was no more hope after seven long months with no leads on her. The finger hovered over the dark-blonde woman with the luminous eyes. "I don't know that one."

"What do you mean?" Anna raised herself from her chair, her voice raised, eyes burning.

"Officer Adams!" Major Steward warned again, and she sank on her chair, exhausted, trembling.

"I don't know that one."

"Did you know all the English women that were held at Ravensbrück?"

"There weren't that many. Only those four. And only the Churchill girl survived. Barely. They were all in our care, weren't they, Dorothea?"

The younger woman nodded, "Yes, Luise, that's correct."

Anna struggled with her thoughts. Yvonne Churchill had testified Pearl Baseden was with the other girls on the train from Karlsruhe prison to Ravensbrück. She hadn't said that Pearl didn't arrive with them.

"I have reason to believe this woman was with the group that came from Karlsruhe prison," Anna repeated in a last attempt to get to the truth.

"She might have died on the way. Or escaped. She wasn't at Ravensbrück," Luise insisted. Somehow, this gave Anna a spark of hope that her friend might still be alive, though she knew there was no reason for hope. Pearl had been lost for over a year now. Anna had to content herself she'd traced her back to the women's prison in Germany in September 1944. Pearl was alive then.

It was time for her next question, feeling this visit was not going to be wasted time after all. She kept a close watch on Suhren's demeanor. More small cracks appeared in the façade, but he could stay out of the limelight of her interrogation for now.

"Why were they shot? I read the resistance women at Ravensbrück were hanged." Anna fought to keep her voice even and managed. There was a quick exchange of glances between Luise and Suhren. Anna saw the slightest of nods.

"That is correct, Ma'am, but hanging was public, so to avoid problems, the English women were taken to the execution wall near the crematorium and shot."

Anna rose half from her chair, her eyes ablaze but she corrected herself this time before Major Stewart could reprimand her and sat down again.

"And their bodies burned immediately?"

"Yes, Ma'am."

Anna looked at Major Stewart next to her. "I want to schedule a trip to Ravensbrück to pay tribute to Maureen, Denise and Madeleine."

"Very well, Officer Adams. That can be arranged." Anna saw concern in the small hazel eyes of her British companion, but turning once more to Luise, fired off her last question.

"Wer gab den Befehl die englischen Beamtinnen zu ermorden?"

Who gave the order to murder the English agents?

A pause, some shuffling, glances exchanged between the three Nazis.

"SS-Sturmbannführer Suhren, Ma'am."

"Liar!"

The Nazi commander seem to wake from his stupor and began to curse in German.

"End of meeting!" one of the guards yelled in English and the three prisoners were quickly taken from the room.

Anna sat very still, her Parker still in her trembling hand. Then she trembled all over and couldn't stop. How different was it to hear the words she'd dreaded all this time from the mouths of the Nazis themselves. Maureen, Madeleine, Denise. Killed in cold blood for their heroism, their love for their country. And Pearl. Still no sign of Pearl.

"How bad must it have been?" she asked softly in the now silent interrogation room. "And the terrible thing is, Suhren still doesn't admit to what he's done. But he will. He must be forced to speak the truth."

"Hopefully he will, Officer Adams, but there's no saying with these criminals," Major Stewart replied sotto voce. "The worst of it is, this is only the tip of the iceberg. We have years of work ahead of us, and many of these crooks will slip through our fingers. That's the sad reality of it. And that's why my suggestion now is to find Jaffe and go for dinner. I know it sounds odd, but we must take care of ourselves in order to navigate this path through hell."

"You're right," Anna agreed, getting up, stretching herself in an attempt to stop the tremors. Then she smoothed her crumpled blue uniform. Major Stewart made a snorting sound, which made her look up in surprise.

"You did well, Adams. From now on I'm going to call you the "Blau Angezogen". That's what we call WAAF women here in Germany."

The Woman in Blue. Anna wondered if she'd ever be able to shake herself free from both uniform and the blues in her soul.

5

THE DINNER AFTER

N ight had fallen around five, as Major Jaffe steered the Box onto the roads of post-war Germany. The passengers were once again silent, enveloped in a mixture of exhaustion and horror.

Some of the truth had been unearthed, a small light of victory in the face of immense darkness. The inky landscape continued to pass by, forever changed by the echoes of history, while Anna felt as if the weight of the revelations the wardresses had just disclosed, rested entirely on her. She knew the pursuit of justice would move forward one step at a time and that she was involved in it now. The knowledge brought her no joy, though it did give her an ambiguous sense of satisfaction.

She wasn't thinking of convicted camp bullies, but of parents and partners and siblings, to whom she would have to explain how their brave loved ones came to an untimely end. How to spare them the worst details, or should they know it all?

"You don't miss anything, do you, Officer Adams? Not a twitch of the mouth, a nervous movement of the hand, a coveted glance?" Major Stewart's voice cut through the thick silence. He was sitting upfront with Jaffe now, as Anna had stated she wanted to sit in the back to sort her mind.

"I guess not," she replied. "It came with the job I had."

"You scan and read people like others browse through and pick from a catalogue." There was admiration in Stewart's voice. "No wonder they called you 'the London spymaker.' Well, if you're serious about becoming a war crimes investigator, that's already a course you can skip. You clearly know how to assess people, though you still must learn not to show your emotions."

"True," Anna admitted, but then added in a sad voice, "I may have picked the most heroic and best women to become agents in France but what good did that do them? So many will never return."

"Don't blame yourself for that, Adams. That was the security systems that failed. Call it laxity on behalf of SOE HQ. The refusal to pick up the signals that circuits had collapsed and agents had been captured. Look at Holland. It was much worse there."

"You seem to forget that I was working for SOE HQ, too, Major Stewart. I was part of the system that failed, and I did too little to ring the alarm bells. So yes, I do blame myself."

"There was so much uncertainty about what was really going on behind enemy lines," Major Jaffe cut in. "Of course mistakes were made, but no one in London deliberately sent agents to their death. It was still all the work of the Nazis."

"You're right there." His softer version of Anna's wartime work helped soothed her troubled mind.

More silence until Jaffe turned off the road to head to a restaurant, filled to the brim with rather merry and not very sober British officers. The only Germans present were the waiters.

Both of Anna's military companions soon joined people they knew at another table, after Anna assured them she was fine on her own and wanted to sort her thoughts. With little appetite, she bit into a piece of beef that was not very tender and picked at some small potatoes swimming in gravy.

"Eat, Ans...!" Her father's voice.

No, no going there. That path is closed.

Anna briefly closed her eyes. She was so darn tired. Shutting out the world, she retreated within, back to the interrogation room, recalling the questions to see if she'd neglected to ask anything. While she sat there with the back of her head resting against the leather upholstery of her dining chair, she got the forbidding feeling she was being watched.

"Don't be daft. Are you going soft in the head now as well, on top of everything else?" she scolded herself, keeping her eyes closed against the brightly lit Gasthaus. She could hear Jaffe and Stewart laughing and talking at the table next to her. She was safe.

But Anna was Anna, and a gut feeling a gut feeling. She opened her eyes to slits to scan her surroundings, not just with her eyes but with all her senses. She may not be a trained agent herself, but she'd been around them for so many years she knew all their tricks. She let her eyes drift from left to right, taking in the room. Yes, the hairs on her arms stood up, her ears picked up the soft rustling of paper.

Who was acting suspiciously in a busy restaurant at mealtime?

A few tables away from her, someone sat hidden behind yesterday's copy of The Times. Trousers with brogues told her it was a man. Cigarette smoke rose from behind the newspaper. Anna couldn't see his face and upper body, but she did detect two small holes in the middle of the paper.

Who was he? And more importantly, was he watching her, or the British officials? Or was she going crazy? Anna decided that if he was a spy, she could hardly be his target. Nobody knew she was here. She'd left her unwanted shadow in London, where she'd constantly felt watched. Moreover, she'd traveled to Germany without an official assignment from the War Office, on the spur of the moment, a free place in a Lysander heading for Berlin. Nobody knew.

But she hoped the man behind the newspaper didn't have his eyes on Major Stewart or any of the other war crime investigators.

Then let it be her. The war was over, and Anna Adams wasn't as dead set on keeping all her personal cards close to her chest. The right people had won. Her people.

Intently staring at the newspaper to show whoever was behind it she was aware of him and his possible spying, Anna's mind worked overtime. Was she seeing too much into it? She heard the stories of the so-called double spies. They'd been the talk of the town back home, suspecting every German to be a possible candidate.

Of course, high-ranking Nazis who were still on the run, were spending large amounts of money to keep the investigators off their tracks. And Nazism hadn't died with Hitler. It was still very much a belief system many hung onto. Assassins wouldn't be hard to find.

Just as Anna was on the brink of joining the men at their table and telling them her suspicions, the newspaper went down. The man was staring straight at her. He was tall and lean, with thinning black hair combed over his scalp, angular cheekbones, his nose was long and thin as well and his lips, bloodless and thin, smiled faintly at her. He folded the newspaper, got up, threw some coins on the table, and left. He moved with a fluidity that sent shivers up her spine. Was he German or British? It was hard for her to determine.

"Miss Adams, we're leaving." It was Jaffe.

Anna was still staring at the man's back disappearing through the rotating door at the Gasthaus' entrance. A beige Mackintosh. Just before he got to the street, he put a black hat on his head and was gone.

"Miss Adams, have you seen a ghost?"

"That was weird." She got up herself, picking up her bag, looking frazzled.

"What was?" Jaffe's voice sounded concerned. "Did we neglect you for too long? Sorry but we hadn't seen the boys since August and ..."

"No, no problem," Anna interrupted. "I'm fine. Let's find a hotel. How far is it to Paderborn tomorrow?"

"It's weekend, remember? We'll take it easy." That was Major Stewart.

"It's no more than a two-hour drive to Paderborn. We'll stay the night over in Dortmund. All arranged at the expense of the British army."

6

AN INTIMIDATING ENCOUNTER

Two days later - Dortmund, 26 November 1945

A t one in the morning, sleep still evaded Anna. The events from the past couple of days, both the start of the trial at Nuremberg and the encounter with the bullies of Ravensbrück, jumbled through her head. But there was more. Being in Germany, the suspicion of being followed, everything weighed Anna down insomuch as it made her toss and turn in the uncomfortable hotel bed.

When she was sure sleep wouldn't come, she threw back the bed covers and got up to fetch a glass of water and an aspirin. Once up and in her dressing gown, she decided to do what she did best. Work.

Sitting down at the small table in her hotel room with the water and the painkiller, she took Major Stewart's gray files out of her bag and chose the one that had Anton Kaindl in bold letters on the cover. She'd already studied the details, but she wanted to make sure she remembered them all correctly before the interrogation today.

Her eyes glanced over Stewart's notes about Sachsenhausen, where cruel Kaindl had been commander:

The Sachsenhausen camp is located 35 kilometers (22 mi) north of Berlin, which gave it a primary position among the German concentration camps. The administrative center of all concentration camps was located in Oranienburg, so Sachsenhausen became a training center for SS officers, who would – after their training - be sent to oversee other camps. Sachsenhausen was used to perfect the most efficient and effective execution methods for use in the death camps. Given that, executions obviously took place at Sachsenhausen. The camp was in use from 1936 until April 1945. It mainly held political prisoners. Of the estimated 30,000 victims at Sachsenhausen, most were Soviet prisoners of war, among them women.

Sachsenhausen-Oranienburg is currently in the Soviet Occupied Zone in use by the NKVD as special camp Nr.7.

THIS WAS nothing new to Anna, but there was a hunger within her to know it all, to remember every detail, to make sure she didn't miss anything. She shuffled through the black-and-white photographs of the camp - emaciated men in striped suits working in a clay pit, more barbed wire and surveillance posts than she cared to see. The last photograph was almost too gruesome - piles and piles of clothes heaped against an outbuilding. The last bit of decency stripped off these prisoners before being forced to wear striped suits until liberation. If they made it that long.

Anna took off her glasses and closed her eyes, rubbing her sore temples.

"I simply can't stand rereading Stewart's description of Anton Kaindl," she said out loud. "I'll make up my mind about him sitting eye-to-eye with him on Monday."

From Kaindl, her mind went to the missing Sachsenhausen agents. So far only one male SOE agent of Section F had returned safely to England, Francis Churchill, Yvonne's husband. Once a flamboyant and charismatic leader, he was now in a terrible state, both physically and mentally, but at least he was alive.

Most of Anna's focus would be on confirming the fate of the man SOE HQ should never have let down. The most brilliant of them all, organiser of several successful French circuits and too elusive to be caught by the Gestapo for years: Peter Suttill.

But he had been caught, probably in June 1943 and after interrogations at the Gestapo HQ in Paris, he'd been sent to Sachsenhausen where it was believed he was either shot or hung in March 1945, just a month before the camp's liberation by the Soviets.

Two other former prisoners had Anna's attention. One was a young boy who had nothing to do with SOE and whose name she'd have to sneak in the conversation. She still didn't know how to do that, as she didn't even dare to mention his name aloud to herself.

Maybe she would just push his photograph under Kaindl's nose and wait to see his reaction. But she was of two minds about this, as she'd had to cut the photograph in two. Which hurt too much. The other half of the photo showed a very young Anna in dark pigtails and a wide smile. Not yet in glasses. The cut-up photograph might create suspicion about the other half.

And Anna was very aware she was only here to ask questions about her Section F agents. Not about unknown boys, let alone agents who'd been part of Section of Polish agents.

But hadn't Sir Owens given her implied permission to also search for Major Henryk "Hubal" Pilecki? He'd asked her what she was going to do about him, adding later that Section P was understaffed with so many missing Polish agents.

She started pacing the room. Why didn't she smoke? This seemed just the moment for it, but any attempt at a cigarette had so far always ended in a huge coughing fit.

Henryk appeared before her out of nothing, just as she'd seen him in the fall of 1942 in the dimly lit, smoke-filled officers' lounge at RAF Northolt where she'd been to see off one of her agents.

All eyes had turned as the door swung open to reveal the dashing figure of ... Anna's family's savior. He was then, as he had been in 1938, the epitome of a hero, tall and ruggedly handsome, a Polish pilot with a presence that could not be ignored. But he shouldn't have walked straight back into her life.

His face, oh that unforgettable face. The strong jawline was chis-

eled and defined, framing a face that bore the subtle scars of countless battles in the skies. The piercing blue eyes held a glint of
determination and a hint of mischief, a testament to his unwavering
spirit and the depth of his character. They were windows to a soul
that had seen both the horrors of war and the beauty of life, a soul
that yearned for something beyond the battlefield. And the eyes had
gone straight to Anna in her blue WAAF uniform. The look in those
eyes had broken her heart all over.

Still pacing the lengths of her dismal, Dortmund hotel room,
where the only sounds were the occasional creaking of a bed in the
next room and the rumble of a lonely car outside, Anna let her mind
linger a little longer on Henryk's physique as if weighing her chances
to ever forget.

Why did she feel so deeply? And why for this man?

He had dark, wavy hair swept back with an effortless elegance,
occasionally falling across his forehead in a way that made her heart
skip a beat. His blue aviator uniform, impeccably tailored, highlighted his broad shoulders and a physique honed through rigorous
training and combat missions. The Gapa, the Polish eagle emblem on
his chest, slightly worn but still gleaming with pride, spoke of his
unwavering commitment to his homeland and his will to defeat
Hitler.

He was no policymaking, staying-safe-in-one's-gentlemen-club
aristocrat. This was a man who shunned no part of the action. A
liberator through and through. And he'd stolen her heart when he
shouldn't have.

Henryk moved with the grace and confidence of the invincible
warrior. But it hadn't been his handsomeness and strength that drew
her to him like a magnet, it had mostly been his quiet charisma.
Never talking much, his whole being spoke volumes, a combination
of humility and strength that endeared him to those who had the
privilege of knowing him. His smile, though rare, was a radiant
display of warmth and charm that could melt even the iciest of
hearts.

And it was as much his character that made Major Pilecki a true hero. He was a man of honor, integrity, with an unyielding dedication to his comrades and the cause he fought for. He was a symbol of hope in the darkest of times, a reminder that even amidst the chaos of war, love and humanity could still flourish.

Oh Henryk, why?

Anna knew confronting Anton Kaindl and learning Henryk too had been tortured to death, would be the hardest truth she'd yet have to swallow. That great, unbreakable spirit broken at last. And he would never know she'd loved him till the end. He'd died thinking she'd married her uppity fiancé, Count Macalister.

Anna was agitated. She sank on the bed, her head in her hands.

"At least I escaped that fate, Henryk." And in a small voice she added, "thanks to you."

Where Henryk had had an unwavering mission in his short life, so had she now. Finally. While there was still breath in her body, Squadron Leader Adams vowed to uncover the whereabouts of every SOE agent who'd disappeared on mainland Europe. Male or female.

Straightening her back, Anna gulped down the rest of the water and grabbed her leather coat. She hesitated as she stared at the Luger lying idly on her nightstand. A present from Henryk, but still never used by her.

A girl like you needs to be able to defend herself.

Anna tucked it in the inside pocket of her coat.

Not knowing where she was heading, but in dire need of some fresh air, away from that suffocating room and her mental agony, she slipped the night key into the front door of Hotel Eisenburg and stepped onto a poorly lit, unfamiliar street in central Dortmund.

At this hour, the city was dusky and deserted but Anna could make out the silhouettes of its many ruins. Most buildings had been bombed into skeletons. Even one of the hotel walls had taken a hit but had withstood the blast. It was cold but dry, white stars flickering in the firmament above her and the crescent of a new moon.

The desolate night air suited Anna's mood. She started walking randomly, taking in great gulps of frosty air. Being outside calmed her senses and lessened her headache. Fear was something from another planet. What could happen to her here that hadn't already happened to her?

Silence reigned. Save for the distant echoes of all-night reconstruction efforts - when had the Germans *not* been industrious? - and the occasional passing vehicle. In yet another war-torn city, Anna sifted her thoughts through the horrors of the past until she felt a heavy unease settle over her.

She quickened her pace, her footsteps echoing against the cobblestone streets. For some reason she'd ended up in a maze of backstreets she didn't particularly fancy herself in. She ought go back to the hotel before losing her way. The sound of her heels made way too much noise against the walls of the abandoned alleyways.

A sense of foreboding gripped her. It was impossible to shake off the feeling she was being followed. Again. Her every instinct screamed danger.

With a racing heart, she slipped into yet another, even narrower, alley, hoping to evade her unseen pursuer. She pressed herself against the cold, damp wall, trying to control her erratic breathing. Her gloved hand instinctively reached for the Luger tucked beneath her coat, a reassuring weight against her side.

I'm not a good shot.

Footsteps drew nearer, their rhythm calculated and deliberate, as they passed the alley where she was hiding. Anna strained her ears to catch any hint of who might be trailing her. Would he return? The silence was excruciating until a faint rustle of footsteps brushing against the pavement reached her ears, and she knew someone was there, lurking in the shadows.

Without even moving her eyelids, she peered into the dim light until she caught a glimpse of a man's silhouette, tall and lean, emerging from the darkness. He moved with a fluidity that sent her into a cold sweat. The gray Macintosh. The black hat. It was him, from the dining room. He was coming *for her.*

Anna couldn't see his face, but the aura of danger around him was palpable.

"*Wer sind Sie?*" Not knowing where she found the courage to speak, she addressed him in German, asking who he was. Her voice quivered with a tremor of fear, her hand on the Luger that would be utterly useless under her command.

The man remained silent. His presence became more menacing with each passing moment. He stepped closer, and Anna's fingers tightened around the grip of her Luger, ready to defend herself if necessary. As a fool would.

"You won't find what you're looking for here," Anna continued in English, trying to maintain her composure. "I'm just an investigator, trying to bring justice to those who committed heinous crimes during the war."

Still the man said nothing. Instead, he reached into his coat pocket and slowly pulled out a folded piece of paper. Without a word, he held it out toward her.

Anna hesitated, her curiosity momentarily overpowering her fear. She cautiously took the paper, unfolding it to reveal a black-and-white photograph. It depicted a group of high-ranking Nazi officers, their faces twisted into triumphant grins as they stood in front of a concentration camp gate.

"What is this?" Anna asked, her voice trembling as she looked up from the photograph to the stranger. He stood with his back to the light, so his features were cast in darkness, the black hat deep over his eyes. Yet he hadn't had any trouble showing himself to her at the Gasthaus.

Finally, the man spoke, his voice low and gravelly. English with a slight German-accent. "You're not the only one seeking justice, Fräulein Adams. There are those who still believe in it, even in the shadows. You may not recognize the man in the middle, but we'll not forget him. Nor will we forget you and your lot."

Anna couldn't decipher the man's true intentions, but one thing was clear: her path had just taken an unexpected turn.

"Gute Nacht, Fräulein. You keep that photograph." And as fluidly and shadowy as he'd arrived, he disappeared again. Anna stood shaking on her legs, the crumpled photograph between her gloved fingers, the damp wall supporting her.

As the German city continued its slow recovery from the ravages of war, Anna Adams found herself entangled in a dangerous web of secrets, double agents, and the pursuit of justice in a world still teetering on the brink of chaos.

And the worst of it all? She knew that man. Just not his name. But she'd seen him before. At SOE HQ. In Sir Reginald's office of all places!

7

THE SACHSENHAUSEN
INTERROGATION

W hen Anna arrived back in her hotel room, she was chilled to the bone. Not from the cold, but from meeting the mean-looking and threatening stranger who warned her with a photograph of some Nazis.

The first thing she did after casting off her coat and gloves, and replacing the Luger in her nightstand, was unfold the photograph.

Four Nazi officers in calf-length black leather coats with the swastika band around their sleeves. Silver-eagled, black caps on their heads. A stone porch entrance behind them also with the swastika. Dachau. The Nazis' first concentration camp, proudly opened by these grinning men in 1933.

All Anna's research braincells went into top gear. The first man on the right was easy to pinpoint, a youngish Heinrich Himmler, the mean eye already history, now dead and deeply buried. She didn't recognize the two men next to him, but she wouldn't rest until she did.

The face on the far left was... familiar. Looking way too young and fair to cause serious harm, seeing him unsettled Anna's already frayed nerves more than she liked. And what harm this man had done to humanity, not he himself but through his death.

It was no other than German Foreign Office Consul Ernst Eduard vom Rath, the Nazi diplomat assassinated in Paris by... Herschel in November 1938. Anna shivered. It seemed like an omen getting this photograph now.

Vom Rath's death had been Hitler's trigger to instigate Kristallnacht. And from there, open hatred of Jews had spilled from the German Reich all over Europe, killing millions. Her family had never been the same. Never recovered.

"No!" Anna said firmly, before turning the photograph over to see if there was an inscription. There wasn't.

"No!" she repeated. "I will not go there anymore. Whoever gave me this photograph must be stopped."

But how was she going to do that? It wasn't like she could tell Jaffe or Major Stewart why she'd been given this photograph in the first place. She couldn't even confide in Sir Reginald.

And what did this stranger want from her? To force her to give up her interrogations of camp commanders? It wasn't like she was persecuting them for their crimes. All she wanted was answers about almost exclusively non-Jewish agents.

And why did she get this now? How had he found her? Or had she become a target as soon as she set foot on German soil?

"Only interrogate Kaindl and back to England as fast as you can," Anna told herself as she switched off the lamp. Still dressed in her uniform, she kept the Luger close to her side.

"First job back in London will be to go through the files at SOE HQ to find out who that man is. Until then I'll say nothing about this encounter. Just need to forget it for now."

AFTER A FEW HOURS of fitful sleep, two cups of black coffee and a new dose of aspirin, Anna was ready to put the previous night away and continue her journey in the Box with the two British officers. The day was frigid and overcast.

"We'd better not stay too long," Jaffe observed, studying the leaden-gray sky. "Forecast is heavy snow."

He directed the Humber to the east, to Paderborn, where Sachsenhausen commander Anton Kaindl was in British custody. Anna, this time in the back, now and then glanced over her shoulder to see if her shadow followed in a car. As far as she could see, he wasn't.

"Don't expect anything out of Kaindl," Major Stewart said over his shoulder. "I've tried to interrogate the fellow twice but he's like an oyster. One word and he clamps shut. But maybe you have more luck, Officer Adams."

"I hope so." Her voice sounded tired. She was in low spirits. Gazing out of the side window she saw they were traversing through moors, not unpretty. Low shrubbery, rolling hills, dotted with farmhouses and cowsheds. Not a sign of the blasted war for once.

The landscape reminded her of the Yorkshire moors, a visit long ago with Henryk. So much passion in the air. It had been spring then. Eternal spring that lasted one week. Suddenly Anna felt a strong pang of longing for home. Home was England. Germany wasn't good for her. Never had been.

A strong breeze picked up and swept through the mauve, heather fields. Crowberry bushes yielded under the weight of the wind, carrying with them a biting chill that even leaked into the Box. Anna pulled her leather coat closer around her slender frame.

"Told you it was a bad day," Jaffe grumbled from behind the wheel.

"Do you want to turn around?" Anna suddenly saw a proper way out of her mission impossible.

"Nope. Now we've come this far, we'd better get it over and done with. And your flight from Berlin is the day after tomorrow, isn't it, Miss Adams?"

"Yes, that's correct." She tried not to sound too elated at the prospect. After the intimidating encounter with the stranger, Anna knew she'd have to reconsider her plans of becoming an on-the-ground war investigator. Once safely back in her flat in Chelsea, everything would look different. She was sure of it.

Tall, leafless trees lined the road leading to the British internment camp, their branches gnarled and twisted like the secrets that had emerged from the horrors of World War II.

The crunching of gravel under the Box's tires was muffled by the pervasive silence that enveloped the area. The camp itself was encircled by a formidable barbed-wire fence that glinted dully in the overcast daylight. Guard towers loomed at strategic intervals, their menacing machine gun barrels pointed outward, a constant reminder of the camp's original purpose. Jaffe had difficulty to find the entrance and Stewart was no help as he hadn't visited this camp before. It looked like a huge place.

"I thought this one was one of the lesser concentration camps during the war?" Anna observed, rather surprised at the size and the degree of security.

"Niederhagen was the smallest camp. A satellite camp first of Sachsenhausen and later of Buchenwald. But don't be misled by the lack of knowledge about this place. It was as gruesome as the other camps. Of the 3900 prisoners, a third perished here," Stewart explained. "And security measures have been upped since the end of the war because of the Nazis it houses now."

"That's all good and well," Jaffe remarked acridly, "but where's the entrance to the damn place? We seem to be going in circles."

Jaffe finally found the gates to the internment camp and steered the Box through. He cursed again. The sky had become a blanket of ominous gray, pregnant with the threat of impending snowfall.

When they got out of the car, the air was thick with the scent of damp earth and decaying leaves, a poignant reminder of nature's indifference to the horrors that had taken place within these walls. The crunch of gravel under their shoes echoed in the quiet, and the weight of the past pressed heavily upon the British visitors as they made their way towards the entrance.

What am I doing to myself? Anna wondered but it was a rhetorical question. Pilecki's parents and sister deserved an answer. It was as good a reason as she could make it.

Soldiers clad in drab, olive uniforms stood guard at the camp's gates, their stern faces etched with the experiences of war. They saluted the Brits as they approached, looking surprised at the woman in blue, but recognizing her as a WAAF officer, a representative of their British government.

Anna thought their eyes betrayed a weariness that could only come from bearing witness to the aftermath of the Holocaust. These eyes had seen too much evil and had no time to process it. She smiled at them, hoping a small act of kindness in these cold and bitter surroundings would be as welcome as the cup of hot tea on their break.

Her breath formed visible puffs in the frigid air as she was ushered through the gates, past the rows of barrack buildings, each more foreboding than the last. The camp's gravel paths were lined with mud, a testament to the countless footsteps that had trodden this grim path. Dilapidated wooden fences encircled small, barren courtyards where former inmates no doubt had been subjected to untold suffering.

Finally, they reached what must have been the commandant's office, a nondescript building at the heart of the camp. Two guards stood on each side of the door, looking as forlorn and frozen as the ones at the gates. Anna also smiled at them, and they smiled back.

"I'm Squadron Leader Anna Adams and these gentlemen are Major John Stewart and Major Angus Jaffe," Anna informed them in her posh English voice. No doubt they knew exactly who the visitors were, as Major Summers, the head of the investigation team at Bad Oeynhausen, had announced their arrival at Anna's request.

"Herr Kaindl is waiting for you inside, Ma'am. Gentlemen, this way please." An adjutant with a nose red from the cold and glittering dark eyes under his helmet, opened the door for them and Anna went in first.

It was a small, spartan room with a table and three chairs. No decorations on the walls. A British flag in one of the corners. An electric heater stood sputtering, warming only the space right in front of it. The cold seeped in through the thin, poorly-insulated walls and though the wooden planks under their feet.

Anna looked around the room. It seemed unlikely the smallish man on the other side of the table was Kaindl, but as the guard had said he was waiting for them, it had to be him. She recognized the round spectacles and receding hairline from his mugshot. The camp commander was just much shorter than she'd anticipated. How could anyone this petite be so dangerous? Napoleon came to mind, who stood at a mere 5'2. This specimen didn't even measure up to that. Well, impressive size was not a requirement for a bully.

He nodded at her as she took the seat opposite him. A guard directed the warmth of the small heater towards her. She studied Kaindl intently. This man may have known two of the most important people in Anna's life. Even if he didn't, he was responsible for what had happened to them.

Due to the receding hair, Kaindl had a high forehead. The ring of dark hair was cropped short. More distinctive were the high cheek-bones over which his red-veined, shiny, skin was drawn tight. Anna thought he resembled a ferret. Not a person to be trusted to give up the truth.

His hands resting on the table were well-kept, the hands of a dandy. His prison clothes, though simple, were ironed and clean. Not a button missing. On entering, Anna's all-seeing eyes had even regis-tered he was wearing shoes with higher heels. Probably to give the impression he was taller.

As it was so cold and remembering Jaffe's warning about an upcoming snowstorm, Anna wanted to get on with it. Without saying anything, she put two photographs of Peter Suttill on the table under Kaindl's nose. One was of Peter, dashing and smiling as ever in 1942, wearing the French-style suit he'd worn on his first mission in October 1942 when he'd been dropped north of Paris. The other one was of Peter in uniform, a major in the British army. Kaindl studied the photos in detail, peering at them through his clean glasses, then shook his head slowly.

"I'm sorry, Ma'am. I don't know who he is."

"Peter Suttill, a British agent, captured in France. Presumably shot or killed in Sachsenhausen in March 1945. Who gave the orders? You,

Herr Kaindl?" This time Anna spoke English which she knew he understood.

The manicured fingers played with the ribbed edges of the photographs. Which infuriated Anna. Peter had been a dear friend, much more than just one of the male agents. He deserved respect. She leaned closer and said in a low, menacing tone.

"Ich wiederhole. Wer gab den Befehl, ihn aufzuhängen?" *I repeat. Who gave the order to hang him?*

She'd taken her target by surprise. He almost jumped backwards, looked at her in horror. The eyes gave her the answer, but she wanted to hear it coming from his mouth. Kaindl recovered quickly and shut tight like an oyster, just as Major Stewart had warned her.

"Ich war es nicht." *It wasn't me.*

Anna cursed inwardly. He'd been too smart for her, and she'd already played the one trump card in her possession. Addressing him in German. Feeling she had nothing left to lose, she put Henryk's picture before him, averting her eyes as she was unable to look at the photo herself.

Next to her Major Stewart shuffled nervously. She gave him a quick glance, hoping to reassure him she knew what she was doing. He shrugged. A man of the letter, it was clear he didn't approve of Anna taking the liberty to ask about a prisoner they hadn't agreed upon.

Knowing by now she wouldn't get anything useful out of Kaindl, she just wanted this interrogation to be over with. So, she was taken by surprise when the tiny commander looked rather reverently at the photo of the Polish fighter pilot in his uniform.

"Do you know him?" Her voice was too eager. She couldn't help herself.

"Yes. Major Pilecki. Polish."

Anna thought her heart would give in as the ferret announced his name.

"What do you know about him?" It was barely more than a whisper.

"He was in Sachsenhausen, briefly in 1943. He was transferred to...," Kaindl paused to think and though Anna hung on his words, she knew he could as well be lying, "...let me see? I think it was Dachau but I'm not sure."

"Is the transfer of prisoners registered somewhere?"

"Yes, Ma'am, we registered everything. But all those files are now in the hands of the victors. You'll have to ask them. I can no longer help you."

"We'll look into it, Officer Adams, don't worry," Major Stewart said under his breath and added rather exasperated, "will that be all?"

Anna hesitated. The torn photo. The young boy. But the atmosphere in the room was so tense, and she was so tired.

I'll be back, Herschel, I promise.

"Yes." She got up. Shot the tiny scoundrel one last glance and hoped he'd get his deserved punishment.

"Let's go home."

8

GOING BACK TO LONDON

The next day - Bückeburg Air Base, 27 November 1945

With the promise to be back, should she be offered a job with the British war investigation office in Bad Oeynhausen, Anna took leave of her driver Major Jaffe and her possible future-colleague, Major Stewart.

The two officers had insisted on seeing her off from the newly erected RAF Bückeburg where Anna was to board a Lysander that would take her to RAF Northolt in London. She was glad her two investigative companions were there as she lifted off from German soil.

Spying around the airstrip for the man in the Macintosh with the black hat, she was relieved to see he wasn't there. Only two other British officials eligible for a few days' leave back home, stood waiting with their overnight bags.

"Take care, Miss Adams! Glad the snowstorm didn't last!"

"See you soon, Squadron Leader Adams."

Smiles, waves, and she was in the air. With a huge sigh of relief. Though it had been only a short week, for Anna it was the welcome end to a harrowing mission in post-war Germany. It was as if this bumpy flight over German woodlands was a crucial moment in her life, symbolizing her journey back to a sense of normalcy after intense investigations and bitterly few results.

Though she hadn't thought it would be a walk in the park, she hadn't foreseen that interrogating camp commanders and gathering evidence of their war crimes would be such a grueling and emotionally draining assignment.

"But I won't give up!" she promised the steamed-up small window that now only gave a view of dark-gray clouds. If post-war Germany had taught her one thing, it was that she'd find her agents, dead or alive, and bring those responsible for their suffering to justice.

Out of habit, she pushed her glasses up her nose, but Anna was too weary to open her bag and read through her notes. *Later!*

Her thoughts lingered on the faces of the Nazis in the Nuremberg courtroom, on the camp commanders she'd spoken to, and one thought nagged at her mind.

How was it possible that a civilized nation in 20th century Europe had become such a brutal and aggressive state?

Anna thought sadly that she'd never be able to give a conclusive answer to that fundamental question. All she could do was help prevent it from ever happening again.

As the ruins of Germany, now blocked by the clouds, faded into the distance, a mixture of relief and sadness washed over Anna. The mission to find her missing agents was a noble station in life, though she still felt she could have done more to prevent their disappearance in the first place.

As the Lysander circled over RAF Northolt – not an airfield Anna was keen to revisit – the weather cleared and the familiar sights of sloping green hills with hedgerow hedges came into view, the proud London skyline glimmering in the distance.

Anna swallowed hard, fought against tears. A sense of both homecoming and alienation. Her journey was far from over, but for now, she had to be grateful to be back on British soil. Alone. Haunted. Determined.

Without looking towards the RAF Northolt's officers' lounge, where no Henryk would make a sweeping entrance and walk off with her heart, Anna hurried outside huddled in her leather coat, her overnight bag and her red officer's bag slung over each shoulder.

Two hours later

Anna fitted her latchkey into the ornate entrance with a black wrought-iron gate leading to a well-maintained, though small front garden, now barren and brown. She looked up at the façade of her Chelsea flat. The decorative stonework and large bay windows unscathed by the war. She'd fallen in love with those windows the first time she came here. They reminded her of the windows of her youth, far away from here. Windows so big they allowed for plenty of natural light. Windows that could see.

Her two-bedroom flat was located on the first floor of a charming red-brick Victorian building on a tree-lined road off Flood Street. Apart from the windows, Anna had chosen the area because the neighborhood exuded an air of sophistication and affluence, which she'd been keen to portray. It was also a popular choice for young officers serving in the military. Easy to reach SOE HQ and right in the center of London.

Upon entering the building, which had six flats in total, she stepped into a cozy hallway with rich, dark, wood paneling and a polished wooden floor. The landlady, a rich aristocrat from Battersea called Lady Arabella Winthrop, had her housekeeper decorate the hallway with framed black-and-white photographs of aircraft and military life, showing she only wanted tenants dedicated to the war effort. Her husband had fought and been wounded in the North African Campaign.

The house was silent but for the sound of a hoover on the second floor. Mrs Parker, the Lady's housekeeper, no doubt doing her chores. The other tenants were still at work or had gone for early drinks to the Special Forces Club.

Anna took a deep breath before opening the front door of her apartment, which she'd once shared with Pearl, but now inhabited alone. Absentmindedly, she grabbed the handful of letters Mrs Parker had left for her on the hallway table before closing her door. Kicking off her high-heeled pumps, she slid into her fur-lined slippers. Both bags landed on the tiled hall floor. As did the leather coat, her gloves, her cap. She left a trail of uniform items behind her, loosening her tie and taking off her jacket. Exchanging them for a comfy cardigan, Anna entered her living room with the stack of envelopes in her hand.

Home.

Home felt so good, even if it was as impersonal as her uniform. No piece of furniture belonged to her. No personal photographs adorned the sideboards. And yet it was home. Her neutral home. A private space.

The living room was spacious, yet comfortable, with high ceilings and intricate cornices. The large bay window with heavy, velvet curtains provided her with a cherished view of the quiet, Chelsea street.

The room was furnished with a plush, tufted sofa and matching armchairs, all covered in a deep shade of burgundy. A Persian rug added warmth to the polished wooden floor, and a simple coffee table sat in the center of the seating area. The walls held a few framed aviation posters and a small bookshelf was filled with Anna's books. Her only private collection, though these days she didn't read fiction novels anymore.

Leaving the mail on the coffee table, she went to her kitchen to make herself a cup of tea. Her kitchen was compact but functional, featuring white subway tiles and wooden cabinets with glass-fronted doors. A gas stove, a porcelain sink, and a small breakfast nook by the window completed the space. The kind Mrs Parker had lit the fires in every room and the flat was agreeably warm.

With the steaming cup in her hand, she opened her bedroom door as if to say hello to the entire house. Only the door that held a small plaque stating 'Pearl's Palace' remained closed. Anna never went in there.

She loved her bedroom. Lady Winthrop had excellent taste. It held a large, antique, mahogany bed, a matching wardrobe, and a vanity table with a mirror. Mrs Parker made sure the bed was always made with crisp white linens. She'd had Anna's reserve WAAF uniform dry-cleaned and hung it on a hanger on the outside of the wardrobe.

Putting the cup of tea on her nightstand, Anna went to wash her face in the adjacent bathroom. The bathroom featured classic white tiles, a clawfoot bathtub with a brass faucet, and an overhead shower. A small window with frosted glass provided privacy while still allowing for natural light. The toiletries and grooming items she hadn't taken with her to Germany lay neatly arranged on a shelf.

Anna was tempted to run herself a bath but felt too tired, so just had a quick wash before returning to her bedroom.

Lying on top of her duvet, huddled in her cashmere cardigan, and sipping her Darjeeling tea, she tried to arrange her mind. And failed.

The bed screamed 'Henryk' at her and the closed door 'Pearl'.

AND THEIR SCREAMS *only became louder in the deafening silence.*

PART II

THE BURDEN OF WAR'S END

LONDON MAY 1945

9

VICTORY FOR ALL?

Six months earlier - London, 8 May 1945

A s the first rays of the May morning sun penetrated the lingering fog, London awakened to a celebratory and surreal atmosphere. The war, that deadly demon that had haunted the country, and London in particular, for six long years, was finally over. Was won. On this momentous day of 8 May 1945, the streets of London became a colourful tapestry of exuberance and relief, a tapestry woven with the vibrant hues of hope and freedom.

Trafalgar Square, at the heart of the city, metamorphosed into a sea of jubilant faces. Union Jack flags waved proudly from lampposts, windows, and public buildings. Even from the small fists of children perched on their parents' shoulders. Red, white, and blue bunting crisscrossed above every square London possessed, displaying a canopy of patriotism.

Even the fountains seemed to dance to the melody of victory, their sprays of water shimmering like diamonds in the morning light. Crowds thronged around the iconic statues. Nelson was towering over them like a silent sentinel, keeping an eternal watch over the ecstasy at his feet.

The buzz and chatter of jubilant voices filled the air, while passing cars and motorcycles honked their horns with joy. Tongues spoke English and foreign languages all at once, a testament to the diverse group of people who'd found shelter from the Continent in Britain's capital. All now came together to share in this moment of triumph.

Soldiers and women in their blue Women's Auxiliary Air Force uniforms and khaki First Aid Nursing Yeomanry uniforms, walked arm in arm, worn out by the long war but now feeling on top of the world. Uniforms mingled with civilian clothing of all classes and ages. They'd all lived through hell, but the Brits had never given up in the face of adversity.

From a vintage, double-decker bus, with the words "Victory Parade" painted in bright colors, an impromptu jazz band played as if their lives depended on it. Their instruments sprouted an endless string of the melodies that had helped the people through the last years of the war. Popular, happy tunes like Bing Crosby's *Swinging on a Star* and Nat King Cole's *Straighten Up and Fly Right*. The music flooded across the square, urging people to dance. Couples twirled and spun, their shrieks of laughter mingling with piano and trombone.

Children, who'd lived in the shadow of the war for most of their lives, ran around in an unknown sense of freedom. They skipped and played hopscotch in the middle of the street, and no one reprimanded them. To every parent, the children's carefree joy was a poignant reminder of the brighter future they had secured.

All eyes went upwards as a squadron of Royal Air Force planes soared in formation overhead, painting the sky in streaks of red, white, and blue smoke. The air show over Buckingham Palace was a majestic salute to King George and Queen Elizabeth for their unwavering resilience in the face of war and the destruction of London.

Minute by minute the crowds grew larger. Everyone took to the streets. Winston Churchill's raspy, much-loved voice, broadcast over loudspeakers and resonated across the city.

"My dear friends, this is your hour. This is not victory of a party or of any class. It's a victory of the great British nation as a whole. We were the first, in this ancient island, to draw the sword against tyranny. After a while we were left all alone against the most tremendous military power that has been seen. We were all alone for a whole year.
There we stood, alone. Did anyone want to give in?

THE CROWD YELLED "NO!"

Were we downhearted?

"NO!"

HATS AND CAPS flew in the air. A sea of Union Jacks waved in ecstasy.

The lights went out and the bombs came down. But every man, woman and child in the country had no thought of quitting the struggle. London can take it. So, we came back after long months from the jaws of death, out of the mouth of hell, while all the world wondered. When shall the reputation and faith of this generation of English men and women fail? I say that in the long years to come not only will the people of this island, but of the world, wherever the bird of freedom chirps in human hearts, look back to what we've done and they will say 'do not despair, do not yield to violence and tyranny, march straightforward and die if need be-unconquered.' Now we have emerged from one deadly struggle-a terrible foe has been cast on the ground and awaits our judgment and our mercy. But there is another foe who occupies large portions of the British Empire, a foe stained with cruelty and greed - the Japanese. I rejoice we can all take a night off today and another day tomorrow. Tomorrow our great Russian allies will also be celebrating victory and after that we must begin the task of rebuilding our hearth and homes, doing our utmost to make this country

a land in which all have a chance, in which all have a duty, and we must
turn ourselves to fulfill our duty to our own countrymen, and to our gallant
allies of the United States who were so foully and treacherously attacked by
Japan. We will go hand and hand with them. Even if it is a hard struggle,
we will not be the ones who will fail."

Squadron Leader Anna Adams hadn't taken to the streets. Dressed to go to the office, she stopped on her way out when she heard Churchill's voice on the radio. Sinking down on her couch in her WAAF uniform she listened to that beloved voice, tears streaming down her cheeks.

When his speech was done, she got up, blew her nose, and resolutely walked to the telephone set in the hallway. There she hesitated a moment but did what she should have done four years earlier but couldn't. She rang a London number.

"Father...?"

"Oh, Anna!"

"I'll come by soon now. I promise. I have to go to work just now."

"Be careful, *mein Kind*. Our ordeal may not be over yet."

"I know, Father. *Ich liebe dich*."

"I love you too."

And she hung up, grabbed her bag, and took a deep breath before plunging into the gathered masses. There was no simple way to get through the dancing and singing crowds. They were like molasses around her. Clinging to her and to each other. Strangers, men and women, started kissing her because of her uniform, thanking her, or just simply wanting to touch her. It was as if she was some kind of celebrity, which was far from what Anna felt.

She saw tears glistening in many an eye and felt her own tears difficult to hold back. They were tears of sorrow for those lost, but also tears of joy and relief.

"The war is over!" Was the sentence on everyone's lips. Now outside and in the middle of it, Anna felt how the people of London, along with the entire nation, had emerged from the darkness into the bright dawn of freedom.

Amid the celebrations, the flags, the music, and laughter, strangers became friends, and a sense of shared destiny bound the city's inhabitants together. Even Anna's heart and mind, though still more on the ravages on the Continent than the gaping holes of London, felt that this liberation was not just a victory over the enemy; it was a victory of the human spirit, a testament to the enduring strength of the people of London, and a day that would forever be etched in their collective memory. The strength of the human spirit. Anna knew the strength of some and how that strength had been tested.

The underground had stopped running or was so overcrowded it couldn't run, leaving Anna to walk the three miles to Norgeby House where F section had its office across the road from SOE's HQ in Baker Street.

Nothing indicated that during the war, Winston Churchill's "ungentlemanly warfare" to "set Europe ablaze" had been organised from these premises. A simple plaque read Inter-Services Research Bureau. And its staff never revealed to anyone on the outside what happened behind those modest front doors.

Anna rang the bell and Dorothy, her secretary, immediately opened the door, looking sad despite her perfect make-up and youthful face.

"Hello Dorothy, anything wrong?" Anna already whisked past her on her way to her office on the second floor.

"No, Miss Adams."

"Then why are you moping?"

"We should be out there celebrating, Miss Adams, not be cooped up here with the past."

Anna turned on the stairs, her hand on the banister.

"Who else is in?" Her dark eyes took in her young secretary who clearly wanted to go out dancing and get drunk with everybody else.

"Just the warden, Miss, nobody else, but you'd told me to be here."

"Off you go, Dorothy. I can make my own tea and see myself out. I'll let Mr. Parks know when I'm gone."

"Are you sure, Miss Adams?" Dorothy's violet eyes lit up and she smiled broadly.

"I'm sure. Enjoy the day! And take tomorrow off as well."

"Thank you, Miss Adams."

Dorothy was already heading for the front door when Anna's voice stopped her.

"Oh, and Dorothy, I might be gone for the rest of the week myself. I'll telephone you."

"Alright. Miss Adams. You take care."

The building was silent and the air heavy after the lively Dorothy Perkins had skipped off, only after applying a fresh layer of lipstick and running a comb through her wavy blonde hair. The young secretary had no idea how many times she'd put Anna's agents at ease with her flair and peppy manners.

Anna on the other hand, was very aware that visitors to Norgeby house, whether SOE staff or secret agents, didn't know what to make of her, the enigmatic girl in glasses and aloof manners. The one who now didn't want to go dancing with the rest. A solitary soul. Though treating her with courtesy, they couldn't wait to turn their back on the squadron officer to have a cuppa and a laugh with Dorothy.

"I deliberately used you for that, dear Dorothy, but I don't think you minded the attention. In fact, I think you reveled in it and rightfully so," Anna mumbled as she passed the now empty Operations room and ascended the stairs and navigated the corridor to a door that simply said 'FA'. France section, Anna. Her code at SOE.

On opening the door to her office, Anna stood still, looking around her modest workplace. This had been her main abode for the past three years. During her first year at SOE, in 1941, she'd begun with a small desk in Sir Reginald's office, when she was still "just his secretary."

But soon her boss, whose French was less evolved than Anna's and who preferred to leave the office early to go to his Club, had by and large transferred more important matters to his "secretary." In

1942, when women started to be recruited as secret agents, Sir Reginald promoted Anna to Squadron Officer and given her an office next to his. After digging through her past.

Six months later, Anna had had her own secretary and a year later, her position had been upgraded to Squadron Leader. Everybody at Norgeby House knew that Anna basically ran F Section and – though not in favor of her – would consult her and not Sir Reginald Owens on important matters. Whether it concerned the improvement in agents' security checks, or the need for more W/Ts, wireless operators, in the field. Anna had her contacts everywhere, from the House of Commons to the scouts in the streets. Nobody knew how she managed to build her network.

When the important circuits in France were infiltrated and signals reached London that agents had been captured by the Germans, both colleagues and family members came to consult with the always-calm and collected Anna, who showed little emotion but seemed to know everything.

And here she stood in the middle of her office with the blackboard still covered with names and codes, and her desk always tidy, only holding a pile of files in the corner and her notebook and Parker pen ready for use. A telephone set and a coat rack by the door. Nothing personal. A mirror image of her functional and impersonal Chelsea flat.

Anna looked around her empty office, blinked twice, pushed up her glasses. She couldn't prevent her shoulders from slumping. The crazy crowds outside were not celebrating *her* victory. She'd lost so much. Too much for her slender, twenty-five-year-old shoulders.

10

THE NEED FOR A PLAN

Anna went to the double front windows and opened them. A soft May breeze entered the room, playfully billowing the gauze curtains. From her window she could see SOE's HQ across Baker Street. A row of plane trees on each side of the road donned their spring attire. Shards of music and joyous people wafted in.

This was London. This was liberation. This should be life at its finest.

She peered through her glasses at the brick stone headquarters through the foliage, musing if there were people inside that building just like her, with their hands in their hair, wondering how to explain to the world all the lives this "ungentlemanly warfare" had claimed.

Anna didn't want to be cynical, but she assumed the the wartime espionage coverup from the city's key players had already begun. It would be up to her to conduct an inquiry into her missing agents' fates. For herself, as much as for their families.

Turning her back on the window, she straightened her shoulders and then her uniform. The glasses were pushed up higher on her nose and with a deep sigh she seated herself at her desk, legs crossed at the ankles. Without hesitating she took the top file from the pile.

On her desk Anna had a box with flip-over index cards. It held the names, aliases, personal data, and passport photo of every F Section agent. It also held the information on when they had gone on a mission, whether returned or missing. Though she knew most information by heart, she now and then took out a card to add or cross out some information.

Though it had been almost nine months since Paris, and the rest of the country had been liberated, of the four-hundred agents dropped into France – many of them just before or directly after D-Day -- some hundred had gone missing, sixteen of them women. Dozens had already been tracked down, but of many there was still no sign.

How she'd wanted to go straight to France at the end of August to find them herself! But her little passport hiccup had prevented Anna from leaving the British Isles.

Now it was time to make the definitive list and act.

HOURS LATER ANNA was fully prepared. After filing the last cards and putting them securely away in her cupboard, she wrote a memo with the most important details, planning on leaving the message at HQ for Colonel Gibbins, head of SOE Operations.

"I'm out, Mr. Parks. You can close now," she called to the warden who was in the backroom with his ear glued to the radio listening to the Victory Parade. Anna could hear the voice of the excited broadcaster yelling over the cheers of the crowds.

"Alright, Ma'am, but there's still someone from Section N upstairs, so my shift isn't over."

"I see, Mr. Parks. I hope you can enjoy some of the festivities tonight. I won't be in tomorrow, nor will Miss Perkins."

"When's Major Owens expected to be back, Ma'am?" Mr. Parks, a short man in his forties came to stand in the doorway, his shirtsleeves rolled up, a cigarette in the corner of his mouth.

"Not until next week, I presume. He's gone to Paris for the victory celebrations with General De Gaulle.'

"Good for him. And good night, Miss Adams.'

"Goodnight, Mr. Parks."

Inhaling the early evening air, Anna was relieved to see the festivities hadn't spread to the doorstep of her office yet. When her stomach rumbled angrily, she realized she hadn't eaten since breakfast, a habit she fell into when nobody nudged her for lunch. Hopefully the canteen at 24 Baker Street would still be open and she could nip in for a crab sandwich.

Baker Street's equivalent of Mr. Parks opened the door for her. The HQ warden was actually called Mr. Blackwell and he was big and ruddy, where Mr. Parks was wiry and small. Yet, they had that same protective attitude towards the special staff at a branch of British intelligence services that had never completely come into its own.

"Evening, Miss Adams. I'm afraid you won't find many people in the office. Special day you know. Who are you looking for?"

"I'd like a word with Colonel Gibbins, but I assume he's not in?"

Mr. Blackwell shook his bulldog-like cheeks. "Afraid not, Ma'am, but his deputy, Sir Rupert Harrington, may be available?"

Anna thought fast. He may not have the authority to help her but at least she could leave her memo with him and ask her burning question – yet again.

"Sure," she smiled at the warden.

"I'll phone his secretary to see if he's available. One sec, Ma'am."

While he made the call, Anna looked around the lobby of the place she'd visited so many times in the past four years. Soon it would be all over. There was no use for the valiant SOE after the war. Yet she knew she'd never forget anything from these years in service of the great Sir Winston Churchill. He smiled down benignly from his portrait on the wall, as if giving her a wink before puffing on his cigar.

"Sir Harrington can see you now, Miss Adams."

"Thank you, Mr. Blackwell." And in a moment of emotion she added, "thank you for always being kind to me. It's meant a lot to me."

"And you too, Miss Adams. I hope by God you'll find your girls."

And up the stairs Anna went, to the deputy head's grand office on the first floor.

Sir Harrington was one of the few high-ranking SOE officials who Anna greatly admired. She often wondered if other staff members would also have preferred him over the stiff, up-in-the-clouds Colonel Gibbins.

Born into a well-to-do London family, Harrington had received a first-rate education at Oxford, which had honed his already brilliant mind. He spoke several languages fluently, including French and German, a skill that had proven invaluable in his clandestine operations throughout the war. He'd been, and probably still was, a banker with Barings Bank, which made him a man of finances as well.

He stood waiting for Anna as she came in and offered her a chair. His tall, imposing stature and salt-and-pepper hair always struck her as "so very British" as it gave him an air of authority and wisdom that commanded respect from his peers and subordinates alike. Contrary to Colonel Gibbins and Sir Reginald, Harrington's sharp, piercing blue eyes were known to miss nothing, but they also held a hint of the countless secrets he'd encountered in this line of work.

Secretly, Anna compared herself to him. The same dedication, the same selflessness, the same feeling of responsibility. And his was much greater than hers.

"Miss Adams, do sit, please. How nice of you to be in the office on a day like this, but there really was no need." Sir Harrington's voice was deep and resonant, capable of both soothing and instilling confidence in those who worked alongside him.

Anna smiled, "the same applies to you, Sir. Why are you not celebrating our victory like the others?"

"Alas, Miss Adams, someone has to hold the fort. What can I help you with?" And then he winked with that dry sense of humor he also possessed, his hand on the bell to ring his secretary. Mrs Eleanor Sinclair instantly stuck her well-coifed, gray head around the door.

"You called for me, Sir Harrington?"

"Yes, Eleanor. This meeting calls for coffee and cream cakes.

There are some black-market goodies Mrs Harrington insisted on putting in my briefcase this morning. I left them in the kitchen. Miss Adams and I need to celebrate this day. And do take a cake yourself."

Turning to Anna, he added, "pardon my manners, dear girl, but you look like a half-starving robin in the middle of winter."

Anna laughed, "I am rather hungry. And you never miss anything do you, Sir?"

"Not when there are hungry women around me. I can sense that from a mile off. My wife always teases me about me insisting she needs to eat but..." Here he dropped his voice to conspiracy levels, "...she's the best of wives until she's hungry. Then she's not safe to be around." He bared his teeth as if imitating a wild animal. They both laughed. With zest, Anna put her own teeth in a full-flavored, spongy crème cake filled with raspberry jam. A delicacy she couldn't remember having had for a long time.

The pleasantries over, Anna opened her bag and handed Sir Harrington her memo. It was a brief overview of the agents who were still missing – one hundred in total – and the possible prisons and concentration camps where they had likely been detained.

"I'd like to travel to the Continent as soon as possible, but..." she hesitated. It was the same old question that lay heavy on her heart.

Sir Harrington finished her sentence for her, "...you need a passport."

"Yes." Anna's mouth became a thin strip. The glasses were pushed higher.

"I'll look into it, Anna. May I say 'Anna' after all this time?"

"Yes, of course."

"And you call me Rupert. Alright?

"I don't know if I can."

He smiled again. "You can do anything, Anna Adams. Calling me Rupert is the least of your challenges."

"That's true, Si...Rupert."

"Well, the matter with your passport is...uh ... a delicate one, but I promise I'll do my best to speed up the process now the war is over."

Anna sighed, "it's just that it's taking so long. There was no need for me to leave England during the war but it's different now."

"I'll pull some strings. I promise. I'll also formalize your assignment to travel to France and Germany in search of missing agents."

"Thank you, Rupert."

Anna felt a lot better. She saw a coy smile glide over the deputy's face, which gave him an almost boyish flair. "I take it you want a real passport. Our department for forgeries hasn't been dismantled yet."

"Yes, a real British passport, please."

"Alright, Anna. I've got to dash out but do drop in early next week. I hope to have positive tidings for you then." He stood up to shake her hand. Then looked at the two extra cakes still on the table. "Here take those with you. There's more where those came from." He wrapped them up and gave her the parcel.

"Now go celebrate your victory, dear girl. You deserve it."

MINUTES LATER ANNA stood in Baker Street with a lighter heart and two delicious cakes in her hand. She knew exactly where she was going next.

11

AN IMPORTANT REUNION

Nestled on one of Soho's cobblestone street corners, where Bateman Street ran into Greek Street, stood a small, specialized bookshop known as Adams Antiquarian Books. This charming establishment, difficult to detect due to its painted shop sign and ivy-covered façade, was a book mecca of days gone by, accessible only to clients who were truly passionate about old books and other written documents.

The bookshop was housed in an eighteenth-century, timber-framed building, exuding the same aura of history and mystery as its owner and contents. Above the door, a weathered brass bell announced the arrival of visitors with a soft, tinkling chime.

Once inside, patrons were transported to another world entirely. The air was laden with the distinct scent of aged leather, yellowing paper, and memories long past. The narrow, sparsely lit space was lined from floor to ceiling with towering wooden bookshelves, each one crammed with books of every size and binding. The shelves bowed under the weight of centuries-old manuscripts, dusty tomes, and leather-bound classics.

The shop's proprietor, a dignified and gentle man named Jude Adams, had come to London as a refugee from war-torn Europe and still spoke English with a pronounced Continental accent. A man of writing and books all his life, Mr. Adams had made it his mission to preserve and share the knowledge contained within these ancient volumes. His wise, deep-set eyes sparkled with knowledge as he greeted each visitor with a warm smile. Jude Adams possessed an encyclopedic knowledge of the books that graced his shelves, and he was always eager to engage in conversations about literature, history, and philosophy. His now-and-then broken English only added to the shop's international charm.

There were literally books everywhere, as the shelves couldn't hold one more copy. And patrons of the shop often brought more to hand over to the beloved Jude Adams. As a result, the place was always in a delightful state of chaos, books stacked in precarious piles on tables and chairs, mingling with vintage globes, antique typewriters, and tarnished brass candleholders. A treasure trove for the vintage lover. A place where the war had never come. Or at least it appeared to have skipped on by.

On the late afternoon of 8 May 1945, soft sunlight filtered through the dusty windows, casting a warm, mellow glow on the shop's eclectic wares. In one of the two well-worn leather armchairs, which were always kept free of books so that a visitor felt beckoned to perch down for a chat or a read, sat white-haired, frail Mr. Adams with a first edition of Emmanuel Kant's *Critique of the Power of Judgment* in his lap. A thin finger with a yellowish nail followed the words on the page as he absorbed them.

The sun gave the bald spot in his thinning hair a golden glow and dust motes swirled around him like dancing fairies. Mr. Adams didn't expect any more visitors at this time of the day and took a moment to immerse himself fully in the wisdom of one of his favorite philosophers.

The shop bell chimed. He looked up through thin-rimmed, dusty spectacles. Blinked. Rose slowly. Was unsteady on his feet.

"Anna?"

"Vati!"

She felt his bony arms around her, the scent of old books and a hint of Eau de Cologne. She tried not to cry but the tears didn't obey. They came and kept coming.

"Mein Kind, mein Kind," he kept repeating, holding her close.

They finally let go of each other and he held her at arm's length, inspecting her in the fading light.

"How are you? You look even thinner than before but much more beautiful. So much like your Mama. God may rest her soul."

"Oh Father. I've missed you so."

"I know, I know. The wretched war. I was so glad when I got your phone call this morning. I could have lived on that for the rest of my life but, see, now you are here, and it is real, and my only wish is fulfilled. God is great indeed. But what am I standing here babbling. Would you like some tea, my dear? I can put the kettle on."

"Just like in the old days," Anna smiled through her tears. "And I've brought something to celebrate with. Look." She showed him the cream cakes Sir Harrington – Rupert – had given her."

"Those look mouth-watering, almost like *Bienenstich*."

Anna was instantly transported to the honey and almond cakes of her youth. Dabbing her eyes and cleaning her misted-up spectacles, she sank in the armchair opposite where her father had sat. Four years and nothing had changed here. He hadn't even changed that much. Just a little more parchment-like and delicate, but the same sharp mind that saw everything but revealed only what was needed.

As her father puttered around in the kitchen, Anna thought it was typical of him not to fire any questions at her. Where had she been in the past four years? Why had she not contacted him when she loved him so much? Anything could have happened to him, to her, and she hadn't given him any sign of life. Not an address. Not a postcard. Nothing about her whereabouts. But that was her father. He never counted his losses, only his blessings. Yet she would tell him all now. No more secret life, no more lies.

But when he sat opposite her, beaming with happiness and feasting on cake and relishing her presence, Anna's resolution wavered. How to tell him she'd made such a mess of it all? His only daughter, his only remaining family.

"Vati..." she begun but before she could prepare the words, he waved an impatient arm.

"Not now, mein Kind, not now."

"But when, Father?"

"Soon, not tonight. Tonight, you and I are going to remind ourselves that we have survived it all. Every step of the way." And as if he could read her mind, which Anna secretly believed her father could, he added, "remember, no regrets, Anna my dear. No regrets. I brought you up to believe you would always do the best you could. And that's what I'm sure you've done. Allow yourself to make mistakes. Don't beat yourself up over them. Rectify them, if you can, but don't punish yourself for your aberrations or you're bound to repeat them. And that's not what you want, right?"

"Oh Father, you're so wise and you don't know how much I needed to hear those words. Because I made mistakes. Deadly mistakes and they weigh me down."

"I can see that, mein Kind. Your conscience is great, which is a gift and a handicap." And with a warm smile he added, "you're a chip off the old block, don't forget."

And as if they'd never been a day apart, father and daughter closed the shop together and walked side by side to her father's favorite pub, The Soho Star on Dean Street, for what they hoped to be a festive dinner.

When they arrived, they found the pub had been renamed "Café de la Liberté" for the occasion. The outside of the two-story restaurant was completely covered in Union Jack flags.

"Time to join the masses, Anna dear. No escape from it anywhere, and I think both of us can do with a dose of over-the-top elation." He grabbed her under the elbow and steered her through the crowds that had gathered in front of the pub, drinking pints of beer, and singing loudly. Anna felt slightly out of place in her blue uniform, but as she was kissed and hugged by strangers, she soon found herself smiling at the jubilation around her. Her father was right. She needed a bit of relaxation.

The pub's large windows, previously obscured by blackout

curtains, were now wide open, allowing evening light and music to waft in and out of the dining rooms. A brass plaque near the entrance read, "Celebrating Freedom, One Plate at a Time."

"Let's worm ourselves inside." Her father who'd been one of the regulars of The Soho Star for years, was quickly spotted by the owner George Winston, a big man in a black suit with an even bigger black moustache and a wide grin on his face.

Coming towards them, zigzagging with great agility for someone of his size and weight through the dense crowds that even danced in between the tables, he escorted Anna and her father to Jude's regular table in the corner by one of the open windows.

"Mr. Adams, what an honor, to serve you and your daughter on this exceptional day," he boomed over the music and the clatter of voices and cutlery on plates. "The usual?"

"Thanks George. Unless Anna wants something else?" He looked with a question mark on his face. Anna shook her head. Vati's lamb stew was fine for her too. She was hungry, even after two cream cakes. And she had to agree with George Winston. It *was* an honor to be seated with her father on this special day.

"The wife was mighty pleased with the first edition of David Copperfield," George Winston shouted in Mr. Adams' ear. Her father just nodded and smiled, unable to raise his own soft voice over the cacophony.

While they were waiting for their meal, a bottle of Veuve Cliquot in a cooling bucket was placed on the tablecloth. The young waiter, dressed in his finest attire, busied himself with opening the bottle and pouring the bubbling liquid in their glasses.

"On the house," he explained, when Anna's father looked rather perplexed, "with the compliments of Mr. Winston and the head chef, Jacques Mercer."

Anna knew the chef who'd been an SOE agent for Section F with three successful missions under his belt. Her father only knew Jacqui, as he called him affectionately, was a war veteran.

She toasted with her father and the moment their glasses touched she saw the depth of his love for her in his eyes. The look melted all the walls she'd built around her heart, like snowflakes in water. For the third time that day Anna felt like crying, but biting her lip, she managed to keep the tears inside.

While she sipped her champagne, which immediately went to her head, she took in the joyous atmosphere around them. The walls were decorated with vintage war posters, each one punctuated by handwritten notes of gratitude from local residents and servicemen who had frequented the café during the war. The decor was a charming mix of pre-war elegance and a newfound hope for the future. Candlelit tables were covered in white linen, and even held a bouquet of fresh flowers as if nothing was rationed today.

The restaurant's staff bustled about with an air of excitement and pride. They had all played their part in the war effort, and today they were here to serve and celebrate.

Café de la Liberté's clients were an eclectic mix. Uniformed soldiers and nurses were seated alongside locals who had endured the hardships of rationing and bombings. Some had tears in their eyes, while others wore smiles that seemed brighter than ever before. Families, friends, and strangers alike shared tables, united by the joy of liberation.

A jazz band played lively tunes at the back of the largest dining room, their instruments filling the air with an infectious rhythm that had people tapping their feet and dancing anywhere they could fit. The music was about the new-found freedom and a life without the anxieties of war.

A conversation with her father was impossible in this noise and Anna understood this had been his purpose. He wanted her to see happiness, to detach herself – if only for a couple of hours – from the stress she was under, and he didn't want her to feel obliged to explain herself.

His eyes had said the words he had been known to verbalize in the past, "when the time is ripe, all that needs to be said will be said."

They relished their food and drank all the champagne, which Anna knew would mean a headache tomorrow, but she didn't care. The hearty lamb stew was followed by Cornish pastries served alongside fresh strawberries and cream. Finally, a decadent chocolate cake adorned with edible sugar flowers finished her off completely.

As the sun set on that historic May day, Café de la Liberté was a beacon of hope, where the spirit of liberation was alive in every smile, every laugh, and every clink of glasses. It was a place where the past was honored, the present cherished, and the future filled with promise.

For just a fleeting moment Anna's heart was full of the liberation around her.

12

SHADOWS FROM THE PAST

Swaying on her legs but with her head full of happiness, Anna, on her father's arm, left The Soho Star around 10 pm to escort him back to his apartment over the bookshop, two streets down. The neighborhood was still crammed with people in spring clothes and uniforms, dancing and laughing and kissing, though the atmosphere was more out of control due to the copious amounts of alcohol now in everyone's bloodstream.

Her father – never a heavy drinker – seemed plain sober, navigating his daughter through the crowds on a steady arm. They didn't talk. But when he got out his key to get through the shop to his apartment above, he turned to her.

"Go home now, dear Anna, and sleep it all off. I hope we will be able to repeat this soon. And be careful. Shadows from the past are still lurking around us."

Anna tipsy and no longer as tongue-tied, blurted out, "what shadows, Father? For sure we've won those over as well?"

The deep-set eyes fixed on her. Anna had difficulty holding her gaze still. Her father didn't answer her question, but his voice had the same undertone of warning as on the phone in the morning.

"If the underground is still not running, get a taxi. Don't go home on foot. Will you promise me that?"

She nodded, confused, her mind unclear. The next moment he took her face between his thin hands covered with age spots and looked deep into her eyes. Where there had been concern there was now only love.

"Thank you, my daughter, for coming to see me on this unforget-table day. You've made an old man very, very happy."

Anna kissed him on the cheek. "I'll be back soon, Vati. Very soon."

"You do that, mein Kind." He stood on the pavement waving as she disappeared into the crowd on her way to the taxi stand.

Finding a taxi wasn't the problem. The problem was no taxi could get through the ever-thickening crowds set on never sleeping through the first night of victory. As her father had predicted, the under-grounds weren't operating either. Anna saw no other option than to walk home which would take her a stiff hour.

I'll be alright, Papa! I've done this before.

With fuel low and purses empty, the citizens had found their way around London on foot during the war. And Anna liked walking. Certainly now. It would clear her mind.

"I'll be safe, whatever Father thinks. There are people everywhere and in such a good mood. No one will harm me," she mumbled, directing her feet towards Chelsea. Soon she wished she'd put on her low-heeled, court shoes, the last good pair from before the war, instead of her high-heeled pumps. Her feet ached and her head swam but she still felt she was making good progress. Just very slowly.

As long as she walked along Piccadilly, there were people all around her. They invited her numerous times to come and dance. Anna shook herself free every time, smiling, and went on her way. Now and then almost losing her balance on her impractical shoes when someone grabbed her with force around the waist. Still, she smiled.

When she came to Green Park, it became quieter, though she could hear the crowds cheering near Buckingham Palace. It was then, as night had fallen completely, with the park only dimly lit, she began to feel less certain. Searching for a black cab on reaching the park exit, she saw none. Just age-old trees and the last of the daffodils in bloom.

Thinking she heard a rustle behind her, she looked over her shoulder rather skittishly but there was nothing. Nobody.

"I'm imagining things. Father shouldn't have put this fear in my head. Maybe he's just being protective," she told herself, clasping her bag tighter to her side and increasing her step, trying hard to ignore her sore feet.

Anna breathed more easily when she came into the lamp-lit street again and entered the large square before the Palace, where flags were waving - music, people, and laughter abundant. Anna gratefully disappeared into the crowds again.

Until she got to Eaton Square Gardens, and the crowds dispersed. The night was chilly and overcast. Anna shivered in her uniform jacket and hurried on, now and then casting a quick glance over her shoulders, or peering across the road, into dark hallways. This must have been how her agents had felt behind enemy lines. Every step taken under the constant stress of being grabbed by the Gestapo.

Their fears had been real, her imaginations were mere phantoms. Her agents had been so much braver than she was. And yet there was someone. Anna sensed it with her whole being, tipsy or not. She saw it in the withdrawing shadow against the stone wall at the other side of the street, hiding behind a tree, slipping into an alleyway.

Either she was going out of her mind, or she was really drunk. Or... there was really someone following her. Despite her fear and the fog in her head Anna tried to get a glimpse of the phantom. Whence came the threat and why now? And what did her father know that he hadn't told her?

Anna felt sad next to being scared. She'd made so many mistakes along the way, most out of self-preservation, some through no fault of her own. She knew she had reason to believe there was a price on her head. And it probably went back a long way.

"Hurry up, darn passport," she said through gritted teeth, terribly relieved to see the Flood Street sign. The latch key slipped into the keyhole; the door closed behind her. She was inside. She was safe.

Shivering all-over, she skipped out of her shoes, seeing her stockings were torn and her heels blistered and bleeding. Getting out of her clothes as fast as she could, she left them on the floor in a trail behind her and limped to the bathroom. After locking the door, she ran herself a hot bath. She almost screamed when her heels touched the water, but she slid into the bath anyway, holding her breath against the sharp, stinging pain.

It was a good feeling to lie in the warm, soapy water. The strain and drain in her body slowly relaxed. Anna closed her eyes but opened them instantly again. Nightmarish images of screaming children and a deluge of icy water coming down from the heavens on helpless, drenched people, being driven forward by uniformed guards with iron rods, flashed through her mind.

"Not that! Not that anymore!" she said sternly, sitting upright and clasping her hands around her knees. *Why is life so difficult?*

In bathrobe and slippers, she was on her way to make a cup of tea, when the phone rang. Anna almost jumped to the ceiling in fright. Inching towards the black telephone in the hallway that kept ringing, she picked up the receiver with shivering fingers.

"Anna?"

"Sir Harring- Rupert, you gave me a fright, phoning so late. Is everything alright?"

"Yes. I tried to ring you earlier but didn't catch you. I thought you would like to know as soon as possible. You're a British citizen. Welcome to the UK, Anna."

For a long moment Anna stared into the receiver, not knowing what to feel. A squeaky sounding "ow" was all she could produce.

"Are you not happy? I had to call in favors from some important folk to get it done after our talk this afternoon."

"Yes, yes, of course. Thank you so much, Si...Rupert. I'm absolutely thrilled."

"Glad to hear it, girl. Never forget you have friends in high places."

And after uttering these mysterious words, he hung up. Anna stood with the receiver in her hand, still shivering, feeling torn in all directions.

What a strange, strange day this had been. What a strange, strange life she had.

Sitting at the kitchen table with her evening tea, Anna wondered who she really was, out of all these lives. For the outside world she was Intelligence Officer Anna Adams, a British subject. She vowed to do her best to live up to the role. What was left of it.

PART III

A DOUBLE LIFE

LONDON 1942

13

THE FIANCÉ

Three years earlier - London, April 1942

The night air was clammy and dense, laden with the palpable tension of unknown enemies lurking in the sky. In almost every street London bore the scars of its relentless battle against the darkness of war. As the clock struck ten, the city was quiet as a nun's convent, save for the distant wail of a siren and the soft padding of a lone patrol officer's footsteps on the pavement. There was no curfew, but Londoners preferred to stay indoors. Just to be on the safe side.

The nightly sirens, mobilizing them to seek cellar or underground, were still in everyone's blood. Brits didn't take well to enemies threatening invasion. That was *not* in their blood. Hadn't been for almost 1,000 years.

Here and there, nightlife made a vague attempt at being resurrected but the joy had gone out of London's heart. Too many casualties, not enough carousing.

The buildings stood silent against the night sky, silhouetted like sentinels, their windows shrouded in blackout curtains, cutting out the warm glow of human life inside. The flicker of a solitary candle behind those curtains told stories of families huddled together, finding comfort in each other's presence as they listened to the radio for news of a world in tatters.

In the city center, the majestic landmarks that once drew tourists from around the globe now stood in stoic defiance, their facades marked by time and the ravages of German bombings. Still unscarred, the dome of St. Paul's Cathedral rose into the star-scattered firmament, reminiscent of the time the ancient fortress guarded the soul of London.

At regular intervals, the drone of distant aircraft engines pierced the air. Though the Blitz was over, and no German bomb had hit London for almost a year, the sound of planes overhead after dark still made for a collective breath-holding. Searchlights crisscrossed the heavens, seeking the invisible foes above.

These days the aircraft were Spitfires, Hurricanes or Boultons – the good guys. If the thud-thud-thud of anti-aircraft guns resounded in the night, it was commonly understood the threat of a German invasion had been held off.

Londoners had new worries. There were shortages of everything, from flour to fuel. And not enough materials to rebuild the city's damage. Yet, amidst the turmoil and uncertainty, everyday life stubbornly continued. City cats with springtime in their blood prowled in the shadows and daffodils stood defiantly in bloom in the parks. Their presence a timeless reminder that once night life had also thrived for humans.

Through the cracks in the blackout curtains, a sliver of moonlight was visible, painting a faint glimmer on the river Thames, another reflection of life flowing on.

In a modest two-bedroom flat in Chelsea, Anna Adams paced the floor of her sitting room in stockinged feet. Still in her WAAF uniform, a frown between the dark brows and continuously pushing the glasses up the bridge of her nose, something was clearly bothering the young flight officer.

She knew she should be grateful. Even pleased. Sir Reginald's persistent probing into her background had revealed nothing improper. Nothing that could stop him from promoting her to flight officer with the WAAF. Someone "senior in rank" to the Head of the French Section of SOE had thwarted Sir Reginald's attempts to make Anna's statelessness a "security issue."

Who that was she didn't know. And most likely would never know. It didn't matter. As long as she got her British citizenship eventually, she would belong somewhere. The longed-for status was a step closer, but the pacing continued. All euphoria about her new official status dampened under her next predicament.

"It can't be. It can't be," she kept repeating but just what *couldn't be* she didn't even dare to state aloud. Staring down at the golden ring with the enormous diamond on her slender left hand, she slipped it on and off her finger as if weighing its weight.

Without consciously knowing where she directed her feet, Anna stopped pacing in front of a black and white photograph featuring a dashing and elegant man dressed in a tailored suit. Anna looked at the photograph as if she saw it for the first time. As if it had just then popped up on her sideboard without her doing.

Count Roderick Macalister, known as "Roddy Resolute" to his friends and foes, stood tall with that air of confident charisma that came with high-born status and his job as a Conservative MP for London's poshest constituency, Kensington.

Who was he? And who was the 'she' engaged to this man?

The man in the photograph didn't seem bothered about answering such existential questions. He just smiled back at her as if he already owned her, heart and soul. Which he did. In a way.

Roddy Resolute's exterior was well captured in the photograph, from the thick sandy hair neatly slicked back with a touch of pomade, the well-maintained mustache, the single-breasted jacket with wide lapels, the crisp, white dress shirt with a tie, the pocket square, neatly folded into the breast pocket, the impeccably pressed trousers, the shoes polished to a shine. It was all there. Shiny as his diamond. Anna swallowed hard, perspiration and panic spreading over her skin under the tight uniform.

Marriage was forever.

The phone rang. She panicked even more but knew she had to pick it up. It could be a call from work.

"Anna?" His voice was as clear-cut as the rest of him.

"Roderick?"

"I'll have Jason pick you up at 5:00 pm from your office tomorrow afternoon. Mother wants to inspect the wedding venue with you. Wear something decent instead of that infernal uniform of yours."

Anna wound the black coil of the telephone cord tightly around her finger. Tighter and tighter until the top of her finger was white as snow and the rest swollen and red. She was aware how Roderick always made her feel inferior, but she heard herself say, "Yes, I'll wear my best dress and the pearls you gave me. Don't worry."

"It's not for me, doll, but you know Mother. The pearls will be fine. I don't think I can cut out time to be there myself, but we'll dine at the Regent Palace Hotel at eight. Be ready."

"I will. Thank you, Roderick."

"Sleep well, Anna. And don't work too hard. Soon all that nonsense with you and the Secret Services will be over. Thank God."

Anna grimaced at the phone. This was the price she was paying for safety. The dice were cast. There was no way back.

"Night Roderick. You sleep well yourself."

Still in the uniform her fiancé hated and she loved, Anna pussy-footed back to her small sitting room and found herself again staring at his photo.

"Why can I never call you Rod or Roddy? No matter what your friends do or your mother with her eternal 'Ricky Dahling.' To me you're always Roderick. Stiff and formal."

The facial expression of the man of many names remained enigmatic, and she suddenly saw he didn't look directly in the camera but off into the distance, making it impossible to read his eyes. Flipping the photo in its golden frame face-down, she put the engagement ring next to it and sat down on the sofa, hugging her knees.

A great sense of relief went through Anna when she heard the key turn in the door and Pearl's high-pitched voice, calling "I am ho-ome!"

Pearl, just twenty, stood in the doorway. Already mature for her age, though small and slight as an adolescent boy, with short dark-blonde hair, sparkling light eyes and very pronounced dark eyebrows, oozing oodles of natural confidence whatever she was dressed in. Slacks and shirts in her free time or the dirty khaki overalls she was wearing now.

Pearl worked as an ATS mechanic in Greenford, West-London, a job she needed but didn't particularly like. A burning cigarette dangled from the corner of her well-formed mouth.

"What's the matter, Anna? You look like the cat had your cream."

Pearl dumped her tool bag on the floor and sank down next to Anna, who quickly shot up to go to the kitchen.

"It's nothing, Pearlie, let me get you your dinner. You must be starving."

"As a matter of fact, I am." Pearl followed Anna to their small kitchen and gratefully accepted a steaming cup of tea Anna had ready under the tea cosy. Her roommate worked long shifts and would have to get up at six again. But Pearl was never tired and was as observant as she was strong-minded and intelligent.

"You haven't answered my question. What's the matter, Anna?" As the light eyes took in her friend, Pearl sat down at their Formica table, her nails black-rimmed and smears on her hands. Too hungry to wash her hands, she picked up her fork and knife to dive into the mashed potatoes with kipper Anna had put on the backburner for her. The cigarette was still smoldering in the ashtray. Now and then, Pearl would take a drag from it before returning to her food and slurping down the tea.

Anna sat down on the other chair also with a cup of tea.

"It's ..."

"...Roderick," Pearl filled in for her, rolling her eyes.

"How do you know?"

Pearl raised one eyebrow. "Perhaps because of a dashing pilot you try to forget all about?"

Anna shook her head slowly but said nothing.

"Then perhaps it is because you've suddenly woken up and realized that Count Roderick Macalister isn't that lovable? No matter his perfect Mammie calls him Ricky Dahling?" Pearl's voice sounded light-hearted but the look in the light eyes was sharp.

"Oh Pearlie, what am I to do?"

For a moment it was silent in the kitchen. The only sound the buzzing of the electric heater.

"What do *you* want, my dear friend? I think that's the question you have to ask yourself and then give it your most honest answer. I mean can you just marry the guy, say thank you for my British citizenship, and divorce him?" Pearl took a deep drag on her cigarette, her eyes on Anna. Anna saw her friend meant it, wanted the best for her. Again, she shook her head.

"That's not my style, Pearl. Besides marrying Roderick Macalister more or less excludes divorce. Can you imagine the commotion that would create? The papers would be all over me and not in a nice way. Plus, his mother would kill me on the spot."

Pearl looked pensive. "True. Not a nice thought." She shoved her plate away from her and lit a fresh cigarette. Through a cloud of smoke she observed, "I needn't say anything more on the matter, my dear. You're the brainiest of us, so you'll figure it out. Know I'll support you either way."

And with a giggle she added, "Just make sure that if you *do* decide to marry your Count, you warn me in advance. If that mother of his catches me with nails like this in the wedding party, I'll be the one who'll get killed." Rising from her chair, she stretched her arms above her head and spraying a shower of gray ashes over her dark-blonde hair, she added, "speaking of dirty nails, I need to get in the bath and then straight to bed. My eyes simply keep disobeying me, wanting to shut for good every time I blink."

Anna stood up to clear the table. As Pearl headed for their shared bathroom, she was singing Billie Holiday's *God bless the Child* from the top of her lungs.

THEM THAT'S GOT SHALL GET

Them that's not shall lose
So the bible said and it still is news.

IT SOUNDED LIKE PROPHETIC WORDS. Anna stood still to listen to her friend's angelic soprano. She couldn't suppress the unwelcome premonition rippling through her. She, the serious one.

14

DEEP DOUBTS

As Anna heard Pearl singing one popular song after the other in the bathroom, she cleared the evening dishes and put out their breakfast plates as both had to leave early in the morning for their respective jobs. With her mind still on her problematic engagement, she suddenly remembered there was another important tidbit of news she'd been wanting to tell Pearl before Count Roderick had become the topic of their conversation.

She finished tidying the kitchen and headed to the bathroom. The girls had no secrets from each other. They walked in and out the rooms of their rental apartment in whatever state of undress they were, having been friends since before the war.

They'd met and clicked at St. Paul's Girl school in 1938. At the time Anna had been all shyness and self-consciousness. Though she spoke her accented English fluently and excelled in all subjects on the curriculum, she'd been quite lonely until vivacious Pearl Baseden had singled her out as a friend.

Pearl was the daughter of a wool merchant, who owned a shop on Oxford Street, a popular girl – more a tomboy than a girl – and often in trouble with the teachers.

One day, during their lunch break, she'd sauntered over to Anna, who was sitting alone as usual, immersed in one of her beloved novels. Anna had looked up into the light, twinkling eyes of the slight figure in front of her. Of course, Anna had studied all the girls in her year and had admired Pearl from a distance. How Pearl dared to stand out and yet – in her own way - followed the rules.

She wore the prescribed white blouse and tie of the school uniform but Pearl wore black pants instead of a pleated skirt. And her dark-blonde hair was cut short and combed back, like a boy's. There was never a trace of make-up on the open, oval face with the perfect skin, and yet Pearl was pretty, very pretty in her own special way. Not that she cared about her looks. All Pearl cared for was excelling at sports, of which she did many.

Surprised and secretly elated that popular Pearl invited her for a chat, Anna had become even more self-conscious about her own studiousness and accented English, but Pearl plopped down next to her on the bench in the school park, crossed her legs like a Buddha, and grabbed Anna's book from between her fingers.

"The Years. Virginia Woolf?" she recited the cover. "Heavens Anna, you read serious stuff. No wonder you're so serious yourself. I never get any further than my brother's comic books and even then, I fall asleep."

Anna had laughed. For the first time in a very long time, she'd laughed out loud. And she'd known, there and then, she'd found the best friend in the world in Pearl Baseden. Her opposite, her challenger, her alter ego.

FOR SOME REASON that first meeting replayed before Anna's eyes as she knocked on the bathroom door, a big smile on her serious face.

"Can I come in?"

"I am naked. I warn you!" Pearl snorted.

Anna sat on the edge of the bath, scooping handfuls of warm water over Pearl's slender back, perfect skin with not a blemish nor birthmark.

"I won't keep you long," Anna said. "I just came to tell you SOE has finally been given the green light to enroll women and I know you've been want..."

Pearl rose from the bath, wet and naked and prevented Anna from saying more by hugging her tightly. Anna struggled to get out of the tight embrace, her uniform already wet. That was not an option with Pearl. She was and always would be the physically stronger of the two.

"Anna, Anna, Anna! I lo-o-o-ve you!" Pearl danced up and down in the bath and almost slipped. "Does it mean I can finally do real work, and no longer have to do silly checking and cleaning of Churchill tanks?"

"Sit down in the bath, Pearl. Look what you've done to my uniform. You've soaked it." But Anna couldn't help smiling at Pearl's delight. It was so pure, so unfiltered. For the hundredth's time Anna wished she was that open and emotionally straightforward. Sad when sad, happy when happy. Like a child. Endless dilly-dallying – this way or that way? - always stood between Anna and the world.

Pearl sunk back down into the hot bubbles, splashing around like a fish. Anna sat down on the edge of the bath, withdrawn, suddenly silent. There it was again. What had she done? Baker Street staff were strictly forbidden to tell anyone outside the office what the secret agents were trained for and where they would be sent to do what.

After much probing by Pearl, Anna told her she had a boring office job at the Inter-Services Research Bureau, but Pearl hadn't been satisfied with the scant information, sensing Anna was not telling the entire truth. And the girls had promised each other never to have secrets between them.

And thus, the cat had come out of the bag, though by letting it out Anna risked losing her job for the information she'd shared. A dilemma that, now on the edge of the bath, fully sank in. Pearl knew about the training at the different training schools Anna visited at times and the questionable warfare practices the agents were taught there.

It all was getting so entangled in Anna's head. She bit her lip, wishing she'd never brought up the news in the first place. But then, if Pearl found out through her current job that agents were being recruited, she'd never forgive Anna.

Anna sighed, remembering the elation on Pearl's face after she – red-faced and ashamed – had given her an abbreviated account of what the Inter-Services Research Bureau or Station IX in reality stood for. Pearl's eyes had lit up and pointing one slender finger in the air, she'd cried out.

"Now *that's* what I want to do, Anna. How on earth did you secure a job there? Oh, you're a deep one! I hope by God they'll start accepting women agents sometime soon."

Pearl probably knew more about what was going on inside SOE than anyone else. A cross Anna had to bear and pray it would never come to light.

"Do you swear on everything that's holy to you I never told you about this recruitment, Pearl?"

Pearl pulled her most innocent face, and as she was quite the actress it was very compelling. She whispered in a hush-hush voice while vigorously rubbing her body dry with the towel Anna had handed her.

"I swear Officer Adams, on my own alive body that I know nothing. But please, please tell me you put my name forward as a candidate?"

"I did. But I can't promise anything," Anna tempered her friend's enthusiasm. "I told Sir Reginald that you're half French through your mother and you speak the language fluently. You may have a leg up on the others."

"Oh Anna, how grand will it be when we both work for the War Office? I'd love that so much and we would be able to work together, wouldn't we?"

Anna looked sceptical. That was not how it worked. If Pearl were recruited, she'd be sent off to different training schools all over the country and then board a plane and be dropped into France.

And that's where Anna felt her breath escaped her. She knew how dangerous the job was. At that moment she wished again she'd bitten her tongue and not said anything to Pearl. What if she went to France and was caught? She didn't dare to think about that scenario.

Pearl had meanwhile put on her pajamas and was brushing her teeth while dancing from one bare foot to the other. With her mouth full of toothpaste, she purred, "a job where I can speak French and learn how to lynch Nazis. Sounds like Heaven to me."

"Pearl, don't say those things!" Anna for once was stern with her friend. "You will only be sent into the fields to gather intelligence, not to get involved in combat." As she spoke the words, she dearly hoped this would be all Pearl had to do. If it even came to that.

With her usual unperturbedness, Pearl replied, "I can still lynch a Hun if I come across one. I'll do it silently and won't spread the word." Pearl grinned like a circus clown, but Anna let it go. She knew the deep hatred the French had for the Germans, having had their country overrun twice in a matter of decades. Her French agents were among the most fanatical to liberate their country.

"Get into bed, Pearl, and stop that lynching nonsense."

Anna followed her friend into her bedroom that was like a Valhalla for strong women. Posters of Amelia Earhart in her Lockheed Vega plane and the spear-throwing Olympics queen Babe Didrikson adorned Pearl's otherwise austere bedroom.

On the dresser stood a framed photograph of her brothers in their RAF uniforms. In another photograph Pearl's parents stood smiling in front of the Eiffel tower. The third photo was of an elderly couple sitting on a bench in a lush garden, which Anna assumed were Pearl's French grandparents. That was about it.

Pearl's room had none of the feminine touches that women their age generally liked and none of Anna's book collection. A bed, a nightstand, a dresser with what could be boy's clothes, a chair and a table with an ashtray. The decorated walls and family photos were all that showed Pearl's personality. But maybe the austere room did as well. Pearl was simple, solid, straightforward.

Still grinning like an enchanted pixie, she said, "Did I ever tell you I used to beat my brothers at climbing trees?" She let herself fall backwards on the bed. The light-blue eyes glittered mischievously. The short mane, still damp, rested on the white pillow. Wherever Pearl was, she was home. Home in her own skin.

"No, you never told me that, but it doesn't surprise me one bit," Anna replied. In her mind's eye, she saw Pearl swinging like a small ape on one arm from a tree branch, grinning from ear to ear. Then two little girls appeared before her, coughing and crying under a leaking tarpaulin. Rain roaring and rage all around her. Anna shook herself from the unwanted flashback, forcing her focus on Pearl again. She, sleepy and unflappable, opened one bright eye that fixed firmly on Anna's heartbreak.

"That bad again? I'm sorry. I shouldn't indulge in happy child-hood memories but know what...?" Pearl sat upright abruptly, wide awake and taking both Anna's cold hands in her own warm ones.

"I'll take revenge on your behalf, darling. Just watch me. The wretched Nazis aren't getting away with this. Over my dead body."

"Don't say that, Pearl. And honestly, I'm alright. Go to sleep. You need it."

Pearl sank back in the cushions and closed her eyes. The long lashes formed perfect black semi-circles on her creamy skin.

With a long-drawn yawn she mumbled, "I can't wait to float down in a parachute over Maman's country. I so hope either Arnold or Jean-Claude will drop me and be proud of me."

Anna nodded to the closed eyes, biting her lip. She too had two countries but couldn't feel the pride Pearl had for her mother's coun-try. Half asleep, Pearl continued talking and dreaming of her glorious future.

"Maybe I can also pay a visit to *grandmaman* and *grandpere* in Paris. If I can sneak away for a day or two. We haven't heard from them in almost a year. No letters have arrived, and Maman is so *anxieuse*. In their last letter they wrote that Paris had changed so much. They didn't feel safe anymore with the Germans keeping a tight control on everything. Maman wanted them to come to England to have them live here, but there's no way to evacuate them now. We'd never thought Hitler would take Par...".

Soon all Anna heard was Pearl's soft and regular snoring. She always enjoyed the best sleep and woke refreshed and revived. How different that was for Anna, certainly now.

The clock struck midnight and still she was wide awake, tossing and turning as if her bed was on fire. Two matters robbed her of any shot at a decent night's sleep. The engagement to Count Macalister and losing Pearl to France. If only her heart wasn't torn in different directions.

Anna had never expected to love Roderick but lately, she wasn't even sure she liked him. And she couldn't figure out what he wanted from her. He who'd turned down a blue-blooded damsel from another ancient family to marry Nobody Anna Adams. What was behind it? Certainly not his mother's wish.

Lady Macalister had lamented enough that her *Ricky Dahling* had let the *wondhaful* Countess Catherine Calverley slip through his fingers. Anna took the full brunt of the mother's dissatisfaction at Roderick's bridal choice every time they met.

"I need my British citizenship, or my job will remain at constant jeopardy," she told the unrelenting fingers of her fluorescent alarm clock. "I'll make my decision after tomorrow. I will."

Which led her to her other, possibly even greater heartache. Pearl. Though she knew as sure as her present pain Pearl was born for the job of secret agent - there would be no one better suited than Pearl Baseden - the risk of losing her best friend, her only friend, ate away at Anna's heart.

It wasn't just that she didn't know how to live without Pearl by her side. She felt as if she was sacrificing her. Sacrificing Pearl for a cause she, Anna, was too cowardly to take up herself.

"But Pearl wants this herself, with every fiber of her being," Anna tried to convince the clock that ticked, and ticked, and ticked.

Oh what a dilemma, a horrible dilemma.

When the clock struck four, Anna was still awake. Then she made a pact with herself. She would make sure Pearl got the very best survival training she could get, and Anna would supervise her progress personally. Sir Reginald could have no objections to that. Anything Pearl needed to stay out of Nazi clutches.

With her mind made up about her engagement decision and Pearl's future, Anna finally fell into a short sleep.

Until the alarm clock sounded three hours later.

15

THE MACALISTER KNOT

The next day - London, April 1942

N estled at the corner of Belgrave Square, The Grand Manor had been London's most luxurious and elegant wedding venue since the mid-1800s. In the midst of wartime, the grandeur of the aristocratic setting seemed surreal - some would say inconsiderate - but was a testament to the immunity of the elite class. The venue was a typical Victorian mansion, with steeply pitched roof lines and multiple gables facing in different directions.

The current owner, a wealthy American entrepreneur called Harold Sterlingfield, had the cream façade overgrown with ivy and added electric sliding doors to its front. He'd resisted his other grandiose plans to further "Americanize" the wedding hall, as he'd been assailed by London's upper crust not to touch the place where their families had tied the knot for generations. Among those defenders of keeping Britain British was Lady Annabelle Macalister.

Lady Annabelle Macalister, a formidable figure in London's high society, stepped out of her chauffeur-driven Rolls Royce with an air of regal poise, her tailored Schiaparelli dress exuding timeless elegance.

The absolute perfect thing to wear on an overcast but agreeable spring afternoon.

Without the door being held open for her by Jason, the Macalister chauffeur, Anna clambered from the backseat herself. She stood gawking up at The Grand Manor while nervously arranging her pearls and pushing the heavy glasses up her nose. Having forgotten the blue suede gloves, she had at least remembered to wear her navy pillbox hat.

"Come on, Anna. I haven't got all day." The slightly nasal but perfectly upper-class voice of her future mother-in-law startled Anna from her rigidity.

"I'm coming, Mrs Macalister." Anna's legs moved as automatons, the high-heeled pumps and tight skirt not helping her already gingerly movements. As always Lady Macalister's ice-blue eyes cramped every muscle in her body when that glance rested on her. The voice didn't make it any better.

"Heavens, girl, I thought you'd been trained to walk with poise. Didn't you tell me you'd been to a finishing school in Switzerland before the war?"

A porter operated the sliding doors for them, as Anna tried to make Mr Petrov proud.

"Yes, Mrs Macalister, my Uncle Benjamin sent me to Le Manoir in Switzerland in 1938." The Lady looked doubtful.

"That school is perhaps not as good as the one I went to in Lausanne in 1918. Château Mont-Choisi. I was trained for three days – three entire days!" A tapered finger with a bright-red nail went in the air and wagged. "To walk with five volumes of Shakespeare on my head. It was torture but it gave me my famously straight back."

Anna thought it useless to defend Le Manoir or her own torture training. The finishing school still left a bad taste in her mouth anyway.

Inside the Victorian building, crystal chandeliers hung from ornate ceilings, casting a warm, ethereal glow over the people present. Anna saw tables covered in white lace and adorned with fresh flowers awaiting today's celebration. Not hers. Not yet.

As they walked into the ornate ballroom accompanied by the owner himself, Lady Macalister let her eyes flit left and right as if she was interested in procuring the place for herself. The Lady owned everything, just with a glint of these hard eyes.

"Can our modest establishment please our Ladyship?" Sterlingfield's American voice was honeyed with flattery. Anna's opinion was not sought. The blue eyes stopped their flitting to rest on the burly owner. "Everyone marries here, dear Harold. Everyone!" she purred with satisfaction.

The corners of the ruby-red lips tightened, betraying discomfort, as the steely gaze turned to Anna. *You yet have to prove yourself worthy of my Ricky Dahling*, was written all over the powdered face. Addressing the unwanted daughter-in-law, the voice no longer purred but pinched. "Anna darling, this venue is positively exquisite. But I can't help but wonder if it's perhaps a tad too grand for someone of your... uh... background."

Anna managed to meet Lady Macalister's gaze with a polite smile, though her insides shriveled like a sponge being wrung out. Her obscure international heritage was no doubt what the aristocratic matriarch was referring to.

"It's indeed a magnificent place, Mrs Macalister. I feel truly fortunate," Anna replied, her accent revealing traces of her foreign upbringing. Harold Sterlingfield rubbed his plump hands, no doubt feeling he had this one in his already well-filled pocket.

The Lady's perfectly painted eyebrows rose, while she ignored the owner but continued to scrutinize Anna, her frosty demeanor undeterred. "Ricky Dahling has been the most eligible bachelor in London for a decade. I just hope you'll fit into our world. It's not easy, you know, being part of the Macalister family."

Anna's gaze remained steady despite her inner turmoil. The dark eyes giving away nothing. She had her reasons for entering into this marriage. Somehow the mother's scepticism only fueled her determination.

"I understand, Mrs Macalister. I assure you I will do my best to be a worthy wife to Roderick."

As they continued to navigate the wedding venue with the American owner on their heels, the tension between the two women charged the air like an electrified wire. Lady Macalister's disapproval and Anna's enigmatic nature clashed in a silent battle for dominance.

Anna couldn't stop wondering if marrying into the Macalister family, for the sake of a British passport and her covert work, was the right path for her. And Lady Macalister, while doubting Anna's worthiness, couldn't fathom her conservative MP son's obscure reasons for choosing Anna as his bride.

Why don't I have a mother to consult? Anna pondered. She only had Pearl. Who wasn't going to tell her left or right, though she certainly didn't approve of Roderick. Perhaps Vati? Anna shook her head without noticing it. Not Vati! Her father would see through this charade right from the start. No! Anna had to disentangle the Macalister knot herself.

AN HOUR LATER, with the brochure for *The Grand Manor* under her arm and the pearls weighing heavily around her neck, Anna slipped out of the backseat of a taxi in front of the Regent Palace Hotel and sped to Roderick's table in one of the corners of London's poshest restaurants.

"Count Macalister excuses himself, Ma'am," the kowtowing headwaiter informed her. "He's been held up at the Houses of Parliament but will be here as soon as he can."

"Typical," Anna mumbled under her breath, instructing her to be on time but always late himself.

"Would Madam care for a sherry?" The waiter, a middle-aged man, with a face as sad as an overweight Bassett hound, busied himself pulling out a chair for her and clearing some invisible crumbs from the damask tablecloth.

"Just a sparkling water will be fine, Gerald. I'll wait for Mr Macalister before ordering anything else."

"Fine, Ma'am. I'll bring your water in a second." Moving away like a flick knife, the waiter disappeared. The irony of only being treated with dignity by serving personnel, Anna thought.

To take her mind off waiting idly for the encounter with her fiancé, Anna took a novel from her bag. She was soon immersed in reading about a fictive heroine do did find her happily ever after. A brief interlude in thinking difficult thoughts.

"Anna!"

The voice above her sounded both authoritative. In her shock, she dropped the book to the floor. Grappling to retrieve it, she dived under the table.

"Sorry," she muttered, bumping her head against the table's edge as she came up again, her cheeks reddening.

"Don't make such a spectacle, Anna. Please!" Roderick hissed in her ear as he placed a loving kiss on her cheek. Louder he added, "how are you, my darling?"

When they were both seated, he took her hand with the engagement ring in his. "Mother told me you were both enchanted with *The Grand Manor* and have already pencilled in a date. I've always wanted an August wedding. Such a golden month."

He stopped talking to her when Gerald appeared to take their orders. Anna quickly withdrew her fingers and squeezed both her hands together in her lap. She let Roderick do all the ordering. Her insides roared, her instinct told her to flee but she sat quiet and still, slowly dying inside while her outside smiled.

As soon as Gerald scuttled away again, Roderick returned his attention to her. The same hard blue eyes as his mother, the same impeccable, unbreakable charm.

"Have you decided where you want to go on honeymoon, my darling? It's going to be a difficult choice in the middle of the war, but I suggest we go to New York. Safe, smart, and sophisticated. Just for three weeks. I have recess so that's absolutely perfect. A friend of mine has the perfect apartment in Manhattan we can stay in for as long as we like. What do you think?"

"Roderick?"

There must have been something in her eyes that stopped the

cascade of questions in which he made all the choices. For a moment he looked puzzled, combed a hand through the thick sandy mane.

"Why do you want to marry me?" She blurted out the words before she could check herself. He looked weary, irritated.

"That again? I thought we were past that stage, Anna. We have a deal, don't we?"

"What deal?" A sliver of life awoke in her zombie-like trance.

"You get your passport. I get an heir."

Anna thought she was going to fall off her chair. What was he saying? Where was this coming from? But she'd opened the can of worms and had to listen to its contents now.

"This is between us, Anna. So, keep it there, understood? You're a secret agent recruiter so you should know when to hold your trap. Mother's never to know this. Nobody else is to know this. It's between us. Outwardly we play the lovey-dovey couple, but we both have our own agenda. And no, there is *no* divorce."

Roderick had turned into a completely different person, gone was the charm and the veneer. But somehow, he didn't scare or intimidate her. He was finally being honest. Hard as a businessman, but honest.

"What agenda?" Anna asked puzzled.

Gerald's arrival interrupted the conversation. Anna hardly tasted what was on her plate but ate mechanically.

"I'm in love with a married woman who can't leave her husband. The scandal would be too big. I want no other woman, but I need an heir to continue the family name." Roderick took a big sip from his Chardonnay, then wiped his mustache. There was a trace of torment in the blue eyes Anna had never seen before. Her own eyes grew wide behind her glasses.

"Why me?" she whispered.

He hesitated. Took another sip.

"Just like you will never know the name of the woman I love, you will also never know who is protecting you, Anna. But let's say, it's someone with a great deal of power who understands the danger you're in. Even within SOE. Even here in England. The trouble with your passport is because people are thwarting the procedure. I guess you know that yourself?"

Anna thought of Sir Reginald and nodded.

"Are you saying you know all about my background?" She was surprised at the levelness of her voice as she said it.

"Yes, I read your file. I have access to these things. My name and my societal connections can give you the necessary protection in marriage, Anna. That will be our deal. And I know you won't cause trouble in my life. You're not that kind of girl."

Anna smiled despite herself and felt strangely better now the truth was on the table.

"Do your father and mother know my story too?"

"No. They never will. They just think I have a loose thread in my head marrying you."

"But what... what if I can't have a child?"

"Why wouldn't you? There was nothing in your medical file that suggested you had feminine troubles."

Anna blushed. Roderick seemed uncomfortable as well.

"No, that's not what I mean," she mumbled, "but if you love someone else..."

"We'll cross that bridge when we come to it. And can we now just toast and enjoy the evening?" Their glasses clinked. Anna swallowed the wine with difficulty.

THERE WAS SO MUCH, so very much, she had to think about. All was not what it seemed but the offer of permanent protection and not being forced to love Roderick Macalister was an attractive prospect.

16

MAURICE SOUTHGATE

The next day, London, April 1942

The next morning, Anna sat at the breakfast table white-faced and with dark bags under her eyes. Shaken to her core by the conversation with Roderick and his suggestions for their marriage, Anna had suffered another sleepless night. Pearl had already left on the seven o'clock bus to get to Greenford. Being alone in the house, she let her head drop in her hands and was close to crying.

"What am I to do? What am I to do?" she kept repeating, while the clock ticked and the office waited. She shook herself from her stupor.

"I need another coffee. I'll get to the office a little later. It's not like Sir Reginald will mind."

As long as she wasn't late for the morning staff meeting at 10:00 am, there would be no problem. Anna sighed as she wrapped her fingers around the coffee mug. It took all her force not to run to the telephone set in the hall and ring Roderick Macalister.

He'll be on his way to the Houses of Parliament. No. Do it now before it's too late. It's already too late.

On and on, her mind cartwheeled over her indecision while her hands squeezed the mug until it almost broke. The ring stayed on her finger.

Minutes later she grabbed her keys and bag and with brisk steps set out on foot towards Baker Street.

I'll marry him. I'll marry him. Her footsteps made the cadenza on the pavement. Her mind made up.

"ANNA, COME IN HERE PLEASE." Sir Reginald's booming voice sounded through the open door next to Anna's office. She was already on her feet on the way to her boss, assuming a potential new female agent had arrived for her to interview.

"What can I do for you, Sir Reginald?"

Never completely at ease in the presence of her impressive superior who always looked at her as if he was about to question her, Anna stood before the bulky desk. Everything was bulky in Major Reginald Owens' office, including the man himself. He looked at her from under bushy, gray eyebrows, one blue eye slightly bigger than the other, the skin on his nose red-veined, his mouth invisible under a swooping gray mustache.

"I want you to take Agent Maurice Southgate to Northolt Airstrip today. I was supposed to see him off myself but there's trouble in paradise."

'Trouble in paradise' was Sir Reginald's euphemism for trouble in the decoding room. Either messages from the agents in the field were undecipherable or worse, a wireless operator was suspected of transmitting under duress while being held by the Germans.

"I see," Anna answered, "but wouldn't Maurice rather be seen off by someone... uh ...senior? Someone he knows better?" It was a known fact at Section F that Maurice was a special case, a friend of Sir Reginald's.

"Are you too busy, Anna?" One gray eyebrow went up in irritation.

Sir Reginald didn't like personal preferences being mentioned. She shook her head.

"Taxi will be here in half an hour. You know Maurice's file?"

"Yes, Sir."

"Do your job, Officer Adams. And report back here when he's safely in the air."

"I will, Sir."

Two parts of this sudden new assignment made Anna nervous. She'd not been to RAF Northolt before to see off agents, only to RAF Tangemere, so she didn't know her way around this new airport. It would make the last checks she had to carry out before the agent could take off slightly more complicated.

But the unfamiliar airport was the least of Anna's worries. Maurice Southgate was her real worry. Tout London was in awe of the formidable agent who had already two successful missions to his name and was considered a SOE champion. Even De Gaulle, generally not in favor of British agents tramping through his country, had summoned the former barrister to share his knowledge of French resistance in the Lyon area.

Before the war Maurice, whose code name was Shadow, had been a successful lawyer with a wife and two small children, part of London's old boys' network. Not really the person one would expect to leave house and hearth to undertake clandestine missions in France.

Anna was still scanning through Maurice's file when there was a tap on her door and the man himself stood before her. Of medium height but strongly built with a Celtic crop of red hair and a pale freckled face, it didn't appear the Londoner would blend in well among the dark-haired, slighter Lyonnais, but Maurice's impeccable French, a credit to his French-Canadian mother and wife, had not raised suspicion among the Germans on his first two assignments.

"Miss Adams, Reggie... sorry I mean Sir Reginald, told me you'd do me the honor of seeing me off." He shook her hand graciously, as Anna rose from behind her desk. She decided she'd show she could handle this.

"Yes. Let me grab my coat and bag and we'll get to the taxi. Have you got everything, Mr Southgate?"

"My logic, my alias, and my will to free France from the Nazis. That's Southgate's Law: logic, alias, will. Would that be enough?"

Anna smiled. As most successful lawyers, Maurice Southgate was a wordsmith.

"I was more thinking of your valise, sir."

"Aha, you meant my personal belongings, or should I say Monsieur Leclerc's underwear and socks?"

"They're yours now," Anna replied trying to rebound his jocular tone.

They were silent in the taxi, bound by the vow not to speak of their work in public. Even a taxi driver could give away that the Inter-Services Research Bureau was a cover up for a spy nest. And Anna wasn't good at small talk. She secretly studied Maurice's profile as he took in the sights of London for that last time in what probably would be a long couple of months. His expression was unreadable, unruffled, and unrelenting.

Arriving at the modest military airport, they stood in the April sun while several RAF airplanes were taxiing or taking off. A lone Lysander had just begun its touchdown, the silver wings glimmering in the afternoon sun. Anna hesitated.

"Have you flown from Northolt before, sir? It's unfamiliar territory to me. We have another hour, so I wondered if you knew where to go."

Before he could answer her a tall, lanky pilot in flight overalls came striding towards them.

"Maurice! What an honor to fly you again. Gibraltar, this time!"

"Harry. What a coincidence, you're my pilot also this time. But you know the name's Joe."

"Sorry, of course!" The pilot slapped his forehead. All secret agents were called "Joes" by their flyers. Pilots weren't supposed to know agent names for safety reasons. But Maurice Southgate was a class apart. Everyone knew Maurice and Maurice knew everyone.

From reading his file Anna knew Major Henry "Harry" Douglas

was the pilot who would fly Maurice in his Short Stirling to Gibraltar. From there the agent was to cross the Mediterranean in a Portuguese felucca.

"I'll see you later, Harry. Let me spend my final hour on British soil with a decent cuppa and Miss Adams."

"Sure. See you in a bit, Joe." The lanky pilot tipped his cap and sauntered back to his plane that stood facing the runway, ready to go other than the sleeping engine.

Anna felt trepidation as she sat opposite the ginger barrister in the officers' lounge with his file open in front of her. It seemed almost sacrilege to assume Maurice would need any more briefing on his mission ahead, but it was her task to make sure.

"Can you go through your alias with me one more time, Mr. Southgate?"

"Sure, why not?" He took a long breath and Anna was mesmerized by the transformation that took place in front of her. Maurice the barrister vanished and in stepped the car mechanic Jacques Leclerc.

In a pure Lyonnaise accent he asked, "Que voudriez-vous savoir sur moi, Mademoiselle Adams?" *What'd you like to know about me?*

Anna smiled but the look in the light-gray eyes across from her was far from jocular, so she quickly kept a straight face. Maurice wasn't playacting. He *was* Jacques Leclerc now.

"Tell me where you were born, please."

"I was born in Lyon, France, on 12 July 1918. Right at the end of the Great War. My parents lived in Vieux Lyon, 5th district. My father worked as a baker until he died five years ago. My mother is a widow who lives with her married daughter, my sister Eugenie, in the countryside outside Lyon. I hardly ever see them these days. From my father, who fought in the trenches in Northern France, I've developed a strong sense of patriotism and a deep love for my hometown."

Anna nodded.

"Does everyone have red hair in your family?"

"*Non, non*! That's why my mother used to joke I'm from the milkman and not from the baker. I resemble my grandfather on father's side. From him I got the striking red hair, light eyes and freckles. And the robust posture. The rest of them are as slim, olive-colored, and dark-haired as regular Frenchmen. My physique landed me the nickname "Le Tigre" by my schoolmates.

Anna was careful not to smile this time.

"Are you married?"

Jacques shook his head where Maurice's eyes showed a shadow of doubt for a moment.

"*Non*. I'm a staunch bachelor and keep to myself. I work in a small auto repair shop that's owned by my friend, Jean Laban. We repair all cars, even German ones. My mechanical skills come in handy to maintain and repair vehicles used in covert operations. The garage is a perfect cover. I live in the small apartment above it so I can keep an eye on all the comings and goings."

The expression changed to Maurice Southgate again and the strong French accent became upper-class English. "Don't worry Miss Adams, I know Jacques Leclerc's every dirty secret and if not, I'll make him confess it to me. Leave that to the lawyer."

"I have no doubt about it," Anna answered. "I'm sorry for the fuss. This is all just the final security checks from a person not involved in your training. I assume, you're also well-briefed on your mission?" She took a sip from her coffee, her eyes on the list she had to tick off.

"Yes. I'm returning as the organiser of the Papillon network because I know Lyon like the back of my hand. I am to set up a new string of safe houses, improve routes for downed airmen to flee over the Pyrenees, contact local French resisters, organise arms and supply drops, organise sabotage of rail and ammunition supplies, contact other networks in the region. Yes, yes, yes. And two new wireless operators for the growing network will arrive during the next full moon. The first woman sent in that function I understand."

Anna nodded again.

"Denise Damerment, code name Chérie. Highly skilled *Francaise*. She's in the final stages of her training at the moment. She'll be a great asset to you. And another female agent, called Maureen Knight will arrive as your courier. She's Irish."

"Great change for SOE, sending women to act as agents in enemy territory." Maurice observed, finishing the last of his coffee, still with that unperturbed, relaxed expression on his face.

"It is," Anna agreed. "I'm going to be in charge of the female agents." As she uttered the words, she felt her stomach contract. Soon she might be sitting here opposite Pearl. Changing the subject, she asked a bit bashful, "do you mind if I check your clothes one more time?"

"No need, Miss Adams. I already did. All French labels, French shoes. I even saw Dr Beryl Davis last week to get my teeth checked. Wasn't a pleasure I can tell you."

"I know all about it." Anna couldn't help a wry smile. "Strangely enough, all our agents find the visit to that lady dentist the most daunting part of their training. I'd thought it would be survival in the wild or learning morse code, but no, Dr Beryl seems to be your absolute nightmare. The reason Sir Reginald always orders a taxi to take the agents to Hamilton Terrace as he's afraid they'll otherwise escape. Did you need new fillings?"

"One. And that was more than enough!" Maurice smiled like a peasant with a toothache.

"Last thing is your security checks. Both bluff and real. You know them by heart, no doubt?" Anna inquired.

"Sure. And I'll remind myself what my coding teacher Mr Larks taught me at Beaulieu. 'Try not to go over 250 letters. Make sure to free your language, vary your transposition keys and don't fall into patterns. Code as if you're making love'." Maurice laughed heartily for the first time. "Not that I'll get much chance at that, as I probably won't be sending my own messages. I'll leave the fun part to Miss Damerment."

It was time to go to the tarmac. Harry was clearly dying to leave, checking his watch every other minute as he stood next to his Stirling. The engine was now roaring.

"Bad weather expected over the Bay of Biscay later today, Joe, so we'd better get going. See if we can beat the storm first."

Anna and Maurice shook hands.

"I'll be fine, Miss Adams. No worries about me. I'll be back in two months with all the news I can gather. Please send my prewritten postcards to Irene and the children. I don't want them to worry about me."

"I will, *Jacques* and good luck!"

She saw him clamber inside the plane that started moving immediately. She waved. He waved back. As she turned her back on the plane to return to the officers' lounge and wait for her taxi, a shiver shot up her back. She looked again at the plane already high up in the blue sky, a silver spot on the horizon.

Don't be silly, Anna, she told herself. *If there's one agent who will stay out of the claws of the Gestapo, it's Maurice Southgate. Never met a more prepared and more conscientious agent in my life.*

But still. But still.

17

BACK TO THE PAST

S till with the jitters in her stomach, Anna made her way back
from the tarmac.

"I'll have another coffee to steady my nerves before
getting back to London," she told herself.

Seeing off SOE's star agent for another mission in France and her
focus on him had pushed all thoughts of her complicated wedding
plans to the background. Now they popped up like deep-rooted
weeds.

Another dinner with Roderick tonight. And then dinner after
dinner after dinner for the rest of her life. It would be a one-and-a-
half-hour taxi drive back to London. Time enough to get used to soon
being Mrs. Macalister.

On opening the lounge door to leave the airport, she almost
bumped into him. Taken by complete surprise she stammered,
"Henryk?"

"Anna?"

"Is it you?" They said it in unison.

She could see his surprise was as big as hers. He was wearing his
aviation overalls so had clearly just landed or was about to take off.
They stood gaping at each other, only a step between them. Frozen

and flustered. How could it be? After three years. She was safely Anna now. Anna Adams. Henryk knew nothing of her secret life, her engagement to Roderick. She'd failed him. Miserably.

"You're the last person I expected to see here." He was the first to find words, while Anna just stared up at him, her knees weak, an uncontrollable surge of love and passion spreading through her disoriented limbs.

"I'm … I'm here because…"

"Come and sit down for a moment. You look like you've seen a ghost. It's only me, Henryk."

Just as three years before, Henryk took the lead, taking the bewildered, grief-stricken girl by the hand. She followed him to one of the booths that looked out over the runway. The self-assured gait as he navigated the place, the broad shoulders and slim waist in gray overalls. Anna swallowed hard as her heart raced, focusing her gaze on the other side of the window where the lights of descending and ascending planes flickered.

Don't look at him. It's too much!

Her life had come to a full stop while everything around her moved faster and faster. But her eyes were drawn to his face despite all the forces in the world. That unforgettable face. The pronounced jawline, the face so masculine and yet tender, the unwavering blue eyes that took her in. All of her. The intensity of their glint seemed to burn straight through her WAAF uniform. The look in his eyes, just for her, broke her heart all over.

Why now?

Neither of them spoke, both just sat there taking in each other's presence. It was as if the waiters knew to keep a polite distance from the electrifying energy around the couple, he the aviator, she the flight officer.

A dark curl fell across his forehead and her heart skipped another beat.

"Great uniform," Henryk finally observed, clearing his throat. "The WAAF uniform suits you."

Anna cast her eyes down, straight onto the monstrous engagement ring. She quickly covered it with her other hand, but it was too late. Even before she could begin her story, she heard the dreaded words from the other side of the table.

"Should I congratulate you?"

"Yes...no...," she stammered. She held back the tears with difficulty. "How much time do you have, Henryk?" Her voice was so soft she was sure he hadn't heard her but looked up when he said.

"I'm supposed to fly this evening, but just for you I can ask the lads to stand in for me."

"Not again," Anna whispered, remembering how he'd stayed with her only to be able to attend her mother's funeral. Henryk hadn't changed, was still as solid as a rock, but she was like the liquid mercury in a thermometer, unstable, fluctuating, unreliable.

A shy waiter came their way.

"The boss asks if you would like a drink on the house, Major Pilecki, and you Ma'am?"

The smile Anna had cherished in her soul lit up Henryk's handsome face. So much warmth, so much charisma was in that smile. He clearly was a regular at RAF Northolt.

"How kind of Mr. Wilson, Jeremy. Make it a strong coffee for me. I need it."

"Coming, Sir. And you, Ma'am?"

"The same for me." Anna managed a small smile.

"Tell me," Henryk urged, bending slightly towards her, "unless it's too hard."

"I'm so sorry," Anna sniffled. "I tried, but I was too late. The war, you see..."

Henryk misunderstood. "Yes, the war's changed everything for everyone." He let out a deep sigh. "Doesn't look like it's ending soon. But hey, that's why it's great to bump into an old friend."

"I'm so sorry, Henryk. I tried to write but I was too late."

"Sorry for what? You don't owe me anything, Anna."

"Oh, but I do. You just don't know," she blurted out, unable to stop a tear from trickling down her cheek. Before she knew what was happening, Henryk reached across the table and wiped the tear away with his thumb. "What's so bad, Anna. You can tell me."

"I can't. It's just too much."

"Start with what's easy. Your uncle? How is he?"

Anna's body quivered all over while her cheek still felt the pressure of his warm thumb.

"He passed." Her voice was toneless.

"Dear God," Henryk exclaimed. From her cast down eyes, she saw him clasp a hand over his heart. "Oh, my dear Anna. Nothing is spared you, is it? I hardly dare to ask about your father."

And there he was, right back in the middle of her past life, tearing open all the wounds without making a single mistake. *Oh Henryk, why you, why now. Why?*

The coffee arrived. Anna stirred her cup absentmindedly. Just to have something to do. To keep the wheels of her life spinning.

"I'm so terribly sorry, Anna. I had no clue. I should've come by Mount Street earlier. It's just been horrible with the war." His hand came across the table again and rested for a moment on hers, the one without the ring.

Anna swallowed. "My father is alright. I hardly see him these days because of the nature of my work."

It was a white lie. She'd only gone by the shop once now two years ago to tell him she would be staying away for security reasons. Her father had asked no questions. He never did. Accepted what his daughter did when she did it. As it was, she could see he was struggling enough with life himself.

Henryk's voice drew her to the present. "May I know the cause of your uncle's passing?" He spoke with such extreme tenderness Anna's shoulders hunched and she couldn't stop the tears from falling. He was on her side of the booth in one big step and sat next to her, his arm around her. "I should have come. I'm sorry."

"No, it was all my doing," Anna sobbed. "I was so wretched after Mutti's death I didn't reply to your letters. Only when I was in Switzerland, I had enough rest to write back. But I wrote to you the day before war broke out, so you never got my letter. Uncle Benjamin died in November 1939. It was all very sudden. He had a heart attack."

"Oh no." Henryk moaned. An agonizing sound Anna didn't know he had it in him. Why did he care so deeply for her and her family when she didn't deserve it? She'd not only deserted him, but she had also become engaged to another man. His kindness hurt. Hurt more than anything in the world.

Just when Anna thought, she'd cut all ties with her past, Henryk "Hubal" Pilecki came marching back in, forcing her to face what couldn't be faced. Every dirty and difficult detail of it.

WITH LOVE CAME PAIN. So much pain.

PART IV

PAST LIVES

GERMANY-POLISH BORDER-LONDON-
SWITZERLAND 1938-41

18

STUCK ON THE POLISH BORDER

As the Grynszpans were herded out of their home, their neighbors, previously friendly and welcoming, now watched in silence from behind drawn curtains. At the Hanover train station, they were met with a chaotic and heart wrenching scene. Other Jewish families, also displaced and frightened, were being loaded onto trains bound for the Polish border.

The train station was crowded as never before. People of all ages and ranks pushed and shoved their way, not knowing where they were going, while the Sicherheitspolizei tried to herd them in one direction. Towards the waiting trains. Children howled, while elderly people stumbled and fell onto the platform, being walked over. The straps of overstuffed suitcases broke, their contents spilling for all to see.

Somewhere above the frantic crowds a pale pink sky announced the arrival of another day, but this morning brought no gladness to the hundreds of Jews suddenly homeless, stateless, helpless. Yehuda Grynszpan did his utmost to keep his family together, using his voice cracked with emotion to spur them on. Sarah and Eva had stopped crying, gaping at the kerfuffle around them with marble-round eyes.

There had been no time to take their stroller so Ansel and her

father each carried a baby and all the luggage. Judith was too flabbergasted to be entrusted with carrying anything.

"Did you bring our passports, Father?" Ansel asked over the
noise, suddenly remembering they were leaving the country for the
first time in her life.

"I did, my girl. They're in my pocket."

With difficulty, they boarded the train. Though nobody wanted to
leave Hanover or home, all Jewish residents suddenly seemed
anxious to move away, afraid to be left behind in limbo.

Ansel helped her father get all the valises, the babies, and her
mother on board. They were lucky to find two seats. Judith was
installed first with Sarah on her lap. Ansel sat down on the other seat
with Eva. The cramming, crying, and coughing around them was
cacophonic. Forcing herself not to think how long they'd have to stay
like sardines in a can, Ansel kept panic at bay. For now.

In the hurry to leave home, they'd been unable to take food and
drinks with them and it didn't look like there would be catering in
this chaos. With foresight Ansel had packed powdered milk for the
babies.

"You do need water to mix the powder." A middle-aged lady
opposite them huddled in an expensive rabbit fur coat took a bottle
of water from her bag when she saw Ansel fiddling with the baby
bottles. "Here, use this. I'm sorry the water is cold. I hope it will
work."

"Thank you so much," Ansel accepted the water. The powder
didn't really dissolve in the cold water, with lumps sticking to the
sides of the baby bottles, but Sarah and Eva were ravenous and drank
it anyway.

"Have a sip yourself, girl. We're in for a long ride. And give some
to your poor Mutti," the kind lady said. "I have another bottle in my
bag."

"Thank you so much." The stranger's kindness touched Ansel
more than the hardship they were up against. It brought tears to her
eyes. She drank gratefully but didn't dare to take too much.

Sarah and Eva slept. Judith seemed to be sleeping as well, her head sunken on her chest, the hat with the ostrich feather falling forward. Ansel tried not to think, not to feel, not to look ahead. She forced herself to keep her mind as blank as an empty canvas. She was numb, but without fear. Ready to survive.

Now and then she would glance over to her father, who was half sitting, half slumped over their pile of suitcases, squeezed in between two other families. She didn't meet his eye. She didn't want to. None of this was his fault, of course not, but she'd have to do this on her own. At seventeen-and-a-half, Ansel felt she would have to fend for herself. For God knew how long, maybe her entire life.

The journey across Germany was endless and horrific. The noise, the stench, the agony permeated the air. Not thinking of anything kept Ansel away from the edge of a break down.

Take one breath at the time. Not too deep. Just enough to fill your lungs and keep the stench at bay. Don't think of thirst, of hunger, of sleep, of pain. Don't think. Don't think.

One time she couldn't help herself and met her father's eye. The loving look he sent her, encompassing his whole family, broke through the fresh shield around her heart.

No, she screamed in silence. *I can't see your love. I don't want love. Not anymore. I want to survive.*

It was deep in the night when the train came to a screeching halt at an unlit, desolate looking station. The sign read *Breslau*. Ansel remembered seeing the name of the town on the topography map at school. On the Polish border, but still in Germany. Weren't they supposed to go to Poland?

The doors opened. Equally grim and black-clad guards as the ones that had wakened them so cruelly in the morning barked orders at the stupefied travelers. Nobody had a clue where they were or what was expected from them in Breslau.

"*Rauss*! Walk! Faster!"

Ansel's tongue was glued to the roof of her mouth. She hadn't had anything to eat all day and just that sip of water in the morning. Everything had been saved for the babies. Weak with fatigue, she took gulps of cold, misty air as if it was food for her soul. After all the hours cooped up in that overloaded compartment, it was a moment of heaven. She moved with the crowds, carrying Eva and her suitcase, on unsteady legs into the dark night.

When they left the station, pelting rain came down on them and the misery was complete.

"Any idea where we're being sent, Father?" she couldn't help asking her elder as he walked beside her carrying Sarah and the three other valises. Judith trailed behind them.

"I don't know, Ansel. I guess we'll be led to vehicles that will take us across the border and then to Warsaw. None of the guards is willing to give us any information."

As they walked the deserted streets of Breslau – her watch said it was two in the morning - and left the town behind, Ansel saw a sign stating Polish border 2 miles. Just when she had adjusted to the fate they'd have to cross the border on foot, as no vehicles appeared, something horrific happened.

Gun shots rang from where they were heading. The crowd stopped moving, uncertain, terrified. Behind them the German guards pushed on. People started screaming and yelling.

"Stop, please stop!"

More shots rang but they went up in the air. The guns weren't pointed at them. Not yet at least.

"They're shooting from the Polish side," her father observed, his voice quivering. "What by Jove is going on?"

"Will they not let us in?" Ansel asked in a tiny voice. *Where else are we supposed to go?* She hugged Eva closer to her, but the baby started crying and woke her sister who joined in.

The long, bewildered trail of people balked, came to a halt. What now? Nobody dared to move closer. The rain intensified, and a cold wind set in. Ansel shivered. And listened. No more orders seemed to be coming from the Germans at the tail end. It was as if they had disappeared in the night, their job done.

The shots rang again. Nobody dared to move closer. It dawned on everyone they weren't welcome in Poland either. Trapped between two countries that didn't want them. The Polish Jews from Germany. It was the worst nightmare.

But God had not completely forgotten them. There was still mercy. On their left side, with tall dark trees behind, they saw large tarpaulin tents, the silvery wet tops of which peaked into the night air. A big red cross at the entrance. The head of the long trail of people with Ansel and her family among them, stumbled over the fields towards the tents.

As they came closer, Ansel saw there were already hundreds of people in the makeshift village and there wasn't place for this many. Two nurses in rain gear stood at the entrance looking at the newcomers with bewilderment. Worry and wear on their faces.

"So many more. What do we do with them? We can't house you all."

Luckily the Grynszpan family was at the head of the group and admitted.

"Families with babies first. Then the elderly," the nurses ordered in broken German. Ansel thought they had an English accent and for a moment she felt hope. England. The land of green hills and plenty. If only they could go there, she would never leave it again.

They were escorted by another young nurse to a small, muddy tent that only held two thin mattresses, no heating, a small oil lamp. They were given a clammy blanket each and a bowl of warm soup. The soup tasted the best Ansel had ever had in her life. She savored it, taking small spoonfuls, the welcome warmth spreading through her stomach.

After the soup, she felt strong enough to change her sisters' diapers, which were soiled from day-long wearing. She didn't have enough water to wash the girls, so she had to settle for quickly putting on dry diapers, and dressed them back into their warm clothes.

One more bottle of warm milk and they both fell asleep. So did her mother, who hadn't even finished her soup. She just shut her eyes, lay down and was gone. Ansel looked at her father in the shimmering light of the oil lamp. His expression was unreadable. They had no words of consolation for each other and remained quiet.

The rain pelted the tent above them and in one corner a big spot spread over the tarpaulin where the water was leaking through.

No thinking of my warm bed on Leibzigstrasse. No thinking of Teddy.

SOMEHOW, Ansel had fallen into a dreamless sleep only to be awoken by her crying sisters. Like an automaton, she came into action. As they'd all slept in their clothes, there was no need to dress, just put on her muddy shoes and open the tent. Her father was out. Her mother didn't move but lay with her face towards the tent wall.

The weather was dry with a weak sun, but very cold. The night's sliver of a moon was disappearing in the pinkish red of the morning light. Where was she? And why? No thinking of that. Ansel set out toward the main tent at the entrance, where she expected the staff to be. No questions of why. Just food and a plan for the day.

When she returned with milk for the babies, a small package of bread and cheese and three cups of weak tea, she saw her father arrive with his arms full of wet wood. It wasn't much but they could make a small fire and dry their clothes.

"You've done well, daughter, going early. People are already returning empty-handed. Food is scarce."

Ansel fed her family, helped her mother sit up, took care of Sarah and Eva.

No thoughts. Just survive!

19

HELL ON EARTH

A month later – the Polish border, 16 November 1938

Ansel opened eyelids that felt heavy and sleep-deprived. She stared into the darkness of the tent. Silence. Just soft breathing of her family members around her. A moment of heaven during hell on earth.

She rose to a sitting position, suddenly panicking, Sarah, Eva! There was none of the grating breath of her sisters' infected lungs. They weren't coughing or crying. Something was wrong.

Ansel struggled from under the thin blanket that was too caked with mud and too damp to provide much warmth. Her hands, covered in black mittens, went to the two tiny bodies beside her. She felt their chests. Thank God, they were breathing. They were alive. They would be well.

For a moment, she let herself sink back on the mattress that was so thin it didn't prevent the freezing ground underneath from creeping into her bones, but thinking time was dangerous time to Ansel. So, with limbs frozen and her body aching of hunger and fatigue, she sat upright again.

In the darkness, she found her shoes and left the tent to stand in the cold of the early morning. A thin layer of snow had fallen in the night, but it held none of its usual magic. It just meant more cold, more misery, more illness.

Before she was fully awake, she stood in line with other shivering camp dwellers on their way to the nurses' tent for their daily portion of tea, bread, and milk for her sisters. This early morning drill held a kind of comforting routine for Ansel. The one moment in the day something positive happened. Some food, a bit of oil for the lamp that was also their only source of warmth.

But soon the dark clouds of the past weeks settled on her, like the threatening snow clouds above her. The terrain where the makeshift camp had popped up had turned into one big mud pool. The fall rains, now in wintery dress, had been incessant and temperatures had been below 0*C since their arrival.

How much longer? Ansel wondered as she shuffled to the big tent. Both Sarah and Eva had fallen ill in the past week but there was no doctor in the camp and the nurses had no medication stronger than aspirin. Their situation was dire, especially as they were underfed and there was no place to keep them warm and dry. High fever, coughing, sometimes too weak to even cry.

And Sarah and Eva weren't the only babies that were ill, or the only camp dwellers for that matter. Everyone was suffering, falling ill... some had already died.

"I'm so sorry, it's pneumonia," Nurse Margaret had said with a face worn with stress and worry. Sarah and Eva's illness was like an inescapable black web over everything Ansel did and felt and saw. The lungs of her lovely, sweet little sisters being filled by the cold and the damp and nothing she or Vati could do to ease their suffering.

Her mother had not woken from her stupor since they arrived in the camp. She only lay on her mattress with her head turned to the wall. If Ansel insisted, she would briefly turn towards her for a cup of tea and some bread. Her mother's eyes no longer had a will-to-live light in them.

Ansel feared for her mother's life as well, but miraculously enough she didn't show signs of any physical illness. No fever, no coughing, no rattling lungs. Just no longer any spark. Which might be as lethal.

"How long still, Vati?" Ansel asked in a moment of despair, but her father had shaken his head, with hair that had turned snow-white overnight. The brown eyes behind their spectacles held a sorrow and sadness Ansel couldn't face.

"I have to go on, I have to save them. I'm young and strong," she told herself time after time, as she plodded on through mud and cold and lay awake listening to her sleeping family members.

"How are your sisters today, Ansel? Have their fevers broken?" Nurse Margaret asked. Ansel had meanwhile learned the kind nurse was a nun, just like Sister Felicia. She was originally from the north of England but had been in a convent in Breslau for decades.

As Ansel accepted the tray with the Grynszpan's breakfast from her, she answered, "they weren't crying this morning and didn't feel terribly hot, so perhaps they're getting better."

"I've asked for a doctor I know in Breslau to come and have a look at them and at some other patients. I hope he will come, but the good man's afraid of what the Nazis will do to him and his practice if he takes on patients from the camp. We've also asked the International Red Cross to send us more staff, but the Nazis are thwarting that as well. I'm so sorry, Ansel, so sorry we can't do more for you."

"It's alright, Nurse Margaret. We are very grateful for your help. Without it we would be literally in the woods."

"There's still no news from the Polish side. We have no idea why they won't let you in. You're all former Poles, aren't you?" The kind, round face of the fair nurse with her friendly, gray eyes and wrinkled face looked as desolate as she must have felt. Tucking an extra piece of bread into Ansel's pocket, she added, "Come back later in the day, dear, when you have a moment. I hope to have news for you. I'm doing my best."

"News about what, Nurse."

"I can't tell you for sure, yet, but we heard of an opportunity to get you out of here and to a safer place. I want your family to be the first.

Your situation breaks my heart and you most of all, Ansel, taking care of them all. How old are you, after all?"

"I'll be eighteen in February, Nurse."

The nurse shook her head but smiled at her warmly. "Go girl. If the doctor dares to show up, I'll send them straight to your tent."

"Thank you, Nurse Margaret. I will never forget your kindness."

"I'm just doing my job, girl. Now, go and feed your family."

From experience, Ansel learned to go back to her family's tent by a circumspect way. As there was too little food for all the refugees, hungry people would try to steal the bread off her tray if she took the main route. She took the path around the camp along the tall pine trees and at the end of the trail, took a shortcut to the gray tent that now housed all they had. The tarpaulin had turned almost ash white from wear and weather. A weak sun was the harbinger of another hopeless day.

As soon as she heard one of her sister's grating cries, Ansel felt overwhelmed by a sense of gloom.

"Hurry up, Doctor," she prayed aloud. "Please God, help us."

But Ansel kept her moments of despair short by forcing herself not to think. Only to act. Cater, clean, cuddle. Ansel took breakfast last. First, she nannied her sisters while her father did his best to get a smoldering and unwilling fire going in front of their tent. After Sarah and Eva, it was time to attend to her mother.

When all that was done, Ansel's tea was cold and the bread almost frozen, but she didn't complain. She had only one hope left and clung to it with every fiber of her weary body and soul. *Go to London. Go to Uncle Bittermann.* London and the rich uncle would make all their sorrows vanish. This hell on earth would be forgotten. A dark shadow in the past to which she would never return.

BY THE AFTERNOON Sarah and Eva's situation had deteriorated. They had a higher fever than before. How high, Ansel didn't know, as she didn't have a thermometer. Her father was on his way to the big tent to ask for one of the nurses.

The small patients, sweet-looking and lovely as ever, just very white, kept smacking cracked lips. Sucking only led to more coughing so Ansel eased the worst of their thirst by pressing a wet cloth to their tiny mouths. Each in turn, each little face so preciously dear.

They were almost too ill to cry now and just lay still, close together to share each other's warmth with all the blankets, except that of their mother, around them.

Unstably, Judith Gryszspan turned around and sat up. It was a totally unforeseen action, but Ansel's heart immediately went out to her ill-in-the-nerves mother. There was no trace of weakness in her gaunt-faced Mutti now, just soft, translucent love.

She caught hold of her two youngest from her eldest with a warm, "Thank you, Ansie," and hugged them tightly to her. Woken from whatever stupor had alienated Judith from her family for weeks, she seemed clear in the head now, while whispering in gentle repetition, "meine Lieblinge, meine Lieblinge."

After kissing the tops of their sweaty little heads, she broke into the Polish lullaby "Lulaj, Lulaj" in her beautiful soprano voice.

> Oj lulaj, lulaj
> Oj lulaj, lulaj
> Siwe óczka stulaj
> Oj, siwe ocie stulisz
> do mnie się przytulisz
> Do mnie się przytulisz

"Go to sleep, go to sleep, close your blue eyes
if you close your blue eyes, you'll cuddle up to me."

Tears streamed down Ansel's cheeks as the babies settled against their mother's warmth and instantly fell asleep. Mutti had sung that lullaby so often to her, as well, when she was small. Though it had always made her curious little mind wonder why Mutti thought her eyes were blue. Ansel had longed to have those blue eyes.

For the first time since they'd arrived in this hell a month ago, the stress fell off Ansel's young shoulders. Her sisters were comfortable. Mutti was back.

When her father walked into the tent a minute later, he beheld the scene of his wife with their three daughters around her and halted in his tracks. Overtaken by the unexpectedness and a deep joy. He removed his spectacles to wipe his moist eyes. Smiled and cried at the same time. A gush of love and hope going through his whole being.

If only this scene had been in the house on Leibnizstrasse, where they belonged. But they were in a cold, muddy tent between Germany and Poland, stuck between two enemies, stateless refugees, unwanted pariahs. And yet, the warmth spread through Ansel as well, a warmth that would sustain her. At least for this moment the hell was outside and her family inside the glow of love.

"The doctor is coming this afternoon. Nurse Margaret is an angel descended from heaven," her father whispered so as not to wake the twins. "All will be well."

Would it be? Could it be? Ansel thought.

But no. It wasn't to be.

While Judith sat and sang to her young daughters, the family waiting anxiously for the doctor's arrival, life slipped out of the girls, quite peacefully, quite imperceptibly. Ansel didn't even register their passing while her mother kept singing the Polish children's songs over and over.

The Grynszpans sat around the oil lamp in a moment of ignorant bliss. Ansel was back in her happy youth, when Mutti was strong and always smiling, a bit untrameled at times but always fun, always lively.

The end of daylight came early and fast. At some point Yehuda bent over his wife sitting with her babies and felt them. He took off his cap, reached out his trembling hand to close their tiny eyelids.

"They're gone, Judy," he said in a broken voice. *"Baruch Ata Adonai, Eloheinu Melech HaOlam, Dayan HaEmet.* Blessed are you God, King of the Universe, the True Judge."

Consumed by a tumultuous sea of emotions, Ansel sat as frozen. Even if she'd willed her body to move, it wouldn't have obeyed. Grief and despair overwhelmed her. Grief for herself, for her parents, but mostly for her precious sisters who would never grow up, never see London, never marry, or grow old.

Dazed and deaf, she grappled with an indescribable sense of loss, so big and unfathomable she didn't know it could exist. There was movement around her, people talking, a doctor, a nurse, medication given to her mother, then an undertaker going out with her father. She registered it all as she sat, handed a cup of tea, given a white pill.

"I am calm. I don't need anything." Some automatic part of herself talked and made sense, while everything else inside her broke into a thousand pieces. She was outside of it all, fighting to find a place where she didn't feel the pain. But she couldn't find it. A thousand knives landed in her tender flesh, and she bled and bled.

Sarah and Eva were gone. Their innocent lives snatched away by pneumonia. For what? Why had her baby sisters been sent to their deaths by Jew-hating Nazis? Anger flared up, balled her hands into fists, but anger was useless. What power did she have?

Better to feel the deep, gnawing ache at the cruel hand of fate; the void, nothing could ever fill again. As Ansel's world crumbled, it left her with a sense of hopelessness and isolation, without any glimmer of solace amidst the harsh realities of their tragic circumstances.

"Ansel?"

She felt a comforting arm around her, someone pulling her close. It was Nurse Margaret.

"I'm so incredibly sorry, dear, but Doctor Braun would have been too late anyway. But don't worry anymore, dear girl, it's all taken care of. Time to say goodbye to your sisters and then I'll help you pack. You have to get out of here as quickly as possible."

Something didn't match up in Ansel's mind, but she didn't ask questions. Meek as a mouse she let herself be escorted to the small fresh grave behind their tent, blinking against the oil lamps that flicked everywhere, reflecting in her glasses.

Some part of her troubled self registered enormous activity going on around her. It seemed out of proportion for the deaths of her sisters. As if the whole camp had come to their tent. She clung to Nurse Margaret's hand as if she was a little girl.

"Try to pray, Ansel," the kind nurse urged her, herself sinking on her knees on the frozen ground and making the sign of the cross. But Ansel had no prayers. Prayers were gone, hope was gone, life was gone.

This was hell on Earth.

20

THE AVIATOR

Steeped in grief and numb with cold and hunger, Ansel couldn't make head or tail of all the noise and commotion around her in the refugee camp. The name Grynszpan constantly buzzed in the air. Did they have a contagious disease? Were they being hunted down because her sisters had died? She couldn't care less. For all she cared, Ansel would lie in that shallow grave with her sisters and die as well.

With both hands bare, she flattened the loose earth on the grave, her tears frozen in the cold winter air.

"Ansel, dear, it is really time to pack." Nurse Margaret's anxious voice sounded above her. She looked up into the dusk air, into that friendly face, not understanding the meaning of her words.

"Are we going to Poland now? We can't leave while Sarah and Eva are just buried."

"It's not that, dear. You are in danger."

"Who isn't? Is the camp going to be evicted?"

"Come to my tent, girl, and let me explain the situation." The middle-aged nurse pulled her to her feet. Ansel stood, shaking all over, clinging to the hand that held her steady.

"It's all so sudden and now with your sisters' passing today, all so very sad and untimely," Nurse Margaret observed. "There's been a murder in Paris that's made Hitler furious. He ordered all the Jewish possessions in German and Austrian cities to be destroyed and set fire to. It's an absolute nightmare. It's been dubbed the Kristallnacht for all the glass that's been smashed."

Ansel shrugged. What did it have to do with her? They were Jewish, persona non grata, already. It couldn't get worse to her family as they no longer owned anything to be smashed.

When they were seated opposite each other with a hot cup of tea and a bun, Nurse Margaret's attitude became even more on edge.

"The man who was murdered in Paris was some Nazi official, but the murderer was...," she paused for breath, "... your cousin, Herschel Grynszpan."

"Herschel?" Ansel woke from her half-conscious state. It was a ridiculous thing for Nurse Margaret to say. Impossible. There was no sweeter and smarter boy than her one-year-older cousin Herschel, son of her father's brother, studying in Paris.

"I'm sorry?" She almost choked in a piece of her bun, "there must be a mistake." But the kind nurse shook her face.

"Your cousin apparently wanted to take revenge for this." The nurse waved her hand around the camp outside the Red Cross tent. "His parents are in a similar camp south of here. He took out his frustration on the first Nazi he encountered in the German Embassy in Paris."

The shock that this was real was a new blow to Ansel's already fragile state.

"What... what happened to him, to Herschel?"

"As far as we know he's in a French jail where he won't be sure of his life. You and your family must leave the camp as soon as possible. The Nazis will hunt down all the Grynszpans. We have no doubt about that. The fury is immense."

"But how?" Ansel's voice was like the squeak of a small mouse.

"There is a brave Polish pilot, the nephew of one of the sisters in my convent. He's offered to fly you to London tonight. Herschel's parents don't want to go to London, so they're being smuggled into

Poland tonight. But as your mother has a brother in London, we hope you will be safe there."

Ansel let her head hang. She didn't know what to say. The surge of grief that had temporarily been held at bay by the new shock, washed over her anew. Now London arrived on the horizon, suddenly, unexpectedly, but what was the point? Sarah and Eva would never see it. The dream had been shattered.

"I can't go. Not now. Let Mutti and Vati go. I'll stay with you." Her eyes must have betrayed what she didn't say aloud.

"Don't worry about your sisters' grave, dear girl. I've already arranged with your father that they will get a proper burial in Breslau Cemetery, next to our convent. He's already given me money and the text for the gravestone. You, of all people, are going to London, Ansel. Then, when all this craziness is over, and Hitler has lost, you come back here and visit their grave. And me."

Ansel was too stunned to reply. The nurse's kindness and reasonableness fought against Ansel's stubborn wish to stay. But she was running out of options. The fear of being caught and locked up by the Nazis won.

"Are only Mutti and Vati and I going on the plane?"

"Yes, there's only place for three passengers on the plane. It's a small aircraft that can easily avoid German aerial detection, I've been told. Go to your tent, neighbours have helped you pack. A driver will take you to Breslau Airport where you'll meet Mr. Pilecki. He will take good care of you."

"I don't know what to say. I'm so confused. My dream and my nightmare on the same day. But the nightmare is worse. I'll never enjoy London without Sarah and Eva," Ansel suddenly sobbed while warm hand of the nurse rested on her shaking shoulders.

"Oh, but you will, dear girl. You will. Give it time."

"I'll be back."

"I'll be waiting for you at Kloster St. Agnes."

Ansel let herself be kissed on both cheeks. She clung to the bit of human warmth Nurse Margret provided, trying to keep her soul alive.

When she arrived back at her family's tent, there was nothing left to pack. Her suitcase stood ready outside their tent. Her mother was sitting outside in a chair someone had brought, huddled in an over-sized fur coat, her face almost invisible in the dim light.

Judith Grynszpan didn't move, hardly seemed to breathe. Ansel hesitated. She was as lost as her mother now, but at least her legs still functioned so she went to stand next to her.

"Mutti?" she asked in a timid voice. No movement. Ansel pressed a quick kiss on her mother's cold cheek, hoping she'd notice Ansel was by her side.

Contrary to her mother, Yehuda seemed all bustling action. He was discussing matters with neighbors, gesticulating widely, his white crop of hair blowing hither and thither in the icy wind. When he was done saying farewell, he turned to his only remaining daughter. The shadow of a tired smile slipped across his face.

"London then..." It was not a question nor a statement. Just an unfinished sentence hanging in the air. Knowing how much his eldest daughter had dreamed of seeing the British capital, he acknowledged the tragic circumstances under which it was now about to happen. Ansel didn't answer. Nothing mattered anymore. London, Hanover, Warsaw. Grynszpans weren't welcome anywhere.

Father and daughter stood on either side of the untouchable Judith. Only two suitcases would accompany them this time, their possessions having further dwindled while in camp. Mud-splattered and in mourning, they waited for the Red Cross van to take them to their unknown destination.

Nothing operated properly in Ansel anymore. Her legs refused to move forward; her lungs refused to inhale; her brain was enveloped in a total fog. But, somehow, she made it to the white van and sat in the back next to the suitcases. Her father and mother sat in the middle, the driver upfront. She didn't look left or right. She didn't look at all. There was nothing to look back at.

After a bumpy ride they came to a flat area where, from four corners, lamps shed a diffuse white glow over a large lawn. A gleaming plane stood on one side of the lawn with its engine roaring.

Ansel's dazed state slightly lifted. She'd never seen a plane close up before. It looked quite innocent but made an awful lot of noise, the rotor blade at the front whirling like a mad spinning top.

"Come on Ansel," her father spurred her on as she halted in her tracks, suddenly frightened. "It will be alright."

She was introduced to a tall man in an aviation uniform, but she fixed her glance on his shining black boots while shaking his hand. Registering that his hand was warm and strong, she was vaguely aware of being impolite, but she was just too frightened and wrung-out to show any manners.

Then something extraordinary happened. The aviator didn't let go of her hand. When the pressure of his palm on hers became awkward, she had to look up to meet his gaze. Wriggling her fingers to free herself didn't work.

Ansel looked into the bluest eyes she'd ever seen. The intensity of their light was as if a light switch was turned on inside her.

"I'm sorry, Miss Grynszpan. I need to see if you're alright. Once aboard my plane you're my responsibility." His voice was strong yet gentle and the concern in the eyes matched their intensity.

"I guess...so," she stammered pulling back her fingers from the firm grip.

"Sit upfront with me. That always helps first-time flyers control their anxiety."

Ansel didn't know how it happened, but gratitude engulfed her. Whoever Henryk Pilecki was, he knew how to deal with nervous tension. He made the flight sound like an adventure only the two of them would embark on. He offered her a hand, a firm, helping hand.

"I'd like that." Her voice gained strength. Her eyes ventured up to take another glance at the tall man's features. He was almost too beautiful, a robust, regal man who radiated a bright light after the long days of mud, and darkness, and too much pain.

A person who looked so confident and strong surely knew no sorrow or loss, only victory. Ansel was spellbound and would instantly have followed Henryk "Hubal" Pilecki to the end of the earth had he suggested it to her.

"Welcome aboard my Lublin R-XIIID." With that same firm touch she'd felt before, the pilot took her hand to help her up the small steps into the plane.

"Strap in. I'll be back in a minute."

He disappeared leaving Ansel alone in the cockpit. She didn't know what he meant by 'strapping in'. Fiddling with the seat belt that looked like a harness, she gave up, her eyes gliding over the impressive switchboard with all its knobs and flickering lights.

Behind her she heard Henryk talk comforting words to her parents. She didn't dare to look over her shoulder for fear of the condition her mother was in. Instead, she fixed her gaze straight ahead, over the grassy runway.

A mixture of warm and cold sweat swamped over her. One thing was sure in all the uncertainty, she'd never experienced a more confusing cocktail of emotions in her life. Too intense for her slender frame, Ansel sat still as a cat in a gutter, expecting the whole world to collapse around her any minute.

"Ready?" Henryk Pilecki slung his tall body in the seat next to her. A smile showing strong white teeth flashed at her in the semi-dark. Without warning he bent over her and adjusted the seat belt, his hands briefly touching her body while he clicked it shut. An involuntary tremor went through her.

"It's alright, Miss Grynszpan. I don't bite. You're safe with me."

I hope that's true, Ansel thought, sitting a little more relaxed in her seat. There was nothing she could change in her situation right now but put her future in the aviator's hands.

"Have you flown to England before, Mr Pilecki?" She had to shout to make herself be heard over the roar of the starting engine.

"Yes, many times. Since I passed my flying certificate three years ago. I've flown all over Europe for the Polish Aviation Corps, but...," he hesitated, didn't finish his sentence. She looked sideways at him at the perfect profile, a dark lock of hair had escaped from under his leather flying helmet. "... I've never flown Polish refugees before. It's an honor. A responsibility."

"Thank you."

The plane started rolling over the grass. A man with two flags stood wide-legged at the end of the lawn. They went straight at him, increasing speed. Just when Ansel thought Pilecki hadn't seen him and they would run the flagman over, the wheels lifted from the ground, and they went up in the air.

Instantly, she forgot her sorrows as the plane rose and rose until they were above the treetops. Though it was completely dark now, she could see small lights below until they flew headlong into whitewashed clouds, and they were enveloped by mist. It was as if entering a magical world where she hung in the air, the plane like a large body around her and next to her the pilot who made all this possible. She almost held her breath in excitement, staring wide-eyed through the windows, enchanted by all that was happening inside the cockpit and outside in that vast space.

"You like it?" Henryk observed. She just nodded, watching how he busied himself with the panels of intricate knobs and switches, sometimes talking into his mouthpiece. But at intervals she felt his eyes resting on her and it made her self-conscious, pushing up her glasses higher on the bridge of her nose, blinking.

No man, and certainly not a man like Henryk "Hubal" Pilecki, had ever looked at her like that. Not that she would have been able to define what it was that was different in the way he looked at her. A special attention, care, concern. It felt good, as if she was protected from evil in that blue gaze in a way she'd not felt before in her life.

Ansel wished their flying adventure would never end. That she could sit like this with him to the end of the world, flying over continents, flying to a land where she knew no pain, no loss. To a land where she wasn't an unwanted Jewish girl from Hanover who'd lost her sisters in a refugee camp on the Polish border.

"I asked if you like flying, Miss Grynszpan?"

Remembering she had been dreaming and not answering his question, she quickly replied, "it's... it's magical, Mr Pilecki. I've never experienced anything like this. You must love flying so much. I totally get it."

"Agreed. I love flying for my country so I'm glad I can help you and your family."

Boom! She was back to reality. He didn't do this for her alone. And it was his duty. What was she thinking? Still, the notion she was flying away from the past felt good, necessary even. But there was that special attention again that disturbed her hopelessly.

"So sorry for your loss." His gloved hand rested a moment on her arm, the warmth of the touch spreading through her like a protective shield. "When Nurse Margaret phoned me this afternoon, I cleared my entire schedule to take this flight."

"Thank you," Ansel mumbled again.

"Not totally unselfish, I have to admit." The white teeth flashed in her direction. "I love London. Any opportunity to go and I'm game."

"Are you also going to London?"

Ansel hadn't thought about it, but had assumed he'd drop them on British soil and return to Poland.

"Yes. I have instructions to get you to London. We land at Gatwick Airport. I understood you never visited England before?"

"No."

The idea he wouldn't just drop them off at some remote airport to find their way to Uncle Benjamin, who probably wasn't keen to see his impoverished relatives, made Ansel breathe lighter. But wasn't it asking too much of this stranger?

"It's not necessary, Mr Pilecki, I think we can find our own way from whatever airport is easiest."

"I told you I like London. I have two days to spend there for myself."

"Sorry, I didn't mean to be rude."

"You're not rude. And the name is Henryk. Mr Pilecki is my father."

"Henryk," Ansel repeated, letting the name roll on her tongue. "Then you must call me Ansel."

"Ansel. Nurse Margaret told me you're going to stay with an uncle?"

Surprised at the information the nurse had given him, she added, "yes, Uncle Benjamin Bittermann. An uncle on my mother's side. It's unlikely, though, he will want to have anything to do with us. Especially after what ...uh... my cousin did in Paris. My father told me Uncle Benjamin is rich and he broke off all contact years ago."

Henryk now sounded surprised, "my information is that the Polish Intelligence Services tracked down Mr Bittermann's London address. He exchanged his Polish passport for a British one this year. There's been a phone call. It's all settled. He's expecting you. I wouldn't fly you to England without you having somewhere to go."

Ansel's mouth fell open, "I...I didn't know."

"It's all arranged. No worries."

21

LONDON

Early the next morning – London, 17 November 1938

Ansel woke with a start when the plane touched solid ground and made a small jump before gliding smoothly over the tarmac. She realized she'd fallen asleep during the flight. Befuddled she opened her eyes. It was dark and the lamps on either side of the airstrip swung in the wind.

"Where are we?"

"Welcome to England." It was Henryk next to her, smiling.

"Oh no, I missed half of the trip. I'm sorry. I was so tired."

"Just glad you caught up on some sleep." He grinned wider, "you trusted my aviation skills enough to doze off."

Ansel peered out of the steamed-up cockpit windows, with little view of the surroundings.

"Is this Gatwick Airport?"

"It certainly is."

She glanced over her shoulder to get a glimpse of her parents, but their shapes were huddled in darkness.

"What time is it?"

Her watch had stopped working in the refugee camp because of the damp.

"Two in the morning. A taxi will take you to a hotel nearby. It's all arranged."

"What about you, Henryk? Will I not see you again?" Ansel realized she sounded like a little girl and quickly added, "you've been so good to us. I'm sure my father would like to thank you properly, with a meal, or something."

"We'll meet tomorrow, Ansel. I have documents from the Polish Authorities I need to hand to your uncle personally."

Ansel fought with herself not to show how pleased she was that they would meet once more before this dashing man disappeared from her life for good. *Don't be such a goose!*

"I could show you a bit of London tomorrow. I have the day to myself." The smile he gave her was warm and exclusively for her. He quickly added, "if your parents agree, of course."

"That would be my absolute dream!" Ansel exclaimed, unable to need to hide her pleasure anymore.

"That's settled then. Until tomorrow, co-pilot."

A final smile and Ansel stepped onto British soil with a flutter in her heart. The past twenty-four hours had brought her the deepest sorrow and the greatest joy.

AN HOUR later they were stepping out of a black taxi in front of the Parkside Inn in Bayswater. Ansel stared up at the symmetrical, Art Deco façade and the burgundy marquee over the front door. It was so pretty. Then she turned to her father with apprehension.

"Can we afford this, Vati?"

"We can, my dear. I have deposited money with an English bank. Some foresight, I suppose. We're not paupers, no matter what you'd think we were after the past month."

Judith seemed to revive a little at the sight of the hotel, doffing up her hat and straightening her coat. She put her arm through that of her husband and the three of them went up the stairs to ring the bell for the night porter.

Ansel briefly wondered where Henryk had gone. He was still checking his plane when they'd stepped into the taxi.

"I'll be there tomorrow morning."

It was a promise she knew he'd keep.

The hotel was nice, not overly posh or grand, but clean and practical. In broken English, Yehuda asked for their reservation, showing the gaunt looking night porter their German passports. The man who had a long face with even longer side whiskers frowned and mumbled something about "wretched Boches" under his breath. Without another word he showed them to their rooms on the first floor.

"Supper was ordered for you by Mr Bittermann. Would sandwiches and tea do?"

"Perfect," Yehuda answered with a grateful bow.

"Coming in a minute, Sir. And breakfast is between 6 and 9 am in the dining room downstairs. Do you care for an English breakfast, or do you prefer Continental?"

Ansel was glued to the night porter's bloodless lips deciphering the accented English, which sounded very different from Miss Perkins's upper-class English at the Friedrich Schiller Gymnasium, but equally mesmerizing and lovely.

"Londoners often speak Cockney," her English teacher had taught them, so she supposed this was what Cockney sounded like. She'd practice hard to get that same accent and belong in London.

Meanwhile the question about the two types of breakfast hung in the air like a string of sausages. Yehuda was clearly at a loss what to choose.

"English Breakfast, of course," Ansel replied in her most proper English. The night porter nodded and left, grumbling his discontent with ignorant foreigners.

She had a room to her own, tiny but clean and well kept. Her suitcase, mud-spattered and with the strap broken, stood next to a wooden cupboard that held five hangers and two boards. The sheets on the bed were clean. A washstand with a towel in the corner. A chair and even a tiny table.

Ansel stood in her battered shoes and in her winter coat, looking around her, listening to the night traffic of London outside. She began to cry, softly first but the tears kept coming, rolling down her cheeks like big pearls. Her shoulders shook. She was so grateful and so miserable at the same time.

"I am in heaven but without my sisters. I'll have to live for them. We have to make this work. The nightmare is over."

A flash of Henryk in his aviation overalls came before her eyes, his beauty and his strength and Ansel stopped crying. She sat down on the bed still in her coat, staring down at the tray of miniscule white sandwiches and the mug of steaming tea. Too suddenly she had landed in a new world that looked safe and solid, but she was broken inside and wasn't sure the pieces would heal again.

ANSEL'S first English breakfast was an utter surprise. Glancing over at her parents who were staring down at their plates in astonishment, she questioned whether she had made the right decision. Huge plates filled to the brim with sausages and bacon, fried eggs with the yokes whole, and slices of fried tomato stared back at them. The oddest of all, a heap of white beans in a red sauce in the middle. It looked more like a dinner than a breakfast.

"I'm sorry," Ansel mumbled as she nibbled on a corner of her toast, but her father dove into the unconventional breakfast with a hearty appetite.

"It's delicious. Best meal ever," he declared. "You must try the *Schinken*, Judy, you'll love it."

A good thing we never ate kosher in Germany, Ansel thought, *or I'd be even more embarrassed about my choice.* The Grynszpans had never considered themselves religious Jews.

Her mother, who'd sat staring at her enormous plate with astounded eyes, followed her husband's example and soon an appreciative "hmmm" escaped her lips. With more confidence Ansel tried a piece of the bacon and even a spoonful of the beans. She had to agree. Though uncommon, their first meal in freedom was a feast. And it was so nice to see her mother's dark hair done up nicely and a faint smile lingering around her lips.

"We'll always have English breakfast from now on," Yehuda declared.

At that moment, the dining room door opened, and Henryk came in. Ansel was struck by his height and presence. She was sure everyone in the room was turning their head to look at the man in his blue aviation suit with the Gapa, the Polish aviation symbol, on his shoulder. He moved like a film star, and he was coming straight for their table.

Her father pulled out a chair for him.

"*Jadłeś,* Mr. Pilecki?" he asked in Polish. If he had eaten, at which Henryk waved a hand. "Just a coffee will do." As he sat down next to her, Ansel was keenly aware of his nearness. The smile he gave her in broad daylight was even more irresistible than the one in the cockpit.

"Slept a bit?"

She nodded, still finishing her breakfast, and wiping her mouth with her napkin. "Like a Polish rose."

"Good sign! And it's dry today. Another London miracle."

As Ansel sat in the back of the taxi, she took in the sights and sounds of London for the first time full of excitement. Whether the journey from Bayswater to Mayfair was short or long, for her it lasted forever. On the seat opposite her sat her parents, while Henryk was beside her, the top of his head touching the taxi's roof. She was filled with a mixture of awe, anxiety, and wonder.

The taxi rattled along a myriad of streets, passing by rows of elegant Georgian and Victorian townhouses, their front-gardens fenced off with neatly trimmed hedges and wrought-iron railings. Ansel marveled at the urban grandeur of the buildings, so different from Hanover's classicism and Neo-Baroque architecture.

Endless rows of men in black bowler hats hurried across bridges and along pavements as if they were all late for work. Umbrella over their arms. The men wore finely tailored raincoats and the women stylish coats with fur collars, their hats perched elegantly on their heads.

The traffic was chaotic with black taxis, red double-decker buses, cars in all sizes and shapes and even the occasional horse-drawn carriage, all contributing to the morning rush hour.

"Nothing like it in the world, right?" Henryk asked next to her. She became aware he had been studying her.

"Is the taxi ever going to move again?" she asked as it seemed they had been standing still for ten minutes.

"Sure. If needed he'll take a backroad. These cabbies know the drill."

Her attention was drawn to the street vendors selling newspapers and fresh flowers on the corners. Newspaper boys were shouting the headlines with great urgency. The aroma of roasted chestnuts wafted into the taxi, despite the closed window, tempting her with the familiar and comforting scent from Trammplatz outside her father's bookshop, Bücherladen im Herzen.

No going there! I'm here now!

"It's like I'm in a fairy tale," Ansel whispered, looking cautiously at her mother, but she saw the same enchantment in her mother's eyes and breathed more lightly.

As they passed through Mayfair, she glimpsed high-end shops with lavish window displays. The storefronts showcased luxury goods that seemed worlds away from her current circumstances. Would she ever enter one of those stores and purchase whatever she wanted, preferably on Henryk's arm?

Ansel's next observation was an eyeopener. London bred people of all different backgrounds, colors, and religions, walking side by side as if God had indeed created everyone equal. Was it true that being a Jew here wasn't a stigma? Could it be?

The diversity offered a sense of comfort and belonging, reminding her they weren't the only family in pursuit of safety and a new life. Though her heart was still heavy with the uncertainty of their future, the recent events of their eviction from their home, and the camp on the Polish border, amid the bustling London streets and with Henryk beside her, Ansel couldn't help but feel a glimmer of hope. Perhaps the city's vibrant energy and the promise of refuge held the potential for a fresh start.

When the taxi finally arrived in Mayfair, she was ready for Uncle Benjamin.

22

UNCLE BENJAMIN

The taxi stopped in front of an elegant townhouse in Mount Street. The three-storey, Georgian house exuded classic charm and sophistication. Ansel exchanged a quick glance with her father, acknowledging they had the same thought. Uncle Benjamin had done well for himself after leaving Kalisz in 1930, an old town in western Poland with a large Jewish community but a lot of poverty.

The outside of the house was partly covered in ivy and the front-door was freshly painted in bright burgundy with brass ornaments and a knocker.

Yehuda paid the cabbie, fumbling with the unfamiliar pound notes. Ansel swayed on her legs, feeling as if the solid London street under her feet was hit by the tremor of an earthquake. Just when she thought she would lose her balance, Henryk steadied her by gripping her elbow.

"You're alright?"

She nodded, ashamed of her weakness. The entire exodus, from Leibnizstrasse to Mayfair, flashed before her mind. Arriving here after a month of sheer agony and an around-the-clock journey over half of Europe, Ansel's whole being was spinning. All she owned in the suitcase at her feet. All she lost still in Germany. Only yesterday they'd buried Sarah and Eva. It felt like a lifetime away.

Henryk took the lead. "Let's find out if Mr. Bittermann is home."

The Grynszpans followed him up the steps to the red door. Her legs felt like rubber and a knot formed in her stomach. Maybe an English breakfast hadn't been a good idea after all. What if the unknown uncle had changed his mind and they were no longer welcome? They had nowhere else to go.

A housekeeper in a black dress and white apron opened the door and gasped at them.

In his best English, Yehuda explained who they were.

"Dear Lord in Heaven," the middle-aged woman with a tight brown bun on her neck and a strict, narrow face with hawklike gray eyes exclaimed. "Mr. Bittermann told me you were coming but I didn't know it was today. Do come in but wipe your shoes on the mat. I've just polished the parquet in the hall."

"Is Benja... Mr. Bittermann home?" Yehuda asked, while they were still standing on the steps of his porch.

"I'm afraid he isn't. Went to the City early as always but I'll make a phone call. We hadn't expected you today, you see. But do come in. Just mind the floor."

They were led into a broad entrance hall with a wooden floor that shone like burned gold and a high ceiling with a crystal chandelier casting a warm, inviting glow. A grand staircase with a mahogany banister led to the upper floors.

"I'm Mrs. Whitman, the housekeeper. For eight years," she added with pride. "Come into the living room and take a seat while I get hold of the master of the house."

Mrs. Whitman seemed a professional, efficient woman who liked her job. As they sat in the spacious room that was decorated with plush velvet sofas, antique Persian rugs and a marble fireplace, a younger version of Mrs. Whitman, with the same features, entered with a tray of coffee cups and biscuits.

She didn't say anything but curtsied for them, which Ansel thought peculiar, and served them coffee with cream. Then she left the room. Henryk had taken one of the armchairs, while Ansel sat perched between her parents on one of the sofas. The house was silent but for a large Frisian clock on the wall chiming nine.

They'd only half finished the strong coffee, when they heard car doors slam in front of the house and a booming voice ordering, "Pick me up at eleven, Charles. I need to be at the Syndicate at twelve."

"Will do, sir, on the hour."

The door was flung open and, on the threshold stood a middle-aged man who had a distinguished appearance. Not just because of his expensive suit but his whole bearing was one of refinement. Ansel recognised the lean, straight build her mother also had and the striking hazel eyes that held a mixture of wisdom and sorrow.

His hair, once jet black, had begun to show streaks of gray at the temples, adding to his air of authority and maturity. The face was framed by a well-groomed beard, another integral part of Uncle Benjamin's dignified-yet-reserved presence.

Ansel instantly liked him and most of her fear disappeared. Before coming over to greet them, Uncle Benjamin looked around the room as if adjusting his eyes to his new domestic circumstances. Finally, he let his eyes rest on his half-sister. Judith struggled to her feet, hazel eyes meeting hazel eyes. She walked towards him with uncertain steps.

"Judith, is it really you?" He didn't embrace her but instead held out his hand. There was warmth in his voice though, as he added, "I'm really sorry for what you had to go through." A moment of uncertainty also slid over the brother's face as if he too had difficulty bridging the two worlds, one of which he'd clearly left behind years ago. He patted her hand with his other hand. A golden ring with a big diamond flashed on his ring finger.

"You're welcome here, Judith. I will make sure you and your family can start again in London."

Ansel noticed her uncle didn't mention her mother's loss. He was so obviously the bachelor, who had no idea how to navigate the waters of maternal loss. Letting go of his sister's hand, Uncle Benjamin acknowledged Henryk with a quick message in Polish, which Ansel understood meant he'd talk with the aviator in a minute about the letter. He went on to shake her father's hand with similar words of welcome in Polish.

"We never managed to meet back home but I'm happy we do now, Yehuda, despite the circumstances."

"Thank you, Benjamin," her father replied. "We'll make our demands on your hospitality as short as possible."

"Nonsense," was the curt reply. "You stay here. I live in this big house with only the staff. Plenty of rooms. You make yourself at home."

Now it was Ansel's turn to feel the intense green-brown eyes on her.

"You must be Ansel?" He addressed her in English while taking her in from head to toe. "I'll call you Anna. Better suits the British sentiment which is becoming increasingly anti-German."

"Anna?" Ansel stammered feeling the pressure of his strong hand in hers. "I like the name much better, Uncle Benjamin. Thank you."

"That's settled then. You're Anna. We'll get to the Grynszpan name later. Awful business with your nephew, Yehuda. Will have more repercussions than we care to think about."

"Yes," her father replied softly, bending his head as if he himself was guilty of killing a Nazi. "It saved us from the refugee camp, so something good came out of it after all."

Uncle Benjamin's eyes made another pass over his relatives. *He's a real businessman,* Ansel-Anna observed. *Time is precious to him.* The glance rested on his sister.

"You're seriously ill, Judith. I'll have my physician come by today. Take plenty of rest. Mrs. Whitman will show you to your rooms. I'm very sorry but I have an important lunch meeting at noon. Will you excuse me as I have a quick conversation with Mr. Pilecki before I have to leave again?"

"Of course," Yehuda answered.

"All right, I'll see you at dinner then. And do rest. All of you."

Henryk rose to his feet, but before leaving the room with her uncle, he turned to her father.

"Do I have your permission to show Ans..Anna a bit of London tomorrow? I fly back to Poland tomorrow night but have some spare time."

"Do you want that daughter?"

"Very much, Vati."

"Then that's settled. And we will take leave of you tomorrow, Mr. Pilecki."

"It's Henryk, sir, if you will."

Henryk turned to Ansel. "I'll be here at ten o'clock."

Beaming she replied, "I'll be ready."

UNCLE BENJAMIN'S house was a dream. Mrs. Whitman took them on a tour so they would know their way around the three storeys. The living quarters had two more sitting rooms, quite identically furnished as the first one, but in the last one it became clear Benjamin Bittermann had not severed all ties with his cultural background.

There were cherished mementos from his homeland, including family photographs of people Ansel had never met, but were pointed out now by her mother with great emotion in her voice. She recognized Babcia Sarah, her maternal grandmother, and Dziadek Isaac, her maternal grandfather.

"That is Maria, your grandfather's first wife, Benjamin's mother. She died when he was ten years old and then he married Sarah who gave birth to me." Her mother kept staring at and touching the photos and family heirlooms while Ansel studied the paintings of Kalisz and surroundings.

"I'll take you upstairs to show you your bedrooms and the bathroom when you're ready," Mrs. Whitman interrupted.

Ansel thought she'd landed in paradise when Mrs. Whitman stopped in front of a door on the second floor with a plaque stating, "The Rosewood Suite".

"Does the bedroom have a name?"

"Well of course, miss, all the bedrooms have. Are you not accustomed to that?" The housekeeper shook her head over so much ignorance.

"No, but I can get used to it," Ansel assured her.

"It's one of the elegant guest rooms, miss, so you're lucky. It's named after the rosewood furnishings, one of Mr Bittermann's favorite woods."

Ansel stepped into a room steeped in an atmosphere of timeless luxury. Everything was adorned in soft and soothing earth tones, with the walls painted in a delicate muted rose that complemented the deep brown hues of the rosewood furniture. Crisp, ivory-colored curtains hung from tall windows, allowing filtered sunlight to gently illuminate the space. Instantly, Ansel felt grown-up, a woman now, no longer a girl.

"Let me show you the ensuite bathroom and then I'll let you unpack." Mrs. Whitman strode across the room, adjusting a vase here and straightening a curtain there.

The bathroom was spacious and spic-and-span clean. A total change from the grubby toilet units that had been hastily assembled in the camp. The marble floor gleamed, while the fixtures were a mix of vintage and modern elements. A clawfoot bathtub stood center stage, with a separate walk-in shower, a vanity with a marble counter-top, and an array of luxurious bath amenities.

Ansel clasped a hand over her mouth to suppress an astonished "ahh." She'd already found out Mrs. Whitman didn't like the display of too many emotions.

"Lunch is at one o'clock. In the dining room." With that the housekeeper withdrew and Ansel was alone in her own domain. A weight heavier than the sands of the sea ebbed out of her.

"This room. This is what I want in my life." She spoke the words aloud as she wandered around admiring every object, every color, every play of the light. "I want to be a rich girl."

Against one wall stood an intricately carved rosewood four-poster bed. Even the headboard was decorated with delicate floral motifs. The bed was made up with fine, high-thread-count linens and plush pillows. Two matching rosewood bedside tables flanked the bed, each with an antique brass lamp that was illuminated, even in the middle of the day.

Sitting down on the bed that felt soft yet with a sturdy mattress, Ansel let her eyes glide over the walls with oil paintings in gilded frames, serene British landscapes and delicate still lives. Above the fireplace, a large, antique, gilt-framed mirror reflected her figure in the midst of the elegant room.

She looked so slovenly, white, and thin, unfitting for this luxury but she would live up to it. Starting today. She'd listen to all Uncle Benjamin could offer her and make sure she fit into London's society. Whatever the price.

23

A TASTE OF LONDON LIFE

The next morning -London, 18 November 1938

As soon as Ansel, now Anna, woke the next morning, she rushed out of bed to open the curtains. It was still dark outside, the street lamps on Mount Street casting a diffuse yellow light over the early morning fog. A big black car idled in front of the garden gate.

The arms of the marble clock on the mantlepiece told her it was 7:30. The house was quiet until the front door closed, and she saw her uncle approach the car with swift steps and get into the back seat. Just like all Londoners Anna had seen so far, he was equipped with bowler hat, raincoat, and umbrella. An Englishman on his way to work.

Leaving the curtains open, she returned to the heavenly bed and dove back under the soft covers. Today she would see London with Henryk. London with Henryk. But as the next thought struck her, she hid under the bedclothes. She had nothing to wear.

"Why didn't I think of that before? I should have said no," she lamented. But a little voice in her spoke up against her lamentation.

Go darn and iron your best dress, girl. Ansel may accept defeat. Anna doesn't, because Anna acts.

In her nightgown, she went to the rosewood armoire that held her modest row of blouses, dresses, and skirts. Three of each. All she'd been able to take. She chose a white blouse with lace trimmings, a pleated navy-blue skirt, and a light-blue merino cardigan. It was dull, it was schoolgirlish, but it was the best she had. Only her stockings needed darning and her sensible brown shoes could do with a good brushing. She'd ask Mrs. Whitman for the ironing board.

"Did you sleep well, Ansel?"

"I'm Anna, Father."

Her father was already in the dining room drinking coffee, waiting for Mrs. Whitman's daughter to bring him his breakfast, and plainly ignoring her remark. Anna's thoughts flitted back to the Leibnizstrasse, where they had had Greta Schmidt who'd kept house for them. But no going back.

"I have, Vati. And you?" Anna took a seat at the unfamiliar breakfast table, wondering if she didn't accidentally sit in her uncle's chair.

"Could have been better. Your mother was very restless. The doctor will come back today with the prescribed medicine. He says she had another nervous breakdown." He looked lost, white, and shrunken, a foreigner in someone else's house.

"I'm so sorry, Vati. Do you think I should stay in and not go sightseeing with Henryk?"

"Not at all, girl. I'm glad at least one of us finds their feet here quickly. And your English is so much better than mine. We need you! Integrate as quickly as you can."

"Thank you, Vati. I will."

And the burden to keep her family safe was once again on her young shoulders. But Anna didn't care. She would do whatever it took to reach the level where she could afford a house like her uncle's and look after her mother and father.

The fog lifted quickly. It soon became sunny and crisp, while Anna paced the living room waiting for Henryk. With Mrs. Whitman's help, she'd done her best to present herself as neatly as possible. Her attire may be simple, but at least it was clean and whole. Henryk would understand she had no means to dress up as he knew where she'd come from. She'd brushed her dark hair until it shone and tied it with a velvet ribbon in a simple ponytail. Her glasses and shoes were clean.

PEERING THROUGH THE GLASS WINDOWS, she saw the taxi pull up out front and Henryk's tall body emerge from the backseat. Despite the lingering self-consciousness about her clothing, her eyes brightened with anticipation as she descended the stone steps of her uncle's residence.

The grandeur of the Mayfair neighborhood and the start of the Christmas decorations surrounding her increased Anna's feelings of excitement and nervousness. Her cheeks flushed as she approached the taxi. Henryk, as always, greeted her with a warm smile that eased some of her apprehension. He seemed genuinely delighted to see her, his eyes focused on her face rather than on her attire. He was dressed in the blue suit of the Polish Aviation Corps. Maybe he didn't care that much about frivolities like clothes?

"Hello Anna, you look much more rested." He took her hand as if it was the natural thing to do. As using her new name, the ring of which she liked very much.

"Yes, I feel much better thanks to you."

"No thanking me. Thank your uncle who's made himself a nice life here."

"True." She smiled back.

"Hop in. First, we'll explore Mayfair. As this is going to be your neighborhood, you'd better get acquainted with it. I love the West End, as well."

Henryk took her to a charming café nestled along a quiet road called Aldford Street. The café's interior was already completely decorated for the holiday season and though Anna was used to

Christmas decorations in Hanover, they were rarely up this early, and this café had a warm and intimate atmosphere.

They chose a table near the window and Henryk took her coat and helped her with her chair. She worried all the customers were looking in their direction wondering who the handsome stranger with the bland girl was.

"Stop it, Anna. Keep your shoulders straight," she whispered to herself while Henryk went to the coatrack.

"What would you like? I take it you had breakfast at your uncle's?" He smiled that mesmerizing smile just for her and her heart cavorted in her chest.

"Yes, just a hot chocolate, I think."

"Excellent choice. I'll join you."

They sat in silence for a while sipping the delicious cocoa that was topped with a big dollop of whipped cream. Her initial self-consciousness slowly gave way to the joy of the moment.

"I know you've just landed, but any ideas what you want to do here?" The blue eyes took her in intently. Anna considered, a wrinkle forming between her dark brows.

"I guess... I guess I'll go back to school if I may. I was going to do my Abitur in the spring next year so maybe I can do a similar exam here. That is, if my English is good enough."

"From what I heard your English is excellent. You'll pass your diploma with flying colors. And then?"

"Oh Henryk, I have no idea. My parents are my first concern at this moment. Mutti isn't well and my father needs to find a job. We can't live on Uncle Benjamin's purse forever, no matter how much money he may seem to have."

"Don't waste that first-class brain of yours, Anna. You're a very intelligent young woman. You must go to university."

Anna blushed under his compliment, wondering how he could know she liked to use her brains. As if he'd guessed her thoughts, he added, "you're special. I saw that from the moment we met. Despite the circumstances. You're studious and brainy but also very sweet. You need to become the shining star you're meant to be."

"Please stop, Henryk. You make me shy." She bent her head, but he tipped her chin with his finger.

"Never be shy about a good set of brains. Dear God, the world needs women with brains. Certainly, if we're heading to another war."

Anna met his gaze; saw he meant what he said. Henryk Pilecki was no flatterer. He needn't be, he was confident enough in himself. There was also concern in the open face opposite her.

"What about you, Henryk? What do you dream of?"

More concern shadowed his expression. "I'm happy with what I do. I like flying. Being the squadron leader of my team would be great. Hopefully in a year or so. But we're preparing for war. It looks like Hitler will invade Poland at some point. I'll be ready to defend my country."

"Do you really think so?" Anna shuddered. Of course, Hitler had taken Austria and the Sudetenland, but would he honestly be so greedy to invade Poland? "I hope you'll be safe. I don't like to think of you fighting in a war."

"I will always be safe, Anna. Always." He said it with so much conviction she almost believed him.

"Come on. Time to show you London." Henryk paid for their drinks and got her coat.

They strolled through Mayfair, which Anna thought was wonderfully picturesque. They passed Berkeley Square, where the plane trees were adorned with twinkling lights.

"It looks so pretty during the festive season," Anna marveled.

"It does. I don't know if your family observes Christmas, but for me as a Catholic, Christmas is the most cherished period of the year."

"We're secular Jews," she explained. "I fully intend to celebrate Christmas now we're in England. It's where Father Christmas comes from, right?"

Henryk laughed out loud.

"You believe in Father Christmas. I'll stick with the Savior of all mankind."

Anna felt her cheeks redden at her ignorance but also didn't miss he spoke as if they were a team. She liked that very much.

"Why is this part of London called 'the West End?' It seems like central London to me?"

"True. It must be a 19th-century thing when this became the upmarket part of London. The citizens wanted to distinguish it as the fashionable area west of Charing Cross. The West End covers parts of Westminster and Camden." Henryk really seemed to know a lot about the city he liked so much.

"Let's take a look around in Hyde Park, or would you rather go shopping?"

Henryk took her arm, and it was so easy to fall in step with him as he adjusted his brisk pace to accommodate her.

"I love parks."

It would be better to be out in nature and not lured to the beautiful displays in the shop windows. She had no money. Only dreams.

"Wait. I have an idea before we watch the swans in the Serpentine." Henryk turned around, and still with Anna on his arm, entered a large department store called John Lewis.

"What are we doing here?" A wall of heat struck her; the shop was hot after the outside cold.

"Nothing much." He directed her to the stationary department. On a table lay a display of notebooks and journals in all sizes and shapes.

"Choose one."

"But why?" she looked up into the blue eyes that held her gaze steadily.

"I want you to have a journal. To symbolize a new chapter in your life and to have something to remember me by."

Anna eyed a burgundy-red notebook with golden lettering the word 'journal' on the cover and a small flap that could be closed with a press stud."

"That one?" He'd already picked it up and marched to the counter.

"But wait. Maybe it's too expensive."

He didn't listen to her.

"Do you have a pen I can use?"

The shopkeeper looked rather suspiciously at the foreigner in his aviation suit. Henryk explained, "I want to inscribe something in it for my friend here. But let me pay you first before you think I'm a scoundrel."

"That'll be 50 shillings, sir."

Henryk paid and got his pen. "Don't look!" he instructed Anna, then quickly penned something on the first page.

"Please wrap it up nicely for the young lady."

She accepted her gift with a pounding heart. He was so kind to her. She held it in both hands, wrapped in striped gold and black paper with a golden ribbon around it. She could not remember having been given such a nice gift.

"Thank you."

"You must promise me you'll write in it. And think of me."

"I will." It fit perfectly in her coat pocket.

"Time for Hyde Park and lunch."

As the day progressed, Anna knew she'd never forget her first taste of London on Henryk's arm. There was Buckingham Palace, the Changing of the Guard, and Trafalgar Square.

Henryk told anecdotes here and snippets of history there, while she was constantly in awe of the iconic landmarks showing up before her eyes. It seemed she'd always known this city in her heart. Always known she belonged here.

Later in the afternoon, when dusk already announced itself, their journey took them to the picturesque banks of the Thames River, where they sat down on a bench with a bag of roasted chestnuts. Before them stretched the Tower Bridge with the majestic silhouette of the Tower of London against the skyline.

Anna's heart was filled to the brim with bliss. And yet melancholy set in. Soon the day would be over, and he would be gone. His notebook the only reminder of the man who'd changed her life for good.

"What about your family? Are you close to them?" she asked, savoring the sweet, buttery taste of her chestnut.

Henryk laughed out loud. Not the reaction she'd anticipated. It had seemed like a normal question.

"Close to my daredevil sister Beate? I'd love to think so, but I haven't seen her all year. Not since she left Poland to report on the Spanish Civil War."

"Is your sister fighting Franco?" Anna was puzzled.

"She may be, though she went to Spain as a war correspondent."

"Heavens," Anna replied. The Pileckis certainly had adventurous blood flowing through their veins.

"What about your parents?"

Henryk laughed again but in a softer way. "My father is a law professor at the University of Warsaw. My mother teaches in kindergarten. Nothing outrageous there. They say they have no idea where the 'two wild kids' came from."

"You're not wild," Anna chuckled.

"I agree, but Beate surely is."

Evening was falling fast. It was time to go home.

"I fly at 9:00 tonight. It's time to take you home." Was there a tinge of sadness in his voice?

"I loved this day more than I can tell you," she spouted in a sudden moment of openness. Henryk turned to face her. His eyes sparkling.

"So did I, Anna. Whatever the future may bring, I'll cherish this day as a keepsake in my heart."

"Will I ever see you again?" She hoped it didn't sound too desperate.

"Yes. I'll make sure to get in touch next time I'm in London. I promise."

The silence that followed was awkward. Something unsaid lingered in the air. Two screaming seagulls flew by and landed in the water under the bridge.

"Come here."

His words were almost without sound. The next thing she knew she felt herself encircled by his strong arms, leaning against his chest, while he rested his chin on the top of her head. She didn't dare to move, hardly dared to breathe, just sat there, not believing, drinking in his nearness, wanting it never to end.

"Why?" she mumbled, "why me?"

He didn't answer. Just held her.

24

THE ADAMS FAMILY

The next morning - 19 November 1938

Anna had hardly slept, not because she was miserable, but because she couldn't stop reliving the day before, a day so full of promise for the future. Even if Henryk Pilecki forgot all about her and she'd never hear from him again, she had that day to cherish. And his notebook.

For Anna,

A jewel in a dark world. Shine bright, dear co-pilot, and remember to always follow your North Star.

Your Henryk

SHE'D LET her fingers glide over the handwriting, even kissed the page carefully so as not to blur the letters. He would be back in

Poland now. Hundreds of miles away from her while she had to go downstairs to face Uncle Benjamin and her parents. Start her London life in earnest.

Wondering what the new day would bring, Anna dressed and combed her hair. The brush halted in mid-air. She didn't recognize the girl in the mirror. Her reflection wasn't a girl anymore. She was a woman now. This woman's name was Anna.

On entering the dining room, she was unprepared to see her uncle presiding over the breakfast table on his own. He was reading The Times in a paisley dressing gown with brown corduroy slippers on his feet. He lowered the paper when he heard her close the door. Her parents weren't present.

"Good morning, girl. Slept well?"

"Yes, thank you, Uncle. Is it alright if I join you or would you rather be alone?"

"Do sit. Have breakfast."

"Are you ill, sir?"

"Never enjoyed a better health, girl. Why?"

"Because you're not dressed."

Uncle Benjamin threw a quick glance over his attire. "It's Saturday, girl. I never dress on Saturday mornings. My luxury."

Anna had paid no notion to what day of the week it was and felt backwards.

"Oh, I had forgotten."

"No problem. Happens to the best. How was your first taste of London?"

She couldn't help her cheeks coloring crimson, hiding her embarrassment as best she could behind the napkin. Thankfully her uncle was quite oblivious to amorous reactions.

"Impressive, Uncle. I really like it. I dreamed of living here ever since I was a little girl, so I'm very grateful to you."

"Ah, that's good to hear. Just remember you're not here for leisure. I want you to start school as soon as possible. Your father told me you were ready to take the Abitur in Germany. I've already made enquiries and you can start at St. Paul's Girls' School on Monday. It will only be a few more weeks until the Christmas holidays but why postpone your schooling until January? I didn't build my business by postponing making necessary decisions."

"On Monday, Uncle? St. Paul's Girl School?" Anna parroted, processing this new information as fast as she could.

"Yes. The seamstress will come today to measure your uniform. It's a rush job but I pay her well to work on Sunday."

"Thank you, Uncle. So, what class will I be in?"

"Heavens, girl, don't ask complicated questions. I haven't studied the English school system. Your father will take you to meet the headmistress on Monday morning. She'll sort it out for you. I just expect you to do your very best."

"I will, Uncle. Thank you again."

"Well, let me continue to read my newspaper now." He disappeared behind the paper not to show his face again, while Anna struggled with chewing her toast. It was as if her life had suddenly come into a maelstrom of positive change, but it was all going so fast, and the current was so turbulent, she didn't know if she would be able to keep up.

In the afternoon, Anna was in for another surprise. She was writing in her journal, or more accurately, daydreaming over it, when there was a knock on her door and Mrs. Whitman came in.

"Your uncle wants to see you in his study, miss."

"Coming."

"It's the door at the end of the corridor." The housekeeper pointed to a door on the same floor as Anna's bedroom. With a hesitant rap, she announced her arrival.

"Come in," came her uncle's voice from within.

He was now fully dressed in a woolen pullover with a white shirt and green tie underneath, beige trousers with a crease. He was sitting in one of the two leather armchairs by the window reading a file.

Her parents weren't present, so she assumed the seamstress

would arrive any minute to take her measurements for the school uniform. She cast a quick look around her uncle's impressive study. The room breathed both knowledge and business. Two walls were filled with bookshelves lined with leather-bound volumes. It also held a massive antique desk, where he no doubt conducted his diamond business. Along one wall stood a glass panelled cupboard with all shapes and sizes of diamonds and, what Anna assumed, diamond cutting equipment.

"Sit, girl. I expect your parents to join us in a minute. I don't know what's holding them up."

Anna panicked. "Have I done anything wrong, Uncle Benjamin?" Had someone seen her being embraced by Henryk on the bench down by the river? But no, it was impossible. Nobody knew who she was.

Her uncle looked at her with a puzzled expression on his face. "What? No? I don't assume you've broken any of Mrs. Whitman's plates, have you?"

"No, Uncle."

There was another knock on the door and her parents came in. Anna was still standing on the Persian rug, wringing her hands. It was the first time she saw her mother again since their arrival. She looked positively sickly. Her father looked worried and weary. Anna immediately felt a pang of guilt over her own happy feelings about London.

Her uncle rose to his feet to draw up two more chairs.

"You sit in the armchair, Judith." He pointed to the other two chairs for father and daughter and sat back in the chair with his file.

"Have you seen the doctor again today, Sister?" Uncle Benjamin seemed to share their concern.

"I have." Her voice was barely perceptible. It was more like a croaking sound. Yehuda answered for his wife.

"The doctor says she must rest as much as possible and eat well. He calls it grief but doesn't think there's anything physically the matter."

"Good, good. You rest, Sister. No need to worry." Uncle Benjamin's short beard went up and down as he nodded.

He cleared his throat. "I called you here because I've pulled some strings. Luckily, I have friends in high places, like the Churchills and the Macalisters. According to the papers, there's an inquisition going on against everyone with last name Grynszpan. The Germans hunt down Jews with that name all over the Continent. But I was told not to underestimate the power of the Nazis here in England, as well. Don't forget that that confidant of Hitler, Joachim von Ribbentrop, is the German ambassador here. That man has a lot of power with British politicians."

The Grynszpans listened in silence. Would they be evicted all over again? Judith shifted uneasily in her chair. She took to staring vacantly out of the window. Anna ached to go over to her mother and give her a hug but didn't dare to leave her chair.

"What can we do?" Her father sat very still and very straight.

"No need to do anything, brother-in-law. It's all settled."

"What do you mean?" Her father asked. Anna sat straighter as well. Her uncle was certainly not a man to waste any time.

"My friends arranged new identity papers for you. Not passports yet because naturalisation takes a lot more time and we haven't got that time, but a name change on paper was a piece of old tackle."

Her uncle smiled for the very first time, as if the burden of housing Grynszpans was off his back. Then he looked a little apologetically as he added, "it had to be decided so fast I had to choose the names for you. I hope that isn't a problem?"

It was Yehuda Grynszpan's turn to laugh. "As long as it is not Mickey Mouse."

"No, you will be Jude Adams, Judith will be Judy Adams and Ansel will be Anna Adams. Adams is a solid name. Has no tinge whatsoever."

"Adams," her father repeated. "I can live with that if it is for a good cause."

Anna Adams, Anna thought, and her heart skipped a beat, *I will never be Ansel Grynszpan ever again. Ever!*

I am Anna Adams.

"I don't know how to thank you for everything you're doing for us, Benjamin," her father said, clearly moved.

"No need to thank me, Jude. Just remember, you won't be able to travel back to the Heimat as these aren't official traveling documents. But I don't think you're planning anything of the sort now your family is safely in England".

Not the entire family, Anna thought sadly. The expression on her father's face showed he was thinking the same thing. Her mother was inside her own mind, not showing any outward emotion.

"We will build up our lives in London," her father assured his brother-in-law.

"Good." Uncle Benjamin looked relieved that his pushing the name change before checking with them had been readily accepted. "And no worries about extending your stay here with me. I'm starting to enjoy not living in this house on my own. And talking Polish again. I was starting to forget my native tongue. And what about you, young lady? Can you live with Anna Adams? It will also be on your school papers, so you'd better not make a slip of the tongue."

"I won't, Uncle. I am Anna Adams from now on."

Only Judith said nothing. A single tear ran slowly down her cheek.

25

ST. PAUL'S GIRL SCHOOL

Two days later - Monday 21 November 1938

Anna felt a peculiar mix of anticipation and anxiety as she and her father walked up the path that led to the imposing façade of St. Paul's Girl School in Brook Green.

The history of the posh private school, with its chalk-white walls and tall, leaded windows was the opposite of the blocky, large-windowed Friedrich Schiller Gymnasium in Hanover. The new school looked both inspiring and intimidating.

Uncle Benjamin had told her she was to meet with Miss Evelyn Sinclair, the head mistress. She would guide Anna into her new academic journey and introduce her to her new class.

As they reached the heavy oak door of the school's main building, Anna's heart quickened. She took a deep breath, her fingers trembling as she adjusted her new black coat that covered the pristine white blouse and pleated black skirt of her school uniform. The red and blue striped tie felt too tight around her slender neck.

Her father, looking very presentable in a new gabardine suit, his white hair combed backwards, and his brow furrowed, placed a reassuring hand on his daughter's shoulder.

"You'll do fine, Ans... Anna." His accented English sounded soft and singsong. "Remember what I always tell you. You'll do brilliantly."

"I hope so, Vati." She wasn't used to saying "father" yet. She was grateful for his presence, his supportive hand on her shoulder. As soon as he stepped away from her mother's side, some of her father's former calm and wisdom reappeared. Anna understood how worried he was about her mother's condition and how he was trying to cope with his own grief as well.

She, Anna Adams, was her parents' only hope now. They wanted her to have a chance at a bright future. She would not disappoint them.

After ringing the bell, they were shown into the school's lobby by what Anna assumed was a secretary. The smartly dressed woman with her well-coiffed, chestnut hair, in a blue lady's suit and high heels, greeted them in a welcoming way.

"You must be Miss Anna Adams, our new student. And you must be her father. Welcome to St. Paul's Girl School." The secretary spoke very nice English. She shook their hands and invited them to follow her.

Anna looked around her, observing that not just the secretary, but the school's lobby had a pleasant, welcoming atmosphere as well. The lamps spread a warm yellow light over the lobby and the air held a scent of polished wood.

It was unusually quiet for a school building. The students were probably all in their classrooms. This was a very different ambience from her sober, unsentimental Gymnasium, where students and teachers were always rushing around.

"Come with me," the secretary invited. "Miss Sinclair is waiting for you." She directed them to an office at the end of the corridor. On both sides of the long hall Anna saw offices with glass windows. They were apparently passing through the administrative block, with typists and office personnel.

"Wait a moment while I check Miss Sinclair isn't dealing with a last-minute case." The secretary entered the brown door with the plaque "Headmistress' and closed it behind her. Anna's heart pounded in her chest as they stood waiting to be called in.

What would Miss Sinclair be like? At first sight, Anna liked the look of the school, but it was all quite overwhelming. And to be taught the subjects in a language she hadn't completely mastered. Could she do it? Both her father and Henryk believed in her potential.

Of course you can do it, Anna Adams, she told herself and straightened her back.

The door swung open and a young person with cropped, dark-blonde hair and flaming red cheeks burst from the room. In her haste, she almost collided with Anna but sped around her without an apology and disappeared down the hallway muttering to herself.

"What was that?" Anna exclaimed, not sure whether this fury was a girl after all. She'd worn pants and looked like a boy. But this was a girls' school, wasn't it?

"Mr. Adams, Miss Adams, please come in."

They entered a large office with tall bookshelves filled with volumes of literature and history. A desk covered in papers and a typewriter stood near the window, framed by a view of the school's well-kept gardens.

Seated behind the desk was Miss Evelyn Sinclair, a woman in her forties with a regal air about her. She had a warm smile and a commanding presence that put Anna at ease, even if just a little.

"Good morning," Miss Sinclair greeted them, her British accent as proper as that of the Queen Consort, Elizabeth. She rose from her chair and walked around her desk to shake their hands. "Apologies for the holdup. An emergency popped up, but it's all been sorted in good humor. You have my full attention now. Please, take a seat."

Miss Sinclair moved with ease and poise, her clothes in dark tones, but chic and couture, her reddish-blonde hair with threads of silver pinned up elegantly. They took the chairs facing the headmistress's desk. Anna couldn't help but admire her easy elegance and manners. What a difference from Herr Schroff at her German school. He had been nothing but loud-mouthed and bullying.

"We're honored to meet you, Miss Sinclair." Anna heard her father say in his best English. "Thank you for being able to see us on such short notice."

Miss Sinclair smiled kindly. "The pleasure is mine. Mr. Bittermann is a well-respected Londoner, so if he asks for a favor, who am I to say no? Now, Miss Adams, I understand you have recently arrived from Germany. Your uncle told me you are quite proficient in English. Is that correct?"

Anna nodded. Her voice was still hesitant but determined now the focus shifted to her. "Yes, Miss Sinclair. I've been studying English for several years. I've never scored anything but "Sehr Gut"."

The headmistress's light-blue eyes twinkled with interest. "Sehr gut" would be the equivalent of an A in our system. That's excellent to hear. We value language skills here at St. Paul's. I realise, though, that you haven't taken subjects such as biology or geography in English, so that will be a challenge for you."

Anna nodded again, wanted to add she was a fast learner but decided against interrupting Miss Sinclair, who continued. "Now, to determine the most suitable class for you, I would like to ask you a few questions so you can demonstrate your proficiency in English. Shall we?"

Excitement and anxiety battled in Anna as she cast a quick look at her father, who gave her a reassuring nod. She took another deep breath. This was her moment to prove herself in a new country, to show she could do it.

"Yes, Miss Sinclair, I'm ready."

EIGHT WEEKS LATER, January 1939

Anna liked living with her uncle on Mount Street and she liked her new school. Working harder than all the other students in her year she already excelled in every subject in the curriculum, coming up top of her class every time.

In the evenings, she read English classics and wrote and rewrote her homework assignments until they were flawless. She made no friends at St Paul's, as nobody is particularly fond of an eager beaver. But Anna had no time to ponder her friendless state. Her entire focus was on passing her exams in the spring and then enrolling in a history program at one of England's prestigious universities.

Hollow inside, she plodded on, ignoring nightmares of rain and cold and pain on the Polish border, shutting out her mother's deterioration into mental illness, and her father's feverish attempts at finding a job that didn't require proficiency in English.

She focused on the successes of her uncle, sought *his* advice and encouragement about her academic achievements, not that of her parents. Anna systematically erased Ansel from her life. The only part she agreed to take with her to her future was the love of books. No longer did she pick up a Goethe, Rilke or Kafka but turned to Dickens, Austen, and everything by Thomas Hardy. She found the books in her uncle's vast library.

"I'm glad somebody reads these books before the silverfish get them all," he'd chuckled. "I meant to read them when I bought them, often on recommendation from my clients, but I never have the time to sit down with a book. You indulge in them, my dear, and become the wiser for it."

Anna still enjoyed reading but her main goal was getting more proficient in English and extending her vocabulary. She often read parts aloud, hoping thus to improve her British accent.

SHE WAS SITTING with a copy of Virginia Woolf's *The Years* on a bench outside in the school gardens during lunch. It was a mild January afternoon. A robin sang its heart out in the leafless chestnut tree above her head. For the rest, it was quiet in the garden. The other students were in the school canteen, eating their midday meal.

Lately Anna had taken to avoiding the canteen as she hated sitting alone at a table, being subjected to curious, and sometimes hostile, glances from her classmates. Outside in the garden, or in the library, being alone didn't matter as much.

Low in spirits, she tried to concentrate on the open book in her hands, but the letters danced before her eyes. She'd read too much. She was so tired. Just for a brief spell she closed her eyes to listen to the mournful, singing robin. Did he or she have heartache as well? Beyond the tall garden walls, the subdued buzz of the big city settled around her like a cloak. She wanted to cry, but her eyes were dry.

If I could just for a moment stop pushing myself on and on, she thought. *Just have a moment of peace.*

On opening her eyes, she saw the girl she'd almost collided with on her first day, outside Miss Sinclair's office, saunter over towards her. Anna got ready to leave the bench and disappear inside. This was Pearl Baseden, a popular troublemaker and trailblazer, afraid of nothing and no one and constantly clashing with this teacher or that. It could only mean trouble if she was heading in Anna's direction now.

Anna was very aware she hadn't made herself popular with her overzealous start at the school, so she weighed her options. Pearl was clearly coming straight for her. If she ran now, she'd be labeled a coward on top of being a highbrow. She stayed put, hiding her head inside *The Years* as if immersed in her reading.

Pearl plopped on the bench next to Anna and grabbed the book from her hands with such a swift and unexpected move, Anna sat frozen, expecting the scorn of the class's de facto leader to land on her head any second.

"The Years. Virginia Woolf?" Pearl read aloud. "Heavens Anna, you read serious stuff. No wonder you're so serious yourself. I never get any further than my brother's comic books and even then, I fall asleep."

Anna took a swift glance at the girl next to her. She sat perfectly poised, cross-legged, smiling.

"Are you not here to scold me?" she asked surprised.

"Scold you? What for?" Pearl raised one dark eyebrow, still smiling. She tossed the book back in Anna's lap. "I just came over to say 'hullo'."

"Oh." It came out rather awkwardly. Pearl was so accomplished, so confident in her own skin, excelling in both sports and banter. But Anna, who in her solitude had become a good reader of her peers' character, now noticed a small crack in Pearl's unflappability.

"Anything the matter?" Anna asked.

"Something is always the matter at St. Paul's. Gosh, I hate this school, don't you?"

Anna's forehead wrinkled. *Hate St. Paul's? No, I love it.*

Pearl didn't wait for her answer. "Got another F for my English literature." She snorted with scorn. "Here we are, you a German and you score straight A's in English. And I, who've lived here my entire life, can't even discern Shakespeare from Chaucer. Ah well, I'll have to lie to my parents tonight. They expect me to do so much better."

Anna listened carefully. Of course, she hadn't missed Pearl's bad mark as it had been highlighted for all to know by Miss Dorkins, the English teacher, that morning.

"I don't suppose I can be of much help since I'm so behind in my reading. But I'd be willing to help you if I could?" Anna, shy about her accented English, said it in a small voice. Without notice, the impulsive Pearl jumped over to where she sat and hugged her.

"Would you, Anna? Oh, you're such a dear. Miss Dorkins said she'd give me one more chance if I handed the assignment in tomorrow. I don't suppose you have time after school?"

"Of course I do." Anna's cheeks colored in excitement.

Pearl laughed out loud, an infectious laughter that had so much mirth. "Isn't it funny, you a foreigner helping me with my English? And I promise you, you'll never be sitting on your own after this day. I'd wanted to befriend you before, but you seemed so sad and so distant. I didn't want to bother you."

Anna smiled, relieved for the first time in ages. The burden of sadness was lifting from her shoulders. Here was lovely Pearl offering her friendship, or at least a bond.

"What happened the day I stood in front of Miss Sinclair's office, and you burst from the room like a charging bull?"

Pearl continued laughing. "Oh my! That was me being an academic, I suppose. But it was a case of wrong time, wrong place."

"What do you mean?"

"Well, you know the French teacher, Madame Hare, all hoity-toity, *parlez-vous Francais, s'il vous plait?*" Pearl did a perfect imitation of the young French teacher who was rather nervous but insisted on the students speaking only French in her classes. It was a new teaching method she adhered to. It led to not only the teacher, but also the students, having no clue what was being said as the conversations were all in a mixture of English and French. Some students just answered Madame Hare's questions in English with a fake French accent. Anna had noticed Pearl's French was perfect.

Anna nodded.

"My mother happens to be French, so we spend all our holidays in Paris with *grandpere* and *grandmere* and I speak quite a mouthful of French. Madame Hare at some point said, *s'il te plaît, ouvre tes livres et conjugue espoir en français* which means, 'please open your books and conjugate '*espoir*' in French'. So, I corrected her by saying, *Je suis désolée, Madame Hare, mais ça c'est très impoli.* She looked at me as if I'd bitten off her head and, in her confusion, turned to English so everyone could follow our dispute."

"She used the informal 'tu' instead of 'vous'?" Anna filled in.

"Exactly! You are such a bright button, Anna Adams!" Pearl beamed, "but Madame Hare doesn't like to be corrected. She's as big a snob as you get. That's why I wanted to get even with her, but it landed me in Miss Sinclair's office and extra French assignments for the rest of the month. I burnt the edges of the papers I had to write and handed them in like that. Just to push Madame Hare's buttons a little further. I made sure, though, that there were no mistakes in my work. My mother, bless her heart, checked everything for me." Pearl looked triumphant.

At that point the school bell rang, and Anna and Pearl got up from the bench.

"So, will you come to my house after class?" Pearl asked, combing a hand through her short dark-blonde hair, the light eyes fixed hopefully on Anna's face. Anna looked sceptical.

"I would love to but... I need to go home directly after school."

"Could I come with you? Give my parents a ring from your house?"

Anna thought of this new proposal. Her uncle wouldn't be home. It would be up to Mrs. Whitman's decision.

"We could try that," she said hesitantly, "I live with my uncle..."

"... on Mount Street," Pearl interrupted. "I know, I found out through Miss Sinclair's secretary. She's the only one in this school who actually likes me. Not for me, but because I bring her Maman's brioche and she's a sucker for French pastries. She told me who you were and where you live."

"Oh." Anna gazed at Pearl in surprise, "why would you want to know that?"

"Why not?" Pearl shrugged. "I liked you from first sight. You're different from the rest. A high-flier. I guess you won't want to marry the first guy you kiss?"

Anna thought back of Henryk and his modest kiss on top of her head. She would have married him there and then but answered, "no, I want to go to university."

"There, you see! I want to be an athlete or fly Spitfires like my brothers, but I don't think I'll be fit for either of these careers so I'm keeping my options open after exams. Probably Paris for a year."

They walked amicably to the next class and without any comment Pearl plopped her satchel next to Anna's and sat next to her. The history teacher, Miss Higginbottom, looked at the two with a quizzical look on her face but refrained from commenting.

Two individualists, Anna thought, though Pearl was quite popular with the others in the class as well.

SHE HAD A FRIEND. From now on her world would blossom. Anyone's world would blossom with a friend like Pearl in it.

26

MUTTI'S DOWNFALL

Two months later, March 1939

Spring was coming early to London. The first daffodils bloomed in the parks and a pair of sparrows squawked in the chestnut tree outside Anna's window every morning. Life was good. She was flourishing at school and at home with Pearl as a friend. Passing her exams wasn't just going to be easy for Anna now, it was going to be fun and exciting.

Uncle Benjamin had suggested she apply to both Oxford and Cambridge for a degree in history. See which university best suited her qualifications. Anna leaned towards Oxford, as it was her absolute dream to study there, but she agreed with her uncle that keeping a second option open was the smart thing to do.

Also, with Uncle Benjamin's help, her father had taken over an antiquarian bookshop in Soho. He was busy going through the inventory and preparing the apartment over it for the Adams family to move into.

"Father, can I not stay with Uncle Benjamin until I go to university?" Anna had pleaded. She didn't look forward to moving to the cramped apartment over a shop now that she'd lived in a nice house in a good neighborhood for the past several months. Soho was lovely but nothing compared to Mayfair, she thought.

Father and daughter had come to the agreement, Anna's home would remain in Mount Street until after the summer holidays, but she'd lend him a hand in the shop on Saturdays and stay for the weekend.

Moving her mother to Soho was also considered something of a challenge. Judy remained the one weak link in the chain, the one who couldn't grasp life by the horns in London. She stayed in her bedroom most of the time, paper-thin and having lost most of her beautiful brown hair and all of her joy.

Most days she stayed in bed, sipping lukewarm tea with the blinds closed and a small bedside lamp giving a shadowy glow in the room. Doctors had come and gone. Medication prescribed and unprescribed. Uncle Benjamin never stopped trying to help his sister in her grief, but nothing worked.

"How are we going to move Mutti to the new apartment?" Anna asked one day at breakfast when she was alone with her father. She simply couldn't bring herself to calling Mutti Mother, whereas calling her father in the English way came out easy.

The new apartment was dark and low-ceilinged, without all the modern facilities Mount Street had. It would mean another major change for her unstable mother.

"I have my worries about it, but I don't want to leave without your mother, she's my wife," her father sighed. "Benjamin has kindly offered to let her stay here. Just like you. But we need to set up our own life in London, can't be dependent on another man's household for eternity. It's been more than four months."

"Have you asked Mutti?" Anna was crumbling her toast, losing her appetite in the sadness of their conversation.

"I tried, many times. She doesn't answer any questions, least of all where she wants to go. She seems to want to go nowhere, only into oblivion. I'm at the end of my tether with her, to be honest."

Anna let her head hang. She felt the same. She avoided that

dusky, smelly bedroom as much as she could and felt terribly guilty as a result.

"I don't know, Father, if moving her is a wise thing. Mutti may not be happy, but at least there's no drama. Moving her to a new place may trigger all sorts of problems. And if Uncle Benjamin doesn't mind..." Her voice trailed off. Mutti was just a problem too big for her to tackle and apparently her father felt the same.

His sigh was full of sorrow. "I wish there was something I could do to relieve her suffering, but she seems to be beyond help."

"I know." Her own bond with her mother was so fragile. She could endure five minutes at most. Every day after school she'd dutifully enter the Mahogany Suite on the first floor to sit by her mother's bedside. The silence and the oppression made it more a chore than a pleasant rendezvous.

Sometimes, on good days, but less and less often, her mother would turn to her and ask how school was. As soon as Anna started talking, her mother's eyes would turn vacant, and she could see her drift off to her own world.

"I'd leave her here," Anna concluded.

"I can't, Anna. Judy is my wife. I'll convince her that it is for the best, easing her into the new situation, so hopefully it isn't too traumatic for her. We are moving, both of us."

ON RETURNING HOME from school that afternoon, Anna froze on the pavement. An ambulance with swaying lights was parked on the curb in front of her uncle's house. She raced down the street as fast as she would, her satchel with her schoolbooks banging against her back. Just when she was almost abreast of the ambulance, it tore off at high speed, its sirens echoing off the walls, screeching her ears.

"Mutti! Oh no, Mutti!" she muffled her screams, not wanting to sound too German in a London street. She sprinted up the garden path, leaving the gate hang open and banged with both fists on the front door.

"Open the door. Where is my mother?"

Mrs. Whitman, white-faced and with a nervous twitch on her face that hadn't been there before, opened the door.

"Oh Miss Anna," she exclaimed in a high-pitched voice, clearly out of control. "Are you home already?"

"I'm home at my usual time. What is with the ambulance. Is it my mother?"

Mrs. Whitman clasped a hand over her mouth, which further frightened Anna. The housekeeper had never been one to show much sentiment, but she was clearly in all states now.

"Yes, an awful accident. Awful. And left to me to clean it all up. I don't know how. I've never dealt with anything like this in my life. My oh my. What a curse she brought on this house. What a curse!"

"What happened, Mrs. Whitman? Please tell me. And where is my father and where is Uncle Benjamin?" Anna was crying now, begging the housekeeper to stop her babbling to tell her what had happened to her mother. "Is she dead?"

"No, at least not yet. She tried to kill herself, the poor thing. But the mess. The mess is too terrible for anyone's eyes."

"Oh no," Anna yammered. "No, no, no. Where have they taken her and where is my father? I need my father!"

"He's gone with the paramedics in the ambulance. In all the distress I haven't even been able to call your uncle. I need to call Mr. Bittermann. Now. But my hands are trembling so much I'm not sure I can dial the number. And the mess. Oh, oh the mess."

"What mess?" Anna became even more frightened. She was still standing on the doorstep, but Mrs. Whitman pulled her inside now and whispered in her ear. "She tried to kill herself. She... she cut her wrists. Oh, oh, the mess. I'm here to clear it but I don't know if I can. I've never seen that much blood in my life. The sheets are certainly ruined. Oh, oh, oh."

Anna sank to the floor in the corridor crying her heart out. *Poor Mutti, poor poor Mutti.* What would become of her now? And of her family?

"There there, child, don't cry. I'll make you a cup of tea if I can steady my hands. And I must call your uncle. Oh, oh my."

Minutes later a trembling Anna sat in Mrs. Whitman's spic-and-span kitchen, while her hands shook so badly around her cup it clattered against her teeth.

"Has she been taken to hospital? Which hospital? I want to go to my mother. I need to be with her."

"Yes, yes, child. We'll arrange all that. Wait till your uncle is here and Charles can drive you to the hospital. I think they said St. Thomas' Hospital, but I was so upset I wasn't listening clearly. We'll ring St. Thomas' and ask if a Mrs. Judy Adams was admitted. We'll do that, but first finish your tea. Ah, there is your uncle. The good man never disappoints."

Uncle Benjamin strode into the kitchen as a general onto the battlefield.

"What happened under my roof?" He barked as if one of them was to blame. Mrs. Whitman explained in a trembling voice how she'd found his sister lying in a pool of her own blood when she'd brought Judy her cup of afternoon tea. She'd immediately called the emergency number and thank God, Jude had been pottering in the garden and had helped her staunch the wounds.

"What on Earth was she thinking?" Uncle Benjamin seemed very angry, but his eyes had a soft sadness in them as if he'd seen this coming as an inevitable doom.

"You, poor child," he said turning to his niece. "Thank God, you've got my strong genes and not those from the Cohen side of the family. Now get your coat. We'll go to the hospital together. I'm not letting you out of my sight. You need a level-headed person by your side when you've got to witness this misfortune. And Mrs. Whitman don't worry about the mess. I'll call a cleaning service and they will take care of it for you. Don't enter that bedroom. Jude can take a different room until he moves to his own place. We'll sort the Mahogany Suite later."

"Thank you, Mr. Bittermann, that's a huge load off my back."

"Take the rest of the day off, Mrs. Whitman, to calm your nerves.

I'll dine out with Jude and my niece, so you don't have to worry about making us dinner. Now young lady, off to the hospital."

ANNA WAS grateful for her confident uncle's presence as they entered the darkened room in St. Thomas' Hospital. The first thing she noticed was her father's figure by the bed, his head bent, both hands on his white hair. He seemed as if in deep prayer, but when the door opened wider and cast a beam of light into the room, he looked up in their direction. His eyes had never been more sorrowful, and Anna's heart ached twice as hard for her gentle-hearted father.

He rose slowly from his chair. An old man, a broken man, but slowly the expression on his face changed from sorrow to shame.

"I'm so sor...," he began, casting his eyes down so as not to meet the steady gaze of his brother-in-law.

"Don't Jude! Stop!" Uncle Benjamin interrupted in a low voice. "You did nothing wrong and, for the record, neither did Judy. She's got her mother's genes. It's run in the Cohen side of the family for generations. I know all about it. They can't help themselves. And we all know what she had to go through. She snapped, that's all."

"I shouldn't have begun about the apartment in Greek Street," Jude gasped, fighting to hold back his tears. "I shouldn't have."

"Well, you did and that's that." Uncle Benjamin didn't like bewailing one's presumed mistakes.

Anna inched physically closer to her uncle who exuded such calm in the middle of her family's storm. Now and then she glanced at the bed that was very still. The bony frame of her mother's body was visible under the hospital blanket. An IV in her hand was attached to a machine that made gurgling sounds.

Her mother's eyes were closed, sunken deep in their sockets. She was even whiter and thinner than before. But she lay peaceful as if she'd crossed a line in the sand, making clear to the world she needed more than bottomless rest in her brother's house.

"It will be a psychiatric ward from now on," Uncle Benjamin observed, for the first time with a tinge of sorrow in his voice. "Whatever's next, I can't have this in my house, and neither can you have it in yours, Jude. You know what happened to Sarah, her mother and my stepmother?"

Anna had never been told what had happened to her maternal grandmother but there had been the hush-hush about her ill fate in her youth. Her father nodded.

Finally, Anna raked together the courage to go closer to her sleeping mother. She perched on the chair by the side of the bed and stared at her face. Would she ever wake again? Would she ever be her mother again? The one that sang songs and curled her hair before letting her go to a children's party? The one who told her stories of wild bears in the Polish woods and sang songs of angels and fairies? Would she?

She knew the answer. There had not even been time to say goodbye to her mother when she was still around. Sort of around. Now she was fully unreachable and would live in her own little world for good.

Her gaze went to her father and uncle. They were all the family she had left. Two men so different and yet both so beloved by her. In that dim hospital room, with her mother barely breathing, a new Anna emerged. She would not be like her mother. Never.

Anna Adams would carve a life for herself free from the tragedy of her past. She would grow beyond it, leave it behind. She would sever all ties with Germany and Poland. Anna Adams was British to the core and would make a good life for herself in London.

A nurse came in and called them to her small office.

"I'm so sorry for what happened. That it could not be prevented," she said with sympathy. "I'll not beat about the bush. Mrs. Adams lost a lot of blood and will be on a water and salt drip for a while. We'll keep her sedated for the pain and her mental agony. Physically we see no reason why she wouldn't recover from her wounds, but the damage to her mental state is severe. We will keep her for observation for three days here. We suggest transferring her to Claybury Hospital and keep her there for as long as she needs. She'll be in good hands. Claybury has the best psychiatrists in the country. They will do what they can to give Mrs. Adams the best treatment available. Give her another chance at life. But it all depends on her will. I must warn you. When a patient of her constitution becomes suicidal, the urge to repeat such action is strong. Prevention is all we can offer, I'm afraid."

"Thank you, Nurse Gabriel, that seems like a sound plan." Uncle Benjamin answered before Jude could say anything. "Please take good care of my sister. We will be back tomorrow morning, but should there be any change in her situation, do not hesitate to call me any hour of the day or night." He stood up to leave the room.

"I will, sir, I promise," Nurse Gabriel replied and turning to the husband. "Please, Mr. Adams, could I have a word with you in private? It concerns the need to place Mrs. Adams under guardianship. I need you to sign the papers."

Anna slipped back into her mother's hospital room one more time and stood looking down at the still figure in the bed. She placed a cautious kiss on the cool forehead.

"I love you, Mutti," she whispered in English, "I promise I'll live for Sarah and Eva and you. I'll make you all proud." And she sneaked out of the dusky room, tears rolling down her cheeks, misting up her glasses. But her back was straight and her will of iron. She had Uncle Benjamin's genes, and her grandfather Samuel Bittermann's genes. She would survive anything.

27

HE'S BACK

Two months later - May 1939

S tanding on St Paul's Girl School's stage in the auditorium, Anna gazed down on the mass of faces below her, spotting her father and Uncle Benjamin sitting front row. She waved with her diploma and saw them clap. Their faces bright with pride.

Nothing but straight A's. Miss Sinclair called her a "star pupil."

"She's only been in the country for six months, with little education in English and look at her. The best student St. Paul's Girl School has had in years. A true accomplishment, Miss Adams. I foresee a bright academic future for you."

Anna thought she'd burst with pride when the audience had clapped and cheered for her. For her alone.

Don't think of the hollowness in your heart. Remember who you do it for, she'd reminded herself in a sudden moment of weakness. Mutti not there. Sarah and Eva not there.

With her help, Pearl had also passed all her subjects with reasonable marks. They stood side-by-side on the stage, smiling broadly. Anna tucked her heavy heart away, deep inside herself.

Mr. and Mrs. Baseden, Pearl's parents, were sitting with her father and her uncle and even Pearl's two older brothers, Arnold, and Jean-Claude, sat amid the audience in their blue RAF uniforms. Anna's eyes briefly scanned for the presence of another aviator, but he wasn't there. She'd heard nothing of Henryk since they'd parted months before. Gradually his personage was fading from her life, leaving only the remembrance of something pleasant in the past.

"When all this official nonsense is done, we'll sneak out for drinks at *The Cloak & Dagger*," Pearl whispered in Anna's ear.

"Go for drinks? But we're minors, they won't let us into a bar."

"Then you haven't reckoned with my brothers. They said they'll do it for me, for us. We'll enter each on the arm of one and pretend we're their girls. That way the bartender will ask no questions. RAF men are cherished customers everywhere. Well, are you coming?"

Anna looked doubtfully in the direction of her family. Wouldn't they expect her to come home for tea with them?

"I could ask my father," she suggested with caution.

"Let me do it for you. I'll switch on my charm. But maybe I don't even need to. Both your father and your uncle like me."

"That's true," Anna agreed. "Who doesn't like you."

"Some of the teachers could drink my blood. Madame Hare for one," Pearl giggled, putting her elbow in Anna's side, and pointing to the sour-looking French teacher who had indeed fought tooth and nail to prevent giving Pearl the A in French she deserved.

The nit-picking Madame Hare kept insisting Pearl was cheating, and her mother wrote all her work for her. But Miss Sinclair had stood up for Pearl in a moment of rare generosity.

"Madame Hare, Pearl told me she discusses her French lessons with her mother, which can only be applauded, but she made all her written and oral work within the framework of the school exams, so I fail to see your point that she cheated. I declare her A in French final."

When the girls left the stage with their class, Anna felt she was saying goodbye to a part of her life that had been a safe and pleasant bubble. With all the turmoil in her private life, St Paul's had been her haven and the friendship with Pearl a blessing.

She walked over to her relatives and accepted their congratulations. Pearl stood behind her with her two brothers as bodyguards. She'd clearly decided to make hay while the sun shone.

"Mr. Adams, would it be alright if Anna joined me and my brothers for a coffee? We'll make sure she's home by ten."

"Would you want that, Anna, or do you prefer to go home?" Her father's face was one big happy smile for his daughter. Home these days for Anna was still with her uncle while her father now permanently lived above the bookshop in Greek Street. The arrangement had worked out best for both.

"I'd like to go for a coffee, Father. I'll see you tomorrow as it is my day to help you in the shop."

"You do that, girl. Have fun." He kissed her on the forehead.

"Not a minute after ten," Uncle Benjamin said sternly. "I want to talk with you about your future tomorrow, Anna. You know I don't like decisions to be postponed any longer than necessary."

"I know, Uncle. I want that too. I'll be home at ten." Anna smiled at him. Their appreciation was mutual. He was the most stabilizing factor in her life, and he played the part with gusto.

ENTERING THE CLOAK & Dagger pub was a new and confusing experience for Anna. It was immensely crowded and full of smoke and chatter and music. She coughed when the fumes hit her lungs and had the urge to turn around and leave. Such an elbow-to-elbow setting was not Anna's thing. But Pearl pulled her along, seemingly like a fish in water.

She must have been here before. Realizing her forthright friend was even more a woman of the world than she'd expected. The way Pearl mingled with the other pubgoers as if she frequented the place daily opened Anna's eyes to what adulthood might mean. One thing was certain, with Pearl around, her own life would always be a surprise.

Within seconds she was holding a tall glass of beer, while Arnold directed her to a not very clean table in the corner.

"Sit and be merry," he shouted in her ear. Anna grimaced but did as he told her, glad to be out of the way of the pushing swarm to take in the lively atmosphere from a short distance. Arnold arranged another chair next to her but didn't sit down on it. Pearl stood in front of the table, in her hand a glass she raised to Anna, a glint of mischief in the light eyes.

"Are you comfortable there?" she shouted.

"I am," Anna shouted back. She was getting accustomed to her new surroundings. The beer tasted bitter, but it wasn't too bad. After two more sips she started to like it and glanced around her with a little more ease.

Until... she thought she'd die on the spot.

Pearl stepped aside and from behind her, out of a corner of the pub, Henryk appeared holding a single red rose in his hand. His smile melted all the worries in Anna's heart. As he approached her, she felt herself wrapped in that timeless smile, forgetting space and time. At that instance, time came to a standstill in the Cloak & Dagger for her and all noise evaporated to the background.

Before sitting down on the chair next to her, Henryk handed her the rose with a little bow. She accepted it, buried her nose in the sweet fragrance, feeling everything to the core of her being. Pearl gave her a wink and disappeared with her brothers to another part of the pub.

"Congratulations, Anna. You're a pro," he said in her ear, his lips brushing her cheek. Anna sat very still while the emotions cartwheeled through her, temporarily too stunned to react. Awash with tremendous joy.

"Where... where have you come from?" she finally managed to bring out.

"I tried to come earlier. Many times." He sounded apologetic. "Training for war has been brutal. I had no time off, but I met the RAF brothers last month." He pointed to Arnold and Jean-Claude.

"We got talking. That's how I found out about Pearl and you. You can imagine it was quite an interrogation." Henryk smiled, then lightly squeezed her hand that rested on the table. Anna edged closer to his side, while Henryk put his arm around the back of her chair.

"They mentioned you and Pearl would graduate today. I told my squadron leader I simply had to fly to England. And Pearl's brothers arranged this meeting."

"You did that for me?" Anna bit her lip. She was completely overtaken by his sudden reappearance in her life.

"I did. I missed you."

"I missed you too."

"Shall we leave this racket and go for a walk? Or do you want to stay with Pearl?"

"I'll tell her I'm going." Anna was already standing up, leaving the half-finished glass of beer on the table, yearning for fresh air, for being alone with Henryk.

"But I need to be home at ten. I promised my uncle." She hated sounding like a little girl now she'd had a taste of adulthood.

"We'll make sure you're in Mount Street at the appointed hour."

When Anna began to explain their departure to Pearl, she waved her away as if she was a mosquito.

"I'll ring you tomorrow, so make sure you have a great story to tell."

The girls kissed each other's cheeks, and Anna thanked Pearl's brothers for their help.

"So, you're okay with us arranging this for you?" Arnold wanted to know. Anna's smile told him enough.

"Have fun," Pearl shouted after them, "and three cheers for my brothers!"

Anna and Henryk stood in the soft,cool May evening with the scent of jasmine and honeysuckle in the air, a golden sun sinking behind the city's skyline. Anna felt a shiver of trepidation go through her.

Henryk was quick to notice her tremor. "Are you cold? Need my jacket?" Without waiting for an answer, he took off his khaki jacket and draped it around her shoulders. It had his scent, his strength, his spirit. Right away Anna felt dynamic and daring as if his energy transferred to her.

Her eyes said thank you, while from her lips came, "you always know what I need." The past months flashed before her: school, her mother's downfall, her father's new place, university lurking.

So much had happened since they parted in November. She'd become Anna through and through, but as Henryk had also known Ansel, the young girl struggled to be seen as well, to be remembered.

"I'm no longer who I used to be...," Anna began, "I'm no longer the driftwood you encountered on that airstrip near Breslau, and yet..." Her voice trailed off.

"And yet?" he repeated, the blue gaze looking deeply into her amber eyes.

"And yet, my life is never smooth sailing, but I'll get there."

"I have no doubt you will, Anna Adams, you'll go places. Mark my words."

She smiled, though with a tinge of melancholy. "Life is more than a good set of brains, Henryk."

"I wasn't only referring to your brains. I just know you'll carve out a remarkable life for yourself. And I hope to be part of it. Always."

"Oh Henryk, you're flattering me." But as she said it, she saw the blue gaze deepen to fierceness.

"I am no flatterer, Anna. Never been. I mean what I say."

His honesty made her humble.

"I want to be part of your life too, Henryk. And not just because you brought my family to safety."

They were walking in the direction of the Thames. Londoners had left their house to stroll in the pleasant evening. Young couples, parents with children in prams, elderly people sitting on benches. Anna felt as if, all of a sudden, she was walking in a dreamworld where the pieces of her life no longer fit. His nearness, his confidence, the words he spoke, it turned her whole world upside down when she was just ready to take a firm grasp on her own life.

For a long spell, they moved side by side without talking and she felt Henryk was struggling with something as well, which was unusual for him, he who was normally so clearcut and candid.

"I'm sorry I didn't write. I should have. I'm just not a writer."

"It's alright," Anna replied. "I haven't written to you either. I could have sent a letter to Nurse Margaret and asked for it to be forwarded it to you."

"How have you been, Anna? Arnold and Jean-Claude told me the basics, but they only heard it from their sister, so it wasn't firsthand."

Anna mulled over his question. *Where to start?*

"Life's been both good and bad. Which part do you want to hear first?"

He didn't answer, then said between his teeth, "come here." He took her in his arms, just held her, as they stood under a plane tree with the lapping water of the Thames nearby. The city thrummed with traffic, a riverboat hooted once, a pigeon flew up with a long-drawn coo-oo-oo.

Anna's senses were buzzing with the noise around her and from Henryk's embrace. She felt every little thing in her whole being, as if she was lifted to a higher plane where sensations were stronger and more vibrant. He held her until she started crying and could no longer stop.

"I thought so," he muttered, his chin resting on the top of her head like during their first embrace. "You may not have had an easy life, but you'll get there. You're a pro."

"What about you?" she sobbed against his chest, savoring the strong arms around her. "Have you been alright?"

"I'm fine, Anna. I'm always fine. It takes a lot to get me down. My little sister got wounded in Spain. We couldn't get any news about her. Only weeks later, one of her fellow reporters sent word she'd recovered. It was a bad time, especially for my parents."

"What happened?" Anna remembered Henryk had told her his sister was a reporter in Spanish Civil War.

"Her car was ambushed by Franco militants. The driver and two reporters got involved in some skirmish. Beate was one of them. She broke her arm, and her face was cut open. Luckily, she survived. It was not bad enough for her to come home, though." Henryk scoffed, "Beate is Beate. Not afraid of the devil. I love her dearly. Just hope she stays alive." He released her from his embrace and Anna dried her eyes, feeling the closeness between them as if they'd never been apart. They continued their walk along the river's shore holding hands. It felt so natural, Anna wondered if they'd ever really parted, their connection was boundless, easy.

"Please don't stay away from me too long." She squeezed his hand. "I don't even know for how long you're here."

"I must fly back tomorrow. I'm really on stolen time. From now on, I'll write to you. Force myself to sit with pen and paper, if needed."

"I'd love to write to you too, but where should I send my letters?" Anna asked.

He felt his pockets. "I'd give you the address of my base, but I have no paper on me." Anna retrieved the leather journal from her bag. She always carried it with her, and it was almost full.

"Write the address in here."

"You still have the journal I gave you?" His eyes lit up.

"Of course. I cherish it."

Henryk scribbled the address on the last page of her journal. "Can you read it? I have a lousy handwriting. Part of why I hate writing letters."

Flight Officer Henryk Pilecki
Białogóra Airbase
Location: Białogóra,
Address: ul. Lotnicza 1939, Białogóra, Poland

Anna tucked the journal back in her bag.

"How about an ice cream?" Henryk suggested.

"I'd love that!"

He bought two cones with strawberry ice cream. They sat on a bench by the river licking the sweet treat and looking out over the water. Anna's heart sang like a nightingale. Higher and higher. She wanted to scream "I love you!" but didn't. British girls didn't do these impulsive things. Unless you were called Pearl. But she was half French and, thus, excused.

"You want to walk home, or take a taxi?" It was an almost prosaic thing to ask but glancing at her watch, Anna saw it was nine 'o clock.

"I wish it wasn't this late already," she admitted rather sadly.

"I'll walk you home. I can take a taxi to Gatwick from your uncle's house."

Another hour in Henryk's presence seemed like bliss.

"Alright," she agreed, finishing her ice cream, "if we must."

"Come here. You have ice cream next to your mouth." And before she knew what was happening, he'd taken of her glasses and his lips landed on hers. A sensation so delightful took hold of Anna, she never wanted it to end.

Minutes later he let her go, but his eyes were locked into hers and she saw passion and love and commitment in the blue gaze. Just for her. Just for her.

And Anna couldn't be British for one moment.

"I love you!"

It came out before she could hold back.

SILENCE.

OH GOD, what had she said?

"I LOVED you from the moment I saw you, Anna. Just you. Only you."

28

ANOTHER LOSS

"Please come and say hello to my uncle before you go. I'm sure he'll be glad to see you again. He mentions you from time to time. Calls you 'that fine Pole'," Anna invited as they reached Mount Street.

Henryk chuckled, "your uncle is quite the character. Alright, a few more minutes in your presence."

She was still fumbling in her bag for her key when the front door opened, and she stood eye to eye with her father. He looked haggard. The hall lamp shone through his thinning white hair revealing his scalp.

"Vati what are you doing here?" Anna was instantly on high alert. Her father wasn't living here anymore and hardly visited, now he was so busy with his shop. He stared from Anna to Henryk, clearly failing to understand Henryk's sudden presence by his daughter's side.

"You're home?" he concluded in bewilderment. "Do come in, both of you. I hadn't expected you, Henryk. Apologies for my disorderly state. We'd only expected Anna."

"I can go, sir, if my unannounced visit is inconvenient."

"No, no, do come in." He made way for them to pass indoors.

"What's wrong, father? Why are you here instead of in Greek Street?" Anna had a bad feeling.

"Come in first and I'll explain. It's all very unfortunate."

He shuffled in front of them to the sitting room, bent and old. Anna's heart pounded in her chest. Something was clearly wrong. Was it Uncle Benjamin? But her uncle was sitting healthy and upright at the table, staring down on the notepad he'd been writing on. He turned his gaze to them, lowering the reading glasses he'd recently taken to wearing.

"Anna. And you, Henryk? How come you're here?"

"Please can someone tell me what's going on?" Anna insisted.

Her father let out a deep moaning sigh, after which Uncle Benjamin pronounced flat out, "I'm sorry to announce your mother passed, Anna. Peacefully, this afternoon."

All life and joy seeped out of her like a deflated balloon. If Henryk hadn't taken her elbow, she would have sunk to the floor like a sack of potatoes.

"Mutti," she whimpered. "What happened to Mutti?"

"Nothing really," Uncle Benjamin was the one to speak again, while her father looked more dead than alive himself. "According to the doctors, she just stopped breathing. She had no life in her anymore. Nothing dramatic but still very sad."

Henryk directed her to a chair where she sat down like an automaton. He pulled up another chair and sat close to her, holding her hand. Anna raised her eyes to her father and her heart broke for him. He looked so lost, so unconsolably sad.

"I'm alright," she whispered to Henryk as she got up from the chair again and on unstable legs walked over to her father. It was Anna who embraced him, instead of the other way around.

"I'm so, so sorry, Vati. I know she meant everything to you, despite all that happened in the last year." He stood like stone, unreachable but Anna tried again, more desperately. "Vati, Father, it's me, Anna, Ansel. Don't leave me as well."

"Let him be for now, Anna. Your father is in shock." She felt her uncle's hand on her shoulder. Turning on her heels, she came face to face with the man who'd been her mentor the past six months, who seemed to understand better what she needed than her own parents.

"But he's so sad," she protested softly, "someone has to help him."

Henryk got up and went over to her father. He led Jude to the sofa and helped him to sit down.

"Cognac's in the cupboard," her uncle instructed.

"Got it, sir." Henryk seemed to steer through this new crisis in her family as if he'd always been there. Doing exactly the right things. Giving her father small sips of the drink. Loosening Jude's tie. Taking off his shoes. Making him comfortable in the cushions. Instructing him to lie back and relax.

Meanwhile Uncle Benjamin returned to his paperwork at the table.

"I'm arranging the funeral," he explained to Anna. "I want to take this burden off your father's shoulders."

"The funeral?" Anna asked nonplussed. "Oh yes, of course, the funeral."

In her inner turmoil she'd forgotten Henryk had to leave until she heard her uncle say, "you can stay here if you want, Henryk. My chauffeur can drive you to the airport early tomorrow morning."

She looked at him with hope in her eyes. Would he... could he stay the night?

Henryk tucked a blanket around Jude and made sure he was asleep, then returned to the light at the table.

"I don't want to infringe on your hospitality, sir, but when is the funeral? I'd like to be present if I may. I've escorted Mrs. Adams here in the first place. I'd like to also escort her to her last resting place."

"You'd be very welcome, son, but what about your work? Can you arrange that?"

"I'll phone my squadron leader tomorrow. Explain the emergency." He turned to face Anna, "do you want me here?"

Tears sprang up in her eyes. He was even more her hero than she'd dared to dream. He really cared for her and her family.

"Thank you, Henryk." She pressed his hands, her tears wetting his fingers.

Two days later

It was pouring with rain as the small cortège left Claybury Hospital in Woodford Bridge for the City of London Cemetery on Aldersbrook Road. The funeral car went up front with the coffin, with only Uncle Benjamin's big black Rolls Royce following. Uncle Benjamin sat in the front with Charles at the wheel, while Anna, her father, and Henryk sat in the back seat.

Anna looked out of the window at the gleaming wet leaves of the trees, wondering where her mother's soul was now. Was she at peace? Was she seeing her, Anna? Was she with Sarah and Eva? All these questions that would never get answers.

At the hospital, a handful of nurses and doctors had come to offer the family their condolences, but it had been a swift and silent affair. Judy Adams, aka Judith Bittermann-Grynszpan, had slipped out of her earthly life as if she'd not been here at all. Leaving no traces, no belongings, no documents. Only memories.

How can one person's life be so full of sadness? She looked at her father's profile and wondered if he'd slide into the same depression now. He hardly ate, didn't talk, and had left it entirely to his brother-in-law to arrange the funeral while Anna and Henryk chose the flowers. He'd only spoken up about not wanting a Jewish funeral.

"I don't mind hymns or even a vicar. I just don't think Judaism brought Judith much joy."

In the end, they decided on no vicar and no speeches. Just a small affair at the graveyard. Remembering her in their own little circle.

Henryk had been Anna's absolute pillar of strength. They'd grown even closer in the three days he'd stayed with them. Though they hadn't spoken of their feelings for each other again, it didn't seem appropriate in this time of mourning, they had an ease and comfort in each other's presence that needed no words. She felt him constantly, close to her and it was enough, more than enough. She just dreaded the day he'd leave, and she would probably not see him for a very long time.

Anna's heart made a small jolt as they drove through the gates of the cemetery and she saw Pearl, drenched and with a small bouquet of peonies waiting for them near the open grave. Pearl, dear, sweet Pearl had cycled all the way through the rain to be with her in her hour of agony.

Henryk acknowledged Pearl's presence, as well, with one of his warm smiles.

"I'm sorry, I'm looking like a wet cat," she apologized as they got out of the car and quickly hid under their black umbrellas the funeral service provided.

"Thank you for coming," Anna was moved beyond words, "Come under my umbrella." She wanted to have her two friends close to her when she was to bury her mother. She had made two friends, which was much more than she'd had for years.

As they stood solemnly around Judith's grave, the white, wood coffin being lowered by two sour-looking undertakers who kept slipping in the wet, upturned soil, Anna became numb from pain and rain. Rain seemed to be part of her mother's descent. The incessant rains in the refugee camp that had ultimately taken the lives of her two littlest daughters. Rain, pelting rain, gray skies and no hope left.

As the earth settled on her mother's grave, she felt Henryk's hand slip into hers giving it soft pressure. It said *I'll always be here for you,* but Anna was beyond consolation at that point.

It was as if, with Judith's final descent into the earth, her gloom settled on the daughter that was left. Anna would have gone down with her in that wet grave had Henryk not stopped her by holding her back. As if he felt her urge to surrender to the burden of her past.

THE PAST finally caught up with her. Anna no longer cared for London, for university, for love, or dreams.

LET ME DISAPPEAR AS WELL.

29

SWITZERLAND

A month later - June 1939

Days had become nights and nights day, and still Anna's listlessness had not lifted. She stayed in her bedroom most days and read ravenously. Reading was her only escape from feeling a full-on failure. Had someone told her she needed help as she was overcome with grief, she would have been surprised.

Grief? No! This uselessness was intrinsic to her. She had her mother's genes after all. It had only been a matter of time to catch up with her.

I'm a good for nothing person, she kept telling herself. *I don't deserve to be happy.*

At her darkest moments, when she lay awake in the small hours of the night, she even suspected her family was cursed. Had not Herschel Grynszpan shocked the world by murdering Ernst vom Rath? Wrath had landed on every Jew in Germany and beyond. Oh life, was unbearable!

Not an attempt from Pearl, not a letter from Henryk, not a visit to her father's bookshop, not even stern looks from her uncle, nothing, broke through her isolation. Nothing reached Anna.

Until one day when she sat alone at the breakfast table toying with her toast instead of eating it, her uncle marched in and took his seat at the head of the table.

"Uncle?" Anna queried. "Do you not need to be at work?"

He shrugged. Mrs. Whitman hastened in.

"Do you need anything, sir? Everything alright?"

Ever since 'the incident' with her mother, as it was now referred to, if ever, Mrs. Whitman seemed to expect the worst. Another sign Anna thought was her family's fault. Mr. Bittermann's loyal housekeeper had lost her composure.

She needed to move in with her father, she knew, but she couldn't leave the Rosewood Suite. It was the only place on earth that still provided some solace to her.

"I'm fine, Mrs. Whitman. Just a black coffee will do. Thank you."

"Coming, sir."

"So," her uncle directed the clear amber eyes on his niece. "I've been racking my brains to think of a way of getting you out of mourning and suddenly this morning it dawned on me. Thanks to my client, Sir Gerald Hamilton."

Anna hardly listened. Her uncle always talked of this client or that, who led an amazing life, went shooting in Africa, or hiking in the Himalayas. What did it have to do with her?

"I suggest you go to Switzerland. Excellent air and fine food."

For the first time in quite a while Anna almost laughed out loud. "Switzerland, uncle? I don't have tuberculosis."

Her uncle looked at her in a puzzled way, his graying eyebrows knitted.

"Who mentioned tuberculosis? People go to Switzerland for reasons other than medical treatments."

Anna bent her head. It was the first time they were discussing her future again since she'd categorically refused to go to Oxford, though she was offered admittance based on her exam results. Her uncle had tried to persuade her to take the prestigious place, but Anna didn't feel up to it.

"There's this finishing school in Lausanne, Le Manoir it's called.

Many daughters of my clients go there for six months or a year. It won't require any academic achievements from you, but they'll teach you how to behave in high society, which is always a good thing. And there will be girls your age, from all different countries. Then you can go to Oxford next year and start fresh. What do you think?"

Her uncle was truly working himself up to sell the new idea to Anna. To her the idea of Switzerland was all so unexpected and outrageous, it confused her. But it temporarily plucked her out of her blue funk.

"I don't know, Uncle. Aren't these places extremely costly?"

"Who talks about money, dear? Your return to happiness is worth a pence or two. Don't worry about that."

"But what will Father think? I can't leave him for months on end."

"Jude also only wants your happiness, Anna. Remember you're his only daughter now. Believe me, he wants to see you at university as much as I do."

"Can... can I think about it, Uncle? It's all so sudden for me?"

"Sure. Just don't wait too long with your decision. You know I like swift deliveries. Sir Hamilton gave me the phone number of Le Manoir's headmistress, a Madame Paul Vierret. Apparently, she's a bit of a stickler for rules, so I won't be able to announce your arrival and then pack you off the next day. Unless she's susceptible to a few extra pence in her pocket."

Her uncle chuckled. Anna had to smile despite herself. She knew Benjamin Bittermann liked flashing his money at times. It was quite harmless and sweet for a man who once had had nothing.

"Thank you, Uncle. Thinking about it, Switzerland might actually be a welcome change of scenery for me. See, I can make quick decisions as well. Strangely enough, the idea of a non-demanding course at a finishing school may be just what I need to get out of my rut. Be away from it all, literally a breath of fresh air. And it will give me time to think about my future."

"I thought along those lines as well. I'll phone Madame Vierret this afternoon. Now I'm off to work and you go through your wardrobe to see what you want to take. Any new garments can be ordered via Mrs. Whitman."

Anna rose from her chair and went over to her uncle. She kissed his whiskered cheek. "Thank you, Uncle Benjamin. You are so incredibly important in my life."

"And you in mine, girl. Don't forget to go visit your father and ask his permission."

"I will. Today."

~

2 WEEKS *later*

Anna's arrival in Lausanne two weeks later introduced a complete turnaround in her life. Her uncle had been right to set her on this path. As soon as the train left Paris for Lyon and she then boarded *Le Train Blue* to the Swiss border, she felt a different Anna emerge. Not frightened Ansel, not studious Anna, but an Anna who didn't care so much about high or low, pain or joy. An Anna who observed and learned. Who couldn't be read so easily by people anymore.

Maybe the continent suited her after all. But Anna knew that wasn't the reason. It was being away from her family. There had been so much grief in the past year and though her uncle navigated the tricky waters deftly, he was part of her inner circle.

Anna began thinking about Pearl and Henryk again, now she wasn't cooped up in her bedroom on Mount Street with no future to be hopeful about. How small and submissive she'd made herself in their presence.

I don't want to be that faint-heart anymore. I want to be strong and courageous like you two are, she thought and wanted to write the thought down so she wouldn't forget it but her journal, not the one from Henryk as that was full, was in her suitcase.

As the southern French countryside flitted by, rows of conic cypresses under bright-blue, cloudless skies, white-washed houses, and yellow and red flowers in the fields, she longed to talk with her friend again. Pearl would love it here. Pearl loved France. She'd often told Anna about the wondrous holidays in her grandparents' summerhouse in Bretagne, and of course, the endless strolls through romantic Paris. Maybe next summer they could travel France together before Anna headed to university.

Pearl had taken a gap year, still training to qualify for the 1940 Summer Olympics in athletics in Helsinki, while helping her parents in their wool shop in Oxford Street.

And then there was Henryk. He became Anna's focus of attention during the last stretch of her journey, as the train chugged into Switzerland. He'd written her twice, dutifully and short, but she hadn't replied. He must think her ungrateful. A non-starter, unreliable, which she'd been. It made picking up her pen and writing to him more difficult by the day.

The train arrived in Lausanne and Anna descended with her modest suitcase that mostly held books. What use was dressing up when one was in mourning?

"Mademoiselle Adams?" A stocky man in a black uniform and an enormous black cap, woke her from her reveries.

"Yes, *oui*," she replied.

"I'm here to take you to Le Manoir. I'm Filippo Maltese by the way. If I don't drive the school car or am polishing it, I'm the handyman. Just so you know." He winked at her, but his face was serious. His accent strong. Maybe Italian.

"Thank you, Monsieur Maltese. Is it far to Le Manoir from the station?"

"Not at all, Mademoiselle. You could easily walk the distance but with your luggage that's not convenient. Plus, you may lose your way in Lausanne's back streets."

Monsieur Maltese was obviously a talkative and jovial man, but Anna sensed something underneath that veneer she couldn't pinpoint. As if he didn't really like his job, just pretended to. Maybe he was an actor?

As she sat in the backseat of the black Renault, and they wove through Lausanne, she saw what he meant. It wasn't the easiest of towns to navigate. Soon they left the built-up areas behind, and Anna saw Lake Geneva shimmer below her. A vast lake stretching out to hazy blue mountains on the other shore.

"Oh, it's pretty here," she exclaimed, looking from the Lake Geneva to the blue topped mountains in the distance. The Alps no doubt.

"Pretty as pretty can be," Mr Maltese remarked from the driver's seat. "Most girls are impressed by the view the first time. So where are you from, Mademoiselle Adams?"

Was this a trick question?

The Grynszpan stain had made her suspicious to answer questions about her origin. Despite the name change. Who knows what was still to be found on documents? She was traveling with a preliminary travel permit. Not even a full passport. Her uncle had pulled all the strings he had but it still had 'born in Hanover' stamped in it. However, the chauffeur's face in the rear mirror seemed genuinely interested. Innocent.

"I'm from London, sir."

"Aha, I see. It's Filippo for you. I hate being called Sir or Mr. Maltese."

"You can call me Anna, Filippo."

"Oh no, no," the chauffeur chuckled. "Madame Paul would kill me if she caught me calling the girls by their first names. No way, Mademoiselle."

"Is she really that strict?" Filippo seemed open-hearted enough to ask him what was awaiting her.

"Depends," he shrugged. "If she likes you, she's all sweet and nice. But don't get in her bad books. So have you lived in London all your life, Mademoiselle?"

Filippo seemed insistent to return to her roots. She could lie, of course but what if he had access to Madame Paul's administration? What would be in her file? What had her uncle told the head mistress? Seeing herself slipping back into submissiveness, Anna straightened her back. There was no going back. Not for her.

"The most important part of my life, I've lived in London, yes," she half-lied.

"Aha, I just thought I heard a German tinge in your voice."

"That's possible. My parents emigrated from Germany to England." Another half-lie.

"Well, here we are, Mademoiselle. I'll get your luggage out of the boot. Madame Paul usually comes out of her office when she sees the Renault arrive with a new student, so you'd better wait next to the car. To prevent misunderstandings, so to say."

The school looked solemn and square. It was a white, three-storey building standing on a small elevation that sloped down on a lawn towards the lake. Red awnings decorated every window.

The rectangular, school-like architecture reminded Anna of the Friedrich Schiller Gymnasium and she wasn't sure she liked the functional look of it. But the view and the surroundings were fabulous. A middle-aged lady in a dark-blue dress with glasses hanging on her bosom from two pearl strings descended the stairs in high heels.

Oh my, Anna thought, *this is what Uncle Benjamin means with high society. I'm not sure I'll ever live up to her standards. The hair's perfect, the make-up flawless, the smile fake.*

"Mademoiselle Anna, welcome to Le Manoir." A cool hand shook hers, celestite blue eyes boring through her glasses. The eyes didn't twinkle but were two ice-cold pools. The corners of the colored lips were turned up just enough to give the semblance of a welcoming smile.

"Thank you, Madame Vierret. It is very beautiful here."

"It is, isn't it?" The headmistress withdrew her perfumed hand, "I'm called Madame Paul by the students, not Madame Vierret."

"Pardon me," Anna replied, aware of the old submissiveness sliding in.

She'd done nothing wrong so far, but Madame Paul already disliked her. She'd have to call some Pearl-energy over herself to withstand the instant animosity she felt between herself and the head mistress. For the first time ever, Anna felt the brunt of being disliked by a teacher.

"I've given you your own room on the top floor. I'm sorry it isn't much, but the school is full at the moment and your uncle contacted me rather late. I'll show you to your room so you can freshen up. One of the girls will come in an hour to fetch you for afternoon tea."

Anna said nothing. She followed Madame Paul through the front door and into the main hall. It looked spacious and light. A school bell tinkled, and a group of girls came giggling from behind one of the doors, but as soon as they spotted Madame Paul they stopped laughing and marched down the corridor, throwing curious glances over their shoulder at the new student.

The room was small but attractive and clean. It had white walls and brown ceiling beams. The window overlooked the lake which was a nice view. A tiny bathroom was adjacent to the narrow bedroom.

"Usually this is a room for the staff, but this one was vacant. I hope it satisfies you?"

Anna nodded and with difficulty said, "Thank you, Madame Paul. It is quite nice."

Filippo stood in the doorway with her suitcase.

"I thought you'd said Room 8, Madame Paul. Sorry to keep you waiting. Emily said you'd gone upstairs."

"Never mind, Filippo. You're here now, so it's all sorted." The artificial smile flashed in Anna's direction. The look the chauffeur gave her spoke volumes. Anna wasn't slow on the uptake.

On seeing her, Madame Paul had decided to give her this maid's room. She happened to know her uncle had paid an exorbitant sum to get her to the school last-minute. Madame Paul most likely had reserved a larger room for her but had changed her mind on seeing Anna.

I am in for a tough ride, Anna thought, reciprocating one of Madame Paul's artificial smiles. This was going to be her introduction to manners in high society. Lie, deceive, never be real.

What a charade!

30

LIFE AT LE MANOIR

Two weeks later - July 1939

For the most part Anna kept to herself at Le Manoir. Her tiny room on the top floor turned out to be more of a blessing than a curse. She could withdraw there without being disturbed, away from the bustle downstairs, and take her time at unraveling her life.

Less than a year ago, Ansel Grynszpan had been a brilliant student at a German Gymnasium with the only negative the increasing Jew-hate around her. From then on, everything had gone downhill, apart from St Paul's, until she'd landed here in Switzerland. In yet another foreign country, with a new identity, and most of her family dead.

And she wasn't even twenty years old. It was enough to make her turn her back on the world for a while, though she wasn't depressed anymore. She was in a reflective state, taking stock, finding out what was left of her.

Le Manoir wasn't a particularly hostile place, it was just impersonal and unwelcoming, despite its emphasis on etiquette and good manners. As Anna saw it, Madame Paul had a rather simplistic view on the potential of her students. At first sight, she divided them in those 'in-the-making' and the 'never-do-well', and thereafter focused her attention on the first category.

Anna had seen it in those hard eyes on arrival. The instant 'never-do-well' stamp on her being, but also the pretension to hide the disapproval because of her uncle's bag of money. Ah well, she hadn't come here to seek the flattery of a moral zealot. She'd come to recover and give her brain a rest. She would have a good laugh about the priggish schoolmarm with her uncle on her return to London.

The lessons held little of Anna's interest and made no demand on her intellectual capacity. She'd never been an artistic person, so flower arrangement and drawing landscapes didn't spark any curiosity. Setting a table to the nines and then conversing politely in French with esteemed guests, who were actually her classmates, was more of a laugh to her than serious business.

The most preposterous lesson of all was Monsieur Petrov's. Walking with five books on your head from one side of the room to the other while Bach blared from the record player and the Russian teacher gesticulating as if he was conducting an orchestra for virtuosi. To Anna's analytical mind, it seemed more like an out-of-control and half-witted children's game.

But strangely enough, all this frippery was tolerable to Anna. It gave her the headspace to sort out her life and plenty of free time to read. Thankfully the school had a good library of mostly-French authors.

With brains that were not otherwise occupied, Anna pursued extending her French vocabulary with Balzac and Flaubert, likewise gave the stuffy Stendhal a try. But even if she afterwards practised her new proficiency at the dinner table, she never seemed to win Madame Paul over to her.

Just like at the two earlier schools Anna had attended, she studied the other students in-depth without making contact. There were girls of very different plumage.

There was the scheming Scottish Sable. The earnest Esther from Austria - who reminded Anna of herself, both her industriousness and her Jewishness. Then there was objective Océane, who came all the way from the United States and was bosom friends with the lively Lili, a red-haired rebel whom everybody liked.

Anna had only had a brief glance of the elegant Edda, a Dutch girl, who moved like a ballerina and made Monsieur Petrov almost do cartwheels of delight during his book-walking class. She'd left the same week Anna arrived.

None of the girls had approached her but some gave her a smile, like Esther and Océane. Lili had come over one day during wild-flower picking to warn her to stay out of Sable's claws. Not that Sable even cast her celestite-blue eyes in Anna's direction. She was way too busy staying at the top of Madame Paul's favorites' list, while making hell for more vulnerable and shy students.

Anna was withdrawn, but not timid. She sent enough foe signals in Sable's direction to keep her distance.

It was a nice balmy July evening and Anna was sitting on a flat stone near the lake, enjoying the sunset and making another failed attack at Stendhal's *Le Rouge et Le Noir*. The book simply couldn't hold her attention and she cared nothing for Julien Sorel's complicated love life.

"May I interrupt for a moment?" A voice with a soft, German lilt asked behind her.

"Esther?" Anna turned to her, "how are you?"

Esther sat on the next stone, pulling in her legs, and wrapping her arms around her knees. She looked disturbed, downbeat. Anna wondered if Sable had pulled another prank on her. Esther was just the kind, gentle person to become that minx's victim.

"Could be better." Esther's light-green eyes fixed gravely on the lapping waves at their feet.

"Want to talk about it?" Anna closed her book and tossed it in the sand. *Lie there Julien Sorel with your impossible problems. Real life is a lot more daunting.*

"I wouldn't if I didn't think I had to." Esther's voice was flat. Anna swallowed. She'd considered Esther to be on a friendly footing with her, though they hadn't really talked. This sounded like forced proximity. But Esther immediately explained herself.

"I've overheard Madame Paul talk with one of the maids. You know how she's anti-Jewish?"

"Yes, quite."

Esther looked even sadder as she said, "as Hitler is whipping up anti-Jew sentiment across Europe, apparently Madame Paul feels emboldened. She said to the maid that 'the two undesirable objects in our midst' should from now on be housed together in Anna Adams room instead of me being on the same floor with the regular students."

"What?" Anna cried out in disbelief. "My room is hardly big enough for one person!"

"That's what the maid replied," Esther sorrowed. "To which Madame Paul remarked, she wouldn't be surprised to see Jews soon be packed together in even tighter places than a decent maid's room."

"It's despicable!" Anna spat. "I'm going to phone my uncle tonight and tell him I'm coming home. We don't need to accept this kind of behavior, Esther. No matter that hoity-toity Madame Paul believes we're vermin."

"Oh, Anna, you're so brave. I can't think along these lines, as I really need to get my diploma here. My mother and grandmother would be absolutely horrified if I walked away without being qualified to run a big house."

"Really?" Anna had never even thought anyone could take this finishing school business seriously, but she'd seen Esther try so hard and being scolded every time. Not because she did anything wrong, but because she was nice and polite and ... a Jew.

"You know what?" Anna said with warmth. "I'll keep my mouth shut for now. We will live together in that room, one way or another, so you can get your diploma. That's more important to me than having to endure Madame's harrasment for a while longer. You're almost done, right?"

"Yes, three more months and I'll go home to Vienna."

"We'll make it work and not say a word."

Anna could see Esther's beautiful sea-green eyes fill up with tears. Tears of gratitude.

"Thank you."

"Nothing to thank me for, Esther. But will Océane and Lili still be your friends?"

"Oh yes. They don't share the anti-Jew sentiment. We've pledged to be friends through thick and thin. Do you want to join in?"

"That's very kind of you but not needed. I like to keep to myself. I do think, though, you three are the only decent ones of the pack."

"But we'll be sharing more, now we're becoming roommates?" Esther begged, looking hopeful. Anna understood Esther thought of her as protection and it gave her a weird deja-vu. Hadn't Pearl been her shield at St. Paul's Girl School? But no, it was different. Pearl was popular. Anna was never going to be the popular one, she realized without bitterness. Popularity was not what she sought in life.

What did she seek? She still didn't know. It was hidden in the folded pages of her, as yet, unlived life.

31

WAR WITH POLAND

Two months later - 2 September 1939

Anna's life at Le Manoir changed drastically after Esther moved in. The space was so small they had to put the two single beds together and stuff their suitcases under the bed, share one cupboard and take turns in the bathroom. It was the first time Anna had to share a tiny space with another person in nearly a year, and it brought back bad memories of the tent on the Polish border with no personal space, no privacy.

Esther was a compliant roommate who made herself as accommodating as she could, but she was a tall, athletic woman - a strong skier and swimmer. She naturally took up space, whether she wanted or not.

They'd agreed Esther would spend as much time with Océane and Lili in their room as the three were best friends. It meant sneaking down the stairs unnoticed as Madame Paul had forbidden the Jewish girls to visit the downstairs corridor where the other girls had their dorms.

The intrusion on her privacy and reflection time was hard on Anna. No matter she liked Esther a lot. She just needed to be alone.

On many occasions, she was on the brink of breaking her promise to stay, yearning to phone her uncle that she'd be coming home.

Le Manoir had been a mistake. Anna more and more felt like a misfit. But she endured, despite a renewed downward spiral into depression. She was just not the person to give up easily.

On a sunny afternoon in early September, the other girls were outside on a fieldtrip. Anna had claimed a headache, secretly hoping she'd have a couple of hours on her own to finally write back to Henryk. Heaving a sigh of remorse, she retrieved Henryk's two short letters from her bag and reread them.

Biatogóra Airbase, 21 May 1939

Dear Anna,

Miss you. Hope you're well. Weather's cold here. Still no spring. Aircraft repairs and reconnaissance flights. Keep safe.

Love,
Henryk

AND THE SECOND LETTER.

Biatogóra Airbase, 20 June 1939

Anna,

Another month gone. I haven't heard from you. Thinking of you. Can't come to London right now. Stay strong.

Yours, Henryk

The brief sentences were more like telegrams than letters. They had arrived – one month apart - when she'd been in the throes of sorrow over her mother's death. She'd read his letters over and over, weighing every word, desperately seeking the connection they'd had when in each other's presence. It hadn't been there.

The first letter had been sort of warm, his best attempt at letter writing. The second had shown signs of not knowing why she hadn't replied to his first one. It was cooler, no longer calling her 'dear' or signing with 'love'. As if she was the one who'd broken their chain by not writing back.

Or had she read too much in it? Sending letters a month apart could be just Henryk's style. Deciding to stick to a fixed schedule to fulfil his promise. Whatever the truth was, her mental turmoil and her insecurity about his continuing feelings for her had put off replying longer...and longer.

UNTIL NOW.

Le Manoir, Lausanne, Switzerland, 2 September 1939

My Dearest Henryk,

I hope this letter finds you well, and I apologize for the silence that has stretched between us. The past few months have been an emotional whirlwind for me. After my mother's passing, I found myself in a deep grief which I struggled to overcome. I retreated to a finishing school in Switzerland to heal and find some solace.

I want you to know that your presence during that difficult time meant the world to me, and I'll forever be grateful for your support. Please forgive me for not reaching out sooner; my depression kept me from doing all the things I once enjoyed, including writing to you.

I miss our conversations, your smile, and the warmth of your presence. I long to hear about your life, your adventures as an aviator, and how you've been coping with the warmongering that has arisen. We're cut off from news of the world here, as the headmistress doesn't allow radio listening, but some of the dire situation in Europe trickles through. Anyway, I hope you can find it in your heart to forgive my absence.

Henryk, I cherish the moments we've shared, and I want to rekindle our relationship. The thought of us growing apart pains me deeply, and I hope you feel the same way. Please tell me about your days, your dreams, and your hopes for the future.

I am gradually finding my way back to myself, though the school in Lausanne disappoints. It's more about table setting and dinner conversation than a real study. As soon as I'm back in London, which I hope to be in just one more month, I'll once again focus on my academic future. I'm still planning to go to Oxford next year. I believe that with your friendship and support, I can face the challenges ahead.

Please write back soon, my dear Henryk. I eagerly await your reply and the chance to rebuild the bond we share.

With all my love,
Anna

NOW IT WAS time to reread this letter at least a dozen times to see if it had everything she wanted to say in a loving way without sounding too needy. Unsatisfied with the result, but seeing the girls scramble back up hill for afternoon tea, Anna resolutely folded the letter and stuffed it in an envelope. She'd walk to the post office after tea and post it. No retracing her steps now.

THE NEXT DAY, *3 September 1939*

"Anna, Anna, come downstairs to the library. It is war, oh my God, it is war!" Esther stood in the doorway, red-faced with huge, frightened eyes.

"War?" Anna didn't understand. "Where, how?"

"War with Poland. Great Britain and France have declared war on Germany because it attacked Poland. Madame Paul called everyone downstairs to listen to the news on the radio."

For a moment Anna sat too dumbstruck to get up and follow Esther. Her brain refused to understand the message. Until the enormity of it sank in and she clasped a hand over her mouth not to scream.

She'd just sent Henryk a letter but now it would never arrive in his hands. All he'd feared had come true. He was flying his plane to fight Hitler. He would crash and die. Why hadn't she seen it coming sooner and sent that letter months ago? At least he would have known she still loved him. Now he would never know.

It was all over. For Anna this message was hugely personal, and she couldn't see the bigger picture of war in Europe. She could only see Henryk. Henryk was in the war. Henryk was the next person she would have to mourn. But she couldn't mourn any longer. She'd lost too many loved ones already. She had to become numb to the pain.

"Tell Madame Paul I'm still suffering from my headache. I need to lie down. I'll come down later."

"Are you alright, Anna? You look white as chalk."

"Yes, yes. Go. I'll be fine." She'd never told Esther or anyone else at Le Manoir about Henryk. Let them think she was just upset by the idea of war.

The next thought that flashed through Anna concerned Uncle Benjamin and her father, both former residents of Poland. She needed to go home. Now! Be with them. And wait for a possible letter from Henryk if he were to send another one. He would never know she'd been tucked away in Switzerland. He'd be looking for her in London.

In a hurry, Anna started to pack, randomly throwing her few belongings into her suitcase, leaving her books behind. What was the use of reading fiction anymore? She'd give her favorite volume to Esther. Daphne du Maurier's *Rebecca*. Somehow the sweetness and innocence of the unnamed narrator of the book reminded her of soft-hearted Esther.

But when she was done collecting her luggage, she sank down on the bed. To phone her uncle she had to go downstairs. The only telephone the students could use was in Madame Paul's office where she strictly monitored all in and outgoing calls. Facing Madame Paul's likely refusal to make the call made Anna lose her nerve.

"What nonsense," she scolded herself out loud. "She's in the library, just go into that pompous office and make the phone call. No matter what she says or does. She has no power over you anymore. Esther will likely need to go home, as well, so my promise is no longer valid. I can finally leave this place. Go home."

THE NEXT DAY Anna slipped into the backseat of the Black Renault to be taken to the station and board the train back to Paris. To her surprise, Esther was already sitting in the car.

The scene at the school had been so chaotic the day before with the girls flying apart like frightened chickens that she'd lost sight of Esther who'd stayed the night with Océane and Lili.

Even Madame Paul had lost her composure, constantly dabbing her eyes and giving confusing orders to send all the students home to their parents. There had been no supervision, and all classes were cancelled on the spot.

Only Filippo remained his usual unfathomable self, driving to and from Lausanne station to drop off girls leaving for home.

"Which train are you taking?" Anna asked, while Esther waved a white handkerchief out of the window to Océane and Lili who still stood in the school courtyard with their arms around each other's waists. Esther closed the window and blew her nose.

"My parents emigrated to Norway a couple of months ago, so I'm traveling on the same train to Paris as you. From there I'll go to Le Havre to take the ferry to Oslo. Is it alright if we travel together?"

"Nice!" Anna smiled and she meant it. Her alone time was done. Apart from her deep concern for Henryk, she looked forward to going home. She'd barely had the decency to shake Madame Paul's hand. But she had and withdrawn it as quickly as she could.

Anna had already forgotten Le Manoir. The school and its horrible school mistress had left no lasting impression on her. But Esther was alright. Esther was nice. Much nicer than she, Anna, would ever be.

Because Anna had decided she was done with emotions. She was done with feeling deeply, mostly pain. From now on she would arrange her life in such a way, she couldn't get hurt anymore. If she got the message Henryk was killed, she was prepared. It would take all her might to keep that ring of iron around her heart, but she would manage it.

ANNA ADAMS HAD ONCE AGAIN REINVENTED herself.

32

FRIENDS IN HIGH PLACES

Two weeks later, 18 September 1939

The news of war with Poland had spread a blanket of uncertainty over London. Though no outward signs of active battle were taking place in the streets - pubs and restaurants opened their doors at the normal hours and there was no food scarcity - the carefree days of the interwar period were over.

The heart of all Britons, but certainly that of the Londoners, was filled with trepidation first, then resolve second. The skies, once the realm of chirping birds and pleasure aircrafts, now echoed with the ominous drone of air raid sirens and the distant rumble of military aircraft.

Londoners hurried about their daily lives with a new sense of purpose. Passengers on double-decker buses carried stern expressions instead of exchanging lively banter. And in the tube stations, the people talked in hushed voices, discussing the pros and cons of joining the war for a distant country on the Continent. The scars of the Great War were torn open.

Blackout curtains started appearing in windows, casting a gloomy shade over the city at night. The streets were dimly lit with only a few strategically placed lamps to guide pedestrians. Shop windows displayed signs like "Air Raid Precautions" and "Keep Calm and Carry On". A constant reminder of the invisible but real war that was taking place.

Sandbags lined the entrances of government buildings, and children practiced air raid drills at schools. Gas masks were distributed to citizens, becoming a common sight even in the hands of the youngest Londoners.

Yet, amidst the tension and fear, there was an undeniable sense of unity. Londoners from all walks of life banded together, forming a collective spirit of resilience. Strangers became neighbors, and communities looked out for one another. BBC radio broadcast messages filled with hope and courage. Once again, the indomitable spirit of the British people shone through.

London's parks and green spaces, once filled with leisurely picnickers and strolling couples, transformed into training grounds for the Home Guard. Men of all ages, some too young to have fought in the Great War, practiced drills, determined to defend their homeland.

Despite the blanket of uncertainty, London's cultural scene persevered. The West End theaters continued to stage plays and musicals, offering a brief escape from the grim reality outside. Jazz clubs and dance halls were alive with the rhythms of swing music. The need for temporary respite from the threat of war was great.

London in September 1939 was a city on the brink, a place where the past collided with an uncertain future. It was a time of sacrifice, resilience, and the unwavering determination of its people.

ANNA WAS SITTING at her uncle's breakfast table reading *The Times* with her black coffee. She was too skinny and solemn, but serene. Uncle Benjamin had gone out to work as if everyone still needed diamonds. Well, probably they did.

Her return home had been marked by contentment. To see her

uncle, her father, and sleep in her own Rosewood Suite. Yet, she was scanning the job postings. With the war going on she needed to make herself useful. Just selling antique books to customers was not how Anna envisioned passing the war period.

But what to do without any qualifications. She spoke several languages, but German wouldn't be in use now. A secretarial post perhaps? She circled a couple and decided she'd ring them later.

I can't type but I can learn it, she pondered.

HER UNCLE'S car stopped in front of the house and Anna checked her watch. How strange he was coming back in the middle of the morning. She hoped he wasn't sick or anything. But before she could wonder about the cause of his return, he was already in the room, still in his fur lined black coat and wearing his homburg.

"Anna dear, do you have an evening dress? I have a soiree tonight to which I can bring a guest. You said you're looking for a job. There will be plenty of interesting folk there who could give you a leg up. Interested?"

Anna looked doubtful. "I'd love to come, uncle, but I don't have an evening dress. Can't I just wear my black mourning dress?"

"No, the invitation says dress suit for men, floor-length gown for women." He threw a bundle of pound notes on the table. "Get yourself a dress. Don't make it too flashy but do chose one of the diamond chokers from the display cabinet. I'll send Charles to pick you up at seven. I'll meet you at the entrance of The Savoy Hotel, as I have back-to-back meetings all afternoon. The event is held in The Savoy Ballroom. You'll love it."

IN HER BLACK satin dress with a warm stole around her shoulders and her uncle's diamonds around her neck and wrist, Anna slipped from the back seat of the Rolls Royce feeling all graceful and grown-up. Mrs. Whitman had done her best to curl Anna's dark hair and pin it up. The glasses were left at home. Her cheeks and lips prettified with a bit of rouge. The high heeled pumps were uncomfortable, but even having to adjust her step added to the excitement of the evening.

Her uncle was waiting for her at the hotel's entrance, standing very straight and spruced-up in his tailcoat and striped pants.

"Anna, you look like a movie star," he greeted her and put his arm through hers, "I'll have to keep a steady eye on you, or you'll be whisked away by one of the notorious London dandies."

"Don't worry, Uncle. I can stand my ground and I don't have the least intention of being whisked away."

"Heard anything more from Henryk?" As always, her uncle was quick to read her mind. Anna shook her head.

"Hmmm," he replied. "Bloody war. But he's no fool. He'll take care of himself. Now come and have a nice evening and forget the war for a night."

As Anna entered The Savoy Ballroom, her eyes widened in awe. The opulence and grandeur of the venue was something she'd never seen before. Maybe in pictures in magazines, but not for real.

The ballroom was an artwork of elegance and luxury, a true reflection of London's high society. Crystal chandeliers adorned with hundreds of candle-shaped bulbs hung from the ceiling, casting a myriad of starry lights over the guests in the room. The walls were painted with intricate gold leaf detailing, and the polished parquet floors gleamed underfoot.

The atmosphere was alive with the buzz of conversation and laughter. Anna, though dressed appropriately, felt both out of place and exhilarated in this sea of impeccably dressed guests.

Uncle Benjamin, clearly in his element, guided his niece through the room with an air of confidence, introducing her to influential figures from the worlds of politics, finance, and society. Names with Sir and Count and Baroness weren't off the air and Anna's analytical mind stored them all, trying to find the connections between them and where she might fit in.

Because, like her uncle, she belonged here. She belonged in the world of brilliance, if only outwardly. She couldn't help but notice

Winston Churchill in deep conversation with a group of admirers, his signature cigar in hand, his voice carrying a tone of determination.

"Here, have a glass of champagne, but only one." Her uncle accepted two flutes from a passing bartender and handed one to Anna. "Drink in some confidence first. Then I'll tell you who to approach for a good job."

The champagne was fizzy and delightful. And it worked its magic. She soon felt her strained nerves relax. While her uncle talked to a bald man with a formidable belly and a gold chain tightened over it, Anna's attention was soon drawn elsewhere.

Across the room, a tall and expensively-dressed gentleman with sandy blonde hair caught her eye. His blue-gray gaze, filled with an air of mystery, locked onto hers. What impudence to stare at her like that! But at the same time a rush of curiosity and intrigue swept through Anna as their gazes continued to explore each other. She couldn't help feeling her heart skip a beat. He stood out by the sheer force of his looks. And he was British to the core.

Wondering whether she was drunk already and seeing too much in his gaze, she wanted to ask her uncle who this handsome stranger was and if he had any idea why the man was looking at her with such intensity.

But her uncle, temporarily, had no attention for her, only for business. Anna wondered if the staring stranger was one of the London dandies he'd warned her off.

As heightened sensations do, she became aware how the music from the orchestra filled the room over the chant of voices and tinkling glasses. Violin-heavy melodies created a warm backdrop to the evening's festivities.

The urge was stronger than her will. Once again, she directed her gaze across the room to see if the intriguing man had lost interest in her. He was talking to an older woman with similar features to him. His mother?

Before Anna diverted her eyes, as if she was intruding on their privacy, she felt them both looking in her direction. Through half-downcast eyelashes, she saw the mother frown. Then she said something with resolve while tapping her son's arm with a closed fan. All the while he held his gaze steady on Anna.

A mix of nervousness and anticipation wound around Anna's heart. She'd entered an unfamiliar world with new rules. An eager learner, she was thirsting to learn the game of attraction. This evening in the lavish Savoy Ballroom seemed *the* place where chance encounters could lead to unexpected beginnings. She was ready to embark on a journey that could change her life. Anna wanted another life. Very, very much.

"Anna dear, this is William... I mean Mr. Thorne. Mr. Thorne basically runs the administration for Chamberlain's War Cabinet. He's chums with both Chamberlain and Churchill. And he's looking for a new staff member." Her uncle's words broke the spell, calling her back to the reason she was in The Savoy Ballroom in the first place.

Mr. Thorne, the man with the impressive belly and gold chain, had an equally impressive baritone voice as he greeted her. He shook her hand, which was like a clamp around her fingers. Then looked her up and down. His eyebrows flashed as he gave her another once over.

The way men look at women at these parties, Anna couldn't help thinking. So different from how she'd been brought up. Clearly a nice dress, a bit of cleavage and one's hair done up gave men permission to inspect every inch of a woman they could lay their eyes on.

But Anna had no time to ponder the predator and prey theme a second longer. Mr. Thorne started firing questions at her as if she was at an interrogation. The paradigm shift from flirting to job interview made her feel more intoxicated than she really was. Her brain wobbled while her heart fluttered. Mr. Thorne might be crude ogling young women, but he was also highly intelligent.

"Done any data filing? Typing? Analyzing charts? Adept at telephone calls? Hostessing? Done any recruiting business?" he boomed, using his stubby fingers to emphasize the job requirements. And when Anna didn't immediately answer, added, "well have you?"

Anna shook her head, peeking at her uncle whom she assumed to be disappointed at this. Mr. Thorne, however, proved a man not easily deterred.

"My friend Benjamin assures me you're a bright button. My own eyes can see as much. Also speaking several languages is a plus. I'd say, come by my office tomorrow and we'll do some tests to see how far you can stretch yourself to fill the position. Would that work for you, Miss Adams?"

"That would be wonderful, Mr. Thorne, thank you so much for the opportunity." He was intense, but jovial and if her uncle approved of him she should try to stay in Mr. Thorne's good books.

After another head-to-toe examination, Mr. Thorne announced, "that's all arranged then. See you tomorrow at ten. Your uncle will give you the details. Now go and enjoy the party, Miss Adams." And with that she was dismissed but with a new job in sight.

33

JOINING THE WAR EFFORT

The next day - 19 September 1939

"Charles, take the young Miss to William Thorne's den."

In no way could Anna have imagined "William Thorne's den" to be the place of her first job interview. Why her uncle hadn't told her that her possible future employment was at a secure and secret location underground, she didn't know. She had to find out by herself.

Charles, who needed to go back to "the Master" as he called Mr Bittermann, showed impatience at Anna's hesitance. Dropping her off at the curb, he pointed to the stairs at the side of the Treasury building.

"Just walk down those stairs, Miss, and ring the bell. There's nothing to it."

But Anna was stranded in the middle of Whitehall. It seemed like such an irregular place for a government office to be underground. Charles turned down his window and growled, "didn't the Master explain, Miss?"

Anna shook her head.

"Mr. Thorne's office is in the same buildings as the Cabinet War

Rooms. They're actual underground bunkers, right underneath the Treasury building."

"Alright. Now I understand. Thank you, Charles."

The adept-but-antsy chauffeur didn't wait for her reply. He was already manoeuvring the large Rolls back onto the road.

A bulldog of a concierge opened the door for Anna. He had the appearance of a bouncer at a nightclub with his wrestler's arms and out-of-joint nose, but he smiled at her with not very clean teeth. As soon as she'd stepped over the threshold, he locked the door behind her with a lot of juggling of his enormous keyring. Then the grin returned to face her.

"Good day, Miss Adams. Identity papers, please."

Anna's cheeks colored. As instructed to all residents, she carried her papers on her, but since the war she was even more self-conscious of the German stamp in it. *Why couldn't she just be British and no longer exposed to hostile glances?* But the concierge handed back her papers with a straight face.

"Follow me, Miss Adams."

They passed through dimly lit corridors, that were constructed in such a maze Anna feared she would never find her way out on her own. Women in navy-blue ladies' suits and men in tweeds hastened past them from one brightly lit office to the next, doors were opened and closed, hushed voices talked and somewhere a radio announcer forecast spells of rain for the City.

Sounds echoed off the walls, and the smell was musky and smoky. Ventilation was scarce thanks to only small, square vents in the ceiling.

Eyeing the smart women's suits, Anna felt out of place anew. She had chosen a tailored, forest-green dress that she hoped exuded professional charm. Her dark hair was neatly pinned back, and she wore her late mother's simple strand of pearls.

The pearls gave off a soft gleam under the dim fluorescent lights. If was as if her Mutti was with her in that weighty moment. Her practical low-heeled pumps clicked on the stone floor. Just when she thought they must be in the center of the earth, the concierge announced, "Mr. Thorne's office."

The Mr. Thorne, who sat behind a solid oak desk piled high with papers, was a very different one than the one Anna had met the day before, wearing a dress suit and drinking champagne. His heavy-set body was squeezed into a tight black suit and his face wore a stern expression as he was immersed in reading a file with a red 'Top Secret' stamp on the cover. A forgotten cigarette smoldered in the ashtray in front of him. Preoccupied as he was, he didn't hear Anna enter.

She looked around the office, not wanting to disturb him, shifting her weight from one pump to the other. Though the low-ceilinged, rectangular office breathed simple functionality, the atmosphere was dense with the weight of secrets and decisions shaping the course of that distant war.

The office had no windows. Mr Thorne's desk was at the far end, facing the door. One wall was plastered with maps of all the countries in Europe, each map marked with colored pins and cryptic annotations. The opposite wall had floor to ceiling cabinets. A coatrack stood next to the door and on the other side a small table, where a radio crackled softly, broadcasting the latest news from the Polish front lines.

After what felt like an eternity, Mr. Thorne looked up from his paperwork, his sharp eyes locking onto her like a hawk on its prey. She'd seen that piercing look the evening before. Mr. Thorne not only ascertained the weight of secrets, but also that of his personnel. Anna withstood the inspection, only just.

Without a word, still processing what he had been reading and what clearly was of the utmost importance, he motioned for her to take a seat in the leather-backed chair opposite his desk.

"Miss Adams, you made it to the nerve center of the British military and government. How brave of you." A narrow smile slid over his clean-shaven face, and Anna saw he was tired. His eyes drooped. Mr. Thorne wasn't young anymore but how old she couldn't guess.

"I did, Sir. I'm glad the concierge escorted me, as it was quite a maze."

He ignored the remark. It was time for business. "Your Uncle Benjamin spoke highly of you. He tells me you are an exceptionally fast learner and proficient in several languages." His voice was gruff but with an underlying curiosity.

She nodded, her nerves threatening to betray her composure. "I am, sir. I graduated from St. Paul's Girl School with top marks and over the summer I did a finishing school course in Switzerland where I brushed up my French. Naturally I speak fluent German because ... uh... I was born there."

Mr. Thorne leaned forward, his gaze unrelenting. "I saw that in your file, yes. Born in Hanover, of Polish descent. You speak Polish?"

"Only rudimentary, Sir, but I could quickly learn it, if that would help."

"We'll see about that later. For now, we conduct most communication with France as our main ally, so French is a must. And about your German background. I advise you not to share that freely. Won't make you many friends. It's that I trust your uncle and know about your family's situation, but we're very alert to German spies as you can imagine."

"Yes, Sir, I hope to naturalize as a British citizen as soon as possible."

"Don't count on a fast procedure there, Miss Adams. The Home Office isn't keen on handing out British citizenship to anyone at the moment. But we'll apply for it. Don't worry."

"Thank you, sir." Anna felt a weight fall from her shoulders, "I'm eager to contribute to the war effort in any way I can."

"We are in need of individuals who can adapt quickly and keep our operations discreet. The war effort requires dedication and discretion above all else. Can you handle the pressure, Miss Adams?"

She squared her shoulders, her determination shining through. "I'm willing to do whatever it takes, sir."

The interview continued. First Mr. Thorne probed Anna's knowledge of languages. He spoke very decent French and German himself.

Then he tested her ability to decipher codes, scrutinizing her adeptness and swift control of the word puzzles.

"Are you willing to work long hours in these underground war rooms? Little fresh air, not the best of food and bad light?" His eyes watched her carefully.

"I am, sir. With each question you put before me, I begin to comprehend the importance of this work. I understand it is not easy, but I suppose it is very gratifying to know that we make a difference. Even if my contribution will be miniscule."

"Bravo!" Mr. Thorne actually clapped his flabby hands together and only then Anna saw a ring. There must be a Mrs. Thorne waiting long hours at home for her husband.

As the interview drew to a close, Mr. Thorne leaned back in his chair, a glimmer of approval in the hawk-like eyes. "Miss Adams, you may lack the formal qualifications we normally look for, but I sense a determination and potential in you that is rare. Welcome to the war effort. You'll start as a junior clerk, and your first assignment will begin on Monday. Your salary will be 12 pounds per month. But if you show the potential I think you have, I'll increase it swiftly. I want to keep a close eye on your progress, so you'll get an office in this corridor. There will be two other girls working in the same office, Betty and Ghislaine."

Anna's heart swelled with pride and apprehension. She had just taken her first step into the secret world beneath the streets of London, where the fate of nations was being decided.

"Oh, thank you, Mr. Thorne. I'll do my very best. I promise."

"One more thing - can I call you Anna? The girls all ask to be called by their first names. Makes them feel younger, I suppose," he winked.

"Certainly, sir. I also prefer Anna to Miss Adams." She thought of the horrible Madame Paul with her Mademoiselle Anna and had the shakes. She was just Anna.

"Give my regards to your uncle. I'll meet him in the Club on Thursday."

"I will, sir. See you on Monday, Sir."

"Eight o'clock sharp! I'll ring the concierge to see you out. And then I need to hurry getting through this pile." He made a dramatic sigh to the stack of confidential files on his desk.

"Good luck, sir, and thank you again."

As Anna followed the chunky concierge to the exit, she felt like she was walking on air. How proud her uncle would be of her. Oh, and her father. But could she tell Vati, or was this a secret assignment?

Still with her mind on the new job, she collided with a man who was just about to descend the steps she'd just taken. She wanted to apologize, staring straight up into the eyes of the sandy-blond stranger from The Savoy Ballroom.

34

MEETING THE COUNT

"Miss Adams? You? Here?"

The man grabbed her by the elbows, so she wouldn't topple down the stairs. Anna was perplexed.

"You know my name?"

How? The uncovering of her identity pushed the likely-accident he'd just saved her from to the background.

"Of course I know who you are," he smiled under his wide moustache, the same color as his hair. His hands were still holding her arms tightly, "any young woman who enters a soiree with the esteemed Mr. Bittermann is in need of further investigation."

Anna scrutinized him. Upper-class English, groomed to the nines, the self-confidence of a successful man. Just the smear of lipstick on his cheek and the skittish look in the blue-gray eyes seemed out of touch.

Don't read anything in it, she told herself. *You're like a spymaster already when the job hasn't even started.* She wrenched herself free, stood taller on her low-heeled pumps, pushed the slipping glasses up her nose.

"And who might you be, sir?"

"My official name is Count Roderick Macalister, but my friends call me Roddy. I'm the MP for the Kensington Constituency and I was on my way to see if Winston had time for a chat. Does that satisfy your curiosity, Miss Adams?"

"You mean Winston, like Winston Churchill?" Anna couldn't help being impressed.

"Yes, of course. Winston's a family friend. I wanted to pop my head around his office door, because Mother is throwing a party at our country house in Surrey this weekend. She asked me to person-ally invite Winston and Clementine."

Ah, Mother. The disapproving woman with the fan.

"I'll better be on my way, Mr. Macalister." She made a movement as if to leave, but he grabbed her elbow again.

"Wait, Miss Adams, such a chance encounter demands a further familiarization, don't you think? Winston can wait. I'm not even sure he's around, as I didn't announce my visit. How about a coffee at Café Royal? My treat!"

"Café Royal?" Anna repeated.

"Ah, of course, you haven't been in London that long. So, you haven't been to Café Royal yet? An absolute must!" He was already directing her towards Regent Street.

"What more do you know about me?" Anna dragged her heels, which stopped the Count in his tracks. He adopted an innocent expression.

"I didn't spy on you if that's what you think. We don't see many new faces at these soirees, so I had to know who the stunning, young woman draped in Bittermann's diamonds was."

Anna wasn't won over so easily. The reminder of how widespread the Grynszpan stain was and the danger it caused made her suspi-cious of people, especially politicians, digging into her origins. The Count seemed to sense her unease and waved it away.

"With my hand on my heart I pledge only private interest in you, Miss Adams. You're safe with me. Absolutely safe!"

His words came out with a little too much emphasis on his noble intentions, but Anna wanted to believe him, awed by this dashing, important aristocrat who was bending over backwards to make her feel special.

"Alright. Just a coffee," she agreed with a small nod. If she was to study complicated personalities to understand their motivations, why not start with this mysterious man?

The Count held open the gilded door to the fashionable establishment at 68 Regent Street. Anna had heard her uncle talk about this popular destination for socializing, dining, and entertainment. She was to enter that world now and she felt herself grow as they stepped inside.

Just one word suited to describe the interior of the Café Royal. It was magnificent. Anna found herself entering another fairy-tale world after The Savoy Ballroom the evening before. Her heart beat faster with delight.

I'm made for this world.

She admired the ornate chandeliers, the gilded mirrors, the plush furnishings. The decor was a combination of Art Deco and Belle Époque, her favorite styles.

"Are you sure you just want a coffee?" the count broke into her enchantment, "if it is your first time here you should try The Grill Room. The Royal is renowned for all its dining areas, each equally unique, but The Grill Room is top of the bill. Absolutely one of the finest dining experiences in London. Gourmet French and European cuisine."

Anna shook her head, "I'm not one to eat large meals but thank you for the offer."

"Alright. Your wish is my command, my lady, but please promise me I may take you to The Grill Room soon."

"We'll see." It sounded coyer than she meant.

They took seats in a cozy booth with burgundy leather upholstery and a shiny mahogany table with a bouquet of fresh flowers in the middle. Side-by-side, they sat on the padded bench and though the Count sat quite near to her, Anna kept her distance, putting her handbag in between them.

Taking in the ambiance around her, it was obvious The Royal was a social hub for celebrities, politicians, and high-society members. She recognized various faces from photographs in The Times. And by reading their body language and non-verbal communication, there was no doubt they had all made it in life.

This was a café exclusively for the elite and well-to-do. Maybe one day she'd fit in here as well.

"Which kind of coffee would you like? French, American, Turkish, Italian? They have everything."

Anna felt the count was studying her as she studied the ambiance around her.

"Just a black coffee please. I'm not that posh."

The Count snapped his fingers and within seconds a waiter trotted to his side. He ordered her coffee and a Courvoisier for himself. As soon as their drinks arrived, he took a large gulp from the short-stemmed, bulky glass and relaxed within seconds.

"I'm sorry to have been so insistent on getting to know you. You really strike me as someone different. Different from other young women. Quite serious, but also with a touch of genius."

Anna turned to face him, found his expression sincere. She laughed. "Genius? I don't think so. I'm just an ordinary girl."

The glasses went higher on the bridge of her nose. She was glad she'd made an effort with her makeup for the job interview. Yet it felt surreal to sit next to this high-class gentleman in the middle of London, sipping expensive coffee from a porcelain cup, seemingly not having a care in the world.

Her mind wanted to wander to Henryk, but she refused to go there. It was too difficult, too painful. And she wasn't doing anything wrong with this man.

"May I ask what you were doing at the Cabinet War Rooms?" the Count asked, offering her a Players Navy Cut.

"Sorry, I don't smoke."

He lit a cigarette with an engraved silver lighter and blew the smoke away from her face.

"And?" he asked.

"I went for a job interview with Mr. Thorne. And I was accepted. I'm starting on Monday as a junior clerk."

"Attagirl! Well done. Having friends in high places is always a benefit, Miss Adams. You may also reach out to me, should you ever need help or advice about something." He pulled out a business card from his breast pocket and put it on the table. The rectangular card had curly, gilded lettering and the family coat of arms, a heraldic shield in crimson and deep blue.

"Thank you. I will." The coffee was better than any she'd ever had before. Anna also tried to relax against the soft back of the bench.

"May I call you Anna?" His eyes flashed with a light-hearted gleam, "of course, you may call me Roderick or Roddy."

"Alright," Anna agreed. "I'm not keen on formalities myself. So, what does an MP do?"

Roderick laughed but not wholeheartedly. "A whole bunch of things but it mainly means I have to be at the House of Commons a lot. And represent Kensington as my constituency. My father, the old Count is in the House of Lords. My future." He rolled his eyes, "it is quite boring work, to be honest. I live for our estate in Surrey, hunting and riding. I'm much more an outdoorsman. And for skiing in Switzerland in the winter and sailing and diving in the still unspoilt Bahamas in the summer."

To Anna it was impossible to imagine such a life. The flash of a memory, of rain and a tent in the pitch dark, babies crying. She pushed the flash away with force. This was her life now. Maybe one day she'd be skiing in Switzerland and sailing in the Bahamas.

"You know what," Roderick's face lit up as he finished his glass. "Why don't you and your uncle come to Mother's party this weekend?"

Anna looked doubtful. "I don't know if my uncle ever goes away on weekends. I haven't even seen him take a day off in the year I've lived with him."

"All the more reason for Mr Bittermann to kick his heels up for a bit. But more importantly, would you like to come?" The intensity Anna had seen before was back in the blue-gray gaze.

"Yes," she heard herself say, "thank you for inviting me. I'd love to come, but I'm not sure I have the proper clothes."

"Proper clothes? Don't make me laugh. My mother's get-togethers are so informal. And for the evening just bring that dress you wore yesterday to The Savoy Ballroom. Picture perfect, I'd say."

"I'll ask my uncle then."

"Tell him Winston and Clementine will no doubt show up. They love a good party. And your uncle is quite chummy with both, I believe. Now I'll be on my mission to make the Churchills come and you go on yours to persuade your uncle. You've got my number. Make sure you phone me tomorrow. I'll be staring at the phone all day in hopes it will ring."

And with that, he paid the bill and helped her into her coat. Anna was so overwhelmed by the sudden invitation, she'd forgotten all about her new job.

"Oh, but I can't come, Roderick. Not this weekend. I'm starting my new job on Monday. I need to be well rested."

Roderick looked at her as if she had lost her mind. "Well rested? Anna dear, learn one thing from me. When in London, you live in the fast lane. The weekend is the weekend and Monday will come by itself. You can dance all night and do your job at eight in the morning. There's nothing to it. Believe me. I live this life."

"I'll try," Anna promised, giddy with anticipation. Within two hours her life had become as exquisite as the heart of a wild rose.

35

THE FINAL BLOW

To Anna's surprise her uncle said a wholehearted 'yes' to the Macalister party at Briarwood Manor in Dorking, Surrey. She had a faint feeling he only agreed to accompany, to make her happy and help his only niece up the ladder of society. But that was not what he said.

"Why not go to Dorking this weekend, Anna? You know I don't like to be idle but who knows, I could even close some business while others go shooting or dancing. The ones that stay behind are most likely the dry souls like me," he smiled, but his amber gaze was serious.

"Thank you, Uncle. I vow I'll make the weekend as agreeable as possible for you so you might consider taking off some time more often."

"Don't count on it, Anna dear. This war business in my Poland makes folks frenzy all over Europe. They all want to exchange their money in the bank for gold and diamonds. I've never been busier in my life. I actually have to travel to Antwerp and Amsterdam myself next week to buy more new stock. All my staff is either traveling or closing deals. It's never been this crazy."

"Do think of your health, Uncle. And I wish I could come with you to look after you but with starting my new job on Monday, I have to stay put."

"You take care of yourself, Anna. I'll be fine." But her uncle's face had aged in the past months. The lines next to his mouth had deepened, his eyes were sunken and he'd lost weight as his appetite had suffered from the stress of work.

DORKING TURNED out to be a typical British village, picturesque and hidden in greenery. Though it was late September, the trees still had their full crown of leaves, and a warm fall sun escorted them along the winding country lanes. Briarwood Manor lay amidst the rolling hills, full of historic charm, only 45 miles from London. No doubt the Macalister family had chosen this village due to its scenic surroundings and accessibility to the city.

Anna saw a manor built in the classic Tudor style appearing at the end of a gravel driveway. Half-timbered walls with white stucco and dark wooden beams. Oh, what timeless elegance and charm! The steeply pitched roof with ornate gables and tall chimneys made it a house fit for a jigsaw puzzle.

"Look at those gardens, Uncle," she exclaimed enraptured. "So beautifully landscaped with perfect lawns. And the flowerbeds! Oh, I'd love to be a gardener here." Her eyes went to the charming rose garden on one side of the manor. Roses of various colors still bloomed in abundance.

Uncle Benjamin was lost in thought. His eyes were focused on the grandeur around him, but his mind was clearly elsewhere.

"Come, Uncle. Let's announce our arrival." Anna tapped his hand and he seemed to awake from his ruminations.

"Let's do that, dear." He got out of the car with some difficulty. "Charles, pick us up on Sunday evening at 6. And take the rest of the weekend off. God knows how much I make you drive me around England all hours of the day and night."

"I will, sir. Enjoy, sir, and Miss Anna, you too."

. . .

THEIR ARRIVAL HAD NOT remained unobserved. As soon as the black
Rolls made a U-turn in the courtyard, Roderick's tall, elegant figure
leapt around a corner of the house. In shirt sleeves and suspenders
he appeared to be truthful to the low-key apparel he had told Anna
the country weekend was going to be. With hands outstretched, he
came their way, his sandy hair windblown, his corduroy pants and
rubber boots showing he'd been working in the garden.

"Mr. Bittermann, what an absolute honor to receive you at Briarwood Manor. Mummy didn't want to believe I'd actually managed to
persuade you to come, well through your lovely niece, of course."

Anna watched the interaction between the two men as they shook
hands. There was a reservation in her uncle that she knew well.
Uncle Benjamin wasn't comfortable on unknown territory. But
Roderick would have none of it. He was determined to win the
diamond trader over with his politician charm. Why Roderick Macalister was extra friendly with her uncle mystified Anna. Did it have
something to do with her?

Their host's attention shifted to her. "Anna, you're looking ever so
charming in that gray dress. Really sets off your eyes. Do come in.
Leave your luggage here. Gerald, our butler, will instruct one of the
footmen to pick your valises up in a second. Absolutely safe here.
Come, Mummy will be waiting with the tea. You're the first guests to
arrive so we'll have plenty of opportunity to catch up on the latest
titbits of news."

An excellent conversationalist, he led them not through the front
door but around the house and onto the terrace. Two silky-white
English setters raced across the lawn and around a pond with water
lilies, yapping and jumping up against Roderick's legs.

"Down Bella. Down Boris!" He ordered sternly. The hounds
reacted immediately and laid down on the stone terrace, paws
stretched out, looking up with mournful eyes at their master.

"They're usually better behaved," Roderick apologized, "but our
gamekeeper is ill and they're not getting enough exercise."

Anna took in all this information while letting her gaze glide over the neatly trimmed lawn. It was a perfect spot for outdoor dining and relaxation, with wrought-iron tables and chairs placed under a pergola covered in climbing ivy. Neither she, nor her uncle spoke, but they nodded at the required moments in Roderick's monologue.

"Sorry about taking you through the backdoor. Before you came, I was trimming the rose bushes, so I need to leave my muddy boots here. All that recent rain has soaked the flowerbeds."

Neither Anna nor her uncle cared through which door they entered. The view of the garden was spectacular enough. Roderick kept conversing without their help. "I think Mummy was talking to the chef earlier, so she may not have noticed if you rang the bell." Anna wondered why there was no mention of the old Count, his father. It didn't seem polite to ask.

Through the pantry and a hall, where Roderick left his boots, he took them to a drawing room overlooking the sloping garden. It was a spacious and elegant room with large windows that let in plenty of natural light. It was furnished with plush, upholstered chairs and sofas, antique tables, and a grand piano. Persian rugs covered parts of the polished hardwood floors.

"Do sit down, please. I'll call for Mummy to join you while I wash my hands. Excuse me for a moment." He left uncle and niece sitting in two armchairs facing the outside view.

Anna peeked at her uncle, saw the dark circles under his eyes. She was worried.

"Are you alright, uncle? You look tired?"

"I'm fine, Anna. I just wish he'd cut the cackle for a moment. That's it with politicians. Their sport is talking, training the tongue muscles. Quite tiresome."

Anna felt an urge to burst out in laughter. Uncle Benjamin said the funniest things, but he was right. The door opened and a lady so elegant she could have stepped right out of a magazine swooped in. It was the lady with the fan. She whirled towards them all perfume and frilly lace. Ice-blue eyes in a fine face, an immaculate figure in an expensive haute-couture dress.

"Ah Mr. Bittermann, Miss Adams, *Ricky Dahling* said you'd already arrived. What an awful, awful entrée. Thousand times my apologies. We have some sick staff, one after the other and it's been absolute chaos since we arrived here yesterday, but that's no excuse to leave esteemed guests like you on your own."

They both rose to their feet to greet her. Draping her small hand in that of Anna's uncle, she purred, "I'm Annabelle Macalister. Please just call me Annabelle. No formalities here." And with a coy smile on her coral lips she asked, "May I call you Benjamin, or perhaps Benny?"

Anna cringed. This was certainly setting her uncle on the wrong foot, but Benjamin Bittermann was not only a gentleman, his long experience in the diamond business had also made him very adept at handling quirky clients.

In his booming voice, he replied, kissing the powdered hand, "I've never been called Benny in my life, Annabelle, but if you call me Benny, I will have to call you Belly."

She giggled with laughter, high and shrill with long exhales.

"Belly? Oh, Benny that's hilarious! You are going to be my absolute favorite guest today! Don't leave my side. Not for a minute."

The ice-blue eyes rested on Anna and the expression changed like a cloud shifting in front of the sun.

Aha, another Madame Paul, Anna couldn't help thinking. The disapproval made the corners of the coral lips go down very fast.

"Anna, dear," she went back to purring. "How lovely that you met my *Ricky Dahling* in what I understand was almost a romantic collision. What a chance meeting and leading all to this!" Her hand hardly touched Anna's and was quickly withdrawn.

"Thank you for the invitation, Mrs. Macalister. Yes, it was a chance meeting."

"It's Lady Macalister, *dahling!*" She tapped Anna's arm just like she had done her son's arm in The Savoy Ballroom.

"Lady Macalister, of course." Anna smiled, feeling the muscles of her face freeze.

The mercurial Lady clapped her hands.

"Tea!" she bleated. "Where in Heaven's name is that lazy maid and where's *Ricky Dahling* gone? I hope they haven't run off together."

Another blast of shrieky laughter followed. Anna didn't dare to look in the direction of her uncle for fear she wouldn't be able to control herself. Of course, she'd read in many of her novels how eccentric the British aristocracy could be, but she'd never experienced them up close.

Soon they sat with a delicious high tea after the lazy maid had been scolded and Roderick had reappeared in clean clothes and with his hair combed. The tea was excellent with fine sandwiches and scones, but Anna felt she had to restrain herself and not overeat. Her uncle hardly touched his plate.

More guests trickled in, among them Clementine and Winston Churchill who immediately got all the Lady's attention. She seemed to have completely forgotten she'd declared Benny her favorite guest.

Uncle Benjamin didn't seem to regret his lost status to the least. Anna was glad to see him strike up an animated conversation with the Churchills. Roderick had been right. The cordial friendship between them was obvious.

Anna stayed close to her uncle, not confident enough to move freely among the unknown guests. Observing the liveliness of the discussions, the delicious snacks, and the fashionable ladies was enough of a feast for her eyes. She wasn't drawn into her uncle's conversation, but at intervals got friendly nods from both the Churchill couple.

"Not remotely charmed by Chamberlain's appeasement stance," Churchill observed, "least of all as it concerns your former home country, my friend. The Poles are our allies."

Her uncle nodded, "thank you for saying that, Winston. I agree. Poland isn't seen as an important country to most Western Europeans, but it may well play a pivotal role now we're engaged in war."

"What's more," the First Lord of the Admiralty grouched, "everyone with a functioning brain knows Hitler's *Lebensraum* won't stop at Poland. Dear God, all these soapbox orators in Whitehall are just ostriches with their heads buried in 'never again.' Papering over the cracks of the Great War isn't going to get us anywhere. The very safety of this country will be at stake soon. That Nazi Führer will want all of Europe for his damned *Lebensraum*. Mark my words."

"Oh Pig, do me a favor. Calm down and cut out the politics for one afternoon. We're at a party, dear. A party!" Clementine interrupted, using her husband's pet name to call him to order. "You're boring our lovely hostess and no doubt that sweet thing at Benjamin's side. His niece, I believe?"

The sophisticated Mrs. Churchill gave Anna a sweet smile.

"You're right, Cat. Not good for my heart to work me up this way." Winston puffed merrily on his cigar, reciprocating with his own pet name for his wife. He studied Anna through the haze of smoke. The gaze was intense but had none of the predatory quality of other men.

"Got the job helping William I heard?" He remarked, taking a sizable sip from his whiskey.

"William, sir? Oh yes, Mr. Thorne. I'm starting on Monday."

The light-blue eyes with small red veins in them continued to take Anna's measure. He nodded his broad face with only a slight movement of the chin.

"Built of the same fine wood as your uncle. Let me give you some unprompted career advice, Miss Adams. Keep your eyes open, keep your ears open. Don't talk too much. Don't dismiss anything as trivial and you'll swiftly rise in the ranks of the secret services. Mark my words."

"Thank you, sir." Anna made a light bow, feeling all flustered by the great statesman's compliment.

"Now go and enjoy yourself, Miss Adams. No use hanging around with the old folks. We'll look after your uncle." He gave her a wink through the cigar smoke.

Anna looked around the room. She needed to socialize but with whom? It felt so much easier to stay in the vicinity of Uncle Benjamin's familiar posture. Just when she had mustered the courage to step across the room, she heard Roderick's highbred voice behind her.

"Ah, my little wall flower. Time to hijack you and introduce you to some friends." Not wasting a moment, he grabbed her by the elbow and steered her through the open patio doors to a group of young people, who stood laughing and smoking on the terrace. The outside table was laden with empty bottles of champagne and scattered glasses. The crowd was rowdy.

"Let me introduce you to my best friends."

Anna was whizzed around the group until she thought she would be dizzy. Everyone asked her questions through one another. *Where are you from? Where did you meet? Where do you live? Do you know such and such?* Clearly intoxicated, they all jumped on her. Some of the men even kissed her cheek as a greeting, while the women looked at her as if she was from another planet. It was a very confusing and unpleasant introduction. Anna didn't remember a single name of the at least dozen drunkards who were introduced to her. To her horror she saw Roderick was as drunk as the rest.

She didn't take part in the banter. Didn't need to. One loud-mouthed joke or remark followed on the other, erupting in the inevitable salvo of laughter and side-splitting. Anna just stood there in their midst, feeling as if she was indeed from another planet. Maybe this lifestyle wasn't what she wanted after all.

Oh Pearl, you'd help me out if you were here, she brooded, now and then smiling to show her goodwill, but spying for an opportunity to excuse herself and go back inside. Back to the safety of Uncle Benjamin. She'd much rather listen to interesting political discourses than this boozy brouhaha.

Roderick probably sensed her unease and slipped his arm around her waist, pulling her towards him. Now she couldn't escape anymore. Ironically enough the need disappeared. His proprietary gesture alleviated some of her discomfort. He held her, he found her important, he wanted her to be there. So, Anna drank the cham-pagne. Laughed at the risqué jokes. Enjoyed Roderick's steadfast arm. She wanted so much to belong. Somewhere.

Soon, they flocked inside for the evening meal that was to be served in the grand dining room. The dining room was as opulent and richly decorated as the rest of the manor. Dark wood paneling along the walls with hunting trophies and family portraits above them. A long, beautifully-laid dining table that could seat at least thirty people. Three huge chandeliers hung above the table, casting a warm and inviting glow.

Anna was instantly taken back to her table setting classes at Le Manoir. This was what Madame Paul had meant. She could see the finishing school lessons had been applied to the rule here. The position of the glasses, the distance between plates and cutlery. Maybe it hadn't been the waste of time and money she'd labeled the experience. If she was to move in these circles.

Smart, forward-thinking Uncle Benjamin!

Anna sat in between her uncle and Roderick. Lady Macalister presided at the head of the table. There still was no sign of Lord Macalister and no mention of him either.

As the evening progressed, one exquisite course followed the other, with a new wine at every change of plate. Anna had never known that so many different wines existed.

Somewhere between the last main course and dessert, a subtle change took place. She noticed that her uncle's smile had become strained, his face pale, and his breathing labored. Concern etched across her features, she leaned in closer to him, whispering in a worried voice in his ear.

"Are you feeling alright, uncle?"

He placed a reassuring hand on hers, looking sideways at her with a soft, loving gaze. "Don't worry, my dear. Just a touch of fatigue. I'm not used to so much partying and rich food."

"Do you want me to ask if you can withdraw? I've had quite enough myself." There was hope in her voice. She was tired too. He shook his head. "I'll sit out the dessert and the coffee. Then we can excuse ourselves."

But the discomfort on his face spoke volumes. He was not well. Anna's heart sank, she panicked. Turning to Roderick she whispered, "can you fetch my uncle a glass of water?"

Roderick snapped his fingers and the footman hastened to their side with a water carafe and a glass. Anna had only eyes for her beloved uncle as his teeth clattered against the crystal. Her anxiety grew and grew. Uncle Benjamin had prided himself on never having been sick one day in his life. Only broke his ankle as a young boy being thrown off his pony. That was it.

THEN, in an instant, the world seemed to stand still. Her uncle's eyes widened, and he clutched his chest with one hand, gasping for breath. Panic rippled through the room as the partygoers realized something was terribly wrong.

Roderick acted without hesitation. Dragged her uncle from his lopsided position at the table and lay him on the floor, unclasping his belt and undoing his tie. Anna, her heart pounding with wild fear, knelt beside him, tears streaming down her cheeks.

No, no, no, Uncle Benjamin. No, no, no!

In the distance she could hear someone calling for help, but in that moment, all that mattered was being with her uncle Benjamin as his strength faded before her tear-filled eyes.

His grip on her hand weakened, but he whispered with all the love he could muster, "Take care ... of yourself, ... my sweet... Anna... my desk... will."

And just like that, with Anna's trembling hand in his, Benjamin Bittermann's heart gave its last beat. The room fell into silence as the realization of the tragedy unfolded, leaving Anna in shock and grief too big for her to fathom.

ANNA'S LIFE, forever marked by loss, had received yet one more blow.

GONE WAS HER WISE, wonderful, worshiped Uncle Benjamin. The one who'd picked her up and gave her strength. The strength she needed.

GONE.

36

THE RESCUE

Ten months later - Chelsea, London, 20 July 1940

Anna sat in the windowsill of her new apartment off Flood Street with her legs pulled in. Her chin resting on her knees. She was exhausted. The movers had just left. The move was over. A new episode of her life about to begin.

Behind her were unpacked boxes and rolled-up carpets. The furniture, the few pieces she'd taken from her uncle's house, stood in their allotted places. There were only the bare basics, a coffee table, a sofa, and a sideboard. She hadn't even wanted to take these, but Mrs. Whitman had insisted, and Anna didn't have the heart to upset the grieving housekeeper even further.

Her amber eyes followed the pedestrians on the pavement, school children wearing gas-masks and women with shopping bags peering anxiously at the sky. War had come to almost the entire European Continent. Everyone expected Britain to be next. Hitler had announced the invasion. So far, he'd been victorious, overrunning every country his Blitzkrieg army invaded.

Operation Dynamo had saved half the British forces at Dunkirk, the success of it putting Winston Churchill at the helm of the government. But real war was still intangible to most Britons. They hadn't been invaded in almost 1,000 years. Would it happen now? And what would it be like? It was a threat so vast and so frightening, the citizens went about their business with solemn faces and skittish steps.

Anna didn't care about the war. Her own life had been a war of losses for two years. No escape, just ache. The sensations of fear and worry that surrounded her left her untouched. If Hitler decided to come, she'd deal with him when he was at her doorstep.

She had nothing to lose. Nothing to win. Life was one day strung together with the next. She was glad when she made it to her bed every night and was granted a few hours of sleep. These days, sleep - oh sweet eye-blink of oblivion - was not even granted to her, interrupted as it was by air raid sirens and nightly visits to her landlady's cellar underneath the flat.

To Anna, war meant work and work meant focus and focus meant a moment of relief from pain and grief. Relief from the immense hole in her heart nobody could mend.

But, as of today, in her own flat with a new job luring, she decided her heart no longer needed mending. The past was the past. The future her own creation. Today was a fresh start, a new beginning at a life in secrets.

And secrets would be all Anna carried about herself. The secret of her hidden past, left behind in Hanover, on the Polish border, in Mount Street, London. No one in her future should know otherwise than that she was thoroughly British. A well-to-do woman with a mysterious past, who was considering the proposal of a man from one of the best aristocratic families in England, Roderick Macalister.

Dressed in her navy WAAF uniform, her makeup and hair immaculate, the high heels her new statement, Anna was fully prepared for her introduction into the top-secret organization Churchill had launched only a week earlier.

It operated under the neutral flag of Inter-services Research Bureau, but its real name was Special Operations Executive, also not a name that disclosed its true objectives. Anna's months working for intelligence officer William Thorne had shown her the length and the breath of the British Intelligence Services and the rivalries between them.

SOE was going to stir up the status quo and would make its own enemies, high and low. The rebel role of SOE played perfectly into the hands of what Anna believed she wanted to achieve. Be part of an organization that, as yet, was unprecedented in history, established by her ultimate hero, Winston Churchill. She adored all he stood for - innovation, boldness, daredevilry. Just what Anna needed to become, rain or shine.

THE DOORBELL RANG. Her taxi had arrived. Zigzagging around the boxes, she grabbed her coat and bag and walked down the flight of stairs, adroit on the high heeled pumps. The tightness of the new navy skirt meant some adjusting as she descended but she soon had the knack of it.

Though the SOE headquarters were on Baker Street, just one block away from her flat – the new location chosen with that objective in mind -, she'd decided to call for a taxi as it started to drizzle. In no way did she want to show up for her talk with Sir Reginald Owens looking like a drowned cat.

The Chelsea apartment in close proximity to the new job meant morning and evening walks, which would be her only relaxation.

The block where 'the very secret office' was located was nondescript. She was led in by a concierge who could have been a brother of the one at the Cabinet War Rooms. This porter also had the muscular build and menacing expression of a night club bouncer.

"Miss Adams? Papers?"

He led her up one flight of stairs to the first floor. Doors to office rooms were kept open. On first sight nothing seemed out of the ordinary. If top secret activities took place here, they were good at hiding them in plain sight.

Officers, men and women, some in uniform some in civilian clothes, walked from room to room, shared files, smokes or a joke. Just like Anna had experienced in her first job. Office clerks had a peculiar longing for hanging out together, also after office hours. But not Anna. And certainly not in this job.

"Sir Reginald is ready to see you." A young blonde woman, clad in the same blue WAAF uniform as Anna's, rose from behind her desk, one manicured hand demonstrative on her hip, her lips very red and shiny.

"I'm Dolly," she said in the Cockney accent Anna had once thought was the height of Englishness. She had no longer the wish to master it. The blonde continued when Anna didn't introduce herself. "I'm Sir Reginald's secretary. You must be Anna. I hope you agree to us using first names. We will all soon get code names so we're more identifiable by the different country sections. Isn't that exciting?" The pretty blue eyes shone with excitement as if Dolly was Cinderella allowed to go to the ball.

Dolly was all pretty and nice. Anna smiled back. A smile not completely genuine but indistinguishable from real for the unpractised eye.

"Thank you, Dolly. You can call me Anna." The hand that shook hers was soft and squishy. Dolly was one of the girls that would fit in perfectly in Roderick's circle, Anna thought. Popular, cheerful, sociable. All the things she was not, no longer wanted to be. And yet, Roderick still insisted on seeing her.

Shaking thoughts of sociability and the pursuit of suiters off, she followed Dolly to Sir Reginald's office at the end of the corridor.

"Why does everyone refer to the Major as Sir Reginald and not Sir Owens?" Anna asked.

Dolly eyed her with an amazed look on her powdered face, the eyebrows raised to her hairline, "Gosh Anna, I have no idea. Never thought of it. We just all call him Sir Reginald. Maybe because he was in the Navy?"

Hardly, Anna thought but didn't say. She already knew the man she was going to speak with. In fact, he'd personally invited her during a visit to his friend, Mr. Thorne. Anna's former boss had been far from pleased SOE was stealing his star employee away from him.

Sir Reginald's deep baritone voice had sounded loud and clear while Anna had listened in from her own office next door to Mr. Thorne.

"I need a trustworthy assistant who is discrete, can break codes, recruit staff, and understands what the hell it means to keep her mouth shut. Not many women can."

"I need her too," Mr Thorne had retorted.

"I suppose you don't want the British bulldog to get involved, Will?" It had sounded like a threat.

Nice friend, Anna had thought.

"Okay. I give up," Mr. Thorne had lamented. "You can have her, Reggie. Just treat her well. The girl's gone through hell and back. Give her a break now and then, even if she doesn't want one."

"Thank you, Will. I owe you one. I'll treat her like porcelain, I promise."

Seconds later, Sir Reginald had put his large, neckless head around the door of Anna's office.

"Would you like a raise, a uniform, and a real job in the secret services, Miss Adams?" He had boomed.

"Do I have a choice?" Anna had replied curtly, as she didn't like to be traded as a piece of cattle at the market by these two high-ranking officials.

"No, not really," Sir Reginald had replied in complete honesty. He'd stepped inside and closed the door. "Mr. Churchill has given us the order to set Europe ablaze. It means we're going to train secret agents who will be dropped into the occupied countries, mainly France. I will be responsible for Section F, and I need you to help me with the selection procedure. Interviewing and testing possible candidates. Are you in, now?"

"Let me talk to Mr. Thorne first, please. I can't just walk out on him. I'll let you know." Anna pretended she had not overheard their earlier conversation.

Sir Reginald had stared at her for a long moment. She hadn't been able to read the expression in the rather bulging, gray eyes but understood he wasn't pleased when he said in an undertone.

"You've got a nerve, Miss Adams. That may be a good or a bad thing. I'll find out."

THAT FIRST CONVERSATION WITH "THE BULLY," as she secretly called Sir Reginald, flashed through her as Dolly led her to his office. He was sitting behind his desk, shouting in a telephone receiver. His fleshy face was rather red and the tone of his voice far from friendly.

"I told you. Just bring him here. I don't care De Gaulle thinks he owns the fellow because he has a French passport. For heaven's sake he was born in Brixton. He's as British as fish and chips."

Anna stood in the door opening, already turning around on her high heels. She'd much rather work in a lower paid, less profile job for kind Mr. Thorne than for this bully.

"Anna!" It was an order from the Navy commander she couldn't ignore. She turned around once again. He was holding a plump paw over the receiver while he called to her. "Give me a sec, please and I'll explain. Take a seat."

Dolly obstructed the door opening, her apparently signature move of hand-on-hip. Anna was caught between two fires. She caved in and sat down in the chair opposite Sir Reginald's desk. He trumpeted his last warning into the receiver. "Tell him I'll call the culprit back. Don't let him escape into French claws."

The bang with which he replaced the receiver didn't bode well for the phone's longevity.

"Miss Anna Adams, welcome. Coffee, tea?"

"Coffee please, black."

"Dolly, make that two black coffee and water and a Rennie for me. Blasted stomach plays up in this stress."

"Coming, Sir Reginald." Dolly was all happy sunshine as she walked away. Anna and Sir Reginald sat watching each other like two bulls in the ring.

"Apologies for that, Miss Adams. But may be best you see my bad side first. I can be impatient when opposed. And these blasted intelligence services all follow their own rules and refuse to cooperate.

We're all fighting the same enemy but make worse enemies at home."

You'll get nowhere near cooperation rubbing people the wrong way, Anna thought.

Reginald Owens may be an impatient bully; he was also a shrewd intelligence officer.

"You think a lot but keep it to yourself, don't you, Miss Adams? A quality I admire and wish I had more of."

"Silence has its advantages," Anna remarked, accepting the coffee from Dolly.

When Dolly had left and closed the door, Sir Reginald said in a softer tone,

"Pray tell me, Miss Adams, how can a young woman of barely twenty be so wise and mature?"

"You read my file, Sir Reginald, you know all that made me." She said it in an offhand way, but it took some effort. She didn't want him to ask the hard things. Knowing him and his position he would probe, though.

"Yes, I did."

He didn't continue. Silence followed until Anna looked up from staring into her coffee cup. The eyes she met were hard but not completely without feeling. He'd leave it up to her what she wanted to say or whether it remained written words in her file. For now.

"So, I understand you are financially independent, Miss Adams? You want to work but don't need the job?"

"Correct. My uncle provided well for me." Her voice was clipped.

"I, too, knew Mr. Benjamin Bittermann. Who didn't, in genteel London?" It was the first time Sir Reginald sounded sincere. Anna swallowed. She didn't want to hear it. She heard it everywhere she went. Her fantastic, all-around loved and admired uncle. Don't touch him. He was *my* uncle. *My uncle alone.*

Again, she had the eerie feeling Sir Reginald could read her mind.

"I don't want to make this any harder for you than it already is. Let's only focus on the security part of your file I'm afraid I need to address. You have a father who goes by the name Jude Adams. Correct?"

Anna nodded.

"Your uncle also provided for your father in his will. He was able to buy the bookshop and the apartment on Greek Street."

Anna sat straighter. Without upping the volume, she said with ice in her voice. "Have you read my uncle's entire will, Mr Owens? Are you that unscrupulous? So, you probably also know he left Mount Street to his housekeeper and provided amply for his chauffeur and his staff. Are you satisfied now with your probing?"

"Anna!"

She was shocked at his addressing her by her first name. The sternness in his voice and face was unambiguous.

"I told you only the security part. Let me get to that."

Anna withstood his glaring gaze. It took more than a retired bully of a Navy officer to scare her these days.

"Your father and you are still not British citizens. You may have adopted the Adams last name, the Grynszpan name also still circulates on your entrance documents to the UK. That is not only a threat to you but to the entire SOE. That – and only that – is my concern."

"Then why did you ask me to join SOE? I was quite happy working for Mr. Thorne."

"Because you're the best of the best Anna Adams. We simply have to find a way to remove the Germanness from you. Not one person inside or outside SOE may court the thought you are a double agent for the Nazis."

"I'm not a double agent. I'm not a Nazi," Anna said in a biting tone. "Mr. Thorne applied for my citizenship months ago, but according to him the Home Office is dragging its heels."

"True. I investigated the case myself."

"What do you want me to do about it?" The whole naturalization procedure aggravated her.

"Two things. Both hard. Both a sacrifice." He was candid, which was not his best side, Anna thought.

"Being?"

"As long as you work for SOE, have no contacts with your father. That way no one can trace you to your past." Anna felt a cold ring close around her heart. Though she only saw her father sporadically because she couldn't stand seeing his hurt reflected in hers, not seeing him at all was cruel. Cruel for them both.

"I'll try. What's the other?"

"Marry the Count. Exoneration accomplished."

"I'll think about it." It sounded just as prim as she intended.

"Good. I thought we could get down to business," he sounded weary, and she knew it was on her behalf. He did care. Did his best to treat her as the porcelain he'd promised Mr. Thorne. She wouldn't crack, though. Not now. Not ever again.

"Now over to the work...," he announced, and they were in safe waters again.

BACK IN HER unpacked flat with a new job that meant a tripling of her salary but also two major sacrifices, Anna was still churning her thoughts. How could she let her father know she couldn't see him for no apparent reason? For an unknown period, perhaps years? The painful sacrifice was front and center on Anna's mind. She wasn't even thinking of a possible marriage to Roderick.

The doorbell rang. Anna's heart made a jolt. She checked her watch. Eight o'clock. Who could that be? Roderick never showed up on her doorstep unannounced. Mostly he let his secretary make their appointments. On rare occasions, he phoned himself.

Suddenly Anna panicked. Her father! There was something with her father and she had just been contemplating not seeing him for God knows how long. What a wicked, wicked girl she was!

"Anna!

"Pearl?"

"Yes, I thought I'd come to your rescue. If the mountain will not come to Muhammad, then Muhammad must go to the mountain. Or something like that. I don't remember."

Pearl hugged her tightly. Anna succumbed to her friend's strong arms. It was so good to see and feel her only friend at a moment like this.

"Well, are you going to invite me into your domain, my friend, or must I stay on your doorstep forever?"

"Sorry. Lost my manners. Do come in," Anna laughed unrestrained. "It's just so good to see you, Pearlie. How have you been?"

"*Comme ci, comme ca* as we French say. I missed you too."

Anna gave Pearl a quick tour of her modest flat before they sat on the couch with a cup of tea. Suddenly it dawned on her. Her face became one radiant smile. As if the sun broke free after a long, long period of rain.

"You *are* my rescue, Pearl! Why don't you come and live with me here in Chelsea? We'll have so much fun. You can have the spare bedroom. We would just have to share the bathroom, the kitchen, and the living room."

Pearl looked at her with her pixie face askew. "Live with you, huh? I like that. Let me think it over."

"You never think things over," Anna laughed, "just say yes. You told me you wanted to move out of your parents' house. This is your chance!"

"Seeing through my mature stance already," Pearl laughed heartily. "My standard answer these days is 'let me think it over.' Blame it on being turned down from taking part in the Olympics *and* from joining the RAF. My ego took such blows, I've taught myself to pretend I think before I act."

"I beg you not to think and just to act," Anna countered.

Pearl picked up her teacup and toasted with Anna's.

"Here's to Anna and Pearl in Chelsea. Long may they live."

PART V

THE SPYMAKER

LONDON 1942-1945

37

JUST FRIENDS

Two years later - RAF Northolt, April 1942

The sun painted bright rays of sparkling lights on the aircraft that stood parked on the side of RAF Northolt's two landing strips. Like allies clustering together, British Spitfires lined up with Polish Lublins, French Blochs and American Lockheeds.

The respective fighter pilots had also gathered in the officers' lounge for a chat and a smoke. A few hours of respite before the bombers and the reconnaissance flights over mainland Europe would continue.

Anna and Henryk sat nestled in a secluded booth in a corner of the lounge, the insignia of their uniforms reflecting in the glow of the ambient, electric lighting. Around them the lounge was alive with the murmur of conversations, the clinking of glasses, and the occasional burst of laughter from fellow officers. The air was infused with the rich aroma of cigars and the lingering scent of freshly brewed coffee.

They soon would have to part ways. But not yet. Please stretch time a little longer. Sir Reginald and SOE could do without Anna for an afternoon. It wasn't like she ever took time off. Then Henryk's mechanic appeared at their booth, a diffident expression on his young beardless face.

"Your Lublin is checked and refilled, Major Pilecki. Ready for you if you're ready."

"Coming in a minute, Gaston."

"Sure. Take your time, Major." With a quick bow he left them to their intimate conversation.

The interruption made Anna check her watch. Unwillingly.

"Golly, we've been talking for an hour. I honestly thought it was only ten minutes." How hard would it be to not hear that beloved voice anymore, the warm timbre, the short almost staccato sentences that had their own rhythm. How could she do without that wondrous smile, those eyes that really saw her. His strength, his confidence. How?

"I know." He reached out a hand and put it over hers. Not the one with the engagement ring. "You and I could talk for a lifetime. But time's not on our side." A shadow darkened his handsome features, the blue eyes took on a gritty glitter. "We have a war to fight, Anna. A life to live. And not to die."

It sounded almost prophetic. Anna shivered. They were coming to the end and there was no way out. She could still hear the echoes of his aviation tales, the urgency and camaraderie among the aviators, as if she were right there with him in the cockpit. She'd been with him in the cockpit once and their tale had started there. But now, this time, their story was laid to rest. The story of 'Anna and Henryk' was already fading into a memory.

She fought her tears. The man across the table from her was the only person in the world who still made her feel she had a human heart, that she was a woman. But when – not if – he walked out of the officer's lounge and flew away from her, there would be no more 'them.' Never again.

Her heart ached with so much pain. She couldn't let it happen. He was her last refuge. Swallowing hard, she tried to tell him, but the words got stuck in her throat. No sound came. Her brain said no. She had no right. She was engaged. She'd let him down. She'd have to live with the consequences. Just like he had said. She had a life to live. A life as Countess Macalister. She'd made her own bed and would have to lie in it. End of story.

"Anna, what's going on?" Henryk leaned in closer, his gaze locking onto hers with an intensity that sent a new shiver down Anna's spine. "Anna," he began, his warm breath brushing against her cheek, "We can't part like this."

"Ohhh Hen...ryk...," she sobbed, "I... I've been so stup...id. I lo..."

"Shhh!" He put a finger on her lips. "Don't say the word. I beg you."

"What am I to do?" she wailed, trying to keep her voice down so as not to alarm other customers.

"I've been thinking..."

Her eyes met his, their blue depths reflecting in the light that fell on their faces. The lounge's ambiance seemed to fade away as she focused on Henryk with all her force. Willing herself to cry no longer. Something was changing, there was an anticipation in the air that hadn't been there. She held her breath, waiting for his words.

"What if," Henryk continued, his voice lowered as if sharing an intimate secret, "we took a little break? Just the two of us? Escape from this madness?"

Anna's heart began to race, and she felt a surge of excitement. The thought of escaping with Henryk, even if only for a short while, filled her with a sense of longing she couldn't deny. Didn't want to deny. Her whole being screamed 'yes!'

Did Henryk know she was only engaged to Count Roderick Macalister as part of her cover, but her heart had never truly been his? He, Henryk "Hubal" Pilecki, was the love of her life. Always had been. But her brain forced her back on to Earth.

She hesitated, her fingers laced so tightly together, the engagement ring pressed into her skin. Her eyes shone but her mouth said, "Henryk, you know about my engagement. We can't just run away together."

He nodded, his eyes showing both understanding and affection. Reaching across the table, his fingertips brushed her cheek in a tender caress. "I'll never do anything to compromise you, Anna. I respect your commitments. We just both need a break. As friends. If you say yes, I'll arrange three free days next time I'm in England."

Anna closed her eyes for a moment, taking in the sensory details around them—the drone of voices, the clinking of glasses, the enticing scents that filled the air. She took a deep breath, then finally gave in to the temptation. "All right, Henryk. Where would you like to go?"

"Yorkshire."

Anna laughed, "why Yorkshire?"

"I've always wanted to see the Yorkshire moors. It sounds like heaven. Away from the war. No other people."

"Alright. I'll arrange it. Let's go to Yorkshire together. Just as friends, for now."

"I'll let Mr. Wilson know when I'm back. He runs this lounge. Give him your number so he can contact you," Henryk instructed. Anna looked apprehensive. Should it be her office number where she was most of the time, or her home number?

"Don't worry, Anna. I trust Mr. Wilson completely. And he's discrete. Whatever number you give him, he won't use it for any other purpose than I tell him."

A warm smile broke all the shadows on Henryk's face. She couldn't help but smile in return.

"Oh Henryk. I would never have thought this would happen in my life."

"Neither did I. It means a great deal to me. A very great deal."

Anna got up, straightened the skirt of her uniform. Henryk rose as well, tall, and manly in his aviation uniform.

"Au revoir," Anna said, "I must go and find Mr. Wilson. To give him my numbers and then he'll also have to ring a taxi for me." She held out her hand. Henryk took it and pulled her to him.

"Is a friendly embrace forbidden?" He asked, his chin resting on the crown of her head. She felt something slip into the pocket of her coat but had no idea what it was.

. . .

THE EMBRACE WAS BITTERSWEET. Anna could feel Henryk loved her as much as she loved him, but her engagement and the war tore them apart once again.

As they held each other close, the soft strains of a Glenn Miller tune played in the background, deepening the melancholy of their parting. Their hug was both tender and full of unspoken longing, a silent farewell to the love they couldn't fully embrace.

Anna's hand brushed against Henryk's overalls, feeling the rough fabric that had seen so much battle in the air. His arms around her were strong and comforting, a temporary refuge from the uncertainty of their promise to each other.

The lounge was filled with the chatter of fellow servicemen and women, but in that moment, it was as if they were alone in the world, grappling with the reality of their situation. Around them, no one seemed to mind their prolonged farewell. War demanded parting embraces of all kinds.

With a final, lingering touch, Anna reluctantly pulled away from him, knowing that duty and destiny once again set them on different paths. The look she gave him was solemn and sad, and she saw the weight of his emotions etched in his eyes.

The first to turn away, she walked off with unsteady steps. Outside the lounge doors of RAF Northolt, an uncertain future awaited her.

Would she ever see him again? And would they see Yorkshire together?

She reached inside her pocket. It was a Luger, a German pistol with a note attached to it.

"For A. May this keep you safe when I'm not around. Love H."

HE ALWAYS THOUGHT OF HER, even by giving her the oddest gift. Though in war time, it might be the best gift there was.

I LOVE YOU, her heart moaned. *I love you so much!*

38

THE CALL

6 weeks later - London, 20 May 1942

Anna was busy. Two female agents had just finished their combat and security trainings at the various SOE schools in the country. One of them, an Irish girl called Maureen Knight, was invited to come to Manetta's, the restaurant in Clarges Street in Mayfair for her final briefing with Anna that afternoon.

For the women, Anna had decided Manetta's was the perfect place to give her last instructions and go through the security checks. The restaurant was a lively enough place not to attract attention, but it also had secluded corners where she could quietly talk with the agents. They would – no doubt – be under great strain and it was nice to offer them a proper British lunch as a last farewell.

Maureen's training report from Beaulieu in Hampshire lay open on her desk. Anna was in her office, reading it with great interest.

∾

From: Training Facility STS 36
By: Captain L. Skilbeck

Date: 30 April 1942

Subject: Post-Training Report - Maureen Knight (Codename: Lara)

Agent Profile:

Name*: Maureen Knight*
Alias*: Lara*
Nationality*: Irish*
Physical Description*: Ginger-haired, 5'8 tall, athletic build.*
Training Summary:
Agent Maureen Knight, alias Lara, has successfully completed her rigorous training as a Special Operations Executive (SOE) agent. This report provides an overview of her training, skills, and performance during her time at the various Training Facilities but was compiled at STS 36, the finishing training school.

Skills Acquired:
Courier Training: Agent Knight has demonstrated exceptional proficiency in courier operations. She excels in maintaining cover identities, covert communication, and has developed a keen sense of situational awareness. Her background as a quick learner has been an asset in mastering the intricacies of courier work.

Wireless Operation: Agent Knight has displayed impressive competence in wireless communication. She is adept at setting up and operating wireless equipment, transmitting and receiving encrypted messages, and maintaining secure radio contact with HQ. Her technical skills and discipline make her a valuable asset in maintaining communication lines.

Physical Conditioning: Agent Knight's athleticism and strength of character were evident in her physical training. She is in excellent physical condition and has proven herself in endurance tests, combat scenarios, and parachute jumping exercises. Her daredevil nature seems well-suited to the high-risk missions she may encounter.

Personality and Behavior:
Agent Knight possesses a strong-minded and humorous personality. She has a quick wit that can defuse tense situations and build rapport with contacts. Her sense of humor serves as an asset in building trust and maintaining her cover identity. However, her tendency to take risks should be monitored closely to ensure mission success and her safety.

Parachute Jumping: One notable highlight of Agent Knight's training was her exceptional performance in para-jumping exercises. Her fearlessness, combined with her physical prowess, allowed her to excel in this aspect of her training. She is undoubtedly an asset when it comes to aerial insertions into hostile territories.

Recommendations:
Agent Knight is a valuable addition to the SOE team, with her unique combination of skills and personality traits.
Her quick thinking and humor make her an effective liaison with local contacts and resistance groups.
We recommend close supervision of her risk-taking tendencies to avoid unnecessary exposure in the field.
Another subject of attention is her accented French. In her cover story her Irish background is incorporated, but we advised her to immerse herself in French society and language to improve her proficiency and "Frenchness." Maureen Knight, alias Lara, has completed her training with distinction. She possesses the skills, determination, and courage required for covert operations behind enemy lines. Her abilities as a courier and wireless operator, along with her fearless nature, will undoubtedly prove valuable in her future missions. We anticipate great success for Agent Knight as she begins her operational assignments.
Security Clearance: Top Secret
Distribution: Top Secret
Signed,
Captain L. Skilbeck
Training Facility STS 36

ANNA WAS STILL PROCESSING the information and scribbling her own notes in the margin when the phone rang. She picked up the receiver absently, her mind on "wild" Maureen, SOE's first female agent. It had been a wonder the black apparatus had been silent for five minutes.

"FA, A speaking. How can I help you?" Using the code name for all in and outgoing conversations was now the norm.

"Miss Adams, it's Mr. Wilson from RAF Northolt."

A physical shock went through her tightly uniformed body. She was catapulted out of her concentration right into chaos. Unprepared for the jolt, her words stuck in her throat.

A quick glance around her office told her she was alone with Dolly, who sat typing at a tiny desk near the door. Anna gave her the go-away-I-have-a-top-secret-call wave with her hand. Dolly rose on the spot and flitted away. Luckily the social secretary was always more interested in an opportunity to smoke and flirt with male agents passing by than typing reports.

Anna returned her attention to the telephone with bated breath.

"Yes, Mr. Wilson."

"Major Pilecki is expected to arrive at Northolt at 7:00 tomorrow morning. He told me to let you know."

"Thank you, Mr. Wilson. I'll be there."

"You do that, Miss, and good day."

"Good day, Mr. Wilson."

She'd managed to sound level and composed. As if she was just dealing with one of the dozens of phone calls she answered every day. But her heart pounded, and her palms were sweaty. She'd arranged everything to perfection weeks ago, but now it was suddenly here...

With no idea how to get through the rest of the day without having a mental collapse, Anna steadied herself by gripping the ridge of her desk. Her hands trembled; the knuckles showed a sickly white through the tight skin, but the diamond ring glittered as never before.

It was suddenly too much. She wrenched the thing off her ring finger and buried it under a stack of papers in the drawer of her desk. She'd deal with that part later.

Forcing herself to concentrate on Maureen's report again, her sight became blurry, and her stomach protested. What was she doing? What was she thinking sneaking away to Yorkshire with Henryk? Everything she'd carefully built up to get away from her past now came crashing down on top of her.

I am not doing this. I am not going to RAF Northolt tomorrow morning. I'm going to phone Major Skilbeck to tell him I'm ready to see Maureen off. I'm going to phone Manetta's to reserve a lunch for two for tomorrow afternoon. I'm going home to Pearl this evening and won't tell her a word.

But it was all to no avail. Before she knew what she was doing she'd grabbed the black receiver again.

"Mrs. Gibbs, is the cottage in Helmsley available from 21 to 24 May?... Yes, my name is Mrs. Smith.... Yes, just for my husband and me... Yes, we'll bring our own car. ... We hope to arrive around 3:00pm. Thank you. Until tomorrow then."

The sweat was still on her palms. The forged identity papers resting on top of the engagement ring in her drawer. Sometimes working in the secret services had its perks.

"Anna, can you come here for a moment?"

As Sir Reginald's sonorous voice sounded from next door, she jolted in her chair.

"Now you'll get it," she murmured. Her shrewd boss sniffed his catch before it even showed its head. He was like a fox waiting on a rabbit at its hole. And she, Anna, was the frightened rabbit now.

Only now, Anna became aware Dolly hadn't returned to her post. Where was that pretty secretary when she needed her? She could have sent her in to Sir Reginald who had a weak spot for the girl and she herself stayed out of his sight when she most needed it.

Plastering her best smile on her face, Anna dragged her feet to the next office. She was relieved to see her boss preoccupied. The deep wrinkle between the gray brows showed he was dealing with a troublesome issue. Probably one of the agents under suspicion of being tracked down by the Gestapo.

"You called for me?"

"Yes Anna. I got an application from another female agent. Take the file with you and see if you think she carries the weight." Without looking up he handed her a slim file. "Now close the door behind you. I'm busy. Oh, and I won't be in the office for the next couple of days. Making a tour of the training schools. Hold the fort for me."

Anna swallowed. She couldn't. She wouldn't be there. She would have to grab the bull by the horns.

"Sir, I wanted to ask you something, but I see you're busy."

"Go ahead," he grumbled as he continued turning the pages in a thick security-stamped file, still with the frown.

"I wanted to ask if I could take Thursday and Friday off. I ... I want to spend some time with my roommate who... who will soon leave as well." The lie came out falteringly but at least it came out.

"Sure. Just make sure to cancel any appointments you may have until Monday. Promised Will Thorne I'd treat you like porcelain, so off you go. Just make sure that lazy bum of a Dolly has enough to type, or she'll be varnishing her nails and batting her eyelashes the whole day."

"I will, Sir, and thank you, Sir. You have a good tour."

"You have a nice long weekend, Anna. You deserve it. See you on Monday."

And with that it was done and there was no way back. As he was out of town, her boss wouldn't phone her flat and find out she wasn't with Pearl. There were no operational obstacles in Anna's way. It was as if the universe was in favor of her secret escape with Henryk, but her heart screamed 'danger'. Very loud and clear. Yet she wouldn't listen. It was too late to listen. She instructed herself as if talking to someone else.

Pack an overnight bag when Pearl's asleep and sneak out of the house before she is awake. Leave her a vague note about a sudden out-of-town emergency. Then deal with Roderick. Feign to suffer from a contagious bug, so you can't go to 'Blossom Time' in the Lyric Theatre with him on Saturday. The mention of a bug is enough to send him running to the hills.

LEAVING a trail of white lies behind her, Anna was at the steering wheel at 5:00 the next morning. She wasn't an accomplished driver, but London was quiet in the early spring morning and Mr. Davis from the rental company told her the Model-T Ford was easy to operate.

Even the birds hadn't awakened yet when she manoeuvred the black car onto the A40 at Shepherd's Bush. She was well underway to RAF Northolt and there was no turning back. By now, she didn't want to turn back.

39

WILDFLOWER HAVEN

Anna's heartbeats were like running footsteps in a dark alley as she stood waiting next to the airstrip at RAF Northolt, anxiously scanning for a Polish plane among the returning British aircraft. The early morning mist was cool on her face, but the anticipation of seeing Henryk again made her body go hot and cold at the same time.

The roar of an approaching aircraft made her breath falter. Intense joy filled her as she spotted his Lublin R-XIII descend gracefully from the sky like a silver-gray dove. Her fighter pilot had returned. Just to be with her.

A few moments after he touched down, Anna watched him emerge from the cockpit, his tall, muscular frame cutting a striking figure against the backdrop of the airfield. Henryk saw her and waved, before returning his attention to the mechanic rushing to his side. He exchanged some information with the technician, slapped him on the back and, slinging his duffel bag over his shoulder, strode towards her.

As he took off his flight helmet, a dark lock of hair blew up in the wind and a warm smile lit up his face. He looked tired but happy, the smile holding a mixture of relief and excitement as he approached her.

With every step he came closer, the years of their friendship flashed through Anna's mind. They had shared dreams and distress, forging a connection that transcended borders and time. She stepped forward, her heels clicking against the tarmac, as his blue eyes locked onto her amber gaze.

"Anna," he said in that Polish-accented voice that always made her heart flutter, taking her ringless hand in his. The warmth and familiarity of his touch sent an electric tingle through her.

"Henryk. You've come." Her voice was barely more than a whisper. There was no need to say more. Not then. The touch of their hands spoke all the words.

He nodded. Still holding hands, she directed him towards the waiting Model-T, where their secret adventure would start.

As Anna drove away from the airfield, she was unable to stop herself from stealing glances at Henryk in the passenger seat. The dawn had broken into a clear May morning, beautiful as the beginning of time.

And he was really sitting there. Every inch of his striking self. She drank in the strong profile with the angular jawline, the two-day beard, the dark hair tousled by the pressure of his helmet, and she found herself drawn to him as if pulled by a magnet.

For a long time, they didn't speak. Neither found the words as their minds raced backwards and forwards. Wondering what had been between them, what could have been, and what was now the great unknown.

Anna didn't find the silence oppressive but wasn't sure where his mind was at. If it was on her at all, or the long nights fighting the Germans from the air, or the short, sweet break he needed from battle.

The rolling green hills and antique villages of the English countryside passed by as they drove north. Henryk rolled down his window and the air inside the car filled with the fragrant scent of hawthorn blossoms. Anna inhaled the sweet scent and knew she'd always remember this moment in time. She, Henryk, the Model-T, and their unspoken love.

She stopped the car in a village called Selby. The hours of early-morning driving after a short night had taken their toll, and her stomach was making itself heard.

"Let's have lunch here."

"I'd love that."

But they kept sitting in the car as if a bigger force glued them to their seats, unwilling to give up the intimacy of being alone together.

This. This moment in time.

Anna's fingers gripped the steering wheel as if steadying herself. She was drowning in the turbulence of her emotions that swung from sheer delight to utter horror about what she was doing. To herself. To Henryk. To Roderick. And back again.

Henryk reached out and peeled her hands from the leather. He brought her trembling fingers to his mouth and kissed them.

"We'll be alright, Anna, if we put our trust in God."

She nodded. A knot in her stomach.

AS THEY APPROACHED HELMSLEY, Anna sat straighter. Henryk had taken over the driving since lunch, which had been a welcome break for her strained driving skills.

"It's the cottage over there, right on the border of the moors," Anna pointed. "Mrs. Gibbs left the key at the pub across the street."

"Just before closing time," Henryk observed. "Great timing."

Their destination, "Wildflower Haven," was a picturesque and petite cottage, nestled almost against the stile to the stretched-out moors beyond the stone wall. The cottage had two storeys and was constructed of local, grey stone that had weathered over the years, blending in with the moorland landscape.

The roof was covered with dark slate tiles that provided a stark contrast to the vibrant greenery of the moors. A white, picket fence encircled the cottage, framing the front garden. The garden was about to explode into a mass of early wildflowers, their colorful heads swaying in the soft breeze.

A stone pathway led to the wooden front door with a wrought-iron knocker. Both the path and the door bore the marks of countless visitors over the years. The windows were all adorned with delicate lace curtains, providing a homely atmosphere.

As they stood inspecting their secret abode, Anna felt a need to exchange more words between them.

"It's quite rustic, isn't it? I like it."

"It looks perfect, Mrs. Smith," Henryk agreed, not letting go of her hand as they headed over to The Moorside Inn for the key.

As they unlocked the door and stepped inside Wildflower Haven, Anna immediately felt enveloped in an atmosphere of warmth and comfort she hadn't experienced for a very long time. Perhaps not since her parents' house on the river Leine in Hanover, all those years ago when she was still a girl. And she felt like a girl once again. A girl and her best friend on an exploration of their domain.

Inside the cottage had the same rustic charm as outside, like a loving embrace from the past. Mrs. Gibbs had lit the fire for them, as it was cool inside despite mid-May. The flickering flames in the stone fireplace cast a cozy glow across the room, inviting them to draw closer both to the flames and to each other.

Worn wooden beams crossed the white-plastered ceiling, adding a touch of history and romance. The walls were white plastered as well, decorated with aquarelle paintings of moorland scenes.

A plush, overstuffed sofa and two armchairs were arranged around the fireplace, their floral upholstery echoing the vibrant wild-flowers outside. A handcrafted coffee table in the center of the seating area held a vase filled with freshly picked wildflowers, bringing the essence of the moors inside.

SUFFUSED in soft light filtering through the lace curtains, a square dining table in the breakfast nook was set for two. It was covered with a linen tablecloth, and decked with fine china, polished silverware, and crystal wine glasses, hinting at a romantic couple's-away retreat.

They wandered further. The kitchen, though compact, was a clean and charming space with exposed wooden shelves displaying vintage crockery and pots. A small, old-fashioned stove and a farmhouse sink completed the picture of domestic bliss. The scent of a freshly baked pie filled the air. Mrs. Gibbs for sure was a thoughtful host. Anna felt her mouth beginning to water.

Upstairs, the bedroom upheld the cottage's atmosphere of pastoral bliss. A wrought-iron bed with a floral quilt stood centerpiece, flanked by antique bedside tables. Through the lace curtains the afternoon sunlight cast playful patterns of light and shadow on the bed, the walls, the beams, the bare wooden floors.

Though Anna and Henryk explored in silence, in that enchanting bedroom far away from war and grief, the silence was laden with the dawn of love. Love permeated everything Anna felt, everywhere she looked. Wild and soft, raw, and real. Unspeakable love.

They looked at each other and she could see it in Henryk's eyes. At that moment she knew without a doubt. Henryk loved her like she loved him. But what to do with love now it was here? Now every corner of this rented cottage seemed to whisper stories of love and happiness, as if the very walls had absorbed the joy of countless couples who had sought refuge here.

"Come here."

Henryk opened his arms and she ran to him. No force in the world could have stopped her. No force in the world was stronger than that love. Love is eternal.

40

RODERICK'S THREAT

Four days later - London, 25 May 1942

"Where for the love of me have *you* been?" Pearl stood before Anna, blocking their small hallway, legs astride and hands on the hips of her overalls, the light eyes furious.

"I told you. I had work out of town. Don't be silly, Pearl. Let me pass. I'm exhausted." But Pearl didn't budge.

"Did you know that hoity-toity fiancé of yours threatened to kill me?"

Now Pearl had Anna's full attention.

"What do you mean... threatened to kill you?"

"He came bulldozing in here meaning to break down the joint unless I spoke up. He was sure I knew where you were, even after I repeatedly told him I didn't."

"Why?" Anna cried out. "I told him I couldn't see him this weekend."

"Yeah, but you apparently told him you were ill. Someone snitched on you, Anna. You were spotted at RAF Northolt sneaking off with you-know-who."

"Oh my God." Anna's legs collapsed under her. It was all too much.

Pearl was at her side in no time and pulled her up. With her arm around Anna's waist, she helped her to the sofa. Now a grin spread over the pretty features.

"Hell, Anna, I didn't know you had it in you but good for you. Just never lie to me again. Remember what we promised each other?"

Anna started crying.

"I'm so sorry, Pearl, of course I would have told you. But afterwards. How can someone have seen me and informed Roderick?"

"Maybe he has a private detective following you. Seems just the type of man to use such practices." Pearl shrugged, "anyway he was far from pleasant and really aggressive. Good riddance, I'd think. And yay to true love."

Anna dabbed her face and accepted the glass of water Pearl had poured her. "It's not as easy as that, Pearl."

"Why not? Roderick will now see you as damaged goods and break off the engagement. Easy-peasy." In Pearl's world right was right and wrong was wrong. "Now tell me where you two went."

In fits and starts Anna told her friend the whole story, leaving nothing out. Until she'd lost sight of Henryk's disappearing plane, that tiny silver spot in the vast blue sky. An open end. Open love.

Even Pearl was silent for a while, chewing on her friend's precarious love life. But the peace was short. The phone rang.

"Yes Roderick?" Anna's voice was calm. Pearl was now in the know and on her side.

"I want to see you straight away, Anna. No excuses."

"I can't see you right now, Roderick. I've just come home. I need a bath and a rest."

He sneered at her refusal.

"Tomorrow night. Not a day later. I'll pick you up from work at 6:00pm so you won't go off gallivanting again."

"Alright. Tomorrow at six. But for your information, I haven't been gallivanting," Anna said coldly. She agreed with him, though. Their fake engagement needed closure as soon as possible.

. . .

A STRAINED RODERICK picked Anna up from Baker Street the next evening. Without a word he led her to the waiting Rolls Royce and more or less pushed her onto the backseat, taking his place next to her.

"Regent Palace Hotel," he snapped at Jason, his driver.

Of course, Anna thought, *where we'd gone after I visited the wedding venue with his mother a couple of months ago. He wants to rub it in, try to make me regret my decision.*

They sat opposite each other at Roderick's private table like two boxers in the ring. All Anna could feel was relief that love had shown her not to marry this man, whom she didn't love and who didn't even respect her. She'd escaped a mismatched marriage of convenience. Roderick Macalister was not even a nice man. She'd been blindsided by her needs.

But as yet, Anna had no idea what cards he was holding close to his chest.

"You know I know everything about your background, Ansel Grynszpan?" His voice was low, the eyes mean.

"The name is Anna Adams, Roderick." She could do haughty. He was studying her intently, turning the stem of his champagne glass round and round over the damask tablecloth.

"To me you are Ansel Grynszpan and putting you on a flight back to Germany would only need my signature. So, what do you want? To be Anna or Ansel? You know Jews aren't particularly liked in Germany. They're all put in camps. Is that what you want with your life?"

Anna's breath caught in her throat. To be able to find her voice, she took a big sip from her glass but choked and ended in a coughing session. Her face was hot and red. People started looking in their direction.

"Why do you do this to me, Roderick?" she finally managed to get out. "I can't imagine wanting an heir with someone you loathe is your type of a happy life either."

"Aha, that," he remarked, raising one eyebrow in irony. "That was only part of the plan. But you haven't answered my initial question. Germany or Britain, what will it be?"

By now Anna had enough experience with the tactics taught at training schools where prospective secret agents were exposed to brutal Gestapo interrogations. She'd read the reports with interest.

Now the initial shock of what Roderick wanted to do to her was sinking in, Anna's rational mind started working again. He could be bluffing about the signature; he could also not be. She had to find out the reason why he simply wouldn't let her go and marry another little sheep that would give him a son and heir.

She decided to confront him directly. "Why me, Roderick?"

But he wasn't giving in. "I asked you a question first."

"Well, that is an irrelevant question. No Jew who has escaped Germany in time wants to return. No higher math there." Anna was developing a level of sarcasm she didn't even know she possessed. But if she'd learned anything from the brave agents she met daily, it was to be bold and fearless in the face of adversity. He'd caught her off guard, but she wouldn't let it happen again.

Food came, lobster in cream sauce, but Anna didn't touch her meal. The smell and the sight repelled her, like the entire Regent Palace Hotel and all it stood for. Roderick took his time eating slowly and mechanically. Finally, he put his knife and fork down, dabbed his mustache with his napkin and focused on her again.

"Money, Anna. That is the answer to your question. Your Uncle left you his trust. Diamonds is big business. The Macalister earldom could do with a financial injection."

"I would never have agreed to marry you without documents protecting my assets," Anna remarked, studying her ringless hands.

"Right." He lit a cigar. "Then you're smarter than I thought."

"I know," Anna couldn't help the sneer.

"So." He blew the smoke straight in her face, but she waved it away with her napkin. "What do you say we two come to an agreement?"

"I suppose any agreement coming from you will be more favorable to you than to me."

She just wanted to leave the restaurant, everything about it made her nauseous.

"I think I have a reasonable offer." He still puffed on his cigar. Anna became even sicker.

"Enlighten me." She was tired, depressed; all euphoria over the days with Henryk had seeped out of her.

"I'll let you go on the condition you don't see that aviator ever again. If you do, you'll be on the next plane to Berlin. No joke." His voice was as marble hearted as his heart, but Anna knew without a shadow of a doubt that he meant what he said. That he would do everything in his power to get her out of the country. This was the real "Roddy Resolute". Head-to-toe.

She thought fast. The war wouldn't last forever. Hitler wouldn't last forever. When peace returned to Europe, she could travel again and see Henryk whenever and wherever she wanted. And she would pressure Sir Reginald to get her British passport in order. Then Roderick could threaten all he wished. As long as he wasn't the sand in the machine preventing the approval of her British citizenship.

"On one condition," she said softly. "That I may let him know."

"I'll want to read that note."

"No."

She got up, grabbed her bag, and walked out of the restaurant without looking back.

She was free from Roderick, but she'd lost Henryk. At least until her affairs were settled, or for the duration of the war.

She was and always would be Anna Adams.

41

ANNA'S SECTION F GIRLS

Three months later - London, August 1942

The spring of 1942 had changed Anna. Gravely and irrevocably. All youthful hopes, uncertainties, dreams, and possibilities had died. With both love and marriage beyond reach, all she had left was her job. And here, Anna would excel. Here she had control. The whole world was in tatters, including her own life, but she would recruit the best female agents she could find and prepare them to carry out successful missions in occupied France.

Now Churchill had agreed women could join SOE in active combat, it was Anna Adams' task to find the best women. Maybe, at some point, her hero would even recognize her efforts and praise her for a job well done.

Years of weathering the pain since 1938 had finally molded a steely, unemotional Anna, who spoke little, saw every minuscule detail, and made no friends nor enemies. Her male colleagues refrained from flirting with her but sought out and respected her advice in security matters. Her female colleagues dreaded her and never invited her to their after-work parties.

Anna didn't care left or right. She was careful not to step on anyone's toes as she smartly worked her way up the SOE ladder until she was Sir Reginald's right hand.

Thus, she not only became responsible for the female agents, but the crucial matters concerning all French agents were known to her. Often her boss left the decision making to Anna, as he left mid-afternoon for his Club or took extended lunches with this MP or that general.

Anna was the hub to whom all spokes of Section F were connected, and she thrived on it, lived for it, breathed with it. Her unsentimental and self-controlled attitude was a great help in separating the wheat from the chaff when it came to the continuous stream of young women knocking on her office door with a longing to join SOE.

The women who reflected Anna's own carefully constructed characteristics stood a better chance in the strict selection procedure. Moreover, Anna now detested romanticism and naiveté. The women she sought had to be strong, level-headed, and fearless. If they wanted to serve their country as secret agents in German-occupied territory, a lack of brains and guts would be lethal.

The office was quiet on a sunny August afternoon. Birds were chirping in the neglected garden outside Anna's open window. Dolly was God-knows-where but Anna didn't care. She preferred to be alone in her workspace, work uninterruptedly, and stay long after everyone else was home. She picked up the next file on her desk, pushing the glasses higher on her nose.

"What?!" she exclaimed. "You must be kidding me. Sable Montgomery has passed her training?"

Anna flung off her glasses, remembering the arrival of raven-haired Sable at Baker Street two months earlier. Apparently, the minx had secured a job as a secretary at Beaulieu training school and fallen in love with one of the Scottish trainers. But that hadn't worked out. It didn't surprise Anna in the least.

She had no pleasant memories of her fellow schoolmate at Le Manoir. Sable was a pest and had a severe attitude problem. But she'd assured Anna she wanted to be dropped into France and do her part. Sir Reginald had vetoed Anna's decision to refuse Sable.

Now she read the report with great interest.

∿

From: Training Facility STS 36
By: Captain L. Skilbeck
Date: 1 August 1942

Subject: Post-Training Report - Sable Montgomery (Codename: The Raven)

Agent Profile:
Name: *Sable Montgomery*
Codename: *The Raven*
Nationality: *British*
Physical Description: *Black-haired, 5'0 tall, slender, wiry build.*
Training Summary:
Agent Sable Montgomery, codenamed The Raven, has successfully completed her rigorous training as a Special Operations Executive (SOE) agent. This report provides an overview of her training, skills, and performance during her final training time at Training Facility STS 36.

Skills Acquired:
<u>Survival and Camouflage</u>: *Agent Montgomery has displayed exceptional proficiency in survival and camouflage techniques. Her ability to blend into the natural environment and sustain herself in the wild is noteworthy. She has shown adaptability and resourcefulness in extreme conditions, making her an ideal candidate for covert missions behind enemy lines.*

<u>Physical Conditioning</u>: *Agent Montgomery has undergone rigorous physical training and has emerged as a strong and resilient agent. Her endurance, combat skills, and physical fitness are commendable, and she can endure challenging situations effectively.*

Courage and Tenacity: Agent Montgomery is known for her tenacious spirit and unwavering determination. She is fearless in the face of danger, which can be both an asset and a concern, as her hatred of Germans may lead to rash decisions in high-stress situations.

Personality and Behavior: Agent Montgomery is a tough and solitary individual. She tends to operate alone and may have reservations about teamwork. Her desire for revenge against the Germans is a driving force in her motivations, but it has also led to her occasionally disregard security protocols. This tendency should be closely monitored during her field assignments.

Team Collaboration: Agent Montgomery may require additional training and support to improve her ability to work effectively within a team. Her self-reliant nature could be a potential challenge when coordinating operations with other agents.

Security Awareness: While Agent Montgomery's survival and camouflage skills are impressive, her security awareness should be enhanced to avoid potential compromises in the field.
Language Proficiency: Agent Montgomery's French is excellent due to having spent a year at a French boarding school.

Recommendations:
Agent Montgomery's skills in survival and camouflage make her an ideal candidate for missions involving reconnaissance and sabotage.
Her courage and determination should be harnessed effectively to achieve mission success, while her ability to make decisions on the spot and change tactics are valuable assets but could lead to unnecessary risk-taking.
Teamwork and communication skills should be emphasized to ensure she can collaborate efficiently with fellow agents.
Sable Montgomery, codenamed The Raven, has successfully completed her training at Training Facility STS 36. She possesses valuable skills in survival, camouflage, and physical conditioning, which make her well-suited for covert operations. Her tenacity and courage, though assets,

should be carefully managed to ensure mission success and her safety. With further development in teamwork and restraint, Agent Montgomery has the potential to become a highly effective SOE agent.

Security Clearance: Top Secret
Distribution: Top Secret

Signed,
Captain L. Skilbeck
Training Facility STS 36

"Well, I guess I'd better phone Manetta's for a lunch date with Sable." Anna shook her head in wonder, but she understood what Captain Skilbeck meant.

"Maybe I was wrong. Maybe Sable Montgomery will surprise us all. It's 1-0 to you, Sir Reginald."

There was a soft knock on the open door. Anna looked up from making notes in Sable's file. In the door opening stood Denise "Danny" Damerment.

Denise, originally French but brought up in England, was a striking young woman - slender but athletic, with chestnut brown hair, always neatly done up in a bun and deep blue eyes that were sharp and observant.

"Denise, welcome." Anna rose from her chair smiling. She was genuinely pleased to see the always agreeable Agent Damerment.

"Officer Adams, I wondered if you have a moment?" Despite her many years in England, Denise still had that singsong French pronunciation Anna adored.

"Sure. I wasn't expecting you until next week, but I can make time. Here in the office, or some place where we won't be disturbed?"

Denise looked doubtful. "I only have a minute, as I still have so much to do before I leave next week, but it's a rather delicate matter." The sharp eyes looked around the office as if searching for a secluded spot.

"You know what?" Anna said in a chirpy voice. "I'll ring for tea and after it has arrived, I'll close the door and pin up the Do Not Disturb sign. Do take a chair." She pointed to the tiny sitting area which held two slender armchairs and a small coffee table.

Denise stirred her tea with care. Anna knew her to be a resourceful and highly intelligent agent. She'd maintain her composure under pressure and think on her feet. Yet she looked disturbed now and Anna wondered what was bothering her.

"It's Maman," Denise disclosed. "I know we're not supposed to say what we're doing and where we're going, but I already had a hard time explaining I'd not be coming home during the weeks of training. Before I left for Inverness, she kept asking why a Woolworth shopgirl would suddenly be invited on an extensive business trip to other stores all over the country. I guess I'm a lousy liar, Officer Adams." Denise had stopped stirring her tea. She now sat with her hands folded in her lap, looking miserable.

"You told me before you and your mother are very close."

Denise nodded. "After my brother joined the Navy and left home, I was all she had left. Maman has never had a job. Papa wouldn't let her, but he is away from home a lot because he is a travelling salesman, so Maman doted on Marcel and me. And now I'm leaving, perhaps for months. What am I to do, Officer Adams? It'll break her heart when I tell her I have to leave home again. And it's not like she's simple. She knows I'm lying and probably thinks I'm up to no good." Here Denise laughed scornfully, "which of course is the truth. Once in France I won't be a good girl, I suppose."

Denise's report had mentioned her dry sense of humor, which often helped her maintain morale during difficult times.

"I understand," Anna assured her. "Reassuring the home front is one of the hardest things the female agents face. For some reason, the male agents can leave home much easier. I never hear them being questioned by their families. Well, I guess the concern about daughters leaving home makes sense, but it doesn't make it easier."

"No," Denise replied in a small voice.

"You know that under no circumstances may you disclose that you're leaving the country. You've already written the post cards from Brighton, Manchester, and Leeds, which I will post to your parents at regular times. There is really no other way than to lie again, Denise."

Anna briefly put her hand on that of her agent and gave it a soft squeeze. She'd had this conversation five times already. No matter how brave and how fearless the agent, when it came to their mothers, they almost broke down.

"I know I must make her believe I'm still in Britain," Denise said, keeping her tears in check. "And it's not like I don't believe in what I'm about to do. I'm fiercely dedicated to the Allied cause and will do what it takes to help free my country from the Germans."

"I know that. You'll be a great wireless operator, Agent Chérie," Anna said using her codename deliberately. "The only advice I can give you about your mother is to stick by your story. Don't change it, keep it simple, don't digress. Tell her to enjoy the time you still have together. Help her focus on that. That will help you both."

"Oh Officer Adams, you're so good at your job. And you're really kind. I will do that. Thank you." Denise got up and looked at her watch, "I have to dash out now, but I'll see you this time next week."

She was already at the door, the spring back in her step.

"Yes, I'll see you off to RAF Tangmere. Enjoy your last week, Denise. You deserve it."

"I will, Officer Adams. Thank you."

AFTER DENISE LEFT, Anna sank back in her leather chair behind her desk, took off her glasses and rested her palms against her tired eyes. What a luxury to have such a loving and devoted mother. And yet, a girl like Denise didn't think twice about undergoing the toughest physical and mental training women could and then be dropped by parachute overnight into France with her heavy wireless set in order to report to London what was going on in Nazi-occupied territory. What grit, what moral fiber, what willpower.

She, Anna, lacked all that. But perhaps she was good at her job. As Denise had said.

PUTTING BACK ON THE GLASSES, she grabbed the next file and saw before her eyes another valiant fighter, Madeleine "Maddy" Bloch. Madeleine was slightly older than most girls, at thirty-five. She'd been a schoolteacher but after her husband was killed in the Blitz and the opportunity had arisen to join SOE, she'd been one of the first to apply. Madeleine was ready for France as well and actually would fly by Lysander together with Denise, on Wednesday's full moon.

They knew each other well, as they had undergone the same training, but Madeleine would become a courier in the Bordeaux region, while Denise's destiny was Paris.

And the third to go, on separate flight a day later, together with a male agent, was Yvonne Churchill, no relation to the prime minister, but certainly as remarkable and strong a personality.

Slim and elegant Yvonne had blonde hair that was usually styled in waves, her eyes green, expressive, an emphatic air around her. The kind of woman for whom every man turned his head. She would have a difficult time not standing out in occupied France.

But Anna had no reasons to fear for Yvonne's safety. Not only was she extremely careful when it came to security issues, behind that beautiful exterior, she hid a force to be reckoned with. Her trainers had applauded her sharpshooting techniques, and she didn't hesitate or struggle to take down a man almost twice her size in hand-to-hand combat.

Yvonne's goal was Lyon, where she'd connect with Maureen. Her main task would be helping downed, Allied airmen escape over the Pyrenees into Spain and get them back to England. Just the job for this powerhouse, who also was an excellent team player.

DAYLIGHT WAS FADING OVER LONDON. Anna needed to get home and cook for Pearl.

One more week. Then Pearl would start her training and be gone. *Oh Pearl.*

One after the other, Anna's girls slipped from her hands and went into France where they had to stay out of the Nazi clutches. All on their own.

"My girls," she sighed as she switched off the light in her office to leave Baker Street HQ and go home for the night.

"PLEASE GOD, bring all my girls back home safely."

42

PEARL FLIES OUT

Two months later - RAF Tangmere, October 1942

A nna was sitting in her small kitchen in Chelsea, sipping a cup of tea and once again reading every word Captain Skilbeck had written about Pearl. Though it was already evening, Pearl was still out, having a last evening meal with her family. Tomorrow night she would board a Lysander at RAF Tangmere and in the middle of the night be dropped north of the Loire River in the Centre-Loire region of France.

What have I done? Anna thought for the hundredth time. *Letting my best friend, my only friend, go?*

There was no way she could persuade Pearl not to go. That bridge had been crossed. But maybe, just maybe, she could find something in Skilbeck's report that would persuade Sir Reginald to withdraw his permission. Though Pearl would kill Anna if she found out.

And Anna knew it was a useless exercise to begin with. Pearl had excelled at almost all parts of her training. She was a highly trained SOE agent now and would work as a courier for Maurice Southgate's network and also assist in sabotage and demolition.

From: *Training Facility STS 36*
By: *Captain L. Skilbeck*
Date: *15 September 1942*

Subject: Post-Training Report - Pearl Baseden (Codename: Barry)

Agent Profile

Name*: Pearl Baseden*
Codename*: Barry*
Nationality: *French/British*
Physical Description*: Short/cropped dark-blonde hair, 5'4" tall, athletic build, light eyes.*

Training Summary:
Agent Pearl Baseden, codenamed Barry, has successfully completed her demanding training as a Special Operations Executive (SOE) agent. This report offers an evaluation of her training, skills, and performance during her intensive training period at Training Facility STS 36.

Skills Acquired:
<u>Combat Proficiency</u>*: Agent Baseden has demonstrated exceptional combat skills, excelling in hand-to-hand combat, marksmanship, and tactical strategies. Her athleticism and physical prowess make her a formidable asset for direct action missions.*

<u>Parachute Jumping</u>*: Agent Baseden has become proficient in para-jumping, enabling her to insert into enemy territory swiftly and covertly. Her precision and adaptability during jumps have been commendable.*

<u>Demolition and Sabotage</u>*: Agent Baseden exhibits a strong aptitude for demolition and sabotage operations. Her knowledge of explosives and her*

ability to cripple enemy infrastructure make her a valuable asset for disruptive missions.

Stealth and Infiltration: Agent Baseden's capacity for stealthy movements and infiltration techniques is impressive. She can operate covertly behind enemy lines, providing valuable intelligence and carrying out covert actions.

Language Proficiency: Due to her French heritage, Agent Baseden is fluent in French, allowing her to blend seamlessly into French-speaking environments.

Personality and Behavior: Agent Baseden is known for her self-reliance and preference for working alongside male agents. Her determination to liberate France drives her, and her occasional lax attention to security protocols has raised concerns. Advice is to add Agent Baseden to a well-established network where she can learn the skills before operating on her own.

Team Collaboration: Agent Baseden may benefit from additional training in teamwork and collaboration. Her inclination toward solitary operations could hinder coordination with fellow agents during missions.

Security Awareness: While Agent Baseden excels in many areas, her security awareness requires improvement to minimize potential field compromises.

Recommendations:

Pearl Baseden's combat skills and proficiency in demolition and sabotage make her an ideal candidate for missions requiring direct action and disruption behind enemy lines.

Her determination and fearlessness should be harnessed effectively for mission success, but her impulsive tendencies should be addressed through continuous training and supervision.

Enhancing her teamwork and communication skills is essential to ensure she can effectively cooperate with other agents in the field.

Pearl Baseden, codenamed Barry, has completed her training at Training Facility STS 36 with commendable skills in combat, parachuting, demolition, and stealth. Her passion for the liberation of France, along with her physical prowess, make her a valuable asset for SOE missions. Careful management of her impulsive nature and a focus on teamwork will be crucial for her continued success as an SOE agent.

Security Clearance: Top Secret
Distribution: Top Secret

Signed,
Captain L. Skilbeck
Training Facility STS 36

~

ANNA'S PENCIL underlined the phrases 'security awareness requires improvement' and 'careful management of her impulsive nature and a focus on teamwork'. Would it be enough to make her boss see Pearl wasn't ready to be sent out?

"Or am I just being selfish?" Anna asked herself out loud. She glanced again at her watch. Past eight. Where was Pearl? And then she let the report fall back on the table and put her face in her hands.

This was the very last night she could ask herself where Pearl was and know she'd come into that door any moment. Not tomorrow night, not the night after, maybe not for very long months. Maybe... never.

"I told myself so clearly not to love another person ever again," she said bitterly, "but here I am. Mourning Pearl, who is alive."

She had to let her go. She had no right to interfere in Pearl's passionate dream to be a secret agent. And gosh was it hard. She would be so lonely and fretting every day about Pearl's safety.

~

THE NEXT EVENING

The taxi ride to RAF Tangmere near Chichester was a tense and somber affair. It wasn't raining anymore but the sky was densely overcast, which was never a good sign to fly agents out, as it had to be clear at the arrival location in order to see where they had to be dropped only by the light of the moon. The streets of London were wet, and a strong fall wind whirled castaway newspapers and brown leaves into the air.

Anna and Pearl sat silently in the back seat, their fingers intertwined, each lost in their own thoughts. South London passed by and then they were heading south in the direction of Guilford.

Anna's throat was dry. Unable to stop herself from stealing glances at her best friend, she wanted to say something, anything. Maybe not even as a friend, but in her position as SOE official. But the words stuck in the dry dust of her throat and Pearl kept staring out of the window, her face illuminated by the occasional passing car's headlights. Her features were a mix of determination and excitement, but Anna could see the underlying unease in the light eyes.

Pearl was never silent, but she hadn't talked much since she came into the door at ten last night. Monosyllabic answers. Anna knew the last farewell to family was the hardest for the agents, so she hadn't pressured her friend but felt even more guilty for being the cause of the separation.

The radio in the taxi played a melancholic tune, the notes hanging in the air like a haunting refrain. Their taxi driver, an elderly Londoner with a weathered face, drove in silence, as if he too understood the gravity of the moment. He occasionally glanced at the two women in the rear-view mirror, one in her WAAF uniform, the other in a tailored coat.

As they neared Tangmere, Anna's grip on Pearl's hand tightened. She almost choked, thinking of all the uncertainties that lay ahead, the dangers that Pearl would face from the moment she parachuted into occupied France. How Pearl's impulsivity and fearlessness could make her an easy target for the Gestapo.

That moment Pearl turned to face her, and Anna saw an expression in her friend's face she'd never seen before. Equal shares of distress and determination. Pearl had never been distressed.

"Anna, promise me you'll take care of things here," she said softly. "Look after my family, and don't forget about me."

Anna nodded, her voice catching in her throat. "I promise, Pearl," she whispered, her heart heavy with the fear of what lay ahead. "I'll do everything in my power to keep the home front safe. You just focus on your mission and come back to us, alright?"

Pearl managed a weak smile and leaned in to hug Anna tightly. The taxi pulled up to the front of the airport, and the driver turned to them, his eyes filled with kind understanding. "Good luck," he said, as if he knew what these nightly rides between London and Tangmere meant.

It was fully dark when Anna and Pearl stepped out of the taxi, and the sky had cleared. Stars twinkled above them, but the wind was brisk and cold. Pearl hoisted her rucksack onto her slender back and took her suitcase in her hand.

"Here, let me carry it for you," Anna offered.

"No, I need to be able to carry it all, though the rucksack will be left at my first safehouse."

They went through the empty entrance hall, past the officer's lounge, onto the airstrip itself, where the Lysander aircraft loomed in the distance.

"You know you won't be alone, Pearl? A male agent, Peter Suttill, is going out as well. This is his third mission, so he'll be able to help you and answer any questions you have during the trip."

"Yeah, I met him. He passed by when I was in Beaulieu. Told me so much. Nice guy. Glad I'm going with a veteran."

"You know he's not going to Lyon but to Tours, right?" Anna didn't want Pearl to think Peter could take her by the hand for long.

"Don't worry, Anna, and don't treat me like a baby. I'll be fine." It came out quite snappy and Anna bit her lip. Tenseness in agents made them snappy. It was nothing personal. But still, it hurt.

"You know I have to go through the final security checks with you?" Anna had to raise her voice as the roaring Lysander was rolling their way. This was all so different with a friend.

"Sure," Pearl agreed and then dropped her stuff and hugged Anna tightly once again. "Don't worry so much, my dear, dear friend. You're doing fine and I'm doing fine."

While her eyes misted up, she checked all the details of Pearl's clothes once again. The correct buttons, French lace handkerchief, no British labels, the French beret, the false papers stating she was Mademoiselle Christine Latour, a French secretary for Citroën in Lyon.

"Tell me once again who you are?" Anna asked.

Pearl rattled off her entire fictious life as if she already lived it.

"Satisfied?" she grinned at the end. "Can I go now, please?"

As they stood on the tarmac of RAF Tangmere, the roar of the aircraft engines now completely drowned out the last words Anna wanted to say. The night air was filled with the pungent smell of aviation fuel, and the dim moonlight cast long shadows across the airfield.

Anna felt coldness crawl up her spine, a feeling of dread that she couldn't shake. She had recruited more than a dozen female agents for SOE, but this seemed so final. Sure, Pearl was a daredevil, fearless and determined, but Anna knew all the risks Pearl did not.

She looked radiant in her brown cashmere coat and black pants. Her cropped hair tucked neatly under the beret, her eyes sparkling, as the Lysander stopped at their feet and Peter Suttill joined them with a friend who was seeing him off.

"I'll change into overalls once inside," Pearl informed them. "I had to wear overalls for so long at the ATS in Greenford, I'll indulge in these French clothes for a bit."

Peter knew the ropes and no longer required the same security measures at the start of his mission from Anna.

Anna turned to face Pearl for the very last time, her heart heavy with worry. She forced a smile, but tears glistened in her eyes. "You take care out there, Pearl," she shouted, her voice eerie and shrill. "Promise me you'll come back in one piece."

Pearl beamed, her confidence unshaken. "I sure will. Can't live life without you, Anna," she shouted back in a voice filled with determination. "I was born for this. *Vive la France*. But I love Britain too."

Anna nodded, but her throat was tight with anxiety. She reached out and hugged her one last time. "Just promise me one thing," she shouted in her ear. "Be very careful, always watch your back, and never take unnecessary risks."

Pearl's strong arms were around her. "I promise," she cried back but her voice was a bit shaky now. "I'll be careful, Anna. I'll come back. I swear."

They held onto each other for a moment longer, two best friends clinging to each other in the darkness of the airfield. Then, reluctantly, they pulled apart. Pearl gave Anna one last, reassuring smile before turning and walking towards the waiting Lysander with Peter Suttill. Her gait, as always, so confident and strong.

Oh, Pearlie!

As Anna watched her disappear into the night, the sound of the engines grew louder, and the plane taxied down the runway. Fear gnawed at her, a gut-wrenching certainty that this could very well be the last time she saw her friend. The weight of her premonition hung heavily in the air, a sense of foreboding that wouldn't leave her.

WHAT HAVE I DONE?

43

EVERYTHING GOES WRONG

One year later - London, October 1943

The London streets outside SOE Baker Street HQ were shrouded in a dense mist that clung to the buildings like an opaque blanket. The sun hadn't shone for days, and the Londoners were wet and weary. War continued to rage on the Continent, and everything was scarce - fuel, food, fabrics. And winter was coming. Another grim winter, where the people of Britain would have to keep their heads down and their spirits up.

Thank God for that indomitable Churchill, who pepped up his people with his mere words:

"Sure I am that this day, now, we are the masters of our fate. That the task which has been set us is not above our strength. That its pangs and toils are not beyond our endurance. As long as we have faith in our cause, and an unconquerable willpower, salvation will not be denied us."

THE BLEAK FALL weather seemed to mirror the prevailing sense of uncertainty and mounting tension inside the Baker Street Office.

As Anna Adams closed her drenched umbrella and stepped

inside the building that still wore the ambiguous Inter-Services Research Bureau sign, she was greeted by a grim looking Mr. Parks, the concierge.

"Morning Miss Adams. Beastly weather, aint it? Afraid there's another emergency. Sir Reginald asks you to come straight to his office."

"Oh Mr. Parks, I could do with a day without calamities, couldn't you?'

"I could do with a bit of sunshine, Miss Adams, *and* fewer calamities." The kind bulk of a man closed the door behind her, but not before spying the street left and right to confirm there were no unwanted customers in his territory.

The atmosphere inside was a stark contrast from the gloomy, deserted streets outside. The air was frenetic, the whole building buzzing with urgency. Amidst the incessant hum of whispered conversations, punctuated by the occasional outburst of frustrated expletives, Anna hurried up the stairs to the first floor where Section F was housed. The heavy weight of responsibility pressed down on her. Her role as the French Section recruiter was more critical than ever. She passed offices cluttered with hastily arranged maps and hushed telephone conversations, and went straight for the office at the end of the corridor.

"You wanted to see me, Sir?" She already stood in her boss's office after her usual three-rap on the door. For once the bulging, red-veined, blue eyes looked up straightaway from whatever he was doing and met her anxious expression.

"Yes, sit down Anna."

"It isn't...it isn't Pearl?" she stammered. Pearl should have long returned from her second mission but kept postponing her safe return home under the pretense France needed her more than England, but every Baker Street officer knew by now that an agent's postponement of return likely meant capture by the Germans and forced messages about their well-being.

"No Anna, for once this isn't about any of our agents but about you."

"What's the matter? You give me a fright."

He looked at her probingly. "No doubt you remember you had a totally different life before Anna Adams?"

Anna felt her cheeks go crimson. Any reference to her life before London made her very uneasy, especially as the longed-for naturalisation still hadn't happened.

"Of course," she replied, studying her nails and avoiding his look.

"I've protected you, Anna. After my initial research into your background, I let it go. Trusted you. But some folks can't stop digging into your past and I haven't got time for all this nonsense. I have enough on my plate as it is."

Anna's mind was torn in every direction. Who was obstructing her path? Was it Roderick Macalister? A double agent? Who?

"What do you mean to say, Sir Reginald? Do you want to fire me?" Better be straight, despite feeling if a knife was placed between her ribs.

"That's the problem. With everything going on right now with our agents in France, you know I can't do without you, but I'd be damned if I didn't believe I could do without the extra hassle."

"I'm sorry. I thought you trusted me, Sir Reginald." Anna got up from her chair, her lips pursed. "You knew my uncle; you knew my background. I am one-hundred percent pro-British and yearn for the day I'll have a British passport. Whoever is doing this to me and you, is wrong." She was very angry now on that elusive stranger who continued to thwart her career.

"Sit down, Anna!" It was an order from the former Navy officer. She sank back in the leather-upholstered chair, exhausted, frazzled.

"I believe you, but you have no clue about the strength of the opposing dark forces. There are still pro-Hitler politicians with great power in Britain and I'm not just talking of Oswald Mosley and his British Union of Fascists. Next to that, we run into double agents every day, even inside these walls. Apparently, Hitler is keen on decapitating every Grynszpan in the world. So, every step you take out there Anna is a dangerous one."

Anna's uniformed body shook uncontrollably in the chair. She was retracing her steps to and from her Chelsea and Baker Street. The shadows she'd seen lurking. Had it been spies? And her father? Was his Jude Adams cover strong enough?

"What am I to do?" her voice was trembling as badly as her hands.

"We have you covered, Anna. As long as you stay on British soil, we can keep an eye on you. I'll try to expedite the naturalization once again, although even that isn't a complete guarantee you'll be safe. Too many people know your real background. Files should be destroyed in your case, so I'm investigating to what extent your file has been distributed among key people."

"Thank you," she managed a wan smile. "Do you think I should no longer walk home but take a taxi?"

"That might be a good idea." He looked almost fatherly at her in her distress. "I trust you, Anna, and you're a darn good worker. I wouldn't know what to do without you."

"Thank you, Sir."

It took Anna an hour to wrap her mind about this new information and calm down. Three times her fingers slipped around the black receiver to dial Roderick Macalister's office, but she stopped herself every time.

She hadn't heard from him after they parted ways with her freedom and his demand to end her relationship with Henryk. Whatever he was up to, she wouldn't be the one who could stop him. That was the one job she should let Sir Reginald do for her. Her eyes nervously spied everyone passing her open office door, seeing potential traitors all around her.

"Stop it!" she told herself sternly. "You are safe. Most probably. Didn't Sir Reginald say as much? Take your precautions and keep your eyes open just as you tell your agents every time. Now, concentrate on them. They are in much more dire conditions than Anna Adams."

. . .

THIS HELPED. She *was* needed. The chaos around the agents on missions was immense. Sixty male and twenty female agents were currently in France, twenty-two of them under suspicion of being captured and infiltrated by the Germans.

Though there had been signals earlier in the year, in the past couple of weeks, the paranoia in the office had become tangible, with every newcomer scrutinized and every message from France met with scepticism.

Anna was certain there was a mole in their own organization but who was it? She had no hard clues, but persistent rumors pointed to Marcel Déricourt, whom she had urgently requested to return to London. He was expected back on the first flight possible.

Sir Reginald continued to leave much of the work to her, but the weight of the fledgeling F Section's operations rested heavily on her slender shoulders. There was no room for error, no margin for hesitation.

Fluent in code writing herself now, her fingers flew across type-writer keys as she composed coded messages for the Signals Office to send out. She spent hours there, waiting for the light flashing on the switchboard which signaled an agent was coming on air. Then stayed there as the code breakers deciphered the message, checking and rechecking their security and bluff codes for any sign of betrayal.

The process, repeated hour after hour, demanded all Anna's mental and intellectual strength, but she continued to be the first to arrive and the last to leave after a few hours of broken sleep. Unless she had to see an agent off, like the day before.

She'd specifically instructed wireless operator Julienne Samson to cautiously investigate the two large networks Anna feared were infiltrated, Southgate's Papillon Network in Lyon, and Suttill's Brouillard Network in Bordeaux.

Pearl was with Peter Suttill. On her second mission, she'd asked to join the Brouillard Network, which had made Anna wonder if there was a romantic liaison between the two agents who'd flown out together first time in October 1942.

"Don't be daft," Pearl had fumed. "I have no time for kisses when I need to blow up bridges." But her cheeks had blushed, and Anna knew enough.

So today, Anna's eyes were fixed on the broadcast board hoping for a message from Julienne. She knew it was too early. It could take days or even weeks before Julienne would be able to take stock and report. Unless she'd already fallen into Gestapo hands when her parachute landed and her message would never come or, worse, be preformulated by the Germans.

"I need to see Marcel Déricourt," Anna sighed, as she returned to her own office after the flashboard had remained silent for another hour. She knew, though, that it was very unlikely she could extract anything from the close-lipped Frenchman who, when in London, walked through SOE as if he owned it.

With each passing hour, as the fate of her agents in occupied France hung in the balance and it became harder to identify the enemies hidden among the allies, Anna's stomach contracted further.

Pushing her glasses up to see clearer what she was reading, light faded in her dimly lit office. The light of the desk lamp was so pale it cast long shadows across the room. Stacks of classified documents and maps were piled high next to her on a wooden table, and a large chalkboard covered with maps and strategic markings dominated one wall.

This was her habitat; this was her war. Though the Allied forces were winning terrain on the Nazis, Anna was losing her terrain. But she would fight valiantly until the end. Even if the military men in the SOE organization considered the loss of agents' lives collateral damage, Anna knew each one of them, their backgrounds, their families, their hopes, and dreams about a free France. She couldn't let them perish on their own in that occupied zone of Europe. She couldn't.

Just when she decided she needed to take a break and get a cup of coffee, there was a tap on her door. In the opening stood Evelyn Sinclair, the Head Decoder from the Signals Office. A few years older than Anna and wearing a FANY uniform, Evelyn's rounded figure looked more maternal than professional.

"What is it, Evelyn?" Anna asked. Evelyn being recruited from the circles of SOE Head of Operations, Colonel Gibbins, she and Anna had a reasonable rapport, but they certainly weren't friends.

Anna respected Evelyn for her exceptional attention to detail and her unwavering dedication to decode even the most difficult 'undecipherable' from the field.

"I think you will want to read this, Anna." The gray eyes with dark lashes held a hint of curiosity but also concern as she put the paper on Anna's desk.

Operation Paris postponed. STOP Expect delays in female recruitment for Loire region. STOP Weather unfavorable for upcoming operations. STOP Requesting further instructions.

"From Agent Damerment?" Anna asked. Evelyn nodded.

"'Operation Paris' is Agent Suttill's network in Bordeaux, right? Is he arrested?"

Evelyn nodded again.

"And the female recruitment must point to the arrest of women as well." At that point Anna grew red in the face. "Pearl," she gasped, "who else?"

"The message doesn't say but wasn't Agent Montgomery in the Bordeaux region as well?"

"She was. Oh my God!" Anna exclaimed.

"It goes on to say that we have to be very careful with droppings in the middle of France at the moment," Evelyn continued but Anna was still grasping the enormity of Pearl's possible arrest and all the horrible consequences thereof. With all her willpower she remained in her function.

"Were Agent Damerment's security codes and bluff codes in order?"

"Yes," Evelyn confirmed, "it doesn't look like Agent Damerment is under arrest. At least not at this point."

"Thank you, Evelyn. Could you ask Dolly to bring me some coffee and a glass of water and an aspirin should you see her?"

"I will, Anna, and I will keep an eye out on any further messages from Agent Damerment or from Agent Samson."

After Evelyn left, Anna's fingers played absently with the flip-over card system on her desk until it stopped at Pearl's card with her picture. Beautiful Pearl looking straight in the camera for her agent photograph, sporting her immaculate gray-green FANY uniform and the angled beret on her short hair. The chin slightly tilted. Unconquerable Pearl.

"Please be well, Pearlie. Please don't give up."

Outside the windows of Anna's office, the streets turned dark. Dusk was coming early and the rain hadn't ceased. How she dreaded going home to the empty flat where her thoughts only circled around her missing friend. And sometimes around Henryk. And sometimes around her father.

There was no comfort in the solitude and though it was unlikely there would come another message from France, she hung onto work. Gulped down the coffee, water and aspirin Dolly gave her, and waved the secretary off.

Anna's office grew darker and darker. The single light bulb giving the crown of her hair a mahogany shine. The offices on the first floor grew quieter and quieter. The only office that was in full operation night and day was the Signals Office where messages from the field could be expected any moment.

Rain tapped rhythmically against the glass panes. Down in the street, there was a coming and going of people under umbrellas returning from work or running a last errand before the night. A sea of black umbrellas. The distant rumble of engines and the occasional wail of an air raid siren were grim reminders of the ongoing war.

Mr. Parks' head showed up around her door. "Anytime soon, Miss Adams?"

"Yes, Mr. Parks. I'm about to leave. But wait let me call a taxi."

"Smart idea, Miss Adams, or you'll be drenched like a wet cat."

But Anna thought of Sir Reginald's words. The rain didn't bother her. Her safety did.

Just when she was about to turn the corner at the end of the corridor to take the stairs, she bumped into a man coming from the stairs above where the Polish Section was.

She nodded to the tall, spindly man, who she had seen on other occasions on the stairs.

"Officer Adams, is it?" He addressed her in a strong Polish accent that evoked a sudden thrill of a memory in her. She was surprised. It was customary that the different country sections never went beyond a passing greeting. Colonel Gibbins might be Head of all of SOE, but the countries operated completely independently.

"Yes, I wasn't aware you knew my name."

"My name is Jan Nowak, P Section."

"Officer Nowak, how can I help you?" Anna thought of her taxi waiting for her but anything Polish intrigued her, so she stopped in her tracks.

"It's your secretary, Dolly, Officer Adams."

Here we go again. Another officer smitten with that minx, Anna thought.

But she was in for a new surprise. The tall man cleared his throat.

"I know it's completely against SOE regulations to exchange information, but it came to my understanding that you may know one of our agents?"

"I don't think so, Officer Nowak. And, I'm sorry, but I'm in a hurry." Nothing Dolly blabbed about really interested Anna. She was already down the stairs when she heard him say, "Mr. Pilecki?"

Anna turned as if stung by a bee. "Is Mr. Pilecki working for SOE?"

The pale-faced, tall man nodded. "People talk, Officer Adams. I just wanted to make sure you knew."

"Thank you for letting me know, Officer Nowak, but it is none of my business. I bid you goodnight."

"He's been caught."

Anna was too much of a hard-shelled spy recruiter by now to show any sign of emotion.

"I see."

She walked on as her stomach cringed inside. But her mind stayed cold-blooded. Who knew about her and Henryk? And how and where had Dolly retrieved this personal information about her? There were moles inside Baker Street. Like they were everywhere.

Her high heels clicked on the wet pavement as she made her way to the taxi. Only then, the extent of the information the Polish officer had given her sank in.

Henryk was no longer a fighter pilot stationed at RAF Northolt. He was doing what Pearl was doing, in his own home country. And now he was caught.

She would lose him too. Though, she didn't even have him anymore.

On her command, Mr. Wilson, the barman at the Northolt Officers lounge, had made loud and clear to Henryk Pilecki that Anna Adams was no longer interested in him.

In the dark of the taxi, while the lights of London flashed by, Anna felt she had lost everything. Everything had gone wrong.

The car windows steamed up from the cold and wet outside. Big drops of water made channels on the outside of the glass. In silence, Anna's heart cried similar big droplets of tears. But on the outside, her eyes were dry.

I'LL MAKE IT RIGHT. *One day I'll make it right.*

BUT HOW?

44

THE END OF WAR IN FRANCE

Ten months later - London, August 1944

T he chimes of Big Ben reverberated through the misty London morning as Anna Adams stood by her window of her Chelsea flat, gazing down at The Times' headline. The headline brought her both relief and trepidation.

"France Liberated!" the bold black letters proclaimed, with a large photograph of General de Gaulle striding down the Champs Elysees with the Arc de Triomphe in the distance. Thousands of people with the French tri-color waving from both sides. Brave French Resistance fighters flocking to the General's side.

Though anticipated after the storming of the Normandy Beaches and the advance of the Americans and the French from the south, it had been a long and agonizing wait. But the news was finally here – France was free. The freedom Pearl, Denise, Madeleine, Maurice, Sable, Julienne, Maureen, Peter, Yvonne, and so many of her agents had valiantly fought for.

This liberation marked the beginning of a new chapter in the war, one Anna had been yearning for. Not as a symbol of victory, but as an opportunity to unravel the enigma that had haunted her for the past two years.

Where were her agents? Who would soon be stepping onto British soil and who would never return? They were simply volunteers having been sent out on perilous missions. Some were dropped into France as many as five times, while others stayed on the ground for years, dedicated to the cause of espionage, sabotage, and resistance.

Yet, somewhere along that treacherous path, many had vanished without a trace, their last communications riddled with cryptic messages or desperate pleas for help.

With France liberated, Anna could finally begin her quest to uncover the truth about what had truly happened and what London had missed or misinterpreted. The war had kept her tethered to the home front, her hands tied as she awaited news from occupied territory. But now, the shackles were loosened, and she could venture into the land of shadows, where secrets lurked, and betrayals ran deep.

If only she had a British passport, which was still an elusive dream.

As she donned her trench coat and retrieved her concealed pistol, Anna felt a renewed sense of purpose. She knew liberated Europe would hold the answers she sought, at least some of them. She also knew she couldn't rely on official channels or protocols. She would be navigating a landscape of uncertainty, terrain partly still held in Nazi hands. Danger would loom at every turn, with trust a fragile commodity.

Descending the staircase of her modest London flat, Anna's thoughts were filled with mental images of the missing agents. She owed it to them to find out what had happened, to uncover the truth that had eluded her until now. Cover-ups were certainly already put into place, both in Paris and in London. Those responsible would be saving their own skins first. Oh, the ugliness of the remnants of war.

Outside, the bustling streets of London carried on, oblivious to the turmoil within Anna's heart. She hailed a black taxi and took the short ride to Baker Street. It was time to find out who she could trust, assemble a team, gather intelligence, and hopefully soon set her forth on a mission that would lead her back to France, back to the shadows where answers and revelations awaited.

"Anna, come here for a minute," the booming voice of Sir Reginald sounded as soon as she hung up her coat. She obeyed immediately, having a few questions for her boss herself. She was surprised to see him donning his full Navy uniform. During the years of the war Sir Reginald had always dressed in formal three-piece suits. He seemed hurried, even flustered.

"I've only got a minute, Anna. Taxi is taking me to RAF Northolt. I'm flying to Paris today. General de Gaulle has personally asked me to go on a victory tour around France with him. Can you imagine? It seems the Free French and SOE have finally buried the hatchet." The bulging-blue eyes twinkled, "Can't wait to taste real Pernod again and dive into a steak de veau."

"How long will you be gone for, Sir?" Anna looked sceptical. She needed him here now there was so much intelligence work to be done. Unless he'd be willing to do her research on the ground. As had happened before, he seemed to guess her thoughts.

"I'm not going for the food and drink, Anna. Not even for the victory tour." He sounded somewhat soberer. "I've rented rooms in Hôtel Cecil in rue St Didier. I'll set up camp as a temporary SOE center in the hope our agents will start showing up there. The BBC has agreed to broadcast the message around France. I'll stay in touch with you about the progress I make."

Anna would have longed to join him on this trip, but her boss thwarted any thoughts in that direction.

"You man the fort in London, Anna. Returning agents may report at HQ. You'll need to take care of them. And in case of definitive answers that agents were killed, you'll need to inform their families immediately."

Anna nodded. "I hope you will be successful, Sir. And that many survived. We're missing 150 agents, fifteen of them women. It's an incredible number."

"Other countries miss many more," Sir Reginald observed drily.

Anna thought it wasn't a competition but said nothing. Her own questions for now would remain unanswered.

"You have a safe trip, Sir. Talk to you soon."

AND WITH THAT the wait began. In both Paris and London, Section F agents began to trickle in, one after the other, but none of the agents Anna so desperately awaited. The trickle stopped at 101. Of thirteen of Anna's girls, there was still no sign.

THEIR SILENCE WAS DEAFENING.

PART VI

ANSWERS NOT GUESSES

BACK IN POST-WAR GERMANY JANUARY
1946

45

MEETING THE BENEFACTOR

18 months later - London, January 1946

The war in Europe had been over for eight months and life in post-war London was slowly coming alive again. Soon SOE would be completely dismantled, and Baker Street HQ would close its doors for good.

Anna was clearing the last things from her desk in the office that had been her anchor point in the past five years. Her assignment would continue for eight more months, not with SOE but with the War Crimes Investigation team in Bad Oeynhausen that she had visited in November of 1945. Only three months earlier. It seemed like a lifetime ago.

She'd been in Germany to try to find out about her missing agents. How fruitless and frustrating that short trip had been. No leads on Pearl or Henryk. Not even on her cousin Herschel. At least she would have more time now. Nine whole months to devote herself to the task.

Her eye fell on the description for her new job before she put the file in her bag.

Job Title: War Crimes Investigator - SOE F Section
Employee: Flight Officer Anna Adams
Assignment Duration: February 1, 1946 - September 1, 1946
Location: Bad Oyenhausen, Germany
Supervisor: Group Captain Tony Summers
Job Description:

Position Overview:
Flight Officer Anna Adams has been assigned the critical role of War
Crimes Investigator within the SOE F Section, tasked with
investigating the disappearances of secret agents who were stationed
in France during and after World War II. Her primary duty is to
uncover the truth behind these disappearances and where possible
bring those responsible to justice, ensuring accountability for war
crimes.

Key Responsibilities:
Investigation: Flight Officer Adams will conduct thorough
investigations into the cases of missing secret agents affiliated with
the SOE F Section. She will gather evidence, interview witnesses, and
examine any relevant documents to piece together the circumstances
surrounding each disappearance.
Collaboration: Anna Adams will closely collaborate with her
supervisor, Group Captain Tony Summers, and other team members
to share information, insights, and progress reports. Effective
teamwork is essential in this endeavor.
Intelligence Gathering: She will liaise with intelligence agencies,
both Allied and German, to acquire any available information that
may aid in her investigations. This includes the interrogation of
captured enemy personnel and the analysis of captured
documents.
Documentation: Flight Officer Adams will meticulously document her
findings, compiling detailed reports that include witness statements,

evidence, and her own analysis. These reports will serve as a basis for potential legal proceedings.

Legal Pursuit: In coordination with Group Captain Tony Summers and legal experts, Anna Adams may initiate legal proceedings against individuals suspected of war crimes or conspiring in the disappearances of secret agents. She will assist in the preparation of cases for potential trials.

Security and Safety: Ensuring her own safety and security is of paramount importance. Anna Adams must exercise caution when handling sensitive information and interacting with potentially dangerous individuals.

<u>Qualifications:</u>

Military background or experience in intelligence work or investigative roles.

Proficiency in gathering and analyzing intelligence.

Strong interpersonal and communication skills for interviewing witnesses and collaborating with colleagues.

Attention to detail and excellent documentation skills.

A firm commitment to justice and accountability for war crimes.

The ability to work under pressure and in a potentially hostile environment.

Discretion and confidentiality in handling sensitive information.

FOR A BRIEF SPELL her determination wavered. The task before her was monumental. Of the 100 agents who never returned, the death of most had been confirmed but the circumstances under which they died and the role the Gestapo and the camp commanders played in it was still largely undocumented.

Eight months was nothing. She'd have to work night and day. But she was prepared for that.

A knock on her door.

"Are you ready, Miss Adams?" The kind and loyal Mr. Parks would see her out for the final time. Dolly had long moved to another secretarial job. The entire building was silent, mute with secrets and unsolved sorrow.

"Do you have a new job, Mr. Parks?" Anna asked as they walked down the stairs.

"Yes, miss, I'll return to the conciergerie at the Home Office, like I did before the war. I'll miss you though."

"I'll pass by one day to say hello," Anna smiled.

"You do that, miss. And take care in Germany. I don't believe all the Nazis are suddenly converted and are little, white lambs now."

Anna shuddered for a moment thinking of the nasty man with the photograph of Vom Rath, who had cornered her in that alley in Dortmund in November. She would not have the protection she had here with her British passport.

"I'll be fine, Mr Parks. I've learned a thing or two about self-protection after five years in the secret services."

"I hope you do, miss. Well goodbye and so long."

"Goodbye."

And the door of Baker Street, that continuous place in her life where she'd spent most of her waking hours for four of her five years in the war effort, fell shut behind her. It was an empty feeling. It didn't feel like relief, it wasn't closure, and it certainly didn't feel like victory.

A large black car drove up to the curb and stopped right in front of her. For a moment Anna flinched, thinking of the man with the photograph, or even Roderick. A stately chauffeur came from behind the wheel.

"Miss Adams?"

She didn't reveal her identity straightaway. "Who might you be, Sir?"

"I'm the chauffeur of the man who calls himself your benefactor, Miss Adams. I will not disclose his name, as he insisted he wanted to do that himself. I may only say he protected you during the entire war."

"My benefactor?" Anna was stupefied. *Who could that be?*

"I was instructed to take you to him, as he has important information to disclose to you, miss. Please take a seat."

Anna thought quickly. Was this man to be trusted? It sounded all rather mysterious and in no way did she want to miss her last evening with her father.

"If I tell you he is ... was a good friend of your Uncle Benjamin, would you feel safer with me then, miss?"

Her curiosity won her over. And a friend of Uncle Benjamin couldn't be a bad person.

"Alright," Anna agreed, getting into the car, "but it will have to be quick as I have an early flight tomorrow and I have still a lot to do."

"It will all get done in good time, miss. I assure you."

Who are you to assure me I can meet my duties? Anna wondered but sank back in the soft leather upholstery and enjoyed the luxury. It was very different from the taxi rides in old, run-down hackney cabs that had transported her through the war.

"Where are we going, sir?" Anna started to be worried again as they left London in the direction of Kent. Wild images of being abducted across the Channel churned in her mind.

"We're almost there, miss. It's Westenham we're heading to."

"Westenham? I don't know anyone who lives there," Anna responded but the fear subsided.

Before her she saw a large classic red-brick country mansion with white-trimmed windows and ivy climbing its walls. The house was surrounded by sloping gardens and manicured lawns. To the entrance of the property stood a wooden sign with a single word "Chartwell."

The driver stopped in front of the house and helped her out. Before Anna made it to the porch, a prim-looking housekeeper in a black taffeta dress opened the front door.

"Welcome to Mr. and Mrs. Churchill's house, Miss Adams."

Anna turned to the chauffeur to see if he'd been making a joke, but he was already reversing the black car.

"Mr. and Mrs. Churchill?" Anna repeated, an alarmed look on her face. "I'm so sorry, I had no idea. I would have dressed more properly for the occasion." She was – as always – clad in her navy-blue WAAF uniform with her beige, duffel coat over it.

"You look fine, miss. Mr. Churchill is very proud of the women still wearing the uniform. Not so many these days. Now, do come in and let me take your coat."

The middle-aged lady didn't let Anna out of her sight. After some more reassurances that this was a low-key visit, she eventually led Anna to a plant-filled conservatory that evidently also functioned as an atelier.

"Miss Adams has arrived, sir. I'll bring in the tea." The housekeeper made an encouraging movement with her chin to convince Anna to proceed.

It was one surprise after the other. The former British prime minister was clad in an enormous white artist smock over his suit, the signature cigar firmly between his lips. In his right hand, he held a well-used artist's palette, in the other a fine brush. The brush seemed dwarfish in the large, paint-covered hand. On the easel stood a half-finished English landscape in full summer.

On seeing her stand in a mild form of shock, Churchill put down brush and palette and started rubbing his hands on a cloth that hung over one of the easel's legs. The paint was still on his left hand as his clean hand came in her direction.

"Anna, you're already here. I can call you Anna? Dear me, I see such a close likeness to Bennie in you. The same serious brow. Exceptional." The handshake was warm, confidential almost.

"Bennie, sir?" Anna asked bewildered.

"My apologies. I still think of him as Bennie. I mean your Uncle Benjamin of course. We were close you know. He sometimes even called me Wins the War," Churchill chuckled, "Mrs. Windemere will bring in the tea in a sec. So sorry my wife is out today. Some Ladies Charity she had to attend. Clementine would have loved to meet you again. Hopefully another time."

"Thank you so much, sir," Anna replied, restraining herself from staring at her hero. Winston Churchill may have lost the 1945 elections to Clement Attlee, but to Anna he would always be her Prime

Minister. Uncle Benjamin had been right. Churchill had won the war for Britain.

As was his policy, Churchill came straight to the point after tea was served. Anna politely declined the generous glass of rum that came with the tea but accepted a home-made biscuit.

"Two things, Anna. First, let me explain why it took so long to get your British citizenship sorted. There were powerful politicians opposing it, among them a gentleman you know yourself. Count Roderick Macalister."

Anna gazed at Churchill in dismay. Her misgivings had been right all the time. It had been her former fiancé who proved to be the obstacle.

"Oh yes," Churchill explained. "Roddy Resolute was very pro-Hitler. All his hanging out with your uncle and other prominent Jewish businessmen was just posing. His father, the old Count, spent most of the war in Germany rubbing elbows with the Nazi party and cashing in as a by-product. Serving a deserved prison sentence for it, too."

Anna nodded, "I read it in the papers. I never met the old Count."

"You've missed nothing I can assure you. As ugly a traitor as Oswald Mosley." Churchill took a puff on his cigar and a swig from his rum. "It may sound strange for a Prime Minister, but my hands were tied when it came to the self-evident naturalization of Jewish refugees. I'm sorry, Anna, but in that respect, I had to navigate treacherous water throughout the entire war. If I pressed too hard, I'd lose the support of people I needed. And I'm not talking of the likes of the Macalisters, but more moderate folk as well."

"It makes me wonder all the more why at some point Roderick considered marrying me," Anna pondered aloud.

The penetrating blue eyes fixed her. "Should the marriage plan have gone ahead, don't believe for one minute he'd ever have mentioned your background again. These people are blue-blooded turncoats. He was after your uncle's network and money. Remember he'd marry Anna Adams and not Ansel Gryszpan."

Anna sighed, feeling miserable at having been used as a pawn on the chessboard. Now they were bringing up this ugly chapter from her past, Anna confided the entire story as Churchill seemed to be in the know anyway. "Roderick told me he wanted an heir which he couldn't get with his married mistress."

Churchill leaned closer and said in an undertone, "there was no mistress, Anna. Roddy Resolute led a promiscuous life, but there were no women involved. The only woman he adored was the one that called him *Ricky Dahling*." Churchill extinguished his cigar in the ashtray with an angry stomp.

Anna shuddered. "I had never... I'm such a goose."

"You're not even close to a goose, my dear. You had him at telling him you'd never marry him without a document protecting your uncle's trust. Oh, I'm sure he contemplated cajoling you into signing the nuptial papers in his favor, but you started to throw up barriers. I think he no longer found you worth his time. Not to forget his mother's staunch dislike of you. That might actually have been Ricky Dahling's decisive reason for giving you up. But not after continuing to throw spanners in the wheels of your naturalization."

"How do you know all this, sir?" Anna was flabbergasted at the particulars he revealed.

"Hmm..." he replied. "Typical Baker Street question. Well, the truth of the matter is, I didn't even have to find out. Countess Macalister told all the sordid details to my wife, just because she was so relieved her Ricky Dahling wouldn't marry you. Of course, Clementine is an excellent interviewer and an even better empathetic listener. My dear wife knew I had an interest in the matter so there you have your answer."

Anna swallowed the last of her cookie with difficulty. The truth still hurt, but it was also comforting Churchill knew the dilemma she'd faced with the Macalister family. And that he understood.

"I'm glad I refrained from marrying him," she confessed. "How naïve of me to think he somehow cared for me when in reality he was only out to use me and then to destroy me." She stopped there, not knowing if Churchill was aware she'd backed out of the marriage because of Henryk.

Having lit a fresh cigar, her host looked pensive but didn't touch on her love affair. "I'd promised your Uncle Benjamin I'd take care of you, Anna, and I didn't want to fail my friend. Truth is, with the anti-forces around us, it wasn't easy sailing. I protected you as best as I could."

"Thank you, sir. I just never knew, or I'd have shown my gratitude earlier."

The blue eyes rested on her, still with that pensive expression. Or was it a tinge of guilt? "I had my own motive for not giving you a British passport. As long as the war went on, I didn't want you to court the idea of leaving the country. For example, by becoming a secret agent yourself. I know all the agents who went on missions had fake identities, but what if you'd fallen in the hands of the Gestapo and they'd wrung your real name, Ansel Grynszpan, out of you? Their methods were barbarous, Anna, absolutely unprincipled."

The blue eyes changed to a thunderous deep gray. "Here in Britain, you and I only had to deal with a couple of salon fascists and double agents. That was bad but not as bad as being caught on the Continent. Here I could keep an eye on you. So, that's why the passport was ready as soon as the war was over."

Anna nodded, "how did you keep an eye on me?"

The eyes flashed blue again and Churchill uttered his typical guffaw. "You, the London Spymaker, asking me how to keep an eye on people? I'm not going to tell you, Anna. Use your imagination. And please, be double careful when you return to Germany for your work. I'll make sure Group Captain Summers has a man watching you."

"Thank you so much," Anna repeated, feeling a gulf of gratefulness spread through her. Her hero had personally looked after her. And she had never known.

"There's another thing, Anna, I want you to investigate before Germany." He stopped, took another puff, seemed temporarily distracted, then continued. "I received a phone call from Odessa, from General Edward Harrington, a good friend of mine. He told me there is an English woman working in a Soviet Red Cross Hospital there who resembles one of your missing agents.

Anna gasped. "Who? I mean... what does she look like?"

Churchill smiled, "I don't know, Anna but I have the same high hopes as you, that's why I want you on the ground there." He looked very serious. "Here's the thing. Our relations with the Soviets are deteriorating fast, as no doubt you know. I'm glad I can still contact Joseph Stalin and he agreed you may land on the military airfield of the 5th Air Army near Odessa. You'd better take that option as soon as possible, Anna, because I'm not sure how long we'll be Allies and able to travel freely to Soviet occupied territory."

"I will. Straightaway." Anna rose from her chair as if Joseph Stalin might stop her that very minute. What if it was Pearl? But how could it be? Why would Pearl or another agent work in a hospital in Odessa? Why not come home? There must be a mistake. But it was one worthy of investigation.

"Ho-ho, young lady," Churchill stopped her. "Haste without thought is never a good strategy. Here take this." He gave her a file. "This holds all your instructions. And a personal letter from me explaining your trip. Now go home, pack and wait for the phone call that announces your flight details. Now I know you're willing to go to Odessa, I'll notify the RAF."

"Of course I'll go to Odessa, sir. I'd fly to the end of the world for a chance to get back one of my girls."

"That's the spirit, my dear! That's the spirit."

Anna got a warm handshake and a pat on the shoulder.

"You come back here, London Spymaker, and report to this old man what you found. Both in Odessa and in Germany.

"I will, sir, and thank you for everything."

The last look Churchill gave Anna was both paternal and praising.

46

SHADOWS ON THE BLACK SEA

Three days later - Odessa, End of January 1946

I n the wake of the war, Odessa, the jewel of the Black Sea, stood as a city trapped between its glorious past and an uncertain future. The war had stamped deep scars on the city and its inhabitants. The once elegant boulevards bore the pockmarks of conflict, flanked on both sides by grand buildings that stood as silent witnesses to the horrors of recent years.

The brisk, salt-laden breeze off the Black Sea carried whispers of a world forever changed. The bustling port, once a hub of international commerce, was now in the early stages of recovery. Cargo ships, battered and weary from the war's tumultuous seas, docked at the harbor, unloading their cargoes of hope and despair.

Odessa had always been a melting pot of nationalities and after the war a new tapestry of characters emerged. Ukrainian families, their faces etched with both the pain of loss and the strength of resilience, walked the same streets as the Russian soldiers returning from the front lines.

Despite the Odessa massacre - the mass murder of the city's Jewish population in late 1941 and early 1942 when it was under Romanian control - Jewish survivors of the Holocaust sought refuge in the city after the war.

The city's cultural soul, never completely extinguished, flickered to life in underground jazz clubs, where the mournful strains of saxophones met the rhythmic tapping of dancing feet. Artists and writers, their creativity fueled by the turbulent times, met in dimly-lit cafes to share their stories and dream of a better world.

Amidst the political backdrop of the Soviet Union, secret whispers of dissent echoed through hidden corridors. Resistance fighters operated in the shadows, daring to defy the iron grip of the Soviet regime. Espionage and intrigue thrived, as spies from competing nations maneuvered for control in this strategic port city.

As winter's icy grip tightened, Odessa became a place of contradictions—a city struggling to rebuild while grappling with the ghosts of its past.

Anna arrived on what surely must have been the coldest day of the century. The Avro Lancaster that had flown her from RAF Tangmere to the 5th Army Airfield just outside Odessa had difficulty landing. Soviet soldiers had made a valiant attempt at creating an ice-free landing strip, but the Lancaster's wheels continued to slide over the runway until the cursing pilot managed to bring her to a successful halt on the field nearby.

"Sorry about that, miss. Must be the worst landing of my career," the pilot apologized. He was a short, stocky man with a rugged appearance, clearly a war veteran. Anna was just happy to survive the long flight and scary landing.

"15° Fahrenheit," the pilot grumbled. "Better get you into a warmer place. Be careful when leaving the plane. The 5th Army Airfield is a slippery slope."

Churchill had taken care of all the details of Anna's, hopefully fruitful, stay in Odessa. She had three days before the plane with the stocky pilot would return for her. Her hotel, Imperial Riviera Hotel on Deribasovskaya Street, was already booked and there was a taxi waiting to take her there.

Anna took in the foreign, port city with interest. It was beautiful despite its scars, the roofs topped with crisp, white snow and the people huddled in fur coats and hats. The easiest way to transport goods and children was by pulling fur-lined sledges, which looked romantic to Anna's war-weary eyes.

People here spoke only a few words of English, but she didn't dare to address the citizens in German, so stuck to English accompanied by arm gestures and facial expressions. People seemed to find her funny, but it eventually got her to where she wanted to be.

The Imperial Riviera Hotel, once a trophy of affluence in pre-war Odessa, stood as a testament to resilience. The majestic neoclassical façade, with ornate columns and intricate stonework, still bore visible holes from shrapnel and bullets in its once-pristine exterior, silent reminders of the Siege of Odessa in 1941.

Anna had little interest in the architecture or the faded elegance of her temporary accommodation. All she wanted was to make the best of the afternoon light to find the Red Cross Hospital and get her answer. Who was the English woman working there?

A helpful taxi driver understood her quest and steered the old, beige Pobeda along Odessa's seafront until they got to a sturdy building with a large Red Cross emblem at the entrance. Anna sighed a breath of relief and effusively thanked the driver who looked at her with a puzzled expression and kept laughing, "da, da, da." Which Anna knew meant yes.

The medical center was nestled along the Black Sea coastline and stood as a beacon of hope and healing in the aftermath of the devastating war. As Anna stepped inside, she found the hospital to be a hive of activity. The hallways echoed with the steady footfalls of doctors, nurses, and orderlies, all committed to healing. Wards were bustling with patients, both military and civilian, while beds lined the wards, each with a patient, some visibly injured, while others stared into nothingness, bearing the invisible scars of trauma.

Anna went up to the reception desk and pulled out her file of missing female agents. On top, she held the photograph of Pearl in her WAAF uniform, taken the day before she went on her first mission. The photo was almost four years old. It was likely that today's Pearl would not resemble this young, fierce-looking agent, but Anna had nothing better to offer.

The receptionist looked up from a document she was reading and seeing Anna's British uniform asked in English "May I help you?"

Relieved to find someone who spoke her language, Anna tumbled over her words and her photographs landed like a fan on the floor. Apologizing she bent and picked them up. Her cheeks red with embarassment.

"I arrived from England today. Mr. Winston Churchill organized my trip. I am here for information about a British woman who apparently works here in the hospital."

"Yes?" The receptionist's face was deadpan. She listened but gave nothing away.

"Could I show you some photographs of women that have been missing since the war and see if you recognize one of them?" Anna thought she should have better prepared this. How to explain to this Russian receptionist why British women might be missing after the war? How much information should she give? If it was one of her agents, how much information had they shared here about their missions in France? If any?"

Without thinking further, Anna placed Pearl's photograph on the counter and studied the woman's face as she took it between her fingers. Long, endless long seconds passed. The same deadpan expression, then a tiny movement of the chin that told Anna she recognized Pearl, but the answer was negative.

"No, don't know her. Sorry."

Thank God, I worked in the secret services and have friends in high places, Anna thought. She may have lost the first round with her clumsiness; she wouldn't lose the second. From her bag she retrieved a sealed envelope that was addressed to Joseph Stalin and had all sorts of posh-looking British stamps, among them 'top secret' and 'confidential'. The receptionist, a bleak woman with frizzy, blonde hair in an oversized cardigan, eyed the envelope with interest and sat straighter as if Stalin was looking over her shoulder.

"I can either go to the military command here and ask for an inventory of the hospital staff or I can give you ten rubles and you show me where I can find the British woman."

"Ten rubles?" Some light in the bleak eyes. It could buy her a week of groceries for her family. Anna handed her ten one-ruble notes which the woman quickly pocketed. The Stalin letter went back into Anna's bag. It might serve her another time in Germany if she had to go into Soviet-occupied territory.

"She works in the kitchen," the receptionist revealed, "but I have never spoken to her."

"Is she on duty today?"

Only a nod of the head.

"And where is the kitchen?"

"Through that corridor to the end, second door on the right."

"Thank you."

Only when Anna was passing through the corridor on her own, she felt how weak her knees were. Pearl was a few meters away. But what if she didn't want to see her? There must be a reason she was hiding in a Red Cross hospital far away from home.

With no clue how to go about the confrontation, Anna saw their entire friendship pass before her eyes. The day on the bench at St Paul's Girl School, Pearl moving in in Chelsea, Pearl in the bath jumping up and down that she was going to be a SOE agent, proud Pearl in her WAAF uniform, terse Pearl boarding the Lysander.

And all the love Anna felt for her. Would it be enough?

SHE WAS STANDING at the sink with her back to the door, scrubbing a large pan. Pearl had never been chubby, but she was now extremely thin, her shoulder blades protruding through her black pullover over which she wore an apron. The hair was longer, still dark blonde but no longer with a shine. She stood bent as if her hips were hurting.

On the other side of the large kitchen a man and a woman were cutting up cabbages. They saw Anna enter and stopped their work, clearly wondering what was going on. A British woman in uniform could mean only one thing. She was coming for the other British woman.

The man said something in Russian to Pearl, upon which she turned slowly. Anna almost took a step back in horror. Pearl's eyes were lightless, as if she was staring straight down the stairs of death. Her face was pale, the skin tight over her cheek bones, the lips a thin, bloodless line of pain. She slowly dried her soapy hands on the floral apron, staring at Anna as if in need of glasses.

Anna wasn't sure Pearl recognized her, but when Anna took a step in her direction, Pearl slipped past her and bolted out of the door. She was limping but could still run fast.

Not knowing what else to do, Anna followed her, calling out to her. "Pearl, please. It's me, Anna. Wait for me." But Pearl didn't stop. She flung open a door and ran into a snow laden garden, slipping on the icy path. Anna still followed her. She saw Pearl rush to a door on the other side of the open space. She opened it and disappeared.

Anna stopped in the middle of the winter-garden, tears running down her cheeks. If it had been possible, she would have dug a hole in that forlorn, frozen garden and disappeared herself. Instead, she sunk down on an ice-cold bench and buried her face in her hands.

What had she done wrong? It was all her fault. Pearl was no longer Pearl.

Anna didn't know how long she sat in the cold but at some moment she felt a tap on her shoulder. She raised her tear-stained face to see a bearded man in a white coat with a stethoscope hanging from his pocket. He was staring down at her with sympathy. In broken English he said, "must be Anna Adams?"

Anna nodded, too spent to reply.

"Come." The doctor tapped her lightly on the shoulder again and repeated, "come."

He led her to the door where Pearl had passed through but there Anna halted in her tracks, unable to face another showdown.

"Come," the doctor reiterated, "Pearl is alright now."

Pearl was sitting in an armchair, wrapped in a large woolen shawl with her legs tucked under her. She was holding a smoldering cigarette in an unsteady hand. On the coffee table next to her stood a half-full glass of water and a pillbox. Anna stood at a distance, swallowing her re-emerging tears, not daring to meet her friend's gaze.

"Sit," the doctor requested, pointing to another armchair. Anna sat down gingerly, while the physician pulled up a third chair. A long silence followed in which a clock ticked somewhere, and a hungry blackbird landed on the branch of a frozen bush outside.

Who was going to speak first? The monosyllabic doctor or her?

Anna opened her mouth, but the doctor waved his hand as if to stop her. So, they sat in silence again. After half an hour with nobody speaking or moving, the doctor got up. He said a short sentence in Russian to Pearl who nodded and closed her eyes. The cigarette lay forgotten in the ashtray next to her.

"Come," the doctor pointed to another door and Anna went with him, casting one quick look back at Pearl who seemed to be dozing.

"I am Pearl's psychiatrist, Dr. Nikolai Ivanovitch Volkov. Miss Baseden is very traumatized, so don't take her behavior personally." Anna was glad he spoke better English than she'd anticipated and that he was taking care of her friend.

"How... how did she get here?" she asked.

"It is a long story. For her recovery it would be better if she told you herself. It would mean she trusts you again. She did talk about you. Many times."

Anna felt a moment of warmth in the cold agony she was in.

"Did she?" His words almost made her cry again.

"Yes, Miss Adams, I was fortunate enough to gain Pearl's trust. It took me a long time but once given, she began to heal. That's why she came straight to me when you suddenly turned up. That is a good sign as well. She knew where to go."

"How... how long will it take her to trust me?" Anna thought of the three days she'd been given. She'd have to phone London to postpone her flight back and postpone her job with the War Crimes Investigation team in Germany.

The grizzly doctor tapped the tips of his long fingers together. "Hard to say. I was just reducing her sedative medication because she's been stable for the past couple of weeks, but I upped the dose a tiny bit right now. Could be long, could be short."

"Can I let her family know she is alive?" Anna returned to her professional self. "Her parents and brothers have been extremely worried, as you can imagine."

She was surprised he didn't immediately answer in the affirmative.

"That is the largest part of Pearl's trauma, Miss Adams. She is rigid with guilt. The poor girl is convinced it is her fault all the agents were captured in France. Her guilt is so big she believes she doesn't deserve to go back home, whether to France or to England."

"Oh no," Anna whimpered, "it can't be her fault."

"Like most agents, Pearl was severely tortured in Fresnes prison before being sent to a German prison. She couldn't take the pain anymore and gave the Gestapo names. Including her own real name. Everything to make them stop. She thinks she doesn't deserve to have survived Auschwitz."

"Auschwitz?" Anna repeated, facts clicking in her mind. That's why Suhren didn't recognize her when Anna went to Germany in 1945. Pearl had never been to Ravensbrück. But how did she end up in Auschwitz?

The doctor studied Anna. "You might as well hear it from me first. When the Soviets came to Auschwitz, Pearl was very weak but free to walk out of a nearby mining sub-camp, Janina and further to southern Poland. Perhaps to a town called Katowice. The Russians had told her and the few surviving prisoners there was help awaiting them. It was the Red Cross. From there she went to Krakow and finally to Odessa, where she's been in the sickbay for almost six months."

"When did she come here?" Anna asked.

"Late March 1945."

Even though her own visit to the Continent was eight months after that time, Anna cringed at the thought Pearl was in fact free and alone during her November 1945 investigation in Germany. The doctor continued. "It was all-hands-on-deck for the doctors and nurses here." The doctor's steel-gray eyes became veiled for a moment. "I've never seen anything like it in my forty-year career. Emaciated, full of diseases, and the worst mental condition humans can be in. But I can tell you every recovery has been a huge boost for us all and we had come so far with sweet, strong Pearl."

"Until now?" Anna uttered with dread in her voice.

He smiled for the first time. "Oh no, Miss Adams. Maybe you are the catalyst we were waiting for."

At that moment the door opened, and Pearl stood there, the wrap hanging half on her shoulder and half dragging over the floor. Anna recognized her friend's eyes for the first time since her arrival. They were light, almost dancing again.

She rose, slowly, uncertainly.

"Pearlie, oh Pearlie!"

Pearl was in her arms, bony and all, but still with that immense strength she'd always possessed.

"Anna, Anna, Anna. You've come for me."

For a moment Pearl broke the embrace to turn to her trusted doctor but holding Anna by the hand. In her normal, light Pearl voice she announced, "Doctor Volkov, this is Anna, my friend. I told you about her."

Anna thought her heart would burst with joy. The kind, older physician was one big smile for his recovering patient.

"I know, Pearl. Isn't it amazing? Your best friend has come all the way from London to visit you."

"How did you know I was here?" Pearl asked, swiveling around again, her expression full of the forcefulness Anna so adored and admired.

"I'm the London Spymaker," Anna joked, "I know everything."

47

BACK IN GERMANY

Two weeks later - Bad Oeynhausen, February 1946

After careful therapy and progress made in the two weeks prior, Pearl was safely back with her overjoyed family. With the key to the Chelsea flat securely in Pearl's pocket, it was time for Anna to leave for Germany.

The parting of the two friends was painful but necessary. Pearl needed to readjust to her life in freedom with the help of her family and a British Dr. Volkov while Anna had to live up to her promise to investigate the fate of some sixty missing Section F agents.

Pearl hadn't talked to Anna about her ordeals, but she had given her a letter to read for when she was out of the country. On the plane to Berlin, it was the first thing Anna retrieved from her bag. Tearing open the envelope she read.

My Dearest Anna,

I hope that when you've read this letter, you will still think of me fondly, my dear friend. My emotions have been all over the place since our reunion, so that's why I have chosen to write you this letter and explain all that happened to me.

In the early days of my recovery, Doctor Volkov advised me to start a diary and at first I thought "Never! That's more something for my friend Anna," but he was right (Doctor Volkov was _always_ right!). Writing is cathartic when the emotions are both overwhelming and comforting.

I still want to apologize from the bottom of my heart for the betrayal that transpired during those dreadful days in Lyon. When the Brouillard Network was compromised, and I was captured by those Gestapo monsters, I felt like I had let everyone down, including you and SOE HQ. The torment at Hotel Terminus by Klaus Barbie still haunts my dreams, and I can never truly forgive myself for breaking, no matter the extent of the torture.

Fresnes Prison was another harrowing chapter, with torture that seemed endless. They ripped off my toenails, burned my flesh with their wretched cigarettes, and forced me to divulge names and my real identity as Pearl Baseden. I was convinced that I had failed us all and that not only would I pay the price in the worst way possible, but that I endangered other agents.

After an agonizing stretch, I was transferred to Karlsruhe, where I endured nine brutal months in that frigid, women's prison. Denise and I shared a cell, and we found solace in speaking French, singing lullabies to combat the loneliness, and even communicating with the other agents next to us, using Morse code with our eating spoons on the bare prison walls. The hunger and cold were excruciating, but at least the overt, physical torture ceased.

Then, one summer day, we were abruptly ushered to the station and onto waiting cattle trains. It was there that I was separated from the other girls, never knowing what became of Peter Suttill, or Maurice Southgate or the girls.

I was transported to a place beyond nightmares, Auschwitz, where I toiled in a paint factory, my body growing weaker by the day from the grueling labor and meager rations. It was a lonely existence, and I kept my spirits alive by singing the songs Denise and I had cherished and by replaying the memories of my happy life in London and France.

I was certain that I would meet my end in that dreadful place, as my hips ached terribly, and intestinal problems plagued my weakened body. Yet, on one icy morning, with no concept of the date or year, the camp was suddenly overrun by uniformed soldiers. We soon found out it was the Red Army.

Our Nazi guards fled, and I managed to come out of hiding from behind the kitchens in the sub-camp

Janina. My journey to freedom is a hazy memory, but I do recall arriving in Odessa, where the Soviet Red Cross offered me the care and nourishment I so desperately needed.

It was in Odessa that I met Doctor Volkov, who insisted that I return to England. At that time, I couldn't bear the thought of facing the shame of my actions and was prepared to become a Soviet citizen, leaving behind my homeland and all that I held dear. But then, you, dear Anna, appeared at the Red Cross hospital in Odessa, and everything changed.

Your forgiveness, your understanding, and your unwavering friendship brought me back from the brink of despair. I am immensely proud of the George Cross bestowed upon me by Mr. Churchill, but it is your presence and your forgiveness that mean the world to me.

Anna, you are not only my dearest friend but also my savior. You have given me a second chance at life, and for that, I will be eternally grateful. I cherish our reunion and look forward to a future where we can heal the wounds of the past together.

With all my love and gratitude,

Your Pearlie xxx

Anna sat with the letter between her trembling fingers for a long time, now and then staring down at Pearl's round, almost childish, handwriting. The words so mature, so Pearl-wise, and then again, she stared out into space on the other side of the plane window. Above the clouds, the eternal sun shone, spreading an orange-red glow over planet Earth below. She had saved Pearl, or better Pearl had saved herself, had been saved by grace.

The euphoria of Pearl's rescue encouraged Anna that she would book good results in Germany as well. Though no other survivors were expected to rise from the ashes.

GERMANY, here I come!

~

ANNA'S OPTIMISM soon withered when she was back at the War Investigations HQ in Bad Oeynhausen. The building was so cold she had to work in her winter coat during the day, with mittens on her hands and a cup of hot coffee to keep her warm inside. Though the team was nice and helpful, the investigations stalled every time and not much had changed since Anna's brief visit in November.

It was a gray and dismal morning in late February when her boss, Captain Summers, sauntered in.

"I know it's off the record," he began, his elongated face with the narrow nose and hawkish eyes resting on Anna's desk, which was scattered with photographs and documents, "but I happened to stumble on some info about the young man whose disappearance seems to interest you."

Anna looked up at him with hopeful eyes. Henryk?

Summers knew she was also looking for the Polish SOE agent as she had brought his name up in the Kaindl interview in November. She said nothing, waiting, holding her breath for what was to come.

"It's about your cousin, Herschel Grynszpan."

Despite the disappointment that it was not about Henryk, she was all ears. She'd tried to investigate Herschel's traces after his arrest, but everything seemed blurred.

"We are now quite sure that after his arrest in Paris in 1938,

Herschel spent the rest of his life in German custody, in French prisons, and German concentration camps. Based on references to him in documents after 1942, speculations are he died in Sachsenhausen concentration camp. However, his death was not confirmed. We believe the SS commanders may have erased all evidence of Herschel's death, because he was supposed to be kept alive to be tried before a German court.

"So, Anton Kaidl must know but will likely never admit the truth?" Anna observed.

"I guess so," Summers agreed. "Question is, is it enough for you?"

Anna nodded. "Have his parents been informed? I lost touch with them after the Polen Aktion."

"Yes. They settled in the Soviet Union in 1939. I sent a note to our colleagues in Berlin, asking them to forward it to Moscow. I can never be sure it will reach them, but I did what I could."

"Thank you, Captain Summers. One day I'll see to it that a remembrance plaque is placed for Herschel outside their Hanover house. Though a Jew murdering Vom Rath was a convenient excuse for the systematic extermination of the European Jews by the Nazis, my cousin can't be held responsible for the entire Holocaust."

"Correct. Just keep your eyes open for reprisals, Anna." Tony sounded serious and Anna remembered he'd been instructed to ensure extra surveillance for her. She was never to travel without an escort and never to leave the hotel after dark.

After Tony returned to his own office, Anna pondered her illustrious cousin. Herschel had always been a bit of a show pony, even as a young boy, but he had a good heart. She believed none of the nonsense that was rumored, that Herschel and Vom Rath had been lovers. She knew her cousin. He'd been outraged at the way his parents had been evicted from their house and sent to live like rats on the Polish border. Like her own parents, the other Grynszpans had been decent, middle-class Hanoverians, not scum of the earth.

She looked at his photo and blessed him.

"May your death not have been in vain, dear Herschel. Your act was brave, though badly planned."

. . .

One case laid to rest.

ANNA'S LIST of agents whose deaths had not yet been confirmed grew shorter by the day. Her days were mainly filled writing reports and sending notifications to family members in England, France, and Canada.

She also visited the remembrance plaques at the concentration camps where her valiant agents had met their death. If possible and the weather permitted, she would lay a wreath to pay Baker Street HQ respects.

The confirmed death of Peter Suttill moved her deeply and she took great effort to write his report and send a copy to his parents.

War Crimes Investigation Division Bad Oeynhausen

March 12, 1946

Dear Mr. and Mrs. Suttill,

I am writing to convey the most regrettable news concerning your son, Major Peter Suttill. It is with a heavy heart and the utmost respect that I inform you of the events that transpired on September 6, 1944.

On that fateful day, your son was taken from his cell in Sachsenhausen concentration camp by members of the Nazi SS, a group notorious for their brutality and ruthlessness. In a stark departure from the methods typically employed by the Germans to execute prisoners,

Peter was escorted to a barren courtyard where he was to face a firing squad.

This singular instance stands out as an anomaly in the grim annals of the war, as gas chambers and piano wire were commonly used to exact a slower and more agonizing end upon countless others. It is important to note that this exceptional method of execution speaks volumes about the extraordinary qualities that Peter possessed.

What sets this tragic incident apart is that he was so admired that SS officers at a lower level formed a guard of honor as he was sent to the execution place. Even the enemy, who were known for their relentless and merciless tactics, could not help but recognize the exceptional nature of your son's character and abilities. The fact that they assembled a guard of honor to oversee his execution attests to the profound impact Peter had on those around him.

In his role as SOE agent in France, Peter Suttill demonstrated unwavering bravery, unparalleled resourcefulness, and an unyielding commitment to the cause. His actions undoubtedly made a significant difference in the fight against the Axis forces of tyranny and oppression. His dedication to the Allied cause and his ability to inspire respect even among his captors is a testament to his remarkable character.

Although this letter cannot possibly alleviate the

immeasurable grief you must be experiencing, I hope it provides some solace in knowing that your son's sacrifices and exceptional qualities have not gone unnoticed. He will forever be remembered as a hero in our fight against the darkness that has gripped the world during these turbulent times.

Please accept my deepest condolences on behalf of the SOE HQ and the War Crimes Investigation Division in Bad Oyenhausen and know that our thoughts are with you during this difficult period. If you have any questions or require further information, please do not hesitate to contact me.

Sincerely,

Flight Officer Anna Adams
War Crimes Investigator
War Crimes Investigation Division

When the letter was stamped and sealed in an envelope, Anna though of Pearl. She had not mentioned Peter in the brief time they had had together.

So, I'm not going to let her know now, Anna thought. *I'll tell her face to face that her Peter was a hero till his very last breath.*

48

THE SHADOW UNMASKED

Six weeks later – Bad Oeynhausen, April 1946

Having visible personal security night and day was a new experience to Anna and one she couldn't really get adjusted to. Though it was usually the same, heavily-armed British corporal who followed her around and kept a polite distance.

She missed her freedom; the corporal was a constant reminder she was in danger and it was weighing on her. One unchaperoned walk in the park couldn't hurt, could it?

The early spring air was so crisp and carried a faint promise of warmth to come. The winter had been long and lonely. She'd been cooped up in that freezing office far too long, surrounded by the stern faces of her British comrades and the ever-watchful eyes of her assigned protector, Corporal Jameson.

She missed the freedom she once had as the Baker Street spymaker, the thrill of danger, and the taste of adventure. What danger could a short walk in daylight do? No doubt there were other people in the park on this nice day.

She didn't say anything, just took her bag and got up from her office chair. A secret agent has ways of disappearing. As she made her way to the park, her high heels were silent on the pavement. The tall trees that lined the avenue were still barren, their branches reaching out like skeletal fingers towards the sky. Anna's duffle coat billowed around her as a gentle breeze rustled through the remaining dry leaves.

Whether it was all the talk about Nazi spies or the memory of the man who'd given her the photo of Vom Rath three months earlier, Anna was on tenterhooks. She couldn't shake off the feeling she was being watched, even though she'd managed to lose Corporal Jameson in the labyrinthine streets of Bad Oeynhausen. The man with the photograph? Could he still be around? Her nerves were on edge, and she instinctively reached for the concealed Luger tucked beneath her coat.

As she entered the park, she looked furtively around her. It was just an ordinary park with mothers pushing strollers and older couples scurrying by, their shopping bags flapping against their thighs.

The once-lush gardens showed the scars of war. Crumbled statues and neglected flowerbeds spoke of a time when beauty had given way to destruction. Anna wandered along the meandering paths, her senses alert for any sign of danger.

As she turned a corner, she saw him. A man leaning against a stone pillar, his dark eyes fixed on her, the same raincoat, the same lean, shaven face, and short-cut hair. No hat this time. Though her heart pounded in her chest, the recognition struck her like a thunderbolt.

It was the man who'd given her the photograph, uttered the threat, the man she'd seen in the Baker Street alleyways. This time she was prepared for Hans Müller, as she'd found out he was called. She also knew he was the organiser of the fascist Werwolf Movement, former Gauleiter in Munich, the headquarters of the Nazi Party, from 1 November 1929. One of Hitler's close confidants, a man who should have been behind bars long ago.

Their eyes locked, and Anna could see the hatred burning in his gaze. He stepped forward, his hand reaching inside his coat. Panic surged through Anna as she knew he was armed and intent on killing her.

Not just yet, flashed through her, though her hand was on the Luger. What was his motive?

"Herr Müller, you here?" she said in German.

He hesitated, clearly hadn't expected her to know his name.

"Fräulein Adams."

"What do you want this time?" Anna asked, her legs slightly wider than hip width, her feet firmly planted on the gravel.

"Your informants," he replied in a low voice, "who are they?"

"I have no idea what you are talking about, Herr Müller. Please explain." Her voice was steady but her hands in her pockets trembled.

"How do you know my name?"

"Aha," Anna sneered. "I could ask you the same. Why are you following me?"

"Because you know as well as I do that Herschel Grynszpan isn't dead. He escaped from Sachsenhausen. One day you'll lead me to him. And then I'll avenge my friend, Ernst vom Rath."

Anna's brain hurt. This information was new.

"Herschel Grynszpan is dead, Herr Müller. I've seen the death certificate," she lied, "so let me go in peace."

She made a movement as if walking away from him, her hand still on the Luger but hoping she'd won the confrontation. Her mind was on the need to tell her colleagues to track down this criminal. And fast.

But before she could turn away from him, a gunshot rang out from behind her. She saw Müller slowly sinking to his knees. Anna turned to see Corporal Jameson, breathing heavily, his pistol still trained on the Gauleiter. Two other British officers stepped forward and grabbed him by the armpits, dragging him to his feet. Blood oozed from his right thigh, but he was not fatally wounded.

"You're under arrest, Müller," the corporal growled, "and you're going to jail for a very long time."

Hans Müller seemed in too much pain to answer as he was led to a nearby military vehicle with the British flag.

Corporal Jameson turned to Anna, looking rather pleased with himself. "I outsmarted the spymaker. The boss is going to be so proud of me, but that was a dangerous game you were playing, Miss Adams, or did you know I was keeping him within gunshot range?"

Anna laughed despite herself and despite the shock. "No, I honestly thought I'd shaken you off, Corporal Jameson. Not my best secret agent side. Yes, you won this round. When I realized who I was up against I was scrambling to find a way to get him arrested but I hadn't figured it out yet."

"We've had Hans Müller on our radar for a while, miss, and hoped he would start hanging around Bad Oeynhausen now you returned. And he did. His personal vengeance about Vom Rath has become his Achilles' heel and he's basically turned himself in with you as the bait. Sorry for that, miss."

"I have no difficulty admitting I was wrong, and Major Summers was right," Anna remarked wryly. "I just wonder how a guy like Hans Müller could travel to London in the middle of the war? I'm sure I saw him outside SOE HQ in 1942."

"That you must ask the boss, miss. I wouldn't know the answer."

With a cup of tea and the occasional shiver still running through her, Anna walked into Captain Summers' office.

"What is it with Hans Müller I didn't know?" she asked.

"I combed through the entire Vom Rath-Herschel alliance at the request of the British government, Anna. People high up in the ranks wanted to know every little detail. That's when I bumped into this Hans Müller story. During his entire reign as the Gauleiter of Munich, he brought up the great injustice done to his university pal. And how every Jew called Grynszpan should be punished for this murder. The link to you and your family was an easy one. There are some third cousins and aunts he also went after. And with horrible consequences. None of them survived the concentration camps."

"But how could he come to London in 1942?" Anna enquired.

"That wasn't him, that was his twin brother, Walter Müller, caught as a double spy when he tried to leave England in 1943. Still in prison in Leeds. Yes, he followed you in England on the request of Hans. That's when the invisible security measures were put into place for you and your father. Also from high up. I don't know who gave the instructions."

"I do," Anna mumbled, and aloud she added. "Heavens, what a story. I truly hope both brothers get their deserved sentence."

"They will. And you're free to go as you please, Anna. We have every reason to believe Hans Müller was a lone wolf."

"Finally, freedom," Anna smiled. But she didn't feel free at all.

49

THE SLOW SLOG

Three months later - Bad Oeynhausen, 20 July 1946

Having traversed Germany for six months in search of answers, Anna was close to exhaustion and despair. Starting with a list bearing the names of the remaining fifty-two elusive SOE agents, among them, twelve courageous women, the ticking off of names had been as slow as wading through molasses.

With less than two months remaining on her assignment, she had four more to go. Forty-eight condolences letters sent to the families. Forty-two responses, the lines in the letters filled with deep grief and some relief.

It was harsh, it was harrowing, it was Anna's private hell. All her colleagues were investigating Nazi crimes and bringing the criminals to justice. She was trying to find people, people she'd met, people she'd seen off, people whose last words on British soil she'd listened to, whom she had promised to keep their families informed. She felt very alone and very small in her monumental task that now inevitably ended in death. They had all perished.

Few of the people surrounding her knew about Anna's secret

mission and even fewer had ever heard of SOE. She remained the mysterious WAAF flight officer in the midst of military men.

With a mere six weeks left to uncover their fates, Anna's foremost task was now to establish the fate of the last four women at Natzweiler Concentration camp, the only German camp on French territory.

Natzweiler had primarily been used for political prisoners, resistance fighters, and those deemed enemies of the Reich. The term 'Nacht und Nebel,' meaning night and fog, indicated the secrecy and disappearance of inmates sent there. Not a trace should be found of them. Perhaps the most difficult task for Anna to unravel in her final weeks.

The agents she was investigating were Vera Rowden, Diana Leigh, Andrée Khan, and Nora Borrel. With the aid of former SOE agent Brian Fieldstone, a survivor of four concentration camps, among them Natzweiler, Anna was close to uncovering the women's fate.

Brian had been assisting the team at Bad Oeynhausen after being heard as a witness at the Nuremberg Trials. A portrait painter before the war, he saw people in pictures. Even during his long months of captivity, he'd drawn sketches of inmates on any scrap of paper he could lay his hands on.

"Show me the photographs of the women you're looking for," he offered, coming into her cramped office and slumping his long, slender frame on the only other chair in the room.

Anna laid the pictures of Vera, Diana, Andrée, and Nora in front of him. He studied them intently.

"This one." He pointed to Diana. "Middle height, wearing a bow in her mousy-blonde hair, like a piece of tartan ribbon, obviously English." He rumbled in his suitcase and drew out a sketch of a woman in a two-piece suit walking briskly with a small valise, the bow bobbing in her hair.

"You saw Diana at Natzweiler?" Anna gasped, wondering why she hadn't thought of asking Brian before.

"Yes, I saw her walking down the Lagerstrasse at Natzweiler."

"And her?" Anna picked up Vera's picture. Brian hesitated. "I'm not sure, but this one yes." He got another sketch out and laid it next to Andrée's photograph. "She looked foreign, dark-haired, caramel complexion. Maybe Jewish?"

"Not Jewish, Indian," Anna corrected. "How many women did you see?"

"I saw three of them walking together. The third may have been Vera but as I was glimpsing at them through an open slit near the ceiling of my cell while standing on my bunk, I couldn't see much. I did hear a lot of chatter outside among the prisoners. Women were rare at Natzweiler, you see. At dinner some whispered they were English women, apparently four of them brought in that afternoon."

"What happened to them?" Anna already knew. She had read the crematorium stoker's testimony, but hoped to hear the truth from an eyewitness who could be trusted not to lie.

"I'm sorry, Anna. I don't know. I was put on a cattle train to Dachau that very evening."

"I thank you anyway, Brian. You've confirmed what I suspected. The girls likely never left Natzweiler. They were killed there. I'm going to request an interrogation with Franz Berg, the crematorium stoker. Before he's hanged."

WITH KENNETH at the steering wheel of the Box, Anna made her way to Gaggenau, on the edge of the Black Forest, where Franz Berg and other Natzweiler staff were being held in a local villa.

On entering Villa Degler, which looked like a typical southern German building including timber and small windows, Anna was seen into Major Bill Birchwood's office, a former intelligence officer of SOE's rival organization, Special Air Service, better known as SAS.

The office clearly had been the Villa's former dining room, with chandeliers hanging from the painted ceiling and large family portraits decorating the mauve painted walls. Along one wall was a row of shelves containing cut glass bowls and an ornamental clock that ticked as if time would never stand still for the horrors it had seen.

"I'm Captain Cameron, the Major isn't in. Welcome to Villa Degler, Lieutenant Adams and Captain Jameson. Please take a seat. I'll fetch Herr Berg for you. He's down in the cellar we've converted into cells."

"I'm not leaving you alone with that monster," Kenneth said between his teeth.

Anna smiled. She'd seen worse criminals than Berg, like Kaindl and Suhren, even the Paris Gestapo leader Hans Kieffer. It was a comforting thought, though, to have another friend and colleague with her.

"Thank you. Make sure you take notes," she advised. "We'll compare afterwards. Two pairs of ears hear more than one."

"Will do, Ma'am."

Anna knew Berg's checkered past from the Birchwood's report. He'd been a common criminal who had found favor with the SS, earning himself a cushy job stoking the crematorium oven at Natzweiler in exchange for his services. Remarkably, he had also become the Kapo of the Zellenbau, the prison block, and was surprisingly well-liked among the prisoners because he shared tidbits of information about the camp with them.

His notoriety had made it easy for Major Birchwood's men to track him down after the war when he had simply returned to Mannheim.

Anna studied the man before addressing him. He was a dark-haired, half-bald man with a rather broad head and smallish eyes under dark brows. Most likely in his early forties. He looked skittish and pale in the warm glow of the chandelier lamps above him. Not meeting her gaze, he seemed focused on one of the cut glass ornaments next to them.

"You mentioned you began working in the crematorium in February 1943. Can you clarify what your responsibilities were?"

"I was responsible for burning the deceased," Berg replied.

"Those who had been executed or hanged?" Anna probed.

"Yes, and also those who had died from other causes," he explained.

"Such as injections?"

"No, not by injection. I mean, I cremated those who had recently died within the camp – in the quarry and elsewhere."

Anna was all too familiar with the grim reality of the quarry, where prisoners were worked to their deaths, their lifeless bodies brought back to the camp each night by their fellow inmates. She had also delved into the identities of the sadistic perpetrators responsible for these deaths, such as Zeuss, Nietsch, Ermenstraub, and Straub, all listed in the reports.

Berg and others had claimed that Peter Straub was the one responsible for pushing the four women to their deaths.

"You stated before that you'd seen these women. Can you confirm that?" Anna tried to calm her queasy stomach, feeling wearier than ever. She laid the photos out on the table. Too many times she'd had to do this, putting the photos of her agents before their Nazi eyes. Berg nodded.

"When was that?"

"July 1944."

"When in July?"

"Maybe the 6th or 7th." Berg sighed, clearly irritated by Anna's terrier-like behavior.

"Tell me what you saw."

"They arrived at dusk, four women, each with a suitcase and a coat," Berg began. Almost the exact same words she'd read in his statement but now repeated in that monotonous voice. "I thought it might be a gathering, perhaps a party, inspecting the camp," he recalled. Anna ignored this. "Where were the women when you first saw them?"

"On the Lagerstrasse," he replied, indicating the pathway that traversed the camp from summit to base. The same spot Brian had told her he'd seen them through the slit in his cell.

"Describe the camp to me."

"It's on a clearing on top of the mountain, quite high up in the mountains. There were 15 barracks buildings in rows, cut into the mountainside. Down from the barracks were the Zellenbau, the disinfestation hut, and the crematorium where I worked." Berg recited the camp layout as a bored estate agent going over the details of the property he wants to sell.

Anna's irritation with the man grew by the minute, but her mind ticked off all the terraces, huts, and the precipitous route her girls would have walked. Their last walk alive.

"What happened then?"

"They were placed together in a single cell in the Zellenbau, but later isolated in solitary confinement," Berg answered.

"Why was that?"

He shrugged, "I don't know. At 6:00pm, Straub commanded me to heat the oven to have it at maximum temperature by 9:30pm. Then I had to go to my own cell and not show my face. I don't know anything else, but I did hear them drag the bodies down as my cell is right next to the crematorium."

"So that was after you disappeared to your cell? Did you see anything?"

"No, not until I was ordered to clean the oven."

"And what did you find?"

"I could still see their forms in ash. There were four female bodies."

"Yes."

"You know they were given an injection with phenol as Doctor Goetz declared in his statement?"

"No, I didn't. I just followed orders. I didn't kill them, I didn't even do the burning."

AFTER BERG WAS TAKEN BACK to his cell, Anna let out a long breath. She promptly composed a note that Franz Berg's testimony aligned with his earlier statements. Diana Leigh, Vera Rowden, Andrée Khan, and Nora Borrel have been determined to be among those SOE agents who met their fate on 6 July 1944, in Natzweiler Concentration camp.

Having confirmed the fates of her last four girls, the only task left in Germany for Anna was to fulfil her mission to inform their next of kin, starting with the somber declaration:

It is with deepest regret that I have to inform you that your... was killed on the date of ... in the camp of...

But not all was done. Back in London, she would start another relentless pursuit to ensure all the murdered SOE agents would posthumously be decorated as war heroes, preferably with the George Cross, the symbol of bravery and heroism.

"Why do you do all this?" Kenneth asked on their way back as night fell over the scarred German countryside.

"It's my personal mission as much as an assignment. I need to know. To be considered 'missing presumed dead' is a devastating verdict of non-closure."

And Anna recalled the bitterly cold day when Major Jaffe had collected her from Berlin and took her to Bad Oeyenhausen in the British zone. It had all begun there, and now it was done. She'd fought her own lonely battle until every lost agent was traced.

THERE WERE ONLY two people she hadn't been able to find, dead or alive.

WHAT TO DO ABOUT HERSCHEL? It had been several months since she'd heard her cousin might be alive, and she'd changed her mind daily as to whether to track him down. She'd put off deciding, throwing herself more fully into the investigations of her agents.

She looked up into the darkening sky and as if Herschel was

sitting next to her in the car, she suddenly heard his voice, chirpy and slightly teasing as he'd always sounded.

"I'm gone too, Ansel. Let it be."

Anna startled as if stabbed by a knife.

"What is it?" Kenneth asked, his voice worried.

"Nothing," Anna replied, sitting up straighter. "I'm so terribly tired I'm hallucinating voices!"

But it wasn't the truth. The message had been clear.

I'll let you go, Herschel but I'll protect your legacy. You were one brave boy!

HENRYK? she asked tentatively.

There was no answer.

50

BEATE GELLHORN

Bad Oeynhausen, The Next Day, 21 July 1946

Anna sat at her cluttered desk in her makeshift office in Bad Oeynhausen, the dim light filtering through dusty windows casting elongated shadows across the worn wooden floor. Her days were now consumed with rounding off her affairs, writing her reports, checking the last facts. The weight of the past still hung like a heavy cloak on her shoulders.

"Miss Adams, there's a visitor for you," Corporal Jameson called from next-door.

Since Hans Müller had been under lock and key for months now, the jovial farmer's son from the Midlands had set himself up as Anna's archiver, which he'd been diligently doing until the very end of her War Crimes Investigator assignment.

"I'm busy," she called back.

As she absentmindedly thumbed through a stack of documents, the sound of heavy footsteps in the hallway outside drew her attention. The door creaked open further, and Anna looked up to see a striking woman standing in the doorway, clad in combat overalls and sturdy boots. Sharp, inquisitive eyes bore into Anna's, and a wave of recognition washed over her. It was the blonde war correspondent from the Nuremberg trials. The scar, the shimmery blue eyes. There was something hauntingly familiar about her face.

"Are you Flight Officer Anna Adams?" the woman asked, her voice low and melodious with a hint of a foreign accent.

"Yes," Anna replied, her curiosity piqued. "Can I help you?"

The woman stepped into the office and closed the door behind her. There was something in her manner so confident and natural, Anna instantly admired her.

"My name is Beate Gellhorn," she said. "I'm a war correspondent with Reuters." She retrieved her press pass from her pocket, waving it in Anna's direction. "I heard you questioned Anton Kaindl, the former camp commander of Sachsenhausen."

Anna nodded, her professional demeanor intact despite the unexpected visitor. "That's correct. That was when I was doing interrogations related to Sachsenhausen, to track down my missing agents."

As if she was a daily visitor, Beate leaned against the edge of Anna's desk, her expression thoughtful. "I've been trying to secure an interview with Kaindl for a while now. I believe he has valuable information about the atrocities committed there, and I thought your connections might help."

Anna considered the request for a moment. She had grown used to dealing with journalists seeking information, but there was something about this war correspondent that made her guard go up. It was as if the past had caught up with her in this tiny office in post-war Germany.

"And why do you need this interview?" she asked, narrowing her eyes slightly.

She saw Beate hesitate for a moment, the blue gaze flickering. "I want to bring the truth to light. The world needs to know what happened in those camps, and I believe Kaindl may hold some of the answers."

Anna studied her visitor's face, searching for her ulterior motives. Her intelligencer background put her on high alert. There was an intensity in Beate's eyes that hinted at a deeper purpose, but Anna couldn't quite put her finger on it. As the seconds ticked by, Beate's lips softened into a wistful smile.

"You know," Beate said, her voice softening, "my brother served in the Polish resistance during the war. He was in Sachsenhausen. I want to see the monster with my own eyes before they hang him. Which won't be long now, I guess."

Anna felt a lump in her throat, her heart pounding as the pieces of the puzzle fell into place. The scar on her face, a remnant of a skirmish in the Spanish Civil War. Beate Gellhorn was the sister of Henryk Pilecki, the man she had loved and lost. The man she had betrayed before the war had torn them apart.

She swallowed hard, her voice trembling as she asked, "Is your brother...?"

Beate nodded, her eyes now filled with understanding. "Yes, Henryk is my brother. He often spoke of you, Anna."

"Is he... is he alive?"

"Yes."

"Oh my god." Anna had to grab the edge of her desk to steady herself. Emotions like a tempest swirled within her. A flood of memories threatened to overwhelm her. Kaindl had said he didn't know where Henryk Pilecki had gone. What had happened? She'd never known what had become of him after they lost contact and 6 months of searching for her agents across Germany never turned up a clue on Henryk's fate.Yet now, here was his sister, standing before her telling her he was alive.

Tears welled up in her eyes as she whispered, "I loved him, Beate. I still do. But I messed up terribly. How did he survive?" Her thoughts rambled from her own feelings to the realization Henryk had survived the war. That he was alive, somewhere.

Beate reached out and gently touched Anna's shoulder, the fierce expression tempering to compassion. "I know," she said softly. "And he loves you too. Can I sit down now? I've been on my legs all day."

"Sure, sorry!" Anna shook herself. "Tea, coffee? It isn't much we have here, but I can at least offer you that?"

"Coffee would be fine. Strong and sweet, if possible."

Anna was just about to go to the small kitchen in another part of the building when Corporal Jameson cracked open the door and stuck his head in.

"Can I get you ladies something?" His eyes lit up when he saw the attractive blonde woman in his boss's office. Anna was about to roll her eyes at her assistant when he said, "Oh Mrs. Gellhorn, can I please have your autograph? I always read your articles in The Observer. I believe you're as much a war heroine as us soldiers, trekking with us from the beaches of Normandy right into the heart of Nazi Germany."

"Sure." With a nonchalant gesture Beate tore a page from her notebook. "What's your name, handsome?"

Anna saw the brazen-faced corporal blush. It was an endearing sight.

"Kenneth Baldwin Jameson, Ma'am." He even made a small bow.

"Alright. Kenneth Baldwin Jameson." She scribbled something on the piece of paper and, together with her press badge, pressed it in his hand. "I've got a couple of other press passes. Just don't misuse it, as it got my name on it, and I'll hang for it." She smiled as she said it which made her features deform because of the scar on her cheek.

"Oh, thank you so much, Mrs. Gellhorn. I'll never part with this. And I will not misuse the press pass. Now let me get you your coffee." Clearly, he had been listening outside Anna's door before he peeked in.

Anna processed the new information fast. So, Beate was married which explained the different last name from her brother and why Anna had not at first connected the dots.

As they sat with their coffee and Beate with a cigarette dangling from her lip, Anna didn't know how to continue the conversation. She felt overwhelmed with guilt over her actions and yet utter happiness that Henryk was alive.

"So did you end up marrying the aristocrat?" Beate was studying her through the plume of smoke.

"No. I didn't. Thank the stars."

"Why not? That's not what you let Henryk know."

Anna became aware Beate knew everything that had passed between her and Henryk.

"The short version would be I didn't love him." Anna was suddenly very tired. "The long version is complicated and callous." She directed her gaze straight at Beate. "He was a very bad man and it appears I narrowly escaped a terrifying fate."

"Henryk doesn't know that," Beate observed casually.

"I know. Is he ... is he with someone?" Anna's voice was a tiny whisper.

"Heavens no, girl. Henryk's got enough on his plate just getting through the day. But he's getting stronger again."

"What happened to him?"

"Well concentration camps aren't exactly five-star hotels and political prisoners, especially Polish prisoners-of-war, got some of the worst treatment from these Nazi hounds."

"Is he very badly wounded then?"

For a moment Beate's eyes became soft. She was clearly seeing him in her mind's eye.

"You know what, Anna? I may say Anna? We Pileckis are made of steel. We don't bend but we can break. Henryk came close to breaking and that's what he can't forgive himself for."

Anna instantly thought of Pearl. Her guilt and self-loathing. The incredible fortitude these bravest of humans had and then being unable to forgive themselves for breaking under the worst strain extended upon them. Very few humans had that strength of character. Peter Suttill had also been one of them. In fact, every one of her agents fell in that category.

"So, where is he?"

"He's still recovering. Found a place in a monastery on the Polish border. It's run by British nuns so he keeps up his English with them."

"Could that be Sister Margaret's Kloster St. Agnes near Breslau, now Wrocław?"

Beate's eyes grew wide. "Of course, I had forgotten how Henryk and you originally met. You know Sister Margaret from the refugee camp. So much for being a well-documented research journalist, right?" Beate rested her combat boots on another chair and lit a fresh cigarette. "So, are you going to use your network to get me inside Paderborn and interview Kaindl?"

Anna realized she was dealing with a pragmatic professional just like she was. Beate wanted to see cash on the barrel, she didn't come for romantic tittle-tattle.

"If my superior, Captain Summers agrees, I don't see why not. I'll ask him." Anna wanted desperately to have her visitor stay, ask her more questions about Henryk, but she felt equally shy and tongue-tied. She had no right to bombard the sister with questions about the man she'd abandoned.

"Could... could I perhaps write a note for Henryk that you give him next time you meet?" she asked with her heart in her mouth.

"Phew," Beate yawned, extinguishing her cigarette, and jumping to her feet, "I have no idea when the next time will be. If I can have that dust-up with Kaindl, I plan to go home to my family after that for a bit. Haven't seen the kids in months."

"You... you have kids?"

"I even have a husband. Can you imagine?" Beate certainly wasn't without a sense of self-mockery.

"Where do you live?"

"New York. Where else?" She said it as if it was the only place a person could decide to live. Anna felt her self-image shrivel in front of so much aplomb. She also got up from her chair, and straightened her uniform as if straightening her sense of self. Something in her must have seemed very vulnerable at that moment because Beate's eyes softened once again. She tore another sheet from her notebook and scribbled something on it.

"Here, this is the address of the Kloster. Why don't you write him yourself?"

"Do you think I can?" Anna was hesitant.

"Can you write?" The sarcasm was back. "Just put pen to paper and see where it gets you. Heavens, the hoops the two of you jump through. It boggles my mind. Can I get back here tomorrow for my answer?"

Anna folded the paper and put it in her pocket. "Sure, and I'm sorry for the pain I caused your brother. I understand if you don't like me."

"I like you alright, Anna. I think you're doing a hell of a good job here. Shows you've got guts where others in places much higher than you couldn't care two figs. I like your spunk. Now use it for your own good." Beate slapped her on the shoulder and marched out, leaving a completely bewildered Anna behind.

51

THE LETTER

After Beate had left, Anna sank back on her chair pulling the slip of paper from her pocket. Sister Margaret floated before her eyes as if she was really in the room, just as Anna had known her when Anna was a broken and lonely seventeen-year-old. The kind round face of the fair-haired nun-turned-nurse, friendly, gray eyes in a wrinkled face. At least Henryk was in good hands.

ANNA READ BEATE'S SCRIBBLE.

Henryk Pilecki
p/a Sister Margaret Alderwood
Kloster St. Agnes
Schlossstrasse 32
Wroctaw, Poland

Underneath she'd drawn a heart. Anna brightened at the symbol. Beate was a hard case, but she was trying to help. Now came the punishing part of writing to Henryk. Or should she try to phone him? She shook her head. It had to be a letter and she had to pour her heart and soul into it. This was her only chance. No encore.

War Crimes Investigation Office
Bad Oeynhausen, August 1, 1946

Dear Henryk,

I hope this letter finds you in sufficient health and good spirits, although I am painfully aware that the world we inhabit is one far from merriment and good fortune. It has been a long and arduous journey since our paths diverged, and I find myself at a crossroads where I must finally muster the courage to reach out to you.

It has been years since our last encounter, and I know that my actions back then likely inflicted profound pain upon you. The fear of retribution from my then-fiancé compelled me to make a choice that haunts me to this day. I pray you can find it in your heart to forgive me for the cowardice I displayed in severing our connection. The only good thing that came from it was that I never married Roderick Macalister.

As I sit here, stationed in post-war Germany, as a war crimes investigator, the weight of the past bears down on me more than ever. My role in the French section of SOE now involves uncovering the fates of the brave agents we sent into France during those treacherous times. It was in this pursuit that I learned of your

suffering and, most importantly, of your current whereabouts. I can hardly fathom the agony you must have
endured during your time at Sachsenhausen, and for that,
my heart is also heavy with remorse.

Your sister Beate came to our office here today with
a request to interview Kaindl, the Sachsenhausen camp
commander, and during our conversation provided me with
the news of your survival and your residence in Sister
Margaret's convent in Wroclaw. Beate's words brought a
surge of emotions flooding back, Henryk. The mixture of
relief and guilt is almost unbearable. The last I heard,
you were in Sachsenhausen and I have tried over and
over to trace your whereabouts this whole time in
Germany with no success. I had nearly given up hope.

As I am stationed nearby in Germany for another
month, the longing to see you, to apologize in person for
my thoughtless actions, is consuming me. But I understand that you may still be hurt or angry at how I
ended things, and I am hesitant to intrude upon your
life uninvited. I do not know if you have any desire to
rekindle our connection or if you even wish to see me
again.

Henryk, you were, and always will be, the love of
my life. The years apart have not diminished the affection I hold for you in my heart. If you would be
willing to entertain the notion of us crossing paths once
more, even if only to offer a chance for me to express

my regret over my actions and admiration for your strength and resilience, I would be forever grateful.

Please know that this letter carries with it a depth of sincerity and remorse that words alone cannot convey. I could travel to Wrocław in the next few weeks, so if you should decide to grant me an audience, I will eagerly await your response.

With the utmost humility and affection,

Anna Adams

P.S. Please pass my kindest regards on to Sister Margaret, as she was so good to me in my hardest times.

It took ten attempts to get that down, but it wasn't just ten drafts. She reread her final letter a dozen times at least, doubting every word, finding it way too formal and standoffish, but not wanting to overwhelm him with what she really felt inside.

Oh, she could have done with Pearl at that moment to help her in this difficult hour, but she had to go this length alone and she knew it. The letter was in its envelope, and she was on her way to the post office. She kissed his name before dropping it in the letterbox.

A long wait began. A wait that could be forever.

AND THEN THREE weeks later the typical telegram style letter from Henryk arrived.

Dear Anna,

Your letter surprised me. I am indeed in Wrocław. It's been a long time. I'd be willing to meet.

Yours, Henryk

She didn't know what to do with his words. They weren't warm by any standards, but what had she expected? That he'd be jumping up and down in happiness that she'd reached out to him? And he had told her he wasn't a letter writer. It started with 'Dear Anna' and ended with 'Yours, Henryk.' Wasn't that enough of a sign that he cared? And he wanted to see her. That was the most important part.

And God only knew what he'd endured. An old friend from the past may be the least of his worries.

Better ask Major Summers for a few days off and plan her trip to Poland before her assignment in Germany ended.

52

THE BLUEST EYES

Two Weeks Later - 1 September 1946

"I'm driving you through West and East Germany and into Poland," Corporal Jameson was most adamant. "I've done enough trekking through this Huns' country to know the roads are full of potholes and pirates. I'm not letting you go on your own, Miss Anna."

"But can Captain Summers spare you, Kenneth?" Anna was now on first-name status with her archiver though he continued to call her 'Miss Anna'.

"All arranged, miss. You give the sign and we're off. Bit of a treat for me, after all these dusty files."

"Then I'd be honored to have you as my chauffeur, Kenneth. It even means I can do some work while we're underway. How long will it take us to get to Wrocław?"

"It's about 165 miles, so in theory only half a day with the Box. But we'd better plan for a whole day or even more, depending on the route we take, road conditions, and any potential delays still related to the war. Road damage and checkpoints, that kind of thing. Brits are not so well looked upon anymore in Soviet controlled territory. I don't want to put you off, but it may be challenging. Or it may be a breeze."

Anna remembered her journeys to Recklinghausen and Paderborn in November, and they hadn't been fun. But they had only stayed in the British section then.

"We'll manage," she said with more optimism than she felt, remembering she still had the letter of introduction to Stalin that Churchill had given her for her trip to Odessa. Flashing that around might be enough to get them through tight spots. She didn't tell Kenneth this though.

"As long as we have hot tea and biscuits," Kenneth grinned.

"Plenty of those."

As they embarked on the journey from Bad Oeynhausen to Wrocław on the following Wednesday, Anna saw a war-torn landscape stretching endlessly before her, every mile a stark reminder of the brutal aftermath of the war. The Box rumbled along the uneven, pot-holed roads, its tires navigating through the remnants of a once-thriving Europe.

Anna sat in the back, clutching her letter from Henryk, her emotions a tangled mix of anticipation and apprehension. The world outside passed in a blur of bombed-out buildings and weary faces.

Kenneth was a good driver, having driven tractors since he was seven. Though the two passengers spoke very little, she felt he was her loyal chauffeur and protector as he navigated the treacherous terrain with that typical stoic, British determination.

The journey was punctuated by frequent stops at makeshift checkpoints, where soldiers in battered uniforms scrutinized their papers and exchanged terse words. Anna found herself thinking of the countless souls who'd once traversed these same roads, both allies and adversaries, in pursuit of their own wartime objectives.

Despite the somber surroundings, there was an undeniable sense of hope in the air. The war may have left scars on the land, but it had also forged bonds of resilience and survival. Anna's heart raced with the prospect of reuniting with Henryk, a beacon of light in a world still emerging from the shadows of conflict.

As they neared Wrocław, her emotions swirled like the dust kicked up by their vehicle's tires. She knew that this meeting could change everything, and she steeled herself for whatever lay ahead, knowing that the past and the future converged on this winding, war-torn road.

Finally, the Box rumbled to a stop in the outskirts of Wrocław, a city that had witnessed both devastation and rebirth.

"Let's check into the hotel first," Anna suggested. "I hope you can enjoy yourself while I'm on my mission." She had not informed Kenneth what the goal of her visit to Wrocław was, only that it involved the possible survival of an SOE agent.

Kenneth hadn't asked questions, as he didn't do now.

"As long as there are pretty missies to look at, don't worry about me, Miss Anna. And I always try the local beer."

"You have enough Polish złotys, Kenneth?"

"Don't worry about me, miss." He grinned as he said it and Anna understood he was indeed happy to be away from the office.

Hotel Belvoir was a charming establishment that offered a refuge from the bustling city center. Nestled amid lush gardens and over-looking the tranquil Oder River, it was just what Anna needed.

But her focus was elsewhere. As soon as she'd left her small valise in her room, she prepared to go out again but lingered in front of the wardrobe mirror. Yes or no to her uniform? Henryk had said her WAAF uniform suited her, but she'd brought a nice dress, dark green with white trimmings. Pearl always said that dress made her look all womanish and grownup. But what if she accidentally ran into Kenneth and she was not in uniform?

She looked at herself in dismay, the navy-blue fabric crumpled from sitting in the car for hours.

"Stop it Anna and just go." Tucking his letter in her bag and taking her key she went downstairs. In the hotel lobby, she asked the receptionist to phone the convent for her, glad the young woman spoke some words of English and didn't seem too hostile.

Stepping out onto the worn cobbled streets, her heart pounded with a mix of excitement and trepidation. The air was crisp, carrying the scent of young spring and a city in healing.

She had arranged to meet Henryk at a small café called Café Belvedere, which lay tucked away in a quiet corner of the city. As she entered the establishment, her eyes scanned the room nervously. The café's dimly lit interior seemed to echo with whispers of the past, a stark contrast to the bustling days they'd once shared, their pre-wartime rendezvous in London and the days of heaven in Yorkshire in 1942.

THEN, she saw him.

HENRYK SAT AT A CORNER TABLE, his gaze focused on the cup of coffee in his hands. Time and imprisonment had etched lines on his face, but the vigor of resilience lingered in his proud posture. That posture, upright and confident, would occupy a noticeable presence in any room, at any time, despite the wounds of war etched into his formidable personality. His body may have been broken, his spirit never would.

He looked up as Anna approached, and their eyes connected in a moment of profound recognition. The bluest eyes. This man. His love.

Her voice trembled as she spoke his name, "Henryk."

He rose from his chair with some difficulty, adjusting something from within the pocket of his trousers. Then stood straight. His expression was guarded yet warm. "Anna," he replied with a steady voice, the shadow of a smile.

When he walked from behind the table to come her way, she understood. Henryk had an artificial leg. As if hit by a club, she grasped the enormity of his pain. The Polish aviator would never soar over the clouds again.

They stood there, mere feet apart, for what felt like an eternity.

The weight of their shared history hung heavy in the air, the unspoken words and unresolved emotions vibrating between them.

But as ever before, as from the most wonderful then dreadful fall in 1938 when they met, Henryk was the first to act. The smile Anna had never forgotten illuminated his plagued face, casting a radiant glow around him, setting his beautiful teeth aglow. He extended a hand, not touching her but inviting her to sit.

She accepted the gesture, and as they settled into their seats, the past and the present converged. There, in that quiet corner of Wrocław, two souls who had weathered the storm of war began to bridge the chasm that had separated them for far too long.

A waitress came to their table, breaking the tense capsule around them but bringing some welcome normality.

"Coffee for me too, please." Anna looked up at the young waitress with a tentative smile. She smiled back, warm and friendly, which helped to calm Anna's overwrought senses. When they were alone again, she could face what she had to face though still with downcast eyes.

"I know the words sound hollow, Henryk, but I am sorry in every respect. For what I've done to you, to us, for what you had to endure... for everything." She squeezed her hands together until they hurt not wanting to cry. "I hope... I hope I may explain what made me decide to phone Mr. Wilson at RAF Northolt and tell him we couldn't see each other anymore. Please?" She quickly glanced up meeting the sincere blue gaze across from her.

"I've been hoping for the explanation." It was said in a matter-of-fact way. Still, it startled her.

"Really?" There was a little hope in her voice.

"Anna, this is you and me. Something bad must have happened. Remember, I know you? The most intimate you."

She blushed at his words and felt a tremor travel through her entire body, the remembrance of their love, their passionate embrace. He hadn't forgotten.

I will not break into tears. I will not break into tears, she kept thinking, steeling herself by sitting up straighter, staring down in her coffee cup.*Let this part be over and done with sooner than soon.*

Henryk came to her assistance. "He blackmailed you. Is it that?"

She nodded and rambled out the entire story of Roderick's threat to transport her back to Germany and to a camp if she didn't comply with his wishes. How he'd been after her uncle's money and company. How she'd negotiated her way out. Giving up the love of her life.

She managed to get to the end of her story dry-eyed, then ended softly, "and look where it brought us. I escaped the concentration camps, but you didn't. I should have gone, Henryk."

"Are you mad?" He was angry, the blue eyes flashing, "you'd not have stood a chance as Ansel Grynszpan. You'd gone straight to the gas chambers."

"So... so you think I did the right thing? I so hoped I could explain everything to you after the war. But then Jan Nowak from the Polish Section told me you were with SOE too and had been captured. I don't know how I got through that day. I truly believed you were dead, Henryk. Dead." Her voice quivered and a single tear did not obey her wish to refrain from crying.

It was a deja-vu. He reached across the table and wiped the tear away with his thumb. The touch sent so strong a sensation through her, she thought her heart would burst and her shoulder blades would grow wings.

"So, you forgive me?"

"What is there to forgive, Anna? I'm glad I now know the truth. I hoped it was something like this."

The breath of relief made the whole world seem beautiful but soon the realization of Henryk's ordeal being much larger than her own, brought Anna back to earth.

"And you, Henryk?" She cast him a quick glance, seeing the darkest of shadows glide over the handsome features. Such pain, such bitterness. It humbled her but made her more than ever sure she was doing the right thing for *her* agents. The truth, the whole ugly truth must be told.

Henryk became restless, a character trait Anna didn't know he possessed. He fidgeted with the tablecloth, his eyes flitting around the small café that, at the end of the afternoon, started to fill up with customers. He seemed uncomfortable with too many people around him.

"If it's too hard, don't tell me," Anna said, already regretting her question.

"It's alright. I just need another coffee."

That triggered another deja-vu. It was apparent Henryk was a regular in Café Belvedere and loved by the staff, just like he'd been a revered guest in the officers' lounge of RAF Northolt. The waitress was at his elbow the moment Henryk looked in her direction.

"Another coffee, Major Pilecki?"

"You read my thoughts, Agnieszka."

"And you, Ma'am?" The waitress turned the warm smile she had bestowed on her war hero and now showered it on Anna. Anyone with Major Pilecki was considered good folk, Anna was to find out. The fighter pilot turned resistance fighter was clearly a celebrity in Wrocław.

With fresh coffee on the table, Henryk was able to focus again.

"As Novak told you, I wasn't flying anymore. I quit the Polish Air Force after your message. The next two months I stayed in Britain for the SOE training. Then I organised the Polish Wolfhound Network. After blowing-up the car of SS officer Hans von Richter, I was caught." Henryk's eyes turned dark.

"Oh no," Anna was sitting on the edge of her chair, her eyes filled with concern. Henryk paused to collect himself, fidgeting with the tablecloth.

"They put me through hell. The interrogations were brutal. They wanted information about my operations, my comrades. But I couldn't break. I couldn't betray our cause."

"Only your fake identity?" Anna asked with admiration.

Acknowledging the spymaker across from him, he smiled faintly, his eyes distant. "Yes, I was Andrzej Kowalczyk, born in Krakow, from a family of intellectuals and artists. Andrzej was a skilled linguist, fluent in multiple languages. He worked as an art historian and curator at a small museum in Warsaw. His position allowed him to move in intellectual circles, gather information discreetly, and establish connections with fellow academics and art enthusiasts."

Henryk changed as he spelled out the life of his alias. He became the intellectual art historian before her very eyes, and she was spellbound. She'd seen this metamorphosis happen in brilliant agents before. They had the ability to incorporate their fake identities into themselves as actors can.

"What was your codename?"

"Józef. After Józef Klemens Piłsudski, the founding father of independent Poland after the Great War. A name to live up to."

Anna nodded. Something about Henryk, whoever he was and whatever he did, would always be great. "When did you arrive at Sachsenhausen?" she ventured to ask.

"Not long after I was captured. Summer of 1943. I was put to work in the Klinkerwerk, the brickwork section. It was impossible to accept my fate. Not when so many suffered under Nazi terror. I had to fight back, to offer them hope."

"But how, Henryk, in a concentration camp?"

"I set up an escape network within Sachsenhausen. We dug a tunnel from behind the soup kitchen, beneath the wired fence. A blind spot in the terrain monitoring. The cook was in on it and let us through the backdoor. Every shovel of dirt was a symbol of defiance. Of our determination to survive."

Henryk's voice was filled with angry obstinacy. Anna couldn't help but stare at him wide-eyed with suspense. His gaze became more intense, a dark, deep-sea blue.

"One night, it was my turn to enter the tunnel. I was so close to escaping. But one of the guard's dogs sensed me."

Anna was holding her breath, not sure she wanted to hear the rest, but Henryk continued, his voice as dark as his eyes, controlled anger in every fiber of his being.

"The dog grabbed me. My left leg was torn apart. There were no antiseptics, and the infection set in quickly. There was no choice. They had to amputate my leg."

Anna's eyes welled up with tears. "That's terri...a terrible ordeal, Henryk. I'm so sorry."

She saw him close his eyes briefly, using all his inner force to control himself but telling her the story seemed to strangely calm him as well. He wasn't fidgeting anymore and the real Henryk, the man almost too strong for this world, bit-by bit rose from the ashes in her presence.

"I don't know why the Nazis kept me alive after my attempted escape. It was usually hanging by piano wire after that. They probably still hoped I would break. Tell them who killed Hans von Richter. They wanted names. I was in the sick bay when the Soviets finally liberated the camp. They took the patients to a real hospital for re-evaluation."

A huge surge of relief washed over Anna, followed by a surge of love so deep, so definitive. "Oh Henryk, I'm so glad you survived. For you, for me, for the world."

Henryk's smile was bittersweet, but his voice was filled with gratitude. "Me too. I have an artificial leg now; I can manage. And I won't stop until I can fly again. Someday." She saw the pain of his torpedoed-dream in his eyes. Not knowing what she was doing she reached out and took his hand. "I'm so sorry. Again. But thank you for sharing your story with me, Henryk. My heart, at least, is at rest now."

Something changed between them as her hand rested in his across the table. As if the world had taken a slight swirl that only they noticed. Anna looked up, gazing into the bluest eyes, their sincere, wise gaze holding her steady, beholding all of her. All the different Annas.

"Trust me," the eyes seemed to say. "Lay down your burden. You have suffered enough yourself, Anna, and your pain is safe with me."

Their corner of the Café Belvedere had turned shady and secluded. They got up from the table as one. Anna moved without noticing it. As she stepped forward, she almost fell into his arms. But he got her, safely, like every other time.

"Your heart is mine, Anna," he said, his chin resting on the crown of her hair. "Come and fly around the world with me."

And she remembered how the first time they'd sat in the cockpit of his Lublin R-XIIID. The year had been 1938, she was seventeen and she'd dreamed of flying to the end of the world with him, and their journey would never stop.

"I will fly with you for as long as we may," she replied, breathing deeper into their warm embrace, thinking of all the loved ones she'd lost and how fickle life was.

"Have no fear, Anna dear. There is no stopping us. Not this time. Not ever. We will last. We have fought all the wars, inside and out. And we won them all."

Their longed-for reunion was filled with the kind of love that weathers all storms, storms of war and separation. As they kissed, their eyes met, and the cafe around them faded away.

The tender touch of lips conveyed a warmth that only years of yearning and uncertainty could produce. It was a kiss filled with the taste of tears shed in solitude, the ache of longing, and the immeasurable relief of finally finding each other back. Alive.

A kiss so sweet, like a slow dance, as when time itself decides to stop and savor the moment. It was a kiss that spoke of once-shared dreams, missed opportunities, and the ultimate promise of a future together.

In that gentle embrace, Anna found solace, comfort, and the reassurance that her love had endured the darkest of times and emerged stronger than ever before.

"YOU ARE *the light of my life, Henryk!*"

53

ALL'S WELL THAT ENDS WELL

K loster St. Agnes was a serene and imposing structure in Schlosstrasse, in the heart of Wrocław, its ancient walls bearing witness to centuries of history. A testament to Gothic architecture, the convent had the typical stone spires and carved facades. Despite being weathered by time and scarred by the war, the building's exterior had not lost its air of solemnity and endurance.

Hand-in-hand, Anna and Henryk stepped through the heavy wooden doors and Anna found herself in a cloistered courtyard, a peaceful oasis amid the chaos of post-war Europe. The April kitchen and flower gardens were just about to burst into abundance, tended to by the dedicated hands of the nuns.

"Let's find Sister Margaret," Henryk announced, as they crossed the courtyard and found themselves in a corridor that was dimly lit by flickering candlelight and much cooler than the warmth of the garden. Time-worn stained-glass windows filtered the sunlight, casting a kaleidoscope of colors across the worn wooden pews of a side chapel. The air was infused with the scent of incense and the echoes of prayers.

"If it isn't Ansel Grynszpan," Sister Margaret exclaimed, clasping both Anna's hands in her own work-worn ones. The nun had aged considerably, snow-white hairs peaking from under her black cap, but the gray eyes were still warm with the care for humanity. Then she laughed out loud. "Oh, my memory is terrible. Of course, Henry told me you're Anna now. Anna Adams. There you go." She drew Anna into a chubby embrace and then held her at a small distance before kissing both her cheeks.

"The uniform is perfect for her, isn't it Henry?"

Anna fell from one surprise into the other. The tactility of the nun and the fact she called Henryk, Henry. After decades in Poland, Sister Margaret had still not lost any of her Northern English accent. Just standing there dumbfounded, Anna felt she needed to react.

"How are you, Sister Margaret? It is so wonderful to see you again. I had never dared to dream we would meet again."

"I'm as well as I can be at eighty. And seeing you, here, in Poland again. Oh, my dear girl. My old heart jumps like a filly in the spring meadow. And this poor young man has been pining for you so much. Ah well, all's well that ends well. Come children. Tea, real English tea is ready, and we even have home-baked scones."

WITH TWO SMALL bouquets of spring flowers, Anna stepped back into the sunshine and walked around the Kloster to the small adjacent graveyard. Henryk had wanted to accompany her, but she had insisted she wanted to do this part alone.

Sinking to her knees onto the soft, lush grass, she placed the flowers on their graves, one for Eva Grynszpan and one for Sarah Grynszpan. Their small headstones simply gave their names and the dates 25 April 1937 - 16 November 1938. They would have been nine today.

In an unsteady voice, Anna sang,

Oj lulaj, lulaj
Oj lulaj, lulaj

Siwe óczka stulaj
Oj, siwe ocie stulisz
do mnie się przytulisz
Do mnie się przytulisz

"Go to sleep, go to sleep, close your blue eyes
    if you close your blue eyes, you'll cuddle up to me."

~

2 weeks later - Soho, London, September 1946

Hand-in-hand Anna and Henryk stood in front of "Adams Antiquarian Books" in Soho. The façade hadn't changed, the sign hadn't changed. War had come and gone, but the bookshop owner had stayed on his post.

"Vati!" Anna called as they stepped inside, the tinkling bell announcing their arrival.

"Anna, my daughter!" Her father, even more shriveled and bent than before, shuffled from the back of his shop into the light. The smile that spread over his wrinkled face when he saw Henryk stand next to Anna was indescribable, but Jude Adams was a wordsmith with no equal.

"Henryk, my son. Bear with me as I try to find words to express the depth of the emotions I'm feeling right now. Seeing you standing here before me with my darling Anna, after all you've been through, it's a miracle beyond measure. You've endured unimaginable hardships, and yet, you've emerged from the darkness, stronger than ever."

Tears welled up in Anna's eyes as her father continued, "I want you to know how proud I am of you. Your courage, your resilience, they are a testament to the strength of the human spirit. You've not only survived the horrors of the concentration camps but have come back to us as a beacon of hope. You've brought light back into our lives." Her father's voice quivered with a mixture of joy, relief, and gratitude.

Henryk reached out and held Jude's trembling hands between his, his grip firm and full of love. "Thank you, Mr. Adams."

AFTER JUDE HAD INVITED the couple to sit down in the worn leather armchairs in his overstocked bookshop and tea was served, he turned his attention to Anna. The shop, once shrouded in sorrow, seemed to burst with his pride and mutual anticipation.

"Now you Anna, my dear daughter, I haven't told you yet what I think of your wartime escapades," Jude began, his voice filled with a mixture of mock and glee as he looked into her eyes. "Yes, yes. I had a visitor who told me what you truly did during the war and why you couldn't see me. That you had to protect me from possible harm. Usually it's the other way around, the parent protecting the child, but you did well, Anna, very well."

"Did Mr. Churchill come here?" Anna was perplexed.

"No, no, child, I'm not that grand but he sent his assistant, which was kind enough. I cannot express how proud and grateful I am for all that you've done. Not just during the war, but particularly going back to Germany to uncover the truth about your missing agents. You've been fearless in your pursuit of justice – it's nothing short of remarkable. You may not have given the families of these poor agents the answers they wanted, but at least they can mourn their loved ones, at least they know.

"Thank you, Vati," Anna felt incredibly warmed by her father's words. They were the last stamp of approval she needed to believe she was not guilty of anything. He seemed to sense her self-doubt.

"You did nothing wrong, Anna. Nothing. With your tireless efforts, your courage, your intelligence – you're an inspiration to us all."

Anna felt close to tears. Her father was so good with words. And again, he sensed the heaviness that was seeping in. With twinkling eyes, he cried, "now on a lighter note, when's the wedding? It's time I handed her over to you, son."

"Oh, I just wish Mutti was here, and Uncle Benjamin," Anna couldn't help adding. Both Jude and Henryk nodded, remembering the family members they had lost.

～

Later that day, Chelsea, London

"Pearlie, I'm home."

Anna raced into the door with Henryk on her heels. Pearl, familiar old Pearl, with her nonchalant feminine beauty and short, wavy hair, clad in wide black pants and a white men's shirt sauntered into the hall, taking in Henryk with her light, intelligent eyes. She whistled between her teeth.

"Oh gosh, Anna, he's still a stunner. Please keep him this time. I want to peek at him now and then if you're not looking." She winked then opened her arms and Anna embraced her. They kissed and hugged tightly.

"Oh Pearlie, oh Pearlie. Now you're both home with me," Anna kept repeating.

"I've got a surprise," Pearl announced and in the doorway appeared none other than Maurice Southgate.

"Mr. Southgate," Anna gasped at seeing the former SOE agent, who had testified in the Nuremberg trials, standing in her flat. "What are you doing here? Everything alright?" When he wrapped his arm around Pearl's waist, Anna's confusion was complete.

"Can we now just say Anna and Maurice, please?" he grinned. "I got a divorce, Anna. My marriage hit the rocks due to the war. These things happen. But believe it or not, Pearl dotes on Christian and Celine."

"I do," Pearl affirmed. "Please come in. We have cake and champagne for you."

AND SO, after the long and gruesome war, Anna found Pearl back in Odessa and then Henryk in Wrocław. Happiness and laughter sounded once again in her Chelsea flat, where they were bound together for good by the enduring bonds of love and friendship.

THE WORLD IS AT PEACE. *Maybe not forever, but at least for now.*

EPILOGUE

As the days turned into weeks, and weeks into months, the bond between Anna, Henryk, Pearl, and Maurice only grew stronger. Together and alone, they had been through hell; the three agents facing capture, torture, and concentration camps, while Anna had sat powerless in her London office, only to find the gruesome truth of her Section F agents in post-war Germany after it was far too late to prevent their suffering.

As highly decorated war heroes, they were often asked to speak about Britain's fight on European soil during the dark days of the Third Reich and the impact SOE and the French Resistance had had on the success of D-Day.

The four friends never tired of telling the world about the lonely fight of hundreds of trained agents behind enemy lines and the hardships they endured to bring peace to Europe. But as instructed by the intelligence services, they never delved too deeply into the secret British, and later American, organizations behind the missions.

Nevertheless, the hunger for information about the mythical SOE grew, as did the call for justice and posthumous decorations.

AND THEN, one beautiful spring day in 1947, on the arm of her father, Anna walked down the aisle. Anna and Henryk exchanged their vows in a small, intimate ceremony in Chelsea Old Church. The historic church was filled with friends and former colleagues, but also Beate and her family, Henryk's parents, Sister Margaret, and Anna's former boss, Sir Reginald, attended.

It was a day filled with love, hope, and the promise of a long and bright future. As they danced under the stars that night, Anna looked at Pearl and Maurice, and her heart swelled with gratitude. They were more than friends; they were family. Together, they had emerged from darkness into the light of a new day.

IN THEIR COZY flat in Chelsea, Anna and Henryk settled into a life filled with love and purpose. Anna worked as a translator and researcher for The Guardian and later the BBC, continuing to uncover the stories of those who had been lost during the war, ensuring that their memory would not fade away.

She left the *Benjamin Bittermann Trust* in the hands of his legal representatives but remained its chairwoman all her life, making sure charities like *The Red Cross* and *Save the Children* received ample donations.

HENRYK, after a long recovery, was able to fly planes again. In 1947, he flew Anna to Australia, where they traversed the huge country in a rented Camper van. He continued to work as an aviation instructor for RAF until his retirement in the 1970s.

Victorious Poland disappeared more and more behind the Soviet Union's Iron Curtain. Before the borders closed for good, Henryk's parents emigrated to England, bringing with them Sister Margaret, who retired to a convent in Yorkshire.

PEARL, always the adventurous spirit, embarked on a new career in photography. She captured the beauty and resilience of the world around her, and her photographs became a source of inspiration for many. She was the most celebrated photographer at the Festival of Britain in 1951 and had expositions all over the world.

Pearl was, and always would be, Anna's best friend. And they spent many holidays together at *L'Indépendance,* Pearl's summerhouse in the Dordogne.

MAURICE, on the other hand, found a renewed sense of purpose in advocating for justice and human rights. As a lawyer, he joined a group of high-profile professionals dedicated to promoting peace and reconciliation in a world still scarred by the war.

IN THE YEARS THAT FOLLOWED, the four continued to support each other through life's ups and downs. They celebrated the births of Sarah and Ben, Anna and Henryk's children, and of Peter, Pearl and Maurice's son. They buried Jude at age eighty-four next to Anna's mother at the City of London Cemetery on Aldersbrook Road.

ANNA HAD FOUND peace within herself, her past finally laid to rest.

I SINCERELY HOPE you enjoyed Anna's story as much as I wanted to tell hers. This is the last "big book" in The Resistance Girl Series but all the "girls" will meet up three years after the war at Le Manoir in The Resistance Girls Revisited.

Please join my Newsletter to follow all the news about The Resistance Girl Series and the new series Timeless Spies. You'll receive the WW2 novella The Partisan Fighter as a gift. Sign up here: https://www.hannahbyron.com/newsletter

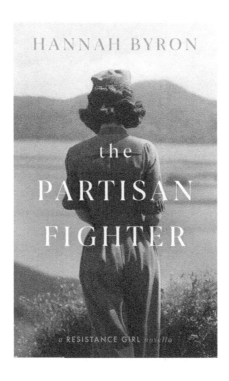

THE RESISTANCE GIRLS REVISITED
CHAPTER 1 THE INVITATION

Le Manoir, Lausanne, 1 January 1948

As the first morning light of 1948 shimmered through the tall windows of her opulent office, Madame Paul Vierret sat perfectly straight in her office chair with a sense of solemn resolution. Forty years. It both felt like an eternity and the blink of an eye since she took on the mantle of headmistress of the posh finishing school on Lake Geneva in Switzerland.

Her gaze drifted to the grand oak desk before her, polished to a reflective shine, bearing the weight of countless decisions made over the decades.

The office itself exuded an air of timeless elegance. Gold-framed paintings decorated the mauve-painted walls, depicting scenes of friendly Swiss landscapes and 19th-century portraits. A crystal chandelier hung from the ceiling, casting a glow over the room and its proud owner. The warm yellow light was the only soft touch to an otherwise stern space.

Beyond the school windows, the choppy waters of Lake Geneva stretched out, the rippling waves shimmering cold and ruthless in the January morning. Across the lake, the majestic Savoyan Alps rose like silent sentinels, their snow-capped peaks piercing the sky. This same dramatic view had greeted Madame Paul each morning for four decades, yet it never failed to stir something deep within her.

Because stirred she was, more so this morning than any other morning. Everyone was still in their rooms, both the staff and the students. Not that there were many present, as most had gone home for the Christmas holidays and weren't expected to return in two weeks. Breakfast would be served in half an hour and by that time Madame Paul would need to be in full control of herself again.

For amidst the beauty of her surroundings, there lingered a dark shadow, a secret carefully concealed behind a mask of impeccable manners and steely resolve, a shadowy secret she allowed to surface only when alone in the sanctuary of her closed-door office.

Madame Paul's celestite blue eyes, sharp and unyielding, belied the turmoil that churned beneath the surface. Her always well-coiffed hair with the role in the nape of her neck, now streaked with strands of silver, spoke of a lifetime spent maintaining an unassailable facade. The tailored navy silk dress hugged her slim figure and the reading glasses on the pearl strings never sported a speck of dust.

For all her years at Le Manoir, Madame Paul knew she'd been a mystery to her students, an authoritarian figure shrouded in enigma. Whispers of her strict demeanor, her unyielding discipline, her sometimes even unfair treatment filled the corridors and the dorms. But none of them fathomed the true depths of her past, the pain that lay hidden beneath that composed exterior.

The Sphinx, she thought, *they called me the Sphinx behind my back. How accurate, how very accurate indeed.*

Lost in thought, Madame Paul's gaze drifted to the polished surface of her desk, where a pristine white paper awaited her attention. It was time to extend an invitation, to reach out to those who had once passed through the hallowed halls of Le Manoir and left an indistinguishable mark upon its history. Upon her history.

With a steady hand Madame Paul picked up her Parker pen and pulled the sheet of paper towards her. But then she hesitated.

Normally her words flowed forth with a sense of purpose and efficiency, but nothing came right now.

Suddenly plagued by one image, one image only, she closed her eyes. A tall, blond girl with sad green eyes staring at her in disbelief. Esther Weiss. The eyes full of tears asked wordlessly why *she* was punished when she'd done nothing wrong? It was a reflection of herself, the mirror she'd looked into before she became Madame Paul Vierret. When she was still Elsie Goldschmidt. Another light-haired, light-eyed Jewess, born for a life in secrecy. A lifetime of regrets.

This was her chance to make amends, to bridge the divide that had long separated her from her former students, to lay bare the secrets that had weighed upon her soul for so many years. And the war, that awful war had ripped open all her scars. Monsieur Paul Vierret in prison for siding with Hitler's Nazi party, organizing the channeling of stolen Jewish property through Switzerland. And she had done nothing. Nothing!

Madame Paul shivered, pulling her fur stole tighter around quivering shoulders.

"Time to make amends." As she spoke the words out loud, her own voice sounded unfamiliar to her, hollow and metallic.

Madame Paul knew the road ahead would not be easy. But for the first time in decades, she felt a glimmer of hope stirring within her heart, a flicker of light amidst the darkness that had long consumed her.

And so, as the dawn of a new year bathed the world in tentative golden hues, Madame Paul Vierret sat in her Le Manoir office, the blue gaze fixed fiercely upon the future, filled with a longing for reconciliation and redemption.

Le Manoir, 1 January 1948

Chères Anciennes Élèves et Amies,

It is with great joy that I extend this special invitation to you to celebrate a remarkable milestone - my 40th anniversary as the headmistress of Le Manoir Finishing School in Lausanne, Switzerland.

Over the past four decades, I have dedicated my time and energy to the education, growth, and empowerment of hundreds of young women who have walked through the doors of Le Manoir and left fully capable to take up their societal places.

In honor of my long career, we are hosting a special celebration at Le Manoir, where former students and friends will come together to reminisce and reconnect about their times under my tutorship.

My steadfast dedication to excellence and ongoing influence on generations of students have nurtured women who courageously assumed their roles as mothers, wives, and societal leaders, excelling in diplomacy and behind-the-scenes empowerment.

Yet, among my most esteemed students, there are those who have demonstrated extraordinary courage as resistance women during the recent war, subsequently forging remarkable careers in peacetime. These women have applied my teachings in diplomacy and etiquette in an exceptional manner to serve their nations. It is my

*express wish to honor this distinguished group of deco-
rated war heroes as special guests during the reunion at
Le Manoir.*

*The celebration will take place on 15 May at Le
Manoir on the borders of Lake Geneva, in the heart of
our picturesque Swiss countryside. Festivities will include
a gala dinner, musical performances, and heartfelt
speeches celebrating both my legacy and those of my
guests of honor.*

*I warmly invite you to join us for this joyful occa-
sion as we express our gratitude and admiration for all
our unwavering dedication and leadership.*

*Please mark the date on your calendars and RSVP by
15 April 1948.*

Avec mes meilleures salutations,

*Madame Paul Vierret
Headmistress, Le Manoir*

She laid down her pen. Folded her hands in her lap and sat like a statue. Outside in the corridor she heard the two maids talking softly while they headed to the breakfast room. Soon it would be time to put her mask in place again but, by heavens, she was so tired of pretending. To be perfect, to be flawless, to be ever confident.

When all this is over, I'll retire," she said as she rose from her chair and straightened her skirt. As her high-heeled shoes clicked on the marble floor, she straightened her shoulders, painted a modest smile on her coral lips and turned the doorknob.

LIFE IS BUT A STAGE!

MACBETH.

⁓

WOULD you like to order the last instalment of *The Resistance Girl Series*? You can preorder it here.

ABOUT THE AUTHOR

Hannah Byron was born to Anglo-Dutch parents in Paris, her heritage weaving together a varied tapestry of European cultures.

Currently based in Holland, she writes gripping Historical Fiction series centered around WW2 Resistance Women.

A former academic, Hannah's transition to full-time writing is a dream come true – or perhaps a sneaky plot hatched by Uncle Tom Naylor, whose heroic D-Day exploits sparked her obsession with WW2 history.

In her bestselling "The Resistance Girl Series", Hannah's heroines traverse Europe much like their adventurous creator. From the bustling streets of Paris to the polder-land countryside of Holland, to the cold maintains of Norway, her stories paint a vivid portrait of wartime heroism and resilience.

Her upcoming series, "Timeless Spies", focuses on female secret agents and their daring exploits in France and Britain during WW2.

With a nod to her lineage and a wink at fate, Hannah's novels celebrate strong women, blending romance with resilience.

Each page pays homage to the unsung heroines of the 20th century, who got dirty in overalls, flew planes, and did intelligence work in the name of liberty and love. These early adopters serve as a poignant reminder of the legacy left by the trailblazing women who paved the way for future generations.

But that's not all! Under the pen name *Hannah Ivory,* she writes Historical Mysteries, whisking readers away on Victorian adventures with the intrepid Mrs. Imogene Lynch.

ALSO BY HANNAH BYRON

The Resistance Girl Series

In Picardy's Fields

The Diamond Courier

The Parisian Spy

The Norwegian Assassin

The Highland Raven

The Crystal Butterfly

The London Spymaker

The Resistance Girls Revisited (preorder)

The Agnès Duet (spin-off)

Miss Agnes

Doctor Agnes

HANNAH IVORY

Historical Mysteries

The Mrs Imogene Lynch Series

The Unsolved Case of the Secret Christmas Baby

The Peculiar Vanishing Act of Mr Ralph Herriot

Printed in Great Britain
by Amazon

41816284R00239